# Shards

## of

## Ember

By: Mitchell Lecoultre

ISBN-13: 9798303060166

ISBN-10: 1477123456

Cover design by: Sienna Arts (https://www.whiterosepublishings-ervice.com/)

Library of Congress Control Number: 2018675309

Printed in the United States of America

# Acknowledgements

As anyone with experience knows, no journey is successful without support. Many people have helped me on this road, mentors, teachers, family, friends, and even enemies, but surely that would be too much to write here. Nonetheless, for those of you who have known me for all my flaws and all my strengths, thank you for your support in this crazy life of ours. Here is to happy reunions and new adventures!

Of course, I would never have made it to this point where I am writing an acknowledgement without the support of my better half, my practical, beautiful, and wonderful wife, Vanessa! You have been there for me through everything from sunshiny days to turbulent storms, and I couldn't ask for a better partner to venture with.

To my mom and dad: No one could have asked for a better childhood. You have given me all the tools I need for success, the wisdom to survive, and a moral compass of immeasurable strength. Truly, I could not have asked for a better set of parents. Thank you!

To my brothers Sean and Ben: Thank you for dealing with a little brother with such patience and showing me how to have fun but also how to navigate this sometimes-rugged life.

To my sister: For the times we shared and the care you gave to me. I hope you are well.

To my friends: Thank you for all the wonderful times together.

Finally, I would like to thank the professionals who helped me complete Shards of Ember.

Elle W. Silver of Elles Editing for the multiple grammatical fixes and wonderful editing service.

Sienna Arts for the amazing cover design: https://www.whiterosepublishingservice.com/

The many beta readers from goodreads.

# Map of The Holliserian Fringe with inlay of the 'New World'

# SHARDS OF EMBER

MITCHELL LECOULTRE

# Part One

# Chapter One
## Alexa

Alexa gazed at the small flames dancing around the dry wood. Transfixed by the furnace of the fire, her keen eyes picked out each crack and crevice within the wood as it warped and shifted under the influence of the heat. The image, aided by the clear crisp night, was immaculate, and like so many other nights before she couldn't help but be awed by the display that nature wrought. An arrangement that had reached the stage she enjoyed the most: a bed of embers. One that not only let out a pleasant comforting warmth but also gave way to a view that felt like she peeked into the very fabric of the universe. And, in the purifying near-invisible flames, one could see details and minutiae that were never within the wood otherwise, even in direct sunlight. Alexa would often find, gazing upon those rich details, that self-reflection became wholly easier, and the light—or dark—of her own failings were laid bare. She couldn't help but wonder, *is it just a trick of the mind or is this the only time I pay attention?*

A sudden swirl of sparks interrupted her thoughts, as Gilneas, her companion, stoked the fire with a stick. "I think we got one … maybe two days before we reach the east end of this cursed forest."

She fixed the stocky black-haired man, mocking sternness. "Well, *sir,* I don't think we will be reaching the end of any forests if you light the whole place on fire."

"What, a man can't enjoy the simpler things in life?"

"Not if those *things* interrupt one of the few moments of peace I get when I am around you."

"Well, Your Highness, I apologize for the interruption," Gilneas said stretching his back in an exaggerated manner. "It's just … staring at this fire makes me think of those delicious little honey biscuits the baker's wife makes. You know the ones?"

She knew of them. They were so much like her mother's biscuits back in Augustia. Bittersweet memories … raids on freshly made biscuits. There, on that stone-tiled floor, Alexa would use tiny pebbles, prized from the dirt-filled grout, to show Bella and Sophia the manner of their heist. They never succeeded. Always chased out of the front door by their mother's stern voice—bits of absconded biscuit following them all the way.

She smiled, a sentimental smile that brought her to the edge of tears. "Yeah, I know of them," Alexa replied.

"It would be a real treat after this particularly cursed patrol, wouldn't it? That and a nice warm bed."

"Yeah, it would be." Alexa's mind struggled to slip away from her nostalgia. The disturbance of her hypnotic view annoyed her at first, but now, as usual with Gilneas, she felt somewhat foolish at her more stoic demeanor when assayed against the more cheerful, joke-filled ranger. His dark, shortly-cropped hair and round face accentuated a near-permanent smile that he wore no matter the occasion. She couldn't help but reflect on the near inexhaustible well of enthusiasm the young man had, even in the face of grave danger.

A need to reconcile for her poor company overwhelmed her. "You remember when you speared that boar!?"

"Hey now." Gilneas smiled. The type of smile he would display when he recognized she was trying to be nice. His brows raised high onto his forehead, in a way that only he could pull off. "That was a fearsome beast. And if I recall your face looked a few shades paler when you heard that … *monster* in the trees."

"Well, in my defense, it was only my second time, *and* it was in an unexplored—potentially lethal—stretch of woodland." Alexa sat up straight, looking him in the eye.

"Yea? Well, the only thing lethal from that trip was the smell of the thing."

Alexa chuckled at the memory. She had been so terrified. Her stomach feeling as if it would explode from the broiling anxiety held within. And, she remembered Gilneas, a veteran from the ranges of the old country, so cool and level-headed, leading her through the experience. She had never been more grateful to her range companion when he had expertly skewered the charging animal. Its squealing cries had pierced her eardrums, and a malodorous stench had wafted into her as the creature died just a couple of meters from her. Truly, an experience that inundated the senses and embedded itself firmly into her memory.

Now they were once again within that same forest that stretched from the sea in the west to a thick range of mountains to the east, Mossgrave as the pioneers called it, although its proper name was Eukaria. Either name belied the sinister truth of the forest, which held an untamed lethality unbroken by civilization. A deadliness that—like the dirt below the moss-covered forest floor—was hidden below a veiled carpet of beauty. Before her mind could wander further and leave Gilneas adrift in the conversation, she replied, "Still, you saved me from a particularly nasty wound that day."

Gilneas paused a moment. "Yeah, well you and that bow of yours have kept me from having to use this spear on more than one occasion." He patted the long-shafted weapon that lay next to him. She looked at the simple tool, and unsure of what to say to his compliment just grunted uncomfortably, leaving them in an awkward pause made more profound by the crackling fire.

In that silence, Alexa looked upon the weapon Gilneas had so lovingly patted. Its ash wood shaft was only fifteen centimeters shorter than him at one and a half meters long. The weapon with its gleaming iron spearpoint, like their duty as rangers, was always held close to Gilneas's chest.

True, Gilneas took to his duties with a light demeanor, but he was deadly serious about his role as a Guardian of the Range. It was in his face every time they swore their oath to uphold the laws of both nature and man. She was proud that her companion was so faithful to their order, and she leaned on his strength and optimism whenever her duty as a ranger became too difficult to bear.

A duty that had brought them across the sea. Pioneers for the burgeoning city-state of Augustia. A governance, which, like many of its competitors, derived its power from the metropolis it had been named after. Now, for the glory of that far-off land, she found herself, along with her biscuit-thieving sisters, going on their second year of a five-year-long pioneer effort in the newly discovered lands. A world that lay across the sea from Augustia and every other human kingdom, big or small.

On those distant shores, after finding nothing but bird and beast, the pioneers had settled Elgion. A growing village with rustic charm, that, although Alexa had learned to love, paled in comparison to the comforts that came with the marbled halls and cobblestone streets of golden Augustia. Yet, even still, Elgion, like Gilneas had pointed out, had far more comforts than the clearing they camped in. They had been 'ranging,' as their order liked to call a patrol of the wilds, for nearly a month now.

One month since she had seen her sister Bella, who had such skill with beasts of all shapes and sizes, that the masters of Elgion named her stablemaster. A profession she had taken to with relish, and, in that demand for perfection, Bella had manifested a stable that housed some of the finest beasts on either side of the sea.

One month since she had seen Sophia, a rather ostentatious Keeper of Stones, who was more likely than not plunging into some obscure text, or—as was her custom—aggravating some official that she considered too 'high-up' for their abilities.

Her primary badge of office, a Shard of Ember amulet, always hanging at her breast. The small fragment pulsating with ephemeral light of unmatched intensity; like a tiny sun blinking in and out of existence.

Gilneas, who was unable to sit in awkward silence any longer, interrupted her thoughts. "And with the weather like it is, ya know hot as Ember's breath, we better count on two days."

Alexa had to shake herself back to the present, taken aback by Gilneas's sudden statement.

"Well … it's good that we stopped at the Farney and refilled our skins." Gilneas held up one of his deer-hide skins and tipped it back, a mock salute to Alexa's observation. "Too bad it's going to be as warm as goat's piss going down."

"You would know, wouldn't you?" Alexa asked jokingly.

"Yea, I learned the trick from Bella."

Alexa pretended to throw a stone at him and watched in amusement as he flinched at the action. "You better watch yourself. Don't matter how many times you saved me; Bella will eat you alive."

"Aye, I know," Gilneas said, a smile on his face.

"Well, if it's all the same to you." Alexa made her way to the makeshift shelter they had set up for the day. Shelter was a generous word for it was no more than a deerskin blanket propped up by some sticks. Still, it would help keep any rain off them, and the deer skin on the ground would help keep any unwanted company from trying to crawl where it didn't belong.

"I think that's a great idea." Gilneas stomped out the fire and the two rangers laid down under their respective shelters and fell fast asleep.

# Chapter Two

## Alexa

It was a hot morning already, the light breeze that fluttered down through the trees doing little to assuage her exhaustion. Already her back was drenched in sweat as they marched through rough country. She shook her head and pushed herself onwards, knowing that even if Gilneas felt the same he would not let his pains discourage her. She stepped on top of a fallen log, covered with moss, and—being sure that no snake or other such creature made its home under the rotten wood—dropped down to the springy turf of the forest floor. A whiff of moss and vegetation caught her senses, a small spark of joy at the taste of nature. Truly, no matter how wild the Eukarian Forest was, it held a distinctive beauty that only nature could produce. *Wait.* There was a foreign scent hidden within the aroma.

She stopped, glancing around. It tasted like wet fur but with a particularly musky bent. Like something that spent little time in the sun.

"What is it?" Gilneas asked, slight apprehension tainting his voice.

Something was wrong. An all-too-familiar trembling assailed her stomach as she tried to tease apart the smell. Wind pierced the upper canopy of oak and pine, caressing her cheek and bringing the aroma of the forest with it. The odd scent was unmistakable now, and Alexa became suddenly aware of the lack of noise. The calls of birds and insects had died away as if retreating from an approaching malice.

Gilneas leaned near and whispered, "Your tension betrays you. What do we face?"

"I am not sure ye—" A brown blur on her periphery stunned her to silence. It was her duty as Watcher to prepare them for threats; to make the call for battle. Gilneas shifted uncomfortably behind her. A brief shadow passed over a bush in front of them, and both rangers fell to the ground. Alexa's stomach hit a moss-covered stone, and a blossom of pain radiated inwards.

"Did you see anything?" Gilneas whispered.

"Not yet." There, hiding in the dense undergrowth Alexa rolled to her side. She unfurled her bowstring and looped the cord around the top horn of her eighty-pound war bow. She flipped the bow around and, whilst steadying the bottom portion of the bow with her legs, heaved the string towards the opposite horn of the bow. Her shoulder muscles complained at the immense effort. With her bow strung she risked a look around, scanning the upper boughs.

Branch and leaf seemed harmless as they rustled softly in the wind, save for a tiny shimmer of light. A reflection of the sun that did not fit with the other scenery. There, about twenty-five meters away, she saw it: eight coal-black eyes staring down at her.

*Iktomids*! A creature that resembled the common wolf spider but through some pressure, natural or otherwise, had grown to a massive size. At about one meter long and half-a-meter wide the arachnid horror carried its weight aloft on eight bristly legs that were known to abrade and infect the skin. Although it shared many of the attributes of its smaller cousins, the iktomid's rear coxa had morphed into a more segmented chitinous appendage. It did not need to spin webs, for its girth and strength helped capture its prey more than any trap.

"Iktomids," Alexa whispered.

Gilneas groaned in disbelief. "What are they doing so far south?" He rolled on his back, scanned the rear of their position, and then rolled back to his stomach. He crawled to within centimeters of Alexa, "Still, looks like they are hungry, and *I* don't want to be dinner. They should flee if we kill or maim a few. Both we and the Balance survive."

She appreciated Gilneas and his focus on their duty to maintain the Balance, a code that dictated rangers should not kill unnecessarily, but perhaps they could dispense with the chivalry in light of impending doom?

Gilneas brought his spear to his side, ready to spring into action. "On your call, Watcher."

A trickle of fear dripped into her heart at those words, and beads of sweat accumulated on her forehead and hands. Her heart pounded in such a way that it felt like a hammer trying to forge her sternum against the anvil of the ground. Another shadow passed on her periphery, and she became aware of the wetness of her palms. *That won't do.* A quick wipe on her trousers fixed slippery hands.

She glanced up to where she had spotted the first iktomid and now saw only a swaying branch. Yet, in the trees and bush, she could hear small betrayals of the gathering foe. Slowly, she reached to her quiver and drew an arrow. A rustle in the brush told her that the hunters were losing their caution. That soon they would set upon their prey. She nocked an arrow, gripping the tensile wood of her bow; the familiar grains of wood steadying her nerves. She scanned the horizon and saw at least three foreign shapes in the upper canopy—none in the brush below. *Curious.*

As quiet as she could manage, she hissed. "I will take the trees. You watch the ground."

Gilneas nodded his agreement. The sun's glare dimmed ever so slightly. She leapt up, bow in hand, and swung around to take aim. The flattened carapace of an iktomid was on a branch straight above them. The beast's head visible, perfect for a shot straight to the skull. *Small targets small misses.* Her Rangemaster's favorite phrase rang in her mind as she steadied her aim.

The string of the bow graced her cheek, and her shoulder complained at the strain of the draw. The iktomid prepared to drop upon her. Its legs outstretched and slivers of saliva dripped from its seven-and-a-half centimeter fangs. She forced herself to breathe; to reach that moment where the body was perfectly aligned. *Small targets*. She let the arrow fly.

It fell to the ground with a shriek, shriveling into a ball of hairy legs as it tried to protect what remained of its ravaged body. Alexa stared at the dying beast, a tinge of fear creeping through her. Scurrying sounds of the enemy pack closed in on them and a tendril of doubt gripped her soul, arresting her into paralysis. Gilneas pushed into her as he thrust his spear forward, cutting the charge of an iktomid short.

"Get your head back in it!" He cried.

*Foolish*, she thought as she grimaced at her broken focus. She drew another arrow, scanned the treetops, spotted a scurrying beast, and aimed. Fear still worked on her psyche, and she fired too soon. The arrow thudded into the wood just centimeters from the beast's face. It scurried to the underside of the branch, where to the creature's folly its left side was still fully visible. Alexa aimed, breathed, and fired, taking the time to lead the target. The shaft drove into the beast's abdomen and flecks of blue blood splattered the leaves behind. Its corpse slammed into the ground with a sickening thud. A surge of adrenaline; A moment of victory clawing back some portion of her fear-riddled mind.

Behind her, the metal of Gilneas's spear whistled in the air, evidently striking true for it was quickly followed by the sound of rending flesh. The third shape she had spotted at the beginning of the engagement made its way down an oak trunk twelve meters away. She fired another arrow which impaled the arachnid's head and speared it to the trunk, the weight of its torso flopping over like some sort of twisted mockery of a leaf.

She heard another grunt from Gilneas. She was about to turn and help the Guardian, but to her right and left the thick undergrowth swayed. Two ripples in the green that drove straight towards them. Enemies who had grown wise to her ranged threat and sought to camouflage their approach.

She drew and fired on the disturbance to the left and was rewarded with a shriek. The shaft impaled into the iktomid, and in its retreat looked like some sort of fish pulling against a hook.

The iktomid to the right still skirted through the undergrowth naught but eight meters away, the distance closing fast. Her muscles ached and she forced a breath as she prepared to draw. Despite the burn, she pulled the war bow back again, aiming into the foliage. She released her shot, the cord snapped against her wrist, and she immediately felt the sting of its eighty-pound draw. Her shot flew over her target, and her heart skipped. She was out of time.

Time, which seemed to speed up as the iktomid closed the distance, Alexa was barely able to duck to the right before the spider burst from the ground, its fangs and front legs outstretched, ready to feast on her. She had not dodged quick enough, and the indefatigable foe slammed into her left shoulder, spinning her in place. Her eyesight blurred as the shock from the impact reverberated up into her skull, her head aching from the jolt.

She had to keep fighting. She put her hand to her dagger, preparing to draw the vicious blade against the iktomid who had hit her. It was close, preparing to strike again, the hissing metal heralding the full return of her faculties.

There, she spotted her foe still turning, caught up in a bush about three meters away. But what she had not expected was the sight of Gilneas. He was perched on the balls of his feet, his knees planted on the ground, and the butt of his spear embedded into the ground. The wicked weapon was at a forty-five-degree angle and a writhing iktomid adorned the blade. Almost like it did not know it had been impaled. To the right of Gilneas, another spider tugged on the leather of Gilneas's waistcoat, seemingly convinced it was feeding on flesh. And behind her range companion, an iktomid was perched on his back. Its fangs were buried into his shoulder, where crimson curtains of blood washed over its hideous maw. A dagger was implanted into one of its eyes. The mangled organ was twitching uncontrollably, vibrating the piercing blade which seemed to cause the creature no pain. The other remaining eyes lay unfocused on their surroundings, a look of contentment glazing over them. There in that beast's visage, a cruel parody of someone finally satiating their appetite played out.

Alexa realized in horror that she had not even known Gilneas had gone down, his screams falling on deaf ears in the chaos of the battle. *If he had screamed at all.* Her breath came raggedly as she saw the iktomid who had charged her uncoil itself from the brush, inspired by the rest of its pack's success.

It scurried towards her, its legs priming for the killer leap it wished to take. In a blur, the beast closed the distance, leaping into the air naught but one-and-a-half meters from its prey. Without thought, she splayed out the blade of her dagger towards the incoming mass of hairy legs and chitin. She thrust hard into the creature's sternum, wrenching it back and forth, warm blood coursing over her wrist and forearm.

Thoughts of her slain companion—her friend and brother—flowed through her as the bloody beast fell away. The other iktomids were still focused on their meal, but she heard more scurrying footsteps closing in. She pushed away the prickle of shame as she considered running. But surely this battle was lost. Surely it was time for her to retreat? After all, Elgion and her sisters would need to know about this. A party of iktomids this far south could spell trouble for the fledgling settlement. The stream of consciousness began to unravel as she saw at least three iktomids work their way down from the trees, making their way to their victorious kindred. Exhaustion claimed her, and her mind—so long in danger—reverted to some form of animal instinct, a mockery of the creatures she had slain.

*Gilneas is dead.* There was nothing she could do about it. He would want her to warn Elgion. He would want her to delay their meeting in that Far Range that awaits them all. She had stood her ground and fought valiantly, but her companion was dead, and she couldn't help but feel that it was her fault. She turned from the macabre sight; her heart grew heavier by the second as she ran south through the trees.

# Chapter Three

## Sophia

The sun shone brightly from the east, bathing Sophia in its morning glow. The amber folds of her Keeper's cloak grew more radiant in the glorious sunshine. The red trim was a beautiful accent to the sun-kissed cloth, and as she stepped over another runnel in the road she smiled at the beauty of the morning. Like so many other days, Sophia, the Keeper of Stones for the village of Elgion, started her day with a walk to the bakers. There she could obtain a loaf of fresh wheat bread from the baker, Jaspin, and his lovely wife Matildy. Already she could smell the baking bread in the twin stone ovens, their chimneys peaking over the top of the baker's hut.

The bustling crowds of Elgion's citizenry prepared for another day on the frontier, unawares or unconcerned about their Keeper amongst them. Sophia, content with the anonymity, stepped onto the small wooden porch of the shop, but before she could reach it, the door opened. A woman, smelling of lavender, ducked out of the entry with three loaves of bread in tow.

"Good day." Sophia greeted the lady, but, as was more common than Sophia would care to admit, the lady just nodded and moved on quickly. *Will the fear of Keepers ever subside?* She shook her head slightly at the quandary and was brought back to task by the delicious smell that emanated from the open door.

"Hey there Keeper, it's a fine day, isn't it?" The baker greeted her.

Sophia replied—ration chip outstretched, "One couldn't ask for better. I'm here for one of those delicious-smelling loaves if you please,"

"Coming right up. I just finished me first batch," Jaspin turned towards an opening on his back wall that gave him easy access to the two stone ovens in his yard. In that yard, he grabbed a massive wooden paddle and fished out a tray loaded with delicious brown wheat bread. The baker swirled around with grace, and with an expert flair delivered the bread to the countertop. The smell wafted into Sophia's senses, delighting her with its delectable fragrance.

Evidently, the joy was all to plain to see, and the baker's wife let out a laugh. Quickly followed by a rather sing-songy voice, "Aye, it looks like you got it right there Jaspin."

"I should think so. I been doing this nigh on ten years now. Seven back in fair ol' Augustia and now—" He paused, furrowing his brows. "Yea three here in Elgion. Gots to be good at something right?"

"Well, you sure have the touch," Sophia said pleasantly. Her mouth watered as she watched the loaves cool just a couple of meters from her. Almost subconsciously she reached for one.

"Hey, let it cool a minute! It wouldn't do if we burnt the hands of our Keeper," Matildy said as she hurried over to the tray. The woman wiped her hands on her flour-stained apron and fanned the bread in a slightly comical fashion.

Sophia smiled broadly at Matildy, ensuring that the woman would know she took no offense at the command. It was—after all—scary for many to talk to a Keeper. A literal messenger to the gods, through the stones and shards that she carried even now. Sophia was acutely aware of the impact she had on people, and ever since her sisters and her had arrived in Elgion she had tried to make the people more comfortable. "Thank you, my stomach was just so eager that I quite forgot the danger."

"That's alright you wouldn't be the first. The other day one of the little ones … Uh, Keldin I think his name was burnt his little fingers on one of me honey cakes," Matildy said as she fished out the largest loaf from the tray. The woman handed the still-cooling bread to the Keeper. The loaf was too hot to touch still, but Sophia assumed the baker was accustomed to such heat. Matildy leaned in and winked. "There ya go, Keeper! A nice fat loaf for ya. Ya know for all that ya do for us."

Sophia smiled again at the lady and tore off a small piece of the steaming bread. She popped the morsel into her mouth and felt the rich, savory, and slightly yeasty taste explode on her tongue, quickly followed by a burning sensation. She blew outwards trying to cool the small chunk within her mouth, making a rather odd scene for a leader of the village. Fortunately for her, Matildy had vanished back into a rear door of the shop, apparently off to see about her famous honey cakes. Sophia was about to walk out of the door with her loaf in hand when Jaspin called out to her.

"Hey, Keeper!"

Sophia turned and swallowed the now-cooled morsel. She prepared to reply, but her struggle to swallow the bread opened the baker up for a follow-up.

"I was wondering if you could look into something for me. Well not for me, perse, but ya know for the village," The baker said, looking a little uncomfortable.

"Certainly. For the village or for you is fine with me," Sophia said winking at the baker.

The man blushed and a smile crawled across his face. "So, ya see it's like this. I went to make my mixture this morning. And wells I'm pretty near the end of the sack. So as is my custom I went to the back to find the flour the miller delivers every week. Well, there is only two more bags back there! And that's not going to last long. So, I gots to asking around, and, well, the miller's boy, Dunkeath, told me that that's what they got. I says to him, what you mean? And he says, look we can get you more next week but we's been asked to ration it as it were. He then leaned in real close like. Ya know like he didn't want no one to hear and says to me … We might not have enough flour to last this year."

The baker paused, his brows raised, emphasizing the seriousness of the issue. "So, I guess that's my favor then. Could you maybe ask around? Ya know with your … powers, as it were, you might have better luck. Surely, we can't be nearly out. I saw the fields down south earlier this year and they were near plump full!"

Sophia looked at him. "Yes, I will look into this. Thank you for bringing it to my attention. And—" She held up the loaf, "Thank you for this."

"My pleasure Keeper," Jaspin replied.

*

Hours had passed since her parlay with the bakers and now, once again, she found herself locked inside whilst the sun shone outside. She had immediately responded to the baker's request, for although she did not show alarm at his revelation, Sophia did consider the matter most urgent. After all, Elgion was a new village on the frontier across the sea from any resupply or support. If they couldn't grow enough grain here, people would starve. It did not escape her notice that as she pondered yet another problem, her sisters battled beasts and the wilderness outside.  Yet secretly she enjoyed these investigations. She loved the thrill of study and discovery, and as a Keeper one of her primary duties was to sort of 'shore up' the administrative machinery of the dominion she was tasked to oversee. And as she had done many times before, for other such issues, she found herself inside the quartermaster's shed looking over Elgion's various accounts.

A ray of sunlight pierced the western-facing windows, and she held up her hand to try and block the blinding light. She stared wistfully at the dust motes that drifted lazily down upon her outstretched hand. The golden beams were a welcome distraction, although she knew they would become somewhat detrimental to her studies. Nevertheless, she took the moment nature provided to take a break and refresh her mind. Her left hand turned, feeling the warmth of the rays bathe her arm and palm. She let her mind drift away from the numbers, sheets, requisitions, port master reports, supply queries, and various other accounts she had piled around her in messy stacks. A garbled mess that reflected her current mental status.

The pine wood chair she sat upon creaked as she leaned back, rubbing her temples in an attempt to massage her overworked brain. A sigh broke forth as she realized—as was her custom—that in her quest for knowledge, food, drink, or other necessities were forgotten. And now, as happened many times before, she felt a headache coming on.

Luckily, she had become adept at her propensity to stay rooted on a problem for many hours and usually prepared some refreshments ahead of time. There on the table was a cup, a small indent on its lip, filled with clear water from the town well. She took a swig from the mug, and although it had become quite warm in the stuffy room, it revitalized her senses. As she placed the cup back down, a trickle escaped to seep into the wooden table.

The droplet of water disappeared into the grains of wood and a voice, one that she had heard more and more often lately, capitalized on her unburdened mind. It spoke at a level that only those who wished to could perceive. "All of this studying is tiresome. I can help you."

She knew this voice; it belonged to one of her more recent acquisitions. A blue stone that held a purplish glow within. A shard of a god, a token of her order, and a magical conduit that she had acquired from a rather shady merchant on the docks of Augustia just two nights prior to their departure to Elgion.

"You want to be the greatest Keeper to live?" The toothless merchant had asked. Alexa tried to warn Sophia away from the man, but something called to her, something that couldn't quite be explained. The man had held the gem; the shard; the token of the god Dolocius there in his hand, tempting her with its beauty. How he had obtained it she did not know, for in the dark alleys and forgotten corners of the world legality and morality are usually forgotten and figuring that at least one moral or legal code was broken in its possession, she had chosen not to inquire about it. Though as was fitting with the god held within the stone, its acquisition was most definitely through trickery or more dubious means.

"Only five gold, Keeper." The merchant pressed, and although one could buy a modest home back in Augustia with such a sum, Sophia held an insurmountable desire in her heart for the stone. She stared for many seconds, fascinated by the slight pulse of the purple within, and the merchant saw her lust. The man held out his gnarled hand with the Magi stone perched centimeters from her face.

There it whispered to her for the first time, a near palpable embrace. "Hello, Keeper. Do not worry … for I am a friend."

Its sibilant tones seduced her, and before she could be seen hypnotized by the object, fished out five gold Augustian marks and handed them to the merchant. Much to the chagrin of Alexa, who scoffed at her sister's behavior. Sophia paid no heed to the complaint and pocketed the stone.

That night, she held the Magi Stone within her grasp, remembering all the tales she had heard of these stones. They had been made illegal by her order, and it was no wonder, for every story—from verbal warnings and dire missives—painted the stone in a negative light.

One written by Grand Keeper Madrios, a founder of her order, had given it the moniker 'Magi Stone' in his earlier descriptions of the godstone but over time began to refer to it as Sorrowstone. Grand Keeper Madrios had very bluntly stated, "Betrayal is his craft. Deceit is his domain. Ember did not foresee his craft. Now we walk amongst the scattered shards of all Dolocius has wrought. We walk amongst the Shards of Ember, and only deceit can be to blame."

Fitting words for one who ended up falling into madness in the end. A downfall that was whispered to have been caused by the Magi Stone itself.

She tried to take those warnings to heart but—enraptured by the stone—the trickster god had worked his magic. She had awoken the next day with a nosebleed and an intense migraine and in the fogginess of her recovery resolved to use the stone more conservatively. In an experimental manner, slowly increasing the time she used the stone with each session, she investigated the gifts bestowed by Dolocius, lord of the Magi Stone. Her discoveries told her that thirty minutes of rubbing the stone would grant heightened perception and increased mental faculties, one hour would give even the dullest of perceivers the ability to hear a butterfly's wings flap, and an hour and a half would grant the user a feeling of light-headedness and, as had happened before on the first night, an intense nosebleed quickly followed by a migraine of epic proportions. Two hours … Well, Sophia did not want to venture a guess at what would happen after two hours of use. In the end, she had come to another conclusion, she understood why Madrios named it the Magi Stone, for in its use one can unlock the mysteries of whatever they set their mind to.

Now, in this quartermaster's shed, she was once again assailed by the voice of a god. A tone that Sophia, as a Keeper, was attuned to. All the stones spoke in some manner or the other, whether through the whispers of the wind or through some intangible voice that hung at the edge of perception. She could feel their presence, not in any physical sense, but in the way one knows of another presence in a room. The presence now was that of Dolocius, who could be made all the more real if she just reached inside one of her many blouse pockets.

"Just one touch will help you with your query." The fractured god whispered. "A boon, for all that knowledge you seek …" She felt something akin to a breath brushing her cheek, and the whisper grew louder in her right ear. "Just reach inside and let me help you."

Intense temptation gripped her heart. Perhaps she could use the focus. Her hand trembled, and slowly it crept along her blouse, driven by her

internal desires. Her mind buzzed with excitement, as the internal workings of her psyche knew that she was at the edge of release. Soon she would
be able to let go and dive back into that which she most desired, the gifts
of that azure gem. At the last moment, some hidden reserve of resistance
took over and her mind crawled its way back to the forefront reclaiming
control.

"No!" she said to herself suddenly, breaking free from the deceiver's
trickery, and as quick as it had arrived its presence was no more. She did
not need such fancies to solve problems. Her body refreshed, she dived
back into her query.

Sophia shuffled some of the scattered parchments around looking for
details on standard wheat production. With excitement she poured into a
document she had found.

*Ankaron Farmstead*

- *32 acres in steading*
    - *4 acres in timber and nature*
    - *4 acres in livestock*
    - *1 acre for commune*
    - *14 acres winter wheat under plow*
        - *8 acres under fallow*
        - *1 acre under used*
        - *12 bushels winter wheat in yield per acre*
        - *168 bushels total*
        - *42 bushels for replanting*
        - *92 bushels for community use*
        - *17 bushels for settlement taxes (by previous decree: ten per-
          cent of full yield)*
        - *8 bushels for homestead law (by previous decree: five percent
          of full yield)*

■ *9 bushels for profit (given to farmstead for enrichment)*

Sophia tutted to herself, yet another rich yield from another farmstead. She tapped her fingers on the table in a rhythmic pattern and started to mumble some calculations to herself. "Let's see one bushel should yield about forty lbs. of flour, and each person, if all other crops fail and they supplement with hunting and fishing, would need about … one hundred and twenty lbs. of flour per year. So, three bushels per person."

She gathered the yield reports for the other six southwestern farms, which spilled across the table, and noted the total community yield was approximately six hundred bushels. She mumbled softly to herself. "So, for those seven farmsteads alone we can feed at least two hundred people on wheat flour alone."

Something wasn't right. A thought sprung to her mind, and she leapt to her feet, spilling one farmstead parchment to the floor. Her Embershard amulet jingled at the disturbance and its crystalline clinking sounded much too loud in the small office. She rounded on a rickety shelf that contained various ledgers acquired throughout the five years of Elgion's existence. "Let's see here, census … census."

She used her finger as a guide, combing for the telltale mark of the governor's seal. "Ah!" she exclaimed, pulling one out with the desired mark. She scanned the document and with defeat souring her voice, she sighed, "Just a request for more fishing boats."

She slammed the copy of the requisition down—its original having long ago been sent to Augustia. She continued her search anew and had nearly reached the end of the parchments when she found what she was looking for, "Ah yes, a census of Elgion … year four."

She shuffled back to her seat, grabbing the fallen farmstead parchment on her way. She threw the papers onto the jumbled mess that had been her investigation and sat in the pine wood chair, which once again complained at the burden. She combed through the census.

*Elgion Census*

- *Year four since ground break*
  - *180 souls devout to the home city*
  - *68 woman grown*
  - *85 male grown*
  - *27 children*
  - *Of the total 12 lacking in full constitution*

Even accounting for growth over the last year, including immigration, which might be around eighty new souls, seven farmsteads should account for all of the necessary yield in winter wheat alone. If she included the other three farmsteads in the less profitable but still arable southeastern farms, bringing the total to eight hundred-and-forty bushels. And, added in the fact that the farmer's families, perhaps six people per farmstead, don't need to be fully included in the total tally she should be approximately at … two-hundred-and-forty souls fed on wheat flour alone. She bit her thumb as she concentrated on the arithmetic. She figured that they should have an excess of forty soul's worth of wheat flour which came out to one-hundred-and-twenty excess bushels of flour!

She sighed heavily, leaning back in her chair. Including the yields from other foodstuffs, say eggs, milk, game, beans, lentils, and forageables they must be well above the required amount. After all, it is only one bread loaf ration per day.

She chuckled to herself and chortled aloud. "We aren't just eating flour alone; we would surely fly away with the next big wind!"

Her wry amusement at her own jest faded, and she resolved herself to her conclusion. Elgion had enough flour for the bakers, so where else could this be failing? She dug for one of the original parchments she had obtained.

*New watermill on Farney River built Spring of year two of Elgion's founding*

*Yield - year four from Elgion's founding*

- *Received 720 bushels of wheat*
- *30 bushels lost to spoilage*
- *Yield 28,800 lbs of flour*
  - *21,780 lbs to the bakers*
  - *1,440 lbs to homestead law (by previous decree: five percent of full yield)*
  - *2,880 lbs to settlement tax (by previous decree: ten percent of full yield)*
  - *900 lbs loss*
  - *1,800 lbs loss to spoilage*
- *One millstone, having fallen on top of a man, was retired for want of curse avoidance. Requisitioned new millstone from local sources.*

And there it was, looking Sophia straight in the face. The miller was skimming off the top by not even reporting the true value of bushels he had received. He should have received eight hundred and twenty bushels. Some corruption was inevitable, but this damn fool had stolen one hundred bushels of wheat which would amount to four thousand lbs. of flour! On top of that, he was claiming a loss of nine hundred lbs., which was a little high, but not unbelievable, for an inexperienced new mill. Sophia breathed heavily. She would need to confront the foolish miller. "I am gonna need some help."

Corruption in the hands of power was a way of life. Yet on this frontier of theirs—this brave new settlement—corruption on this scale was foolish, and Sophia had no time for fools. She gathered up her cloak and swung it around her back, draping it over her shoulders. The amber of its folds glowed in the sunlight from the window, its red trim sparkling like rubies. Handling this particular corruption might not be as easy as just marching straight up to the miller and demanding the lost flour. That could end with bloodshed or plausible deniability. No, she needed a show of force, to catch the miller unawares and thus blindside him with his guilt. Who better to help with such a task than Bella and her right-hand man, Blythe?

# Chapter Four

## Sophia

Sophia buckled the brooch to her cloak and surveyed the fruits of her labor. It was a jumbled mess that reflected the chaotic nature of research. Although she wished to confront the miller for his crime, leaving such a mess behind would not do. She set about gathering up the parchments and various records she had used. She filed the documents away back onto their respective shelves, taking extra care to ensure that the pioneer orders for Elgion's exploration mission, a wax-stamped document signed by the High Magistrate of Augustia, Trelion III, remained as the paramount document within the quartermaster's records.

After placing the final parchment back on the wooden shelves, she stood looking upon the small office with her hands on her hips. She thought she should request a copy of Keeper Kaldin's book: *Keeper's Stones and Living Things*. In her search for the missing grain, she had stumbled upon some ideas for the future prosperity of Elgion. For one, the rich yields of the southern farmlands warranted an increase in farming grants for the Elgion citizenry, and Sophia thought they could offer some sort of reward, possibly silver, for chopping down some of the timber acreage on current and future farmland. She nodded. Elgion's builders would welcome the extra logs.

She smiled. Something that usually occurred whenever she got lost in her studies. But the thought of having to deal with the corruption her research had revealed made her sigh and with a final nod to the parchments she swept around and went towards the door. She took a moment to smooth her blouse and tidy her hair before going out onto the streets of Elgion. Breathing in to calm her excited heart, she embraced a more stoic demeanor. Although she wished to obtain a more friendly rapport with the citizenry of Elgion, it would not do to show the folk of the village the more frantic behaviors she exhibited whilst in the grip of thrilling research. After all, it was best—as with all authority—to show a picture of utter calm. For if a Keeper were to appear panicked, the villagers would believe the sky were to fall. She placed her hand on the door, took one big breath, and allowed her previous smile to drop, but not so much as to disappear completely. With her mental and physical preparations complete, she pushed open the door and stepped out into the street.

Although rays of light had crept through the windows, Sophia was blinded at first by the brilliance of the afternoon sun. She held up her hand to block the intense rays and stood planted for a moment on the porch of the Quartermaster's shed, which was no more than a platform of wooden planks with a slight cloth overhang to protect from the elements.

"Hey there, Keeper." An elderly voice called out. She turned to look at the source, and to her right sat the quartermaster on a much stouter-looking pine chair than the one she had been given inside. He leaned back into the chair, putting his hands behind his head as he greeted her.

She replied courteously to the man's greeting, "Hello there."

The man paused a moment, fixing her with his gaze, almost as if he were inspecting her. "Did ya find what you were looking for?"

"Yes, I did," Sophia replied curtly only to quickly correct course. "You, um, keep good records."

The quartermaster grinned, "Aye, well all I gots to do is *keep* count!" He guffawed at his joke, slapping his knee while doing so. Sophia had to swallow back a feeling of near embarrassment at the joke, smiling politely to fend off any offense.

"Regardless, they are quite ... tidy."

"Yes ... yes, they are. And thank you, mum. But you should thank them there clarks across the street. Theys the ones who make such good records to begin with," the man said pointing a gnarled sun-kissed hand across the street to a long rectangular wooden building. The clarks, the name granted to any scholar or scribe within the realm of Augustia, were housed within that space. There those scribes and scholars could write or copy various manuscripts for the benefit of Elgion. And, if those clarks were of a less fortunate disposition, some housing.

"Yes, they are efficient in their work. But I have some business at the stables. Thank you, quartermaster," Sophia said smiling at the elderly man.

"Off to the sister then? Well, it's my pleasure, Keeper. Good day," he said with a smile of his own.

Sophia liked the man and the many other frontiersmen and women that inhabited Elgion. Even in the light of difficult pioneer living they found humor and happiness in small things. She truly did feel blessed to be their Keeper and made a note to make an arthritis tincture of willow bark and bloodshade for the quartermaster. She still had an ample supply of willow bark in her apothecary, but the bloodshade, a rare berry similar to nightshade that felt and looked like blood when crushed, would be harder to find. She resolved to drop by the Ranger's Hall, after her visit with Bella, to see if they had any stock she could borrow.

She stepped off the porch and onto the road. A soft rain the previous night had softened the ground, and a few carts and the typical foot traffic of people had turned it into a sloshy hellscape of mud. She hitched her trousers up slightly and started her walk north to the stables. To her left one of the Warriors of August, who guarded the Armory, nodded at her as she passed. The armory, being the only fully stone building in town, held the town's weaponry as well as the silver, gold, and other treasures that would eventually be shipped back to the mainland. The warrior who nodded at her was accompanied by two others, all dressed in the livery of Augustia, and equipped with heavy spears and armor. Their crest, a golden sun over a semi-circle of wheat, adorned their tunics, matching the radiance of the afternoon sun and hiding the heavier—uglier—mail that lay

beneath. Their shields lay propped against the walls of the armory and Sophia could make out the little sunburst tendrils that ringed that symbol of
Augustia, that beacon of light. Truly, she was glad to have the guard, who
under the command of Guard-Captain Alexander Vitrusian lived up to
their hallowed title, The Warriors of August.

She nodded back at the guardsmen, passing a small well on her right.
She pushed into the crossroads of Elgion. To the east, a curving loop of
mud and muck carved its way around the many homes that made up the
residences of Elgion's citizenry, a loop that had been informally named
Hook Street due to its fishhook shape.

To the west, the intersecting road split the armory and a large warehouse that held the various goods that Elgion received through production
or trade. At that moment, strong workmen unloaded another cart, bringing
in pots of oil and bags of coffee.

What she wouldn't do for a cup of that coffee right now. But she
guarded that desire knowing that a fortune must have been paid for such
a luxury.

The port that brought in such goods was about three kilometers to
the west at a natural harbor on the southeast corner of Deinos Bay and
held both of the local inns on the road to its wares. Deinos bay was so
named for the massive reptiles that glided across its calm waters. The
scaled monstrosities were so large that they on occasion took down smaller
fishing boats, along with any unfortunate souls aboard. Yet, with the help
of the larger sea-going vessels of Augustia's navy, many dared the trip
across that monster-infested bay. For overseas trade was too great to pass
up, and Elgion alone provided vast quantities of treasures, gold, and silver
even without these operations being fully fleshed out. Sophia had even
sent a full crate of Maidenstone, the milky white stone of the god simply
known as the Maiden, back to the capital. That small white rock had

bountiful healing properties that ranged from simple headache relief to the mending of lethal wounds.

Just yesterday she had cured a young boy's rash by taking a honey poultice that had small bits of crushed Maidenstone mixed within and applying it as a topical analgesic. She did not say to the grateful family that such an ointment would be worth its weight in gold, even though it only required a sprinkle of the precious white gem. Truly of all the Stones, the Maidenstone was the most beneficent. Even the whispers that an adept Keeper could hear when using the stone—those tiny glimpses into the fragmented gods—soothed the soul. Whereas stones such as her Shard of Ember could feel omnipotent and, if unprepared, quite terrifying. Regardless of its uses, she knew that the quantity she had sent back to the mainland could have been traded for a sum of coffee that would have kept her caffeinated for the greater part of a decade.

Yet she'd sent it for free, knowing that the fortune she had sent would only serve to further Elgion's value in the eyes of the Augustian council. A value that could see Augustia sending regular trade ships to these shores, drowning Elgion's citizens in whatever luxury they desired.

She pushed on through the crossroads, which were a quagmire of ruts and runnels that crisscrossed in undiscernible patterns.

"Hey there Keeper!" one of the merchants of the marketplace to her right called out. "Come, buy a taste of home," he said, holding up a ceramic pitcher, its lip indented in the characteristic fashion of the town's potter.

Two children ran from the market stalls, the sweet honey cakes of Matildy in their hands, giggling as they rushed toward Hook Street with their recently purchased treasures. Sophia had to dodge as one of the kids slipped in the mud in front of her, a look of fear growing on her face as she recognized the Keeper.

"It's alrigh—" Sophia began to say with her hand outstretched, but the child had darted off as quickly as they could. She pushed on, and the merchant called again.

"This here pitcher comes all the way from fair Augustia."

"No, it does not Barnabus, and you know that. That indent on the lip is the sign of the Kiln master. Stop hawking local wares as 'foreign' and then up charging them."

Barnabus, one of the few tradesmen that plied their trade in the market stalls, looked abashed and quickly hid the aforementioned pitcher. He stammered slightly and chose to remain quiet instead.

Matildy, who had just sold the honey cakes to the children, laughed. "I told ya Barnabus, that that was a stupid sales pitch!"

Another merchant, a rather exuberant mustachioed man, that Sophia couldn't quite recall the name of, called out to her. "How about a juicy venison roll to keep those keen eyes strong?"

Sophia paused, and her mouth watered at the thought of the delectable morsel. Her hip pouch jingled slightly, the coins inside calling out to her as if they wanted to be spent. "Oh, why not."

The man clapped his hands together and, opening up a wicker basket, fished out a still steaming bread roll stuffed with juicy brown venison. Sophia made her way to the man's stall. "How much?"

"Just one copper, mum," the man said.

A copper was the smallest increment of Augustian currency, and although it was made of poor-quality iron and not copper, and was fair trade for a lunchtime meal. She fished one out from her pouch and traded the man for the roll. She took a bite, and the juices of the venison burst, filling her mouth with the rich gamey taste of Elgion's wildlife. For a brief second, she simply enjoyed the taste. A smile graced her lips, and she held the roll up to the man in thanks before moving northwards up the street.

She slipped on a newly made runnel in the street and heard a duck quack in what seemed like laughter at her clumsiness. The ducks belonged to the fletcher whose yard lay on her right, the evidence of the most recently dispatched duck apparent in the feather debris lying around the crotchety old coot. The man sat upon a rather large piece of upright firewood, and he eyed her with his one good eye, dirt and grime caked heavily on his features. The man did not stare long and grumbled to himself as he bent back to his task, applying glue to one of the many arrows that would go to the Rangers.

Just past the grumbling old man lay the blacksmith's forge and hut. A rather different breed of individual, the smith was a jovial fellow, who was always open for a bit of conversation and a laugh. His large open fire reminded Sophia of the many winter days in which people would gather around the smith's forge, listening to his extravagant tales and trying to escape the winter cold. The blacksmith, like the quartermaster, fought off the difficulties of the frontier with laughter and joy and Sophia had found herself drifting closer to his firepit on many a day, enthralled by one of his stories.

To Sophia's left, the Ranger's Hall lay where the complement of the town's Rangers made their home, trained, and butchered their kills. A small corral with a couple of mares fronted the northern corner of the building, and one could see the two wings that flanked the central hall of the building jutting off into the west. As she looked down the alley, past the northernmost wing, the smell of the tanner's pits wafted into her. Oddly, the scent of animal urine made Sophia feel a pang of sadness at the sight of the large building, which rivaled the great hall in size. Her sister, Alexa, was out on the range for the better part of the last month and the pain of distance weighed on her. The stern and composed nature of Alexa was a great comfort when Sophia felt lost, and the memories of childhood antics could always make her cheer up in the darker times.

Like when their father had ordered a finely wrought vase, which came packaged in a crate stuffed with hay. He had proudly displayed the treasure to Alexa, Bella, and Sophia, saying this here is all the way from Xeeland, a merchant city-state known for its high-quality trade goods. Sophia remembered Alexa nodding along with their father. But as soon as he turned around Alexa looked over at Sophia and raised her brows twice in rapid succession as if they were both in on a mischievous secret. After some more caterwauling about the necessities of such a purchase, their father took his vase into the kitchen to show their mother. Alexa leapt into action as soon as he left.

"Quick! Get inside." She called to her two sisters. And, not one to question a spontaneous moment, Bella leapt into the box, forcing a tuft of hay into the air at her jump. Alexa looked at Sophia and jerked her head towards the crate, urging her to join Bella. Under pressure from her older sister, she clambered into the crate, and once inside tried to make herself as comfortable as possible.

Alexa looked down into the box. "Alright when dad comes back, you two jump out screaming. I will knock on the box."

Both Sophia and Bella nodded, and Bella grinned so wickedly that Sophia thought her more of a gremlin than a little girl. They waited in that crate for what seemed like forever, trying desperately not to squirm in the uncomfortable situation. Before long, their dad came back into the room, calling behind him about some fact or another regarding the vase.

"That's right it's near fifty years old!" His voice grew louder, his heavier steps pounding closer to the crate.

"Hey girls." Their dad called as he stopped just a couple of meters from the crate. And just when Sophia felt like she was going to burst from the trembling excitement, Alexa rapped the side of the box twice with her knuckles. Sophia and Bella leapt out of the box, pushing the lid high into the air. Their father started in excitement, a tiny tinge of fear in his eyes and a rather excited yelp on his breath. The vase, still in their father's hands, went flying into the air, the lid of the crate and the finely wrought vase both testing the will of gravity. Time seemed to slow as they all watched the objects fall back to Telaea—stunned to inaction. It slammed into the stone floor and miraculously did not break. It rolled a few times and stopped at Alexa's feet. There, their older sister reached down, dusted off the vase, and handed it back to their dad.

"Here you go Dad. You should be more careful."

Their father's brows rose, and Sophia feared whatever wroth was about to issue forth. But their father, who was at times graced by good humor, burst into laughter. In turn, the sisters laughed, and before long their mother joined them in the now hay-strewn room. Together the family laughed, sharing a moment that only those of close kinship could obtain.

She smiled at those bygone days and realized the Ranger's Hall now lay behind her. There, just past another crossroads of Hook and Main Street, the stables stood on the edge of town, a monument to the frontier lifestyle. The property was composed of a stout but long barn, a pen for sheep/cows, a wooden shack in which Blythe, Bella, and the other two stable workers lived, and a large corral that gave the horses and oxen that helped build the town plenty of rich grazing ground.

At the far western end of the corral, Sophia could see Bella riding full gallop on one of the more spirited horses. Sophia approached the fence line that encompassed the corral, and—for a time—just watched. Bella's red hair, almost always worn in a messy bun, contrasted with Sophia's longer ponytail.

The messy bun danced wildly on her scalp, loose strands of autumnal-colored hair bobbing up and down with the horse's gallop. The compact frame and bundles of corded muscle kept Bella's riding posture firm and resolute. Sophia watched the smallest of the sisters' ride with grace, a quality that helped affirm her position as Stablemaster of Elgion.

Before long, Bella spotted Sophia, who was leaning on the fence at the southern edge of the corral, and a smile brightened her face. Quickly, Bella turned the beast with skill, and Sophia couldn't help but notice how rapidly the horse, Precious, a muscly brown mare with a white diamond on its chest, obeyed her commands. In just seconds, horse and rider closed the distance, and Bella, always one for a show, skidded the horse to a stop.

"Woah there." She leapt from the saddle, and looking all the more like some dashing rogue, landed with grace, walked all but three paces, and leaned her elbow on a fence post close to Sophia. Bella smiled and with little pause after the commotion launched into her greeting. "Hey there sister, what brings you all the way out here to see little ol' me?"

"What? I can't just come and visit," Sophia said, stretching her hands out in mock astonishment.

Bella raised her brows. "Right. Last time you came and *visited,* I ended up in some cave in the eastern quarries digging for Maidenstone." Bella pushed herself up and crossed her arms nodding as she spoke again, "Not my favorite thing to do, ya know?"

"No, no, not anything like that. I swear. I just might need your help with a little *civil* matter. And well, maybe the presence of that big ol' stable hand of yours."

Bella fixed her sister with a stony gaze, trying to decipher whatever quest she was going to be sent on. Evidently done with her probing investigation she yelled out over her shoulder, "Blythe!"

Sophia could see the stable hand, Blythe, come running from the barn, a bundle of riding gear still in hand. Bella turned to pat Precious on the head, not noticing her protégé approach. "You remember Precious, don't ya?"

Sophia smiled. "Of course, who wouldn't remember such a fine beast."

Bella looked back at her sister with narrowed eyes. "This is not a *beast*. She is a queen amongst mortals." The jingle of the riding stirrups Blythe carried grew louder as the lumbering man approached at a gait, but Bella was far too distracted by her adoration of Precious to hear.

She yelled again over her shoulder, "Bly—!" But her yell died on her lips as she turned to see Blythe, a dark-haired man of immense stature standing there before her, riding gear in hand. His arms, which seemed too long even for his long frame, held the equipment in his hands like a child presenting a toy to their parents.

Bella fixed him with a look that bordered between amusement and surprise, and with little chance for others to speak launched into a set of orders, "Oh, there you are. What are you doing with all that? Whatever, doesn't matter, I need you to take Precious here and walk her before end of day. Also feed her some oats, because she has been such a good girl." Bella pulled at Precious's bit and handed the 'queen' off to her stable hand. Without a word, Blythe moved off to obey.

Before he could get far, Bella called out again, "Oh, and Blythe … don't feed her that swill we got from the miller the other day. Feed her the good stuff we got from Barnabus." Blythe simply nodded and then continued with Precious in tow. Sophia, as she had seen in times past, noticed how easily he directed Precious.

Bella looked up to the sky, observing the position of the sun. "Looks like it's near closing time. You hungry?" And without awaiting Sophia's response, she made off towards the living shack.

Inside, Bella offered Sophia a quarter loaf of bread, some boiled carrots, and a strip of dried venison.

As Bella situated herself across from Sophia, on the small wooden table that was buttressed against the back wall of the shack, she launched into a query, "So, what's this that's got ya bothered?"

"Well, that miller who provided you with the *swill* oats is what has got me bothered."

"What, did he drop another millstone on some poor fellow?" Bella asked between a mouthful of bread.

Sophia took a small bite of her own loaf before responding. "No, but I am thinking you, me, and that fellow you bark at so much could go have a chat with him."

Bella swallowed, and brought her hand to her chin, rubbing it softly. Suddenly she snapped her fingers like she had discovered a secret. "Ya know I did hear something mighty suspicious around those parts the other night."

Sophia did not reply, choosing to let her sister speak, and took the opportunity to eat one of the unseasoned carrots.

Bella continued, "So, I was tracking another group of those raptors. Ya know the two-legged lizards you scholarly folk have taken to calling saurians?" Bella pointed her hand towards Sophia like she was directing her to speak.

Sophia, used to Bella's sort of rapid conversational style, understood that the question was not rhetorical and nodded.

Bella launched back into her story. "Well, anyways I was tracking them all into the evening and of course the wily fellows made good their escape, darting off over a hill on the northern plains never to be seen again. I was pretty far out by the time I gave up the chase and decided to head back." Bella paused, tearing a large hunk of the dried venison off in her mouth, pulling back on the dried meat as she bit down.

Bella pointed the half-eaten stick of meat at Sophia and continued. "Well as me, Precious, and Blythe were heading back, we of course had to cross the Farney Ford near the mill." Bella then leaned in a little closer, like she was telling a secret, "Well, as we did so we could hear some mutterings and some hollering on the other side of the mill. They must have not known we were there, because they didn't try to hide their doings. At first, I figured, 'Ah well,' the miller was just behind tonight and had a late shipment of flour go out. But something told me there was more to it. So, I had Blythe, Precious, and Scout go on ahead." Bella paused here, biting another hunk of the dried meat.

Scout was Blythe's favored horse. Sophia, finished the last carrot, enjoying the flavors of the summertime harvest before she asked, "Did you catch sight of what the miller was shipping?"

"It was hard to make out in the dim light, but it looked like bags. Probably flour my reckon, and he had some fellas I didn't quite recognize. They looked like sailors and when they had finished the sailor folks took off with the whole lot, cart and all! But like I said it was much too dark to make out a whole lot." Bella's eyes widened. "He's skimming off the top, isn't he?"

Sophia smiled broadly, happy that her sister had figured out the riddle. "Yes, I believe so. But before we make any wild accusations, I was hoping you and that behemoth of a man could help me ask some questions."

Bella grinned mischievously. "A little *interrogation* huh?"

Sophia sighed at her sister's choice of words. She hated that she had likened her to some sort of thuggish government official and then clarified her reasoning. "Not an interrogation. But if I go there on my own, I will either be forced to use the stones in an obvious manner and thus terrify the entirety of Elgion with exaggerated tales of what little sorcery I would have to use. Or I will be left in the lurch as the miller and his sons use their own intimidation and numbers to hide their secrets in the comfort of their own home."

Bella nodded; her eyes narrowed. Just then Blythe walked into the shack, having to duck low under the doorframe to enter.

Bella didn't give him a moment's rest. "Blythe, grab some food and saddle the horses. We got somewhere to be!"

# Chapter Five

## Sophia

An orange glow illuminated the dry grass that spanned a wide plain in front of them. The setting sun lit the landscape in a red-orange hue, reminding Sophia of the Embershard amulet hanging at her neck. Her horse felt tremulous under her untrained mounting, and even the easy track that led toward the Farney Ford felt difficult to manage. Still, Bandit—or whatever this horse's name—was getting her there much quicker than on foot.

Bella must have sensed her sister's difficulties and with a low whistle brought Sophia's horse back to task. Its ears perked up in response to the stablemaster's call and in an instant straightened its gait, making for a much smoother ride. The track was no more than a patch of grass that had been trampled underfoot by frequent use and now was taking the shape of a simple dirt road. This track led on eastwards towards a quarry and, on another fork, some ways north towards the lumber camps of the Eukarian forest. Its usability decreased as it left Elgion.

Bella tapped her shoulder. "Hey, ya still there? We are here."

Sophia shook her head, shrugging off her daydreams, and in the falling gloom of evening, recognized where they were. A watermill was built on the edge of the Farney River, which stretched all the way north to its source somewhere in the hills of the Eukarian Forest. The large wooden construction supported a large waterwheel that churned in the waters below, a silo for grain, and a squat wooden house that was occupied by the miller and his family. Although it lay about five kilometers from Elgion, the ease of grinding grain under the power of water made it viable for use, and since the second year of Elgion's founding, had been grinding the grains produced in the rich southern farmlands into much-needed flour.

Flour that was being stolen in vast quantities. Blythe took the reins of their horses and led them to a small hitching post within the yard of the mill. Sophia struggled to see as the darkness of night dropped its curtain over the land, and although she could make out light under the entry of the mill, it was difficult to see any sign of the miller or his family.

"You are going to need me for this." A sudden whisper formed within her mind. The surprise of Dolocius's voice made Sophia pause.

Bella, who had been silently at her side, paused, a look of consternation on her face. "What's wrong?"

"Nothing, just making sure I got my plan right in my head," Sophia replied. Dolocius laughed, but not in any way that could be heard outside of Sophia's thoughts.

"You lie? To your sister? Oh, Keeper whatever shall we do with you?"

Sophia tried to hide the amazement she felt at the Magi Stones' reach. It was incredible how 'active' the azure stone was, how often it tried to speak to her. The other stones were faint whispers if they were ever heard at all. More like the soft caress of wind than a direct voice within your mind.

The front door opened wide, and a light burst forth from the mill. A gray-haired man, brandishing a torch, called out, "Who goes there!?" To Sophia's surprise, a tinge of anxiety-induced fear trickled into her heart, and her hand grasped the outside pocket where the Magi Stone lay.

"You, see? You want my help." Dolocius beckoned. Wrestling with the twin adversaries, one a god that spoke only in her mind and the other a terrified miller, Sophia succumbed to the god's request and plunged her hand into the pocket. She fished out the blue stone and tucked it away into a pocket at her stomach that helped conceal what her hands did from the outside. There she rubbed the stone gently, allowing the tingling sensation of Dolocius's boon to course through her.

With the incessant crooning of the Magi Stone silenced she replied to the miller, who had swayed the torch back and forth trying to make out who stood at his door in the dark. "It is your Keeper," Sophia said with formality.

"Keeper!? I count three of yous and last time I counted there were only one Keeper in Elgion," the miller replied gruffly.

Sophia sighed. "I have the stablemaster and her stable hand with me."

The miller made a very audible harumph and stepped down off the twin steps that fronted his door. "What you want?"

Sophia rubbed the stone more vigorously as she tried to contain her anger. "We want for nothing, but come on business for Elgion. Now, it is late, and we have ridden far. And unless you have lost your hospitality all the way out here on the edge of civilization, I believe it still customary to offer guests a place to sit and rest before you harangue them."

"Ember's breath! I didn't mean no offense Keeper," the miller replied, shocked at her sudden change in tone. "Come inside, come inside." He stepped off to the side and beckoned for them to go through the door.

"Thank you," Sophia said with a nod as she entered the house quickly followed by Blythe and Bella. The miller followed them, dousing the torch against a dirt patch in the yard and placing it in a basket near the steps.

Once inside, they found themselves around a table, much too large for the small room they were in, flanked by a rather nervous wife who was not too pleased with having the Keeper and the Stablemaster in her home.

She busied herself by bringing fresh bread and drink to the table. "What pleasure it is having you come out here to visit." She said barely hiding her scorn. Blythe dove into his hunk of bread, scarfing down a large portion with one bite. "Plenty of, um, bread …" The miller's wife said in awed frustration.

"We will compensate you for what we have eaten lady," Sophia said politely. The lady, cowed by her politeness, nodded abruptly and hurried off into a room dimly lit behind the miller. The miller did not seem aware of his wife's troubles and instead occupied himself by drizzling honey over his own bread.

"It is good bread is it not?" Sophia asked with a leading inflection.

The miller paused and put the honey-covered spoon down. He looked up at Sophia, and she swore she saw a twinkle of fear—or guilt. The man took a bite of his honey-covered bread and with two quick chews swallowed the treat in a rather painful-looking manner. "Aye, it is … So what brings you out here Keeper?"

"Bread!" She said suddenly, causing the miller to jump from both the suddenness of the word and from abruptly pointing her own hunk at him. "Bread is the nature of our visit." The miller's wife reentered with a clay pitcher of well water. The wife went around the table pouring water into clay cups set in front of each of them, a small indent on the rim of each cup plain to see. The Magi Stone was taking effect and with alarming alacrity. Her god-infused perception made every small error, every tiny abnormality, stand out like wine on wool. The table had already been set for five, but only the miller and his wife were present. The miller's sons could not be far and although their absence was concerning, she pressed on. "You see, bread might be lacking soon. And I would hate to know what would happen come the winter without it."

The miller raised his eyebrow at this, feigning surprise.

Sophia smiled at the man and continued. "You see, I heard from our rather *opinionated* baker that he simply does not have enough flour to make bread for everyone."

The miller snorted. "Well, that baker is a fool."

Sophia fixed the miller with her gaze waiting for his indignation to drop. "Whether he is a fool or not, this made me curious." She paused allowing a faux smile to ripple across her face. "You know how curious us Keepers are." Her grin widened, a subtle threat, pushing tension into the air of that room. The Magi Stone showed Sophia every hand twitch and tiny tremble of frayed nerves between the miller and his wife. The woman looked at her with a thin veil of curiosity and fear. Sophia did not wish to frighten the wife, but the miller was plainly hiding something, and at times the difficulties of honesty needed a sprinkling of consequence—and fear—to ensure their will was carried out.

The miller spoke slowly. "Well, yes, you are known for that."

"Yes … yes *we* are," she said with a hint of threat in her voice. She paused, allowing for the tension to mount even higher before she delivered her accusation. "And some of us are known for our, shall we say … gluttony?" She leaned back fixing her eyes on the honey-covered bread. The miller scoffed, but Sophia continued. "My investigations have led me to believe that someone in the provisioning of bread may be gluttonous." Her voice now rose in tempo and volume. "So now, *miller*, can we stop with the games and arrive at the truth!" Her Embershard amulet took on a faint glow, mirroring the increase in her intensity.

"I-I-I don't know what you mean," the Miller spluttered. The effects of the Magi Stone were now in full force, and Sophia swore she could hear a faint creak of floorboards. The near imperceptible sound emanated from the room the wife had entered for the well water, and which now lay ominously shrouded in shadows. She did not see anyone, nor did Bella or Blythe show signs they had heard anything untoward in the room. Yet, there in those shadows, Dolocius had told her, not in direct terms but through something akin to the sensation of touch, that someone or something lurked.

The miller's sons were sure to be strong, being in the profession of grain millers. Perhaps he had hidden a backup plan in his sons, in the dark, ready for ambush. After all, it was certainly wise to prepare a contingency plan for strangers arriving at your home at such a strange hour.

Regardless she pressed on, capitalizing on her position. "You know exactly what I mean, sir." She paused a moment, looking at the wife, who writhed in apparent agony at her predicament, and back at the stunned miller.

With the accusation planted, it was time to twist the knife. "I am sorry folks," she said with a genuine look of sorrow at the miller's wife. "But my sister and I simply wish to know the truth, and your sons hiding in the dark will not stop us." The last words were loud enough to be heard through the house. She was rewarded with a muffled whisper and the shuffling of feet in the adjacent room, whatever ambush lying in wait now blown.

"You see my sister and I are of one mind," she said jerking her head to the left where Bella sat. Bella chose that moment to grin, bringing her hands above the table, a whetstone and a rather nasty-looking dagger in hand. With malevolent force she drew the blade across the oiled stone, its sound echoing throughout the room.

"And well Blythe here, he does whatever my sister wants."

Blythe dipped his head in ascension his girth accentuated by the fact that he hunkered over his nearly finished loaf of bread.

The miller closed his eyes and with an audible sigh relented. "Look, I'm sorry." Heaviness now in his voice, he reopened his eyes and relayed his regret. "It's just that last year was a hard year. What with the stone falling on poor Thomas and all. He was a good mill hand and now he's under the ground. We have been giving his widow some extra money so she can get more than just what the ration chips allow. Figured we owes it to her. And well I guess I wanted to make it up somehows is all."

Sophia recognized the placid courage, a common trait of those on the frontier, of a man facing down his accuser and admitting the truth. Yet still, this man had been skimming off the top for a while now. And it was also true that this most recent year was the most egregious. She allowed her silence to work its magic on the guilty miller.

Suddenly the wife spoke, "Please Keeper forgive us! We didn't mean nothing by it!" The miller had hung his head in shame, choosing not to support or dismiss his wife's plea.

Sophia held up her free hand, palm outwards, calming the room. "My sister and I are not unreasonable. All we ask is to show us where the stolen goods are, or if they are gone the coin you made from their sale." Her voice was slow and deliberate as if to accentuate each point. "We can see about getting Thomas's widow some additional accommodations."

A moment passed with the miller's head still downcast, before his wife nudged him into action. The Miller sighed. "I can show you where the missing flour is Keeper … and I gots about three silver coins here from the sale of what else is left." He pulled the coins out and placed them on the table. He yelled over his shoulder. "Boys! Come on out now!" From out of the darkness came three large boys, a product of a miller's life, their heads held low in shame.

"Great," Sophia chose that moment to pull her hand off the Magi Stone revealing both of her hands to the crowd. She clasped them together in front of her, harder than she had expected. She had meant the gesture to be one of goodwill, but she had done it much too quickly and with too much force. The wife jumped back in fear, her hand held over her mouth. Sophia felt her left-hand tingle, filled with the desire to feel the cool Magi Stone radiating up her forearm. In forcing her hand to release the stone she had exerted some force, causing rapid motion. "My apologies lady, it has been a long day."

"It's quite alright Keeper," the miller's wife said, her face pinched. "We could hole you folks up in the extra room for the night … so you could go with my husband to rectify this; first thing in the morning."

Sophia looked calmly at the wife. "Thank you for your hospitality. As a sign of our goodwill and mutual understanding. Also, we owe you for the food and board. Hows about you guys keep one of these silver coins?" She pulled the other two away slowly, allowing them to scrape across the wood.

The wife grabbed the coin quickly muttering her gratitude. "Oh, Maiden's blessings Keeper. Well, I mean more than she probably does already. You being able to talk to them and all, I mean."

Sophia chuckled, smiling pleasantly at the woman, and with more warmth in her voice asked, "Blythe, could you be a dear, and help this woman with our sleeping arrangement?" Without a word Blythe rose to his feet, his head nearly scraping the roof. One of the miller's boys, the apparent youngest, had his mouth agape at the behemoth of a man.

"Boys, go and help your mother," the Miller said, tapping his finger on the wooden table. Blythe, the boys, and the miller's wife all disappeared into the gloomy room in the back. When they had left, the miller looked up at Sophia, showing her his eyes, which were threatened with tears.

"Sir, I promise no harm will come to you or your family," Sophia said calmly.

The miller breathed a sigh of relief.

"I could even talk to the governor about some way for folks like you to make some extra coppers." She said with a hint of enthusiasm in her voice.

"Thank you ... Keeper," the miller said.

"But, if you are ever caught selling the town's grain again ... Well, I would hate for us to have to come visit you again," Sophia said flatly.

The forlorn miller simply nodded and then left his head bowed in surrender.

# Chapter Six

## Bella

The morning air was crisp, a sign of the changing seasons. A light mist blanketed the ground, and dew lay heavily on the grass. The life within the small grove of oak and maple trees was just waking up, and songbirds sang out a beautiful chorus of melody. Squirrels and hares darted away from the newcomers, the fear of being prey lay paramount over their morning hunger. It was a beautiful place to be, and Bella breathed in heavily, enjoying the fresh air. She always found the first-morning chill from summer to fall to be quite refreshing, though with notes of sorrow. For that brisk touch heralded the changing seasons, and the abundance of life would fall away into the somber notes of winter. Yet for now the sky was clear in the dawn light, and it promised to be a warm and pleasant day.

Nature's beauty invigorated her, and she saw Sophia too was smiling—ever so softly—at the pleasantness of the morning. Her sister looked radiant in her amber gold cloak, which sparkled in the morning's early light. Sophia had, as she always did, worn the simpler attire granted by her order, a blouse, a vest, and a cloak fastened at its nape by a brooch. All of this was adorned by the ever-present Embershard necklace, and the only non-Keeper-oriented clothing was a pair of simple riding pants and boots.

Yeah, Sophia's outfits were simpler. Not like that uncomfortable-looking smock that some of those old codgers in Augustia wore. Even so, Sophia was still weighed down by a heavy cloth vest along with a blouse that held many pockets, each one loaded with stones, vials, and other such trinkets. The mark of a Keeper.

Bella's reflections on her sister's clothes made her look down at her own clothing, a dirty tan blouse and rugged riding pants. It was enough for even Bella's lower standards to feel a flush on her cheeks. She looked back at her more regal sister, partly in embarrassment and partly in wonder.

Sophia must have noticed Bella's gaze because she slowly turned to her, her brown eyes peeling off the miller and his boys.

Deciding it was best to say something instead of just awkwardly staring back, Bella yelled, "Hey! It's a fine morning!"

Sophia, apparently unphased by Bella's staring, replied with matched enthusiasm, "Yes! Yes, it is! Elgion is blessed this time of year." The Keeper upturned her head; her red ponytail falling loosely between her shoulders and closed her eyes. Bella watched as Sophia let go of her reigns and raised her hands towards the air, appearing to soak up the surroundings. Slowly, the Keeper let loose a shuddering breath, as if she had been in a moment of meditation, and as her hands dropped back to her sides Bella was delighted to see a look of pure joy ripple across her sister's face. "I sure hope Alexa returns with a few nice fat rabbits. I see the beasts scurrying about here and there, but bah … you know me. I never was a hunter."

"If I know Alexa, we will be eating venison and hare for weeks after her return," Bella replied, a somewhat sad smile stealing across her face. Alexa and her range mate, Gilneas, had been out longer than was usual, even for a sojourn into the cursed Eukarian forest. The lateness of their sister's return was causing anticipation amongst them, and no matter how many 'tasks' Bella busied herself with, the anxiety mounted.

It mounted even though Bella had kept herself beyond busy in the chaotic time of Summer. Within the month that Alexa was gone, she had sunk a new fence around her stable yard, captured three local bovines, gathered fleece for the coming winter, and, most excitingly, found herself chasing off a group of Saurian raptors who had ravaged three of the townsfolk's sheep just five nights prior.

Bella had pushed herself, Blythe, and the other stable hands to the edge of night hunting that pack. In the end, they had to turn back as the confounded lizards had doubled back on their own trail, throwing their pursuers off, and promptly disappearing over a rise in the hills never to be seen again. Nevertheless, much was discovered about the elusive animals' behavior. How they never moved in straight paths, always turning and wheeling. And how they were very selective in their direction almost like they were driven by more than just instinct.

Those raptors, bipedal lizards with arms nearly as long as their legs and a stature that rivaled that of a horse, had quite cleverly ambushed the three sheep furthest from protection, efficiently devoured the meat and bone off their kills, and were off before anyone was the wiser. It wasn't until the morning, when the poor farmer had nearly burst down the stable house door, before anyone was aware of the crime. Bella had ridden to the sheepfold and found that all that remained was a smattering of offal and woolly skin, husks of their former owners. It was hard not to admire them.

An admiration that was enhanced by curiosity, for Sophia—in days past—often mentioned talk of bones discovered by intrepid explorers. Bones that were ancient and by their makeup must have belonged to some 'great lizard.' Sophia, as was her custom when in the thralls of academic conversation, went into great detail about the various hypotheses and discoveries of the world's academics. Even going so far as to praise a Keeper from Argolon.

"Some of my more exuberant colleagues believe those bones and the beasts that live here are from the same family tree! And some, an Argolonian of course, even believe they are intelligent! Like as in being able to rival us in speech or other such crafts. Of course, she *is* an Argolonian, so, her logic is slightly flawed, because how would a race without the capacity to build ever rival us? Nevertheless, some of her observations are ... intriguing."

Bella smiled at her sister that day and had simply replied, "I don't know if these animals are smart enough to shape a blade, but they do seem to move with purpose."

Now, here they sat on the edge of civilization, wondering about their sister and about the mysteries of this new world they came to just two years ago. Mysteries like the saurians, who were being spotted more and more frequently in the years since Elgion's founding. A songbird, twittering as it flew, dived in front of Bella, throwing her mind back into the present.

"You will find it all there, Keeper." The miller panted as he slammed what appeared to be the last bag onto the now bulging cart.

Sophia scanned the bags, her face rigid like stone. "There is forty pounds per bag, correct?"

"Yes, Keeper, that's right. And well, I get about a bag per bushel."

Bella couldn't resist a cheeky grin as she heard her sister ask the leading question, although she surely knew the answer.

Sophia smiled. "It would appear, sir, that your debt has been repaid. Let us not meet again under such circumstances."

With those words the miller nodded, a small grin alighting his face. "Thank you, Keeper, and thank you, mum," he said as he nodded to Bella. His gaze flashed over Blythe, but whatever he saw made him decide not to comment.

"I believe your name is Garreth, is it not? I heard your wife call you so." Sophia asked.

"Um, yes it is mum."

"Would it be alright if I called you so in the future? A token of our new partnership in the goodwill of Elgion?"

The miller, flustered by the generosity of the statement, stammered, "Uh, yes that would be alright Keeper. Um, may I call you by yours?"

Sophia smiled, more mirth in it than during the investigation, but still a façade. "Garreth, I am a Keeper and for all the years that hold me in the promise of the stones, I cannot allow for that to be so. Truly, it is not against you but against the guidance gifted to us from my order." She brought the Embershard necklace to bear and let the amulet catch the light before she tucked it back into her shirt.

"Certainly, Keeper, I understand." The miller bowed.

Bella had always admired the way that Sophia could tease out emotions from people. Her gifts from either stone or insight were astounding, and Bella had watched Sophia bend many to her will, generally a will that aimed for good. The miller—in comparison—had been an easy will to bend, and Bella wondered why this man who stole nearly 4000 lbs of flour was being let off rather easily. Still, the manipulations, no matter what they were used for or if they were a craft of the Keeper's order, did feel somewhat wrong. It didn't help that Sophia had a certain air of pomposity about her, which was definitively demonstrated by her insistence that she and Bella remain mounted.

Perhaps a trick of authority. Regardless of the reasoning behind the decision, it was really beginning to chaff for they had been in the saddle for about an hour. Now with all the flour loaded, Bella looked down at Garreth and his sons. Two of which appeared to have no lingering animosity, but the oldest son did not share the same conviction. His mouth was curled in a rictus of malice, and his fists were clenched as he tried to hold in his anger. Dunkeath was his name, and Bella marked him there in her mind.

"Mum!" Blythe called out suddenly, pointing north through the grove of trees. Bella fixed her eyes towards Blythe's warning, and there she could see a lone figure prodding through the tall grass. They were only one and a half kilometers from the old mill and not too far from a northerly bend of the Farney River that would lead towards the Eukarian Forest, but still, a lone person out this far was cause for concern. Bella glanced at Sophia, and a near imperceptible nod from her sent Bella cantering off toward this new threat. She cleared through the trees, Blythe shortly behind, and could see that the figure appeared to be exhausted, nearly falling over with every step. What in Ember's breath was a person doing out here? She placed her hand on her axe, a weapon she preferred in the saddle, calming herself with its touch.

The figure raised its head, and Bella could see it trying to raise its hands in recognition. Yet those hands only rose to their chest, falling as if gravity was too much to overcome. Bella was covering the ground quickly, and fifteen meters from her goal she made out the figure who dared to be out so far. Alexa! Bella increased her pace, dismounting smoothly in the last few seconds. "Sister! What are you—"

"Gilneas," Alexa said weakly as she reached her hands out. Bella barely caught her as she fell and nearly toppled herself. Blythe came in to steady them both.

Alexa spoke hoarsely again, "Gilneas."

"It's alright sister, we got you now." Worry filled her voice. Alexa looked as if she had seen the worst of it. Her clothes were filthy, and grime covered her face. There was a gash on her left shoulder that appeared to have taken an ill turn. Alexa's bow was still strung, which was odd as a ranger would know that a strung bow would get weak with time.

Alexa noticed Bella's stare and through a faint smile on cracked lips responded to the querulous gaze. "I-I … couldn't restring it if I let it loose."

Bella laughed without mirth. "Sister, what in all of the Maiden's blessings are you doing out here?" She looked around at the countryside. A vast plain stretched off to their north, leading all the way to the foothills of Mossgrave, but Bella saw no one around. "Alone?"

Alexa, her weight supported, gained some small semblance of strength and replied more powerfully. "Gilneas … h-he is gone." Her voice trailed off and she looked back up into Bella's eyes, a flash of terror stealing through them. "We must get back to Elgion. I … I have news." Her head dipped, exhaustion claiming her, and before Bella could reply Alexa had fallen into sleep.

# Chapter Seven

## Bella

Bella raced with her sister draped across the saddle. Alexa was incredibly warm to the touch, and by the time they had reached Sophia's apothecary, she was sweating profusely. A scorching fever had taken hold of the lone ranger, which was only made worse as they raced into town. Townsfolk scattered at the sight and sound of their horses, some of them crying out in fear—or anger. Bella did not care because she could feel the heat radiating off her kin. They pulled alongside Sophia's home, which doubled as the town apothecary, located on the easternmost bend of Hook Street. Blythe quickly dismounted and rushed to Precious' side. Bella lowered Alexa into Blythe's arms, and he jolted through the now-open door of the home. Sophia guided him to a back room that she had fashioned into a sort of observation room for the ill or injured.

In that space, Sophia lit some candles, placing them on sconces and holders strategically placed throughout the room. "Help me with her clothes, we need to see if there is a source to this infection. Blythe, can you gather us a bucket of water and some rags?"

Blythe nodded and quickly darted out of the room. They undressed their sister, and Sophia's deft hands felt under the skin for lumps or contusions working from the head down. Bella watched Sophia's probing hands as they discovered the source of the fever, an abrasion that resembled a starry sky, raised bumps of lighter-colored flesh acting like stars as they were surrounded by a blackened void of corruption. The blackened rot was taking over the skin in front of her left shoulder.

Sophia paused when she saw the wound. The pause was minute, and she recovered with slight exasperation. "We need to clean around the wound, as well as elsewhere to ensure there are no additional infections."

As if on cue, Blythe burst through the door with a water bucket; half its contents spilt in his haste. A few rags draped over his shoulder. Bella moved to intercept him, stealing the bucket and rags, nodding to him in silent thanks. As Bella set about Alexa with the soaked rags, she suspected that venom had caused this wound, but what kind of bite would appear like that? She wracked her brain trying to consider what type of beast could cause such a wound.

Iktomids. The hairs on their legs have been known to abrade skin, and Alexa must have gotten into a pretty rough tumble to have venom enter her wound. Bella had cleared the larger debris from the shoulder wound and was beginning to cleanse more intimately in the crevices of the abrasion when she heard the clatter of drawers opening and closing.

Sophia was rooting around in a dresser, which held multitudes of small drawers, most likely containing the herbs and Maidenstone that was frequently used in the apothecarial trade. Bella had never seen her sister move so quickly, and it frightened her. If Sophia, a Keeper of the Stones, was worried, then it did not bode well for Alexa's prospects.

Bella continued to scrub away the grime. The water Blythe had brought was filthy after just a few soaks of the rags. "Blythe!"

The ambling giant appeared suddenly at her side, as if ready to be called. Bella simply nodded to the bucket, and he understood, sweeping it up to be replenished. A fragrant smell of herbs filled the room, as Sophia ground some healing balm in her mortar and pestle. Bella could see ample quantities of Maidenstone and echinacea and she could smell yarrow flowers and goblin's finger. The irony of using a fungus that had a similar appearance to the hands of such a wretched creature was not lost on her. Still, it was a proven fever breaker.

Blythe reentered the room with fresh water and Bella resumed her task of cleaning away filth from Alexa, all the while searching for additional wounds. She only found some scrapes, cuts, and a rather nasty bruise on her stomach. Nothing unordinary for a ranger who had just returned from a month-long ranging.

Sophia—her grinding complete—chanted, "For the Maiden is wise and we offer to you for good health, Alexa, who in your eyes has fallen ill." The words seemed to fill the room, and Bella could feel a slight thrumming whip through the air like insects buzzing about them. Sophia approached the bedside and generously applied the paste to the wound, interlacing it between the blackened rot. "I ask for your mercy, oh Maiden, bring us your boon and we will continue to walk with grace," Sophia's voice soon resonated with an inhuman-like quality, as if from an other-worldly source.

She repeated the phrases a few more times while applying the paste throughout the wound. All the while Bella continued to cleanse the sickly hot skin. Bucket after bucket was brought, as Blythe carried out the old filthy water and replaced it with new. Several minutes passed in which Bella scrubbed every centimeter of her sister. Yet, in her fear and worry, she did not stop even when the job had been thoroughly done. Instead, she scrubbed vigorously trying to work away the pain of her emotional turmoil.

Suddenly, Sophia put a calming hand on her shoulder. It made her jump, breaking her free from her trance. She looked up into Sophia's eyes, the comfort in them, stilling her rapidly beating heart. She gathered herself and realized that in her trance she had rubbed her own hands raw, a feat accentuated by Alexa's scoured skin which glowed red from the intense cleaning it had undergone. Bella looked back up at Sophia, feeling much like a child looking for guidance. Sophia gestured with her hand to a basin of cold water and without a word demonstrated by dabbing a rag and holding it to the head.

As she fell into that small but still useful task, her nerves settled. Alexa's labored breath eased, and the skin felt slightly cooler than the inferno it had been earlier.

Sophia brought a blanket to cover Alexa, save for the corrupted shoulder. With the blanket in place, she turned away from the bed and increased the tempo of her chants, the words dying to a single repetitive phrase, "Maiden! Grace us with the boon of your mercy!"

Raising her hands towards the sky, Maidenstone in hand, her arms quivered as if under strain. Bella held her breath as the very air in that room seemed to fill with a presence, the chants taking on a will of their own and seemingly repeating themselves before Sophia had even spoken them again. The sound became near deafening, and Bella dropped the cold cloth in awe at the sight. Sophia's eyes rolled back into her head. Hands clasped above her; towards the heavens. With her mouth agape, she crushed the Maidenstone between the vicelike grip, repeating the incantation one more time, almost at a whisper, "Maiden. Grace us with the boon of your mercy."

The room became deathly quiet for what felt like ages. Bella was about to speak again when, almost beyond any sensation, she heard something at the edges of perception. "I hear you …"

Chills ran up Bella's spine. The voice was not from anyone in that room, nor from anyone she had ever met. A voice that belonged somewhere else. Somewhere greater than here. Sophia collapsed to her knees. Bella ran to her side, catching her before she lost her balance completely.

"Sophia," Bella called, tears streaming down her face. "Sophia … wha-what was that!"

Sophia's voice was a hoarse whisper. "The Maiden, Hyclepius." She opened her eyes fixing Bella within their window. "Of course, you probably knew that, but you just have never heard her before. She has answered us," Sophia said with a smile gracing her lips. "Give me a moment and we can continue our labors." They sat for a time, Bella holding Sophia in her embrace. With great effort, pressed her hand to the floor to push herself up. She spoke more firmly now as she gained her feet. "I think … I think I will be alright. You may let me go. Thank you."

"Will *she* be alright?" Bella queried as she nodded her head towards the bed.

With strain still in her voice the Keeper replied, "This mercy I asked for can be fickle, but I think we have bought ourselves a chance. Only time will tell now."

Sophia gently pulled Bella's hands away from their steadying grip, and with a slight stumble, she regained her footing. "But for now, sister, we have work to do. Let us continue to try and break this fever."

For several hours they continued their work. Sophia had settled into a routine of examining the wound and then studying a ponderous tome, titled *Hyclepius's Teachings,* that lay open on a desk at the back. Occasionally she would find something of interest in her studies and it would cause her to try a sprinkle of healing ointment or simply a closer examination of some hideous crevice of the now scarring tissue. All the while, Bella continued to reapply the cooling cloth, in silent observation of both her sisters.

Blythe had brought some dried venison for them to eat in the early afternoon as well as some light broth for Alexa. Bella ate her ration, but Sophia barely touched hers. Blythe held Alexa's head up as they spooned the light broth into her mouth. A reassuring cough oddly gave Bella a sense of hope. "There ya go, you will be right as rain in no time." Bella said with emotion rich in her voice.

The afternoon dwindled, and Sophia had settled into her desk hunched over her medical tome. Bella had eventually fixed the cool cloth with a simple headband and settled into a chair near the door, just observing. Her sister mumbled to herself, but exhaustion and caution had kept Bella from interrupting. Sophia also rubbed something inside of her vest with increasing vigor. After an hour of this repetitive behavior, the Keeper suddenly stopped and brought her hand to her face, turning to Bella. Blood seeped through the cracks between fingers, and Bella rose suddenly, fear once again creeping in.

She rushed over to Sophia's side, knowing that Keepers had worked themselves to death on more than one occasion. "Sophia, what in Ember's breath is this?"

The exhausted Keeper looked up at her sister and pulled the hand away from her nose, a rivulet of blood escaped past her lips. The rubbing had stopped, and a look of what appeared to be shame crossed her sister's face. "I think … I think I need to rest now. There is nothing else I can do tonight." She paused for a moment glancing at Alexa, "Can you sit with her tonight? You or Blythe?"

Bella could see the pleading look in that face. "Of course, me and Blythe will stay here. And, if sleep takes me, that ox of a man will not fail." Blythe, quiet and gentle as ever, nodded solemnly, an understanding that he would not fail held heavily in the action.

Sophia grinned, although it faded quickly as exhaustion stole across her face. "Thank you. I will return in the morning."

Sophia left the observation room surely to seek rest in her private quarters. Bella stood for a while, wondering over her sister's sudden ill turn. Sophia had worked herself ragged in her attempts to keep claim over Alexa's life, but the frantic rubbing, the near maniacal mumbling, and the sudden bloody nose had her mind tumbling with worry.

Blythe gently placed one of his massive hands on Bella's shoulder. "Come mistress, you should sit down … conserve your strength."

"Aye, I think I might," Bella replied smiling at the big man. She liked Blythe, but she had always felt their kinship was more like that of a wolf pack. Her being the leader and him being a loyal follower for the good of the group.

Her mind was now set firmly on the task at hand, and she took up her vigil over Alexa, allowing the exhausted Keeper time to rest. She claimed the chair closest to the back window and Blythe propped himself against the wall adjacent to Bella. The night wore on in silence except for one fit of coughing. At the sound of the productive cough, the duo sprang up; their eyes wide open; the fear of death heavy on them. They wiped away the worst of the phlegm and propped Alexa on her side using a heavy wool blanket. With Alexa's breathing back to normal they had sunk back into their seats. Shortly afterward, Blythe had fallen back asleep with his head tucked between his knees. Bella content with allowing the big man to rest, settled back into her vigil of worry. She sat in silence for hours just watching Alexa's chest rise and fall. Every breath was a blessing. A couple of times the exhalation did not come quickly, the specter of death looming over that crowded room.

The raspy breaths came at random intervals, punctuating the slow creeping minutes in relative darkness. Otherwise, the room was silent, except for the forlorn cry of some wild thing carried in by the evening chill. Dawn would be falling on her in a few hours. The sounds of birds could be heard. The faint edges of gray light were beginning to eke out over the plains of Elgion.

Unable to keep her exhaustion at bay any longer, she tapped Blythe on the knee. Although he grumbled rather loudly at having to wake, he stood and shook the sleep from his face. He nodded and she knew that the stable hand wouldn't fail her. Without moving from the chair she had been perched in all night, she leaned back and let sleep take her.

# Chapter Eight

## Bella

Bella woke to a beam of golden dawn light piercing through the open back window. She rubbed her eyes and arched her back, stretching the soreness gained from sleeping on a hard-wooden chair. Sophia had already risen. Her normal manner of calm dignity restored. Blythe stood behind the Keeper holding tongs, scissors, and a basin of steaming water with white cloths draped over its side. They stood over Alexa's bed and Sophia used tongs to pull away crusts of Maidenstone ointment. Particularly difficult sections of ointment were first cut away then washed thoroughly. Blood ran thick when the broken flesh was removed, accompanied by a sickening crackle. As Sophia pulled away sections, they were cleansed by one of the many still steaming cloths in the hot basin. She then reapplied the frothy paste from last night, once again invoking the Maiden, although now nearly at a whisper. In mimicry of her lighter tone, Sophia also didn't apply the paste as generously.

Bella rose from her seat, content with watching the two work. From her vantage point, the wound appeared lighter in color. A desired contrast to the deathly black of last night.

Sophia, noticing her sister, turned and said, "I think … all will be well. Alexa just needs a few days to recover." Bella nodded and couldn't help but smile. She embraced the Keeper suddenly. Sophia, shocked at first, slowly returned the embrace.

*

For the next two days, Bella would wait with Alexa at night, giving Sophia some much-needed rest, but during the day she had to keep herself occupied. Since she could not tolerate sleeping the day away, Bella found jobs throughout town. On the first day, she and Blythe made sure the stables were in good order under the other stable hands. Although neither of the duo could find any fault in the care of the grounds, they still made sure Precious, the other prime horses, and Scout, Blythe's favored stallion, were exercised and given good oats. After a time at the stables, a few stray sheep meandered by. Blythe, one of the sheep in tow, went into the village to ask about them. He returned, discovering that they were from a communal pasture just outside the eastern part of town. The devilish beasts had broken out and eaten a few heads of cabbage in the neighboring garden. Bella and Blythe helped the townsfolk recapture all their lost livestock and reset the broken fence posts.

On the second day, Bella wandered the streets, without Blythe in tow. She hadn't risen near lunchtime, sleeping much longer than the previous night. With a hot wrap of venison and fresh bread in hand, Bella spotted a gang of workers who were pushing a rather overburdened timber cart through the ruts of Main Street. There were three other carts behind, all loaded with similarly sized logs.

Feeling rather adventurous, Bella called out to the foreman, "Hey there, fella! You need an extra hand?"

"Only if you don't want to be paid," the foreman replied rather gruffly.

"Sure." Bella scarfed down the rest of her venison wrap. The warm juices ran down her chin, and she grunted contentedly.

The foreman stood shocked; rather unsure of what he had heard, but, as he regathered himself, he simply shrugged. "Oi, I won't stop you helping me, but don't go telling your sister if you lose a finger."

"Don't worry sir, there won't be any fingers lost today … Unless you want them to be." Bella grinned mischievously as she turned to the foreman. The man stood agape as he saw Bella cleaning her nails with a wicked knife she had produced seemingly from thin air. "Well, if there isn't anything else," she pointed the dagger toward the deck of logs. "Shall we?"

"Uh, yes that would be fine," the now flushed man said quickly, ready to be done with the exchange. Bella chuckled and set herself to work. They pushed each cart through to the clearer port road, only able to move one of the brutish timber carts at a time. After they had cleared the cumbersome carts through, they tried to coax the large draft horses into solely pulling the load. Bella knew the lead beast personally, Bruno she had called him, and he was a stubborn oaf. She chuckled as the foreman yanked on his reigns to no avail, cursing as he did so. Bella always kept treats for the more stubborn beasts of burden, and she rooted around for one of the carrots she carried in a shoulder-slung satchel. She had watched him pull for the greater part of a minute before she ambled over towards Bruno, holding out the carrot. When Bruno reached for it, she only walked slightly forward keeping the carrot ever in sight of the horse's gaze. Slowly but surely, the heavy carts began to creak forward. She surrendered the carrot only after the caravan had gotten a proper move on.

The port was only three kilometers away, down a gently curving path to the shore. The first trip out to the port took the better part of an hour, and the afternoon sun had been cruel on horse and human alike. Sweating and consigned to their drudgery, the caravan moved towards a staging site. The logs would eventually be carried out to the middle of the wharf where a rather sturdy crane was moored. The crane would be the only way to load such heavy cargo on the fat holds of ships from the capital.

The port was not impressive. Made up of three rickety wooden warehouses that lined the portside road. Each warehouse had its massive twin doors towards the sea. The wharf, where the logs would be carried, jutted out into Deinos Bay and was one of the first constructions Elgion had made. Haste brought on by the desperate desire to ensure that trade and supplies could flow easily into the settlement. Three berths—one for large and two for smaller craft—were nestled against the right side of the wharf. On the opposite side of the wharf, a brace of jetties—now empty save some rigging and tackle—lay in wait for the fishing craft that trolled the rich waters of the bay. Bella noticed that most of the dockworkers were lazing away under shade trees or the overhangs of the warehouse fronts. A few swarthy members amongst them could be seen repairing nets and tackle.

They had made their way to the crane, and the foreman of the caravan exchanged a few words with the port master. The port master, a slender man with an exuberant mustache, gestured with both hands at the dockworkers. "Hey, you lot! Time to earn your keep!"

The dockworkers ambled over to the carts and both the caravan crew and the dockworkers unloaded the logs onto the empty plot. Bella grabbed one of the hefty iron hooks that were used to gain a stronger purchase on a log and hooked it to the top of their first target. The foreman called out a quick count of three and together they heaved the log onto their shoulders. With the strain of the timber's weight, the team hastily moved to the empty plot using the hooks to guide the log gently down to the ground. The last three logs went just as quickly and already a timber deck base was taking form.

The rest of the afternoon was spent moving back and forth between a log deck that had accumulated at the Farney River landing and the plot by the sea. A task made possible by the ability to float logs down that wide river from the lumber camps to a southerly bend in the river, which lay not far from the mill. By the time the sun was drifting down to the horizon, they had moved a deck of twelve logs. Bella had found the work to be cathartic and had enjoyed the camaraderie with the other workers. Few words were spoken, but the hard labor forced the team to cooperate or suffer.

When the last log had found its mark, the port master called out to the caravan crew, "Will y'all be taking a drink before you head back?"

"You ain't gonna charge us like you did last time are ya," the caravan foreman called back with a wolfish grin across his face.

"Only for you, ya fat bastard," the port master called back. His own expression looked like one only shared between friends. Soon, flagons were passed around the worksite and the team of workers shared in a rather stout ale.

Bella winced with her first sip of the stuff, but that did not stop her from downing another three full flagons before the port master called out, "Alright you lot, looks like time's up. If you want to keep up the drink it won't be from my hand." The port master grinned and he and the caravan foreman made their way into one of the warehouses. A warehouse where mock quarters had been built for the dockworkers who had no family or home in the village proper.

It seemed they were going to continue their soiree inside, but she needed to head back to resume her vigil on Alexa. By now, Sophia would be wondering where she was. Even so, she ensured that the pack horses were fed, watered, and properly quartered for the night before she began to head back into town with the remainder of the caravan crew.

"Goodbye, Bruno," she said as the huge beast munched happily on some hay she had found nearby. As they began to make their way back to town, Bella's mind drifted. She realized that she'd drunk more than she originally intended, but recent events had her feeling careless at the moment. The stout bitter ale warmed her stomach and relaxed her nerves. In the company of the workmen and women, she couldn't help but take a few flagons, and she figured if the port master hadn't closed down the festivities she might have kept on consuming. Most likely finding herself arm in arm with some like-minded soul singing songs from the old country. Which would lead to reminiscing about what they all missed about home. She knew that it would most likely end in a fight when some hapless fool would say the wrong thing, or, more likely, when some uninteresting fool would try to charm her. Luckily for everyone, the port master did run out of ale or … at least ran out of free ale for the carousing crews. Most of them had sobered up on a chilly evening walk back to the village.

The walk was only a few kilometers on a slightly uphill path, but the team found themselves in the dark by the end of the journey. At first, the workers admired the vibrant oranges in the sky as the sun dipped below the horizon, and then they caught glimpses of the first stars as the light faded. Some of the workers—used to this kind of evening stroll—lit torches to help the crew on their way. As they passed by the warehouse in town, the workers split off to their respective homes saying their farewells along the way. Bella made her way back to the apothecary, breathing the cool night air deeply, and glancing up at the stars.

As she entered the apothecary, Sophia, looking rather impatient, was sitting in the front room eyeing her with some semblance of scorn. "Well, sister I'm glad you could finally join us."

Bella simply looked at her, not quite ready for the admonishment.

Sophia continued, "Blythe is already in there, and I am rather worn from today. She seems to be doing ok, but I must get some rest." She rose to her feet, the sounds of tiny glass vials and clinking stones sounded loud in the silence.

"I'm sorry, I got caught up with something," Bella said, her eyes downcast.

Sophia simply nodded and stepped into her bedroom, closing the rather stiff door behind her.

Bella sighed deeply, already feeling the strain of the night's labors upon her. She was exhausted and couldn't imagine being able to stay observant through the night without Blythe's help. She entered the medical room, seeing her still prone sister and a rather tired-looking Blythe rise from his chair when he saw her.

"Hello mum," Blythe said, his hand to his chest in respect. As Bella stepped closer, Blythe, like a nurse briefing a doctor, said, "She seems better than before."

That may have been true, but as she looked closer, Bella did not see the Alexa she knew and loved. All her life she had looked up to this now helpless figure, and all her life she had known Alexa to be relentless. A force of will and strength that now seemed so fragile. It made Bella feel small and anxious. She wanted to lash out, she wanted to go out into the forest and rip the fangs out of the bastard spider that did this. She slammed her fist on the table next to her sister, making Blythe flinch; although, in the manner of someone accustomed to such outbursts.

Bella breathed deeply, trying to master her emotions. "She does look better Blythe, but she is still lying here isn't she!" Her voice rose in intensity as she spoke. She felt scornful of the man and felt an urge to smack him across the face. Instead, she glanced up at the fellow, his face staring down at the ground trying not to incur her wrath.

She stomped to the front of the room again and slammed her fist into the wooden wall. Instantly, her knuckles began to bleed. The pain served to sober her even further, from both the alcohol and her anger. As she peeled her gaze from her bloody middle knuckle, she turned slowly towards Blythe. She looked at the forlorn soul and sighed deeply once again.

"Blythe, I am sorry. I-I just am tired and stressed from all this." She sat heavily in a chair propped against the entry wall.

"It. It's alright mum. I would be upset meself," he said rather meekly. His obeisance helped calm her, regret already stealing into the crevices of her consciousness.

"How about I take the first watch, and you get some rest?" Bella asked with more empathy in her voice. Blythe nodded, producing a small straw pillow and cloak from the far-right corner of the room. He laid them out against the wall that held the back window, rustling around until he found a comfortable spot and closing his eyes when he finally did so.

Bella marveled at his preparedness and her thoughts filled her with sorrow, knowing that she reacted poorly to the situation. She did not know if it was from the strong drink or just her nature. She had a temper; a spirit that reacted instead of stopping to think of the situation. The tumultuous combination had gotten the best of her more than once.

For many minutes afterward, she fretted over her behavior, trying to justify her actions. And when those justifications could not be found she turned to self-loathing. The mental game was exhausting, and she found that only an hour had gone by before she could barely keep her eyes open. So, instead, she stood, pacing the room, falling into a rhythm that was in tune with Alexa's breathing. She kept up the patrol for another hour and a half before she was forced to shake the big man awake. He looked at her, bleary-eyed but understanding. When he had risen to a sitting position, she immediately slumped in the chair falling into a dreamless sleep in just seconds.

# Chapter Nine

## Bella

"Bella." A hoarse whisper called out to her.

She tried to restart her faculties. The call of birds floated through the open window.

"Bella." The whisper croaked again, and she shook her head, hoping to jump start her mind. It was daylight outside, and the smell of morning dew was heavy in the air.

When her vision settled, Alexa had her head turned towards her. There, still lying on her back but with her eyes open, Alexa smiled, a weak but genuine smile.

"Bella, it's good to see you," Alexa said, her voice cracked and dry from days of neglect and illness. Bella smiled warmly at her sister; their eyes locked in the embrace that only love can bring. She rose slowly and crossed the distance to the bedside, kneeling when she arrived. Blythe stood by ready to help, for he knew that he should have been more alert. Alert enough to wake Bella up before Alexa's barely audible voice did, the fear of Bella's scorn made him fidget ever so slightly.

"It is good to see you too," Bella said warmly. She touched Alexa's cheek, which was still slightly warmer than it should have been. The two sisters sat in silence for a moment, just locked in each other's comfort.

"Sophia must be told, she must see you!" Her sudden urgency startled Blythe. "Blythe. Don't just stand there, go get the Keeper!" The huge man hurried out of the room, seeking the target of his quest. A few moments passed before the sound of clinking vials could be heard, proceeded by Sophia rounding the corner into the observation room. Alexa raised her head slightly at the sight of her other sister, and her smile was infused with new vigor.

"I thought you would be awake sooner, what took you so long?" Sophia asked.

"Well, I thought I needed a vacation from you two," Alexa replied.

"Is that so?" Bella asked with amusement.

"Yes, it is so. So, why bother such a nice nap?" Alexa replied, holding her hands palm-up and doing her best to shrug.

"That felt like more than a nap," Sophia said matching the humor of the moment.

"Yeah, maybe so," Alexa said. Bella and Sophia looked at each other, puzzlement plain on their faces, expecting more to be said. Sophia was about to speak again when Alexa interrupted, "Maybe so … maybe so. Still, it was awfully nice having the two of you dote on my every need. In fact, it wasn't a nap at all. More like a rare vacation!"

Bella grinned and Sophia—so stern at first—suddenly burst out laughing. The dam that had held all the tension and worry for the last few days broke, and she joined her sister in the merriment. Before long, as painful as it must have been for her, Alexa chuckled as well. There in that stuffy observation room, the three sisters felt a moment of kinship that was sorely needed. Together they laughed and smiled, just enjoying one another's company, and although little else was said the three took several minutes before they had regained enough composure to decide on their next move.

"We best get your Rangemaster here, she has been worried sick about you," Sophia said with red cheeks inflamed by laughter. "By the Maiden, we should probably get the governor and the captain of the guard as well! Blythe, there is a silver on the desk in the foyer for all your help the last few days, but could I ask you for one more favor?

"Anything, mum," Blythe replied.

"Could you rouse our town's *esteemed* leadership and have them come here at once?"

Blythe nodded and began to head for the door, but he paused, obviously debating something within his mind. He nodded again, "Mum, it ain't necessary to pay me for this. Y'all are the closest to kin I got over here."

Bella's heart sank at the words, and a tumble of regret ripped through her as she thought of her reproof of him this morning.

Sophia replied, "Maiden's blessings on you Blythe." For a split second, the two held each other's gaze, a Keeper and a stable hand, a moment of understanding passing between them. He nodded once again and headed out the door, no sound of snatched coin to be heard.

"That there is a good man ... Welp, there is much to do!" Sophia exclaimed, clapping her hands together. The Keeper rushed off, going out to prepare the observation room for the more illustrious company they were to receive. Bella still holding Alexa's hand, looked at her recovering sister and saw that she had closed her eyes once more, her energy spent on letting them know she was ok

Leaving Alexa to rest, Bella walked out into the foyer. Sophia, an obsidian stone in hand, poured over a rather different-looking tome than the medical journal from before. "What do you plan to do with that?"

"Well, I intend to use just enough to get her awake and a little more cognizant of her past," Sophia had replied as she glanced at the book.

"What about the book?" Bella asked.

Sophia paused and looked at the cover as if she had forgotten its name. "Ah, *The Stones and The Divine,* well it's a rather helpful guide for us Keepers when we haven't done a thing in a while. A sort of ... recipe book if you will."

Bella moved closer to her sister, the book splayed out now on the desk of the foyer, the silver coin meant for Blythe precariously perched at the edge of the desk. She looked down at the tome and saw a rather beautiful drawing of a man in flowing robes, holding an orb filled with a mosaic of tiny images.

"What's that he's got there?" Bella asked.

"I have no idea; it is simply this particular writer's view of what Mosyneta looked like."

"A smart-looking fellow then," Bella said.

"Yes, a smart fellow indeed. It is said that Mosyneta was told by Ember to record everything that went on between the gods," Sophia said as she brushed her hand against her fire-orange Embershard amulet. "Surely, you recall the tale the bard had told us a few nights before we left Augustia?" Sophia looked up at her sister inquisitively.

Bella nodded in response. She did in fact recall the night in that tavern. A rather eccentric bard told the tale of the one necromancer—if he could be called that—who had ever been successful. His success stemmed from the fact that he had cobbled together the corpses of several bards and poets who he knew would be long-winded in their retelling of their memories. The Night of the Bard, as it was called, was a successful assault against the garrison at Sutheath in which the reanimated corpses were goaded in the night to march on the gates of the small keep. The guards on duty that night, which were hampered by heavy fog, ran in terror when they saw the rotting abominations approach. Fearfully many recalled the assault as if they were brave but outnumbered and regretfully had to retreat.

"However, the truth is quite different," the bard had said with a flourish, "for not a drop of blood was spilled nor was a single 'zombie' slain. So, who's to say whether those zombies were there to slay or just to parlay?" With a wry smile and a wink the bard had ended the tale. "So, as we think of our loved ones, we should always remember The Night of the Bard. For if we are drained of coin to pay our favorite signer, we may find ourselves brained by the dead with a zinger!"

Bella had laughed heartily at the bard's jest and had indeed paid the man a full silver coin. Yet the real truth was that the guards of Sutheath

Keep ran from a bunch of dead caterwauling bards and poets who were shambling towards them in the night.

Her reverie brought on by Sophia's question ended and with memory served, she replied, "The Night of the Bard."

"That's the one. Hence, it's more common name, Necrostone." Sophia held up a black-faceted gem. She placed the stone back on the table in front of her. "I, however, do not wish to raise our sister from the dead, but just…spark her awake."

"Well, I mean … it would help to hear the story in full. Right?"

Sophia looked at Bella with a mentor's patience. "Yes, but, a word of caution, the lords of this here town are about to be upon us, and if our dear sister did anything *untoward* on her recent journey … it would be best if they didn't know that."

Bella looked up, pondering the conundrum Sophia had posed. "Aye, I can see the logic," Bella relented, stepping back to watch her sister work.

"Necrostone has been widely used by Keepers and sordid sorts for years," Sophia said. "And, although it sounds quite malevolent, this stone is no more than a conduit to the god's own recollection of events. If we were to give a full dose to Alexa, she would recall everything, including her own thoughts."

Bella nodded. "Well … how can I help?" They prepared the room for the arrival of the town's leaders. The group had begged or 'borrowed' three fine chairs and propped them against the walls of the room. They had also hung sage up throughout the room and closed the windows, filling the air with a pungent aroma. Within half an hour, all the guests had filtered into the room.

The Governor, a rather pompous-looking fellow, had entered the room with an air of superiority, his fine purple cloak wafting the herb-filled air as he swept it onto his lap when he sat. Excited to see the spectacle of a godstone in action he sat forward in his chair. The Guard-Captain,

Captain Alexander Vitrusian, who was a scarred veteran of some far-off war chose not to sit but seemingly stood in guard near the entrance. His stoic face betrayed no emotion. The Rangemaster, Master Erin Apararius, who was the only other to have visited Alexa during her fever-filled sleep entered quickly, taking her seat. Her manner was that of one who did not want to disturb. The sign of someone capable of delegating tasks on subjects that she had no knowledge of.

There was a quiet fascination in the Rangemaster's eyes. The curiosity of one with true intelligence. She was a rather stout woman but of a decent height, her hair was neatly trimmed. A golden-brown crown that was pulled taut over her scalp. Bella could see a small trickle of sweat escape from that rigid construction. The sweat served as a reminder of the stifling heat that had consumed the room once they had closed the windows. Although she wished she could just be with her sisters, she liked the Rangemaster and remembered how she had not disturbed Sophia or Bella as they had worked over Alexa the first day. She had simply entered the room and held a respectful distance for many minutes. After she was satisfied with what she saw she simply said, "Let me know when she wakes."

All the attendees watched in silence as Sophia approached Alexa with the Necrostone raised high. "Memory, serve us this day. Let us wake this individual, Alexa, and hear her once again. Mosyneta, I beseech you," Sophia spoke loudly in that small room, and her voice seemed to penetrate Bella's mind. She felt a trickle of memories—old and new—flood back to her, thoughts of the golden sun on dew-kissed mornings and the faint whisper of their mother, so beautiful and kind. "Mosyneta, with your wisdom allow us the grace of your memory," as she spoke, she pointed the small black gem towards her sister. A wisp of smoke drifted from the god-stone, swirling its way through the room, lazily curling its way to and fro until it found purchase in Alexa's nostrils. Bella looked on in a sort of dread fascination at the sight of another god answering the pleas of a Keeper.

The smoke injected deep into Alexa's mouth and nose. She opened her eyes as if she had been jolted awake. Her sclera was prominently displayed, as her eyes opened to unnatural proportions. She sat up stiffly coughing into her fist as she did so. The room held its breath in anticipation of what would happen next.

Alexa looked around the room. "What's happening?"

Sophia replied gently, "It's alright sister."

"Wh-where am I?"

"You are still here in my apothecary. And you are still safe."

Alexa, reassured by her sister's words, seemed to relax and accept her situation. Yet the governor, who shuffled constantly at the excitement of the godstone's happenings, drew Alexa's attention. Alexa began, "What? What are they—"

She was cut off abruptly by Sophia. "They are of no importance sister. We cannot waste time right now." Sophia smiled at Alexa and with her most soothing voice implored her, "We need to know what happened to you."

Alexa closed her eyes, taking a long pause before collecting her thoughts. Finally, she nodded. With one more deep breath, the ranger recounted her story, her voice monotonous feeling not entirely her own. "Gilneas and I took dried venison and hardbread for our jou—"

Before she could even finish her first sentence a sneering voice interrupted, "Surely we don't need to hear every detail." The governor's voice while not quite malicious was condescending all the same. The monotonous retelling interrupted; Alexa sat with her eyes glazed over, the magic of the stone being waylaid, causing her to sit like some sort of zombie. Sophia shifted uncomfortably, trying not to show anger at the man's interruption.

"Governor, the magic of the gods cannot bend to your whims. Since we are asking for divine recollection, you must expect that recollection to be perfect," Sophia replied. "With that said, Alexa let us jump ahead and start with what waylaid you," Sophia spoke gently.

The governor sighed and leaned back in his chair. "Very well."

Alexa, the glaze in her eyes fading, once again nodded. With heavily furrowed brows and obvious strain evident on her face a monotonous speech poured forth, retelling the event that she had endured. Bella couldn't help but smile at Sophia's subtle reproof of the governor. The diplomatic nature of her stalwart sister was in stark contrast to the very colorful description she had for the man in private.

The others betrayed little emotion, but Bella could plainly see that their patience was slightly frayed by his interruption. Slowly the chastisement faded, and the party settled in as they listened to Alexa. She recounted the iktomid ambush and the subsequent retreat from the Eukarian forest. Alexa told the company of the days and nights she had trudged through the trees and plains. Although the telling was without intonation or inflection, the descriptions of how the infection slowly consumed her wits and will, felt painful to hear. She ended the story at the rendezvous with Bella and Sophia outside of the miller's grove.

With her mission complete, Alexa simply said, "That is all." Her glazed eyes faded completely, and for a brief moment, Bella could see the real Alexa in those brown eyes. The frightened ranger spoke, emotion back within her inflections, "Where … where am I?"

Sophia rushed to her side, realizing that the magic of the Necrostone had ended. As the godstone's penetrating smoke released its hold, Sophia helped Alexa back down to the bed. She brushed a calming hand across Alexa's forehead.

"Wh-where?" Alexa asked faintly.

"Shhh, it's alright," Sophia said as she continued to rub her forehead. Only a few seconds passed, and the ranger fell back asleep.

Sophia turned and addressed the group. "Necrostone takes a heavy toll on our minds. She must rest for a time."

The governor piped up with a little more humility in his voice. "That damn forest has been the bane of my existence. First, my beloved daughter and now iktomids seek to root us out!"

The members of the impromptu council shifted nervously. Everyone recalled the loss of the governor's daughter in those cursed woods, and everyone still remembered how his wife had forced the governor to name the forest in honor of their daughter.

Bella recalled the haunting eulogy the mother had given. Her grief was not reflected in tears but in utter hollowness, a desolation of the will to live.

"At least she will be remembered," was how she had ended that speech, and everyone there had felt the weight of the words. Now, not only was the governor reminded of his daughter's death in every report from the northern lumber camps but also the people had taken to calling the rich timberland cursed.

The Guard-Captain stepped forward, his boot clinking heavily on the wooden floor. "We must find out what happened. We need to send out a scouting party."

The Rangemaster replied quickly, "I agree, but it might be folly to act too quickly. For my rangers have not all returned." The Guard-Captain nodded at the Rangemaster, obvious respect in the gesture.

"When will those rangers return?" Sophia queried.

"Well, I still have three parties out, but they are slotted to return by week's end." The Rangemaster replied.

Bella blurted out, "By week's end! That is far too long to wait. You heard her, why would the iktomids be so far south? Something must be driving them."

The Rangemaster fixed Bella with her gaze. "Stablemaster, I respect your opinion, but rushing off into a known peril without full force would be foolish. Especially if we will need to range north of the forest to see what hugs our borders."

Bella clenched her fists, anger swelling within her bosom.

Sophia moved to her sister's side placing a calming hand on her shoulder. Her voice matched her calming touch, "So, folks, what can we do?"

"Well, I can send a complement of eight rangers out to scout the forest and its northern border, but as it stands if I send that many now, we will have none to defend ourselves," The Range Master replied. The Guard-Captain raised his head slightly as if to indicate agreement.

The governor chimed in. "We need to keep our citizens safe, and rushing off into danger is not how."

"It sounds like danger is coming for us," Bella said, anger souring her voice.

The governor sighed. "If you're quite finished interrupting let us come up with a plan of action." Bella raged at the reproof, but once again Sophia squeezed her shoulder tightly warning her against rash action. The governor, content that no interruption would come, continued. "We shall wait for the rest of the rangers to return and then we will scout the forest."

"When they are sent out, I will disperse my guards where necessary to shore up any gaps left by their absence," the Guard-Captain stated. The Governor and Range Master nodded. As Bella raged internally, Sophia and the others hammered out the minutiae of the scouting expedition. The voices droned on, and Bella drifted into her own thoughts. Not but a few minutes of discussion had passed when she abruptly stood, brushing Sophia's hand aside. "I must see to my stables." With the company looking on in astonishment Bella rushed from the room, a ball of fury.

# Chapter Ten

## Bella

The machinations of Elgion's main street at midday were a cooling draught for Bella's heated blood. She had stormed out of the apothecary and plodded her way at a furious pace all the way to Main Street. Now she was at the crossroads in front of the market. There a cart laden with flour turned the corner towards the port-bound road with what must have been one of the last shipments of summer wheat. The miller, accompanied by his two youngest sons, looked over at Bella. His eyes told her that he was well aware of the leniency he had been granted, before his gaze lingered long, he nodded curtly and pulled the pack horse onwards.

Her blood cooled slightly by the simplicity of it all and stepped on towards the town well. She pulled the well's bucket up and poured herself a cooling draught into one of the many clay cups scattered about for communal use. With a sigh, she leaned against the stones of the well. The sun-kissed her skin, and the warmth of the summer sun radiated into her bones. Her rage slowly dissipated as she allowed the moment of calm to take hold.

"Damnit," she yelled suddenly, the rage from the leader's inaction boiling up to the surface again. Her curse, having escaped past her lips, made two rather wealthy-looking clarks jump slightly at the unexpected bark. She held up her hands and placation, mouthing a silent apology to the two men. She struggled to understand why they couldn't just send out a scouting party now. What's the trouble? Three maybe four folks into the forest COULD figure out what in Ember's breath was going on. As she watched the two clarks head back to their quarters with steaming venison rolls in hand, a plan formed in her mind.

In her mind's eye, she imagined taking Precious, Blythe, and Scout north into Mossgrave, laden with supplies. How hard could it be?

Her triumphant resolution was interrupted by a hand tapping on her shoulder. She bolted to a standing position from the well, twirled around, and dropped her right hand to her dagger. The figure before her held his hands up in placation. "Pardon my foolishness."

The figure wore the sun-kissed livery of a Warrior of August with a rather heavy-looking ax strapped to his belt and a stout round shield slung over his shoulder. "Me and the lads heard what went on in there," he said with his hands still raised. "It isn't right. Well, it isn't right not at least checking on it, is it?" He paused, allowing his question time to ferment in Bella's mind. He smiled slightly, hands still raised and carried on. "You see, I think you and I are of a like mind on this. Why should we wait until something comes down and stoves in our 'eads?" He raised his eyebrows.

Bella measured the man for a time, blowing a strand of rebellious red hair away from her eye. Although she had seen him before on patrol, this encounter made her truly take in his visage. He was an old fellow with a gray bread and mustache that ringed the mouth. His brown eyes were friendly but the wrinkled baggy skin that surrounded them told her of a stress-filled life.  He looked like a stout warrior, but not one who cared about advancing up the ladder.

"And what makes you think you know my mind," Bella inquired.

"Well pardon me mum, but like I said, me and the lads heard what happened in there. The most- clear of which was a rather loud stablemaster voicing their opinion." He grinned, lowering his hands a fraction and shaking them as if to suggest no trouble.

Bella moved her hand away from her dagger, realizing the old guard meant no harm. "So, why are you telling me this?"

"Hmmm, I guess I was thinking that we could make an arrangement," he said in the practiced manner of a frontiersman making a bargain. Suddenly, he shook his head, "Oh! Where are my manners? This here is my nephew Godwin." He stepped to the side gesturing with both hands to a blonde-haired blue-eyed youth. As Godwin smiled sheepishly and waved, the old guard continued, "And I am Godfrey. We both gots our name from the same old man, Godson. Which makes no sense, since he was more of a son of a bitch than a son of a god." He beamed at his jest waiting for a response to the comedy.

Bella hid her genuine mirth at his joke and once again measured the man. She could find no cord or string that she could pull on in his mannerisms that she didn't like. He wasn't someone that she thought would be great, but on taking stock of him he measured out to be the better quality of frontiersman she could find. And Godwin, well his company would be welcome anywhere for he was a handsome muscle-bound young man. "Well Godfrey, if you want to walk with me that would be fine."

*

The creaking sound of the leather saddle felt much too loud in the night air. The worn leather of the seat rise rubbed uncomfortably on her palm as she gripped it tightly, trying to prevent excess noise. The cantle and skirt of the saddle were tucked firmly into her armpit. While her rear hand held the stirrups and strings. No amount of grip or steadiness could prevent the sound of old leather as it shifted from her steps. The intermittent squeaks from the dry material felt like they pierced into her soul and broke her wish that she could convey every piece of equipment with naught but a whisper. A wish that was nigh impossible, for the equipment and gear of a one-week-in and one-week-out trip through the wilderness could not be transferred without some commotion.

She had woken Blythe from his cot in the stable house. Now Godfrey, Godwin, Blythe, and herself saddled and equipped the horses. Fortunately for them, no other stable hands had decided to bunk there for the night, probably preferring a warmer livelier bed at the Broken Flagon Inn, a raucous institution located on the western port road leading out of town. Without hesitation, Blythe had readily agreed to her plan not only because he was unnecessarily loyal to the stablemaster, but also because he was seemingly worried about the dire premonitions that Alexa's god-enhanced story provoked.

And so, with the weight of premonition on their hearts, they had started their preparations for the unsanctioned journey by loading saddle bags with rations and survival gear. Dawn was still far off, and the pervasive weight of night's darkness held the air to a stillness drenched in dread. Every disturbance of that eerie silence felt amplified, and Bella was eager to get on the road before someone came along.

Suddenly, she heard a thump and the jingle of metal behind her. Blythe had tripped on a small stone, tumbling helplessly to the ground. "Damn it, Blythe. You alright?" Bella whispered in a rather harsh venomous tone.

"Sorry," he called back mutely. His effort to regain and rebalance his feet sounded louder than the original fall, especially since Godwin had bent over to help him to his feet. Which made his own gear clink and rattle in the dark. Bella glared at the two men.

A sound pierced that near-perfect darkness, the unmistakable fall of feet. Fear shot through her veins as the sound was copied in a steady march towards them. She ducked using the saddle as a pseudo shield, more out of instinct than rational thought. Blythe, Godfrey, and Godwin crouched near her, and the group stayed motionless as the footfalls grew louder. When the sound of the steps felt like they could not come any closer they stopped. Metal fasteners and joints creaked in the dark as the stranger settled at their location.

Bella's arm ached as the awkward positioning that the saddle landed on strained her muscles. The pain radiated up her shoulder as the time rambled on. Whoever it was, they did not carry a torch or light of any kind with them, which made Bella curious as to their motivations. Her arm drifted downwards as the strain on her muscles became unbearable. Metal creaking pierced the darkness again as the stranger shifted their weight once more. Hidden in that sound she allowed the saddle to drop down slightly more, giving solace to her beleaguered muscles. It felt like an eternity, an affrontery to her physique. Her throbbing bicep evoked outrage at the egregious amount of time that had passed. What was this bastard doing? When Bella felt like she couldn't handle the strain anymore, the footsteps once again resumed. For a few more *painful* seconds Bella held her pose while the footfalls receded in the distance.

After the threat had passed beyond earshot, they all tangibly relaxed. Bella rested the saddle on the ground shaking her arm to try and dislodge the pain that had taken root.

Godfrey sighed heavily and an audible click could be heard from his ankle as he stood once again. "What in Ember's breath was that about?"

Bella replied, "I have no idea but let's get out of here before we have to play Sly Fox again."

*

The group made their way overland. Bella felt more comfortable as they gained some distance from the town and the metal-footed stranger that came so close to discovering them. Godfrey had inspected the location of the stranger's vigil but found nothing of concern nor any sign that they would be followed. Safe in the knowledge that they had made their escape from the village unnoticed, they marched on, passing through the plains north of Elgion. A land that consisted of groves and thickets of oak and maple that interspersed a sea of grass and brush. Birds, hares, and foxes could be seen on their journey, and the company had little to complain about as they rolled over the sunlit plains. Bella felt some exhilaration from the freedom of their trip and smiled as they trod along.

Godfrey talked nearly nonstop throughout the day, only stopping to raid a raspberry bush that he had spotted. Bella found his constant chatter more comforting than annoying, although his horsemanship was somewhat lacking. Without proper preparation, Bella had to saddle Godfrey and Godwin with two of the pack horses, Kedwin and Lilith. The stout but lumbering beasts were already stubborn in their manner, but to place an untrained rider on them was almost comical. Numerous times Godfrey had to raise his voice as his horse, Kedwin, cantered sideways away from the group. The act would be topped off by a rather grumpy Godfrey digging his heels into the side cursing, "Hey! Ya mangy beast what's a matter with you?"

The journey, punctuated by Godfrey's rather entertaining mannerisms, brought them along a moderately well-worn track. A well-worn track that eventually led to the base of a range of foothills that were blanketed in a thick oak, maple, and pine forest.

As they came close enough to the forest to make out individual trees, Godfrey opined, "Mossgrave, a bitch of a place if you ask me."

"That 'bitch of a place' is the reason for this journey," Bella replied.

"Pardon me, mum, but that don't change how I feel 'bout it. Some say it's haunted."

Godwin shuffled uncomfortably in his saddle, as if he was made squeamish by the prospect of a haunted forest. Bella turned to look at the young man, who knowing he was being stared at, blushed heavily.

"The only thing haunting that place is myths and fairy tales," Bella tried to devalue Godfrey's foreboding comments as much for Godwin's sake as for her own. Yet the old veteran would not be dissuaded.

"An ol' one-eyed lumberjack told me that he once heard a banshee wailing in them woods. 'Course nothing ever came of it 'cause he ran back to camp right quick when he heard the caterwauling. But he swears it was a banshee and he should know. He been hearing foreign sounds in trees the world over!" He said the last statement with a grand gesture of his arm as if to encompass all of creation.

This made Kedwin steer heavily to the left as his weight was flung in that direction. The horse unsteadied him and took him off the track once again, making him curse. "Damn you, you stinking beast. Blythe it's your turn to ride. I am sick of this mangy thing ruining me good stories." Godfrey dismounted, taking his turn to walk his mount instead of riding it. They did so to preserve the strength of the companies' horses. Blythe, after a slight nod from Bella, remounted Scout effortlessly. Godfrey's stories slackened after he had been disarmed by Kedwin and the party moved in relative silence for the next couple of kilometers.

"Should we make camp here mum?" Blythe held his hand out towards a clearing in the grass. It was nearing sunset and Bella was beginning to wonder at a place to camp.

It was a near-perfect spot to settle in for the night, Elger's Landing, thirty-or-so kilometers north and east of Elgion. Bella surveyed the landing, which consisted of a fork in the road, a clearing that was worn down to dirt, and the remnants of campfires dotted throughout. Those campfires were used by the loggers of Mossgrave when they were trying to float logs down the Farney River.

She thought about the portmaster and the caravan work boss, smiling at the thought of their easy-going demeanor. She made a mental note to visit the docks when they returned. A fork in the road darted off to the east, never climbing but still hugging some steep hills that at times turned into a rocky cliff face. The eastern track was the reason for this landing. Not only did the landing offer distance from the noisome falls but also gave a reprieve for those lumberjacks who wanted a break from the dense forest.

The other part of the fork went out west, winding its way up the hills. The track disappeared in the trees after a switchback that was about three-quarters of a kilometer up

In the early days of Elgion, the loggers tried dropping the timber from the falls themselves but soon discovered that more than half their trees were either damaged or disappeared beneath the roaring pool below. Thus, they were forced to make the trip down the hillside path to bring the bounty of the forest to Elger's Landing. At present the landing was vacant, but some of the fires had warm coals still within their bosom. They used those fires to make camp and heated up a hearty helping of carrot, cabbage, and venison stew. In the further legs of the journey, they might be forced to eat the more resilient rations. So, Bella had authorized Blythe to cook the more perishable rations for comfort and efficiency.

They spent the night in relative peace, regaled by Godfrey's stories. They restarted their trip early in the morning, taking the western hillside fork up the hill. It took most of the morning to reach the summit, and they rested near the first logger's camp to revitalize the horses as well as themselves. Godfrey was glistening with healthy sweat from the uphill venture, and he heartily dug into a loaf of bread. None of the loggers were near this first campsite, but the signs of habitation from the previous night were readily apparent. Either the loggers were working in tandem at a specific site or at this time of day were still deep within the woods.

After their respite, they skirted a track that narrowed between the hill's continually steepening edge and the ever-closer forest. Godfrey gladly remounted on his steed and exclaimed rather exuberantly at Kedwin's first errant step. "Woah there friend! I know we had our disagreements but let's not be hasty."

Godfrey's eyes grew comically large, and Bella struggled not to laugh at the man whose fear was readily apparent on his face. Nevertheless, Kedwin, Godfrey, and all the rest carried on for another couple of hours until they reached the upper portion of the falls, above Elger's Landing. Bella tutted in amazement as if the grandeur of the images before her were unbelievable. It overlooked the plains of Elgion, a view that stretched out over golden fields, rolling hills, and green groves. Hawks and eagles swooped overhead crying out at their prey below. Miniscule rainbows flecked in and out of existence, adding to the majesty of the view, as water splashed around the top of the falls. Godwin and Godfrey had both led their mounts to the water for a drink.

The two men took the opportunity to drink heartily from the clear water and refill their waterskins. Blythe looked at her, obviously desiring her permission to do the same, but not wanting to dismount if she didn't want to stop. Bella smiled at him and nodded. He dropped to the ground quickly and raced with Scout over to the clear water.

She led Precious to the water and as she was allowing the horse a hearty drink from the cool water, she drank in the sights, feeling awestruck at the lack of civilization in that vast wilderness. *How long would it remain so pristine?* Her thoughts conflicted on the matter. After all, she was a pioneer herself and helped expedite the very civilization she hated seeing grow on vistas such as this. Yet also, she couldn't help but strive for that growth—that frontier, to push the bounds of what was capable. No matter how many times this thought came to the fore, she never came to a satisfactory answer. Instead, she just acquiesced that *hopefully* she and the other pioneers would uphold some moral standards as they conquered the wilds.

After a break enjoying the majesty of the falls, they turned north and quickly were surrounded by denser spruce and fir trees. They traveled until the piercing light in the trees faded, finding themselves at a camp on the northern bounds of the logger's range. It consisted of no more than four cabins arranged in a semi-circle around a circular clearing. The entrance to the camp had a wide clearing to their right where log decks normally lay but were currently bare. The rich aroma of sawdust and sap saturated the air, and the warm air buzzed with myriad insects.

As they made their way up the entrance track on horseback, a young woman and a boy no bigger than a toddler greeted them warily. The boy was full of vigor and eyed their mounts with the awe that only a child can have. Godwin, a smile upon his face, dismounted his steed and helped the boy up into his saddle. He did not allow the boy to ride but just let him experience what it felt like to be mounted. Bella had noted that the mother's hand had initially shot up in protest at the action, but when Godwin turned towards her the hand had drifted down, pretending that it had not moved in the first place. The mother, her face slightly flushed, only watched with a smile as her son whooped in delight at the experience.

During the child's revelry of his first horse ride, the loggers of the camp came out from the trees, their day's labors coincidentally concluding near the party's arrival time. Four burly men, looking rather haggard, trudged through to where the company—save Godwin—remained mounted. The father of the awestruck boy was a surly man with forearms the size of a small tree.

"What brings you all out here!?" he said with a deep voice that betrayed some small annoyance.

"We are on the business of the Guard-Captain of Elgion," Bella said quickly, stilling any outburst from the talkative Godfrey.

The surly logger eyed them for a time. His two companions closed ranks behind him, and before long his wife risked a glance at Godwin. Godwin was remounting his horse, and as he straightened in the saddle his armor shone in the fading light. The wife's gaze did not linger long, but the evidence of her desire stained her face red.

The husband's face flushed in anger, ironically matching the shade of his wife's cheeks. "There ain't enough for the lot of you." He paused for a moment, eyeing Godwin malevolently, "You can make camp near us, but we folk struggle hard enough as it is without you city folk coming out here and eating up all our food."

Bella looked at the logger who had not broken his gaze on Godwin and simply stated, "Very well. Thank you."

There was no reason for bloodshed or confrontation, and admittedly Bella did not want to see what the burly loggers were capable of. Bella circled her hand above her head to indicate that the company should move elsewhere, and they turned their mounts towards the currently empty log deck clearing near the entrance. After they had lit a fire and were settling in for the night, the final logger who was an older man with greying hair, approached them with a pot of steaming stew.

"What you got there," Godfrey had said to the man, his eyes glinting noticeably in the firelight at the sight of the stew. The old man said nothing but simply placed the pot on the ground and held out a wooden bowl and spoon to Godfrey. Warily, Godfrey grabbed the bowl and held it out for his serving. The logger slapped a rather viscous-looking concoction into the carved wooden bowl, and a rich flavor filled the air. There were traces of hazelnut, chestnut, mushroom, wild onion, and ... *was that grouse or maybe ... squirrel?*! Whatever it was, the combination of flavors made her mouth water.

Before Godfrey could even raise his spoon, the logger had moved on to Blythe, holding another bowl out to the big man. Just as quickly, he slapped a serving into the bowl of the now dumbfounded Blythe.

"Gods above! That is good!" Godfrey exclaimed. The compliment did not slow the old man down, and when he had served them all, he scooped a hearty portion in a final bowl and sat next to them around the fire. Bella nodded at the man who in return dipped his head near imperceptibly, and the whole of the group ate in relative silence. The sounds of slurping and wooden spoons scraping the more resilient chunks of food were the only thing to break the silence. The old logger did not seem to care much for the jealousies of his compatriots, and, after the pot was thoroughly scraped clean, he simply nodded again at Bella and headed off to his cabin. The party, full of delicious stew, quickly fell asleep around the fire covered in the lighter hide blankets they had brought.

At dawn's light, they continued their journey northwards through the forest. The logger's camp lay not far from the Farney River and for a few kilometers, they were able to stay mounted as they traveled along a rocky shrub-filled beach. Beavers and ducks darted between rocks in the swiftly flowing river. Dragonflies and gnats happily droned over the shallower parts of the river, weaving an inscrutable dance through the reeds. Squirrels and chipmunks raced against the heralds of the coming winter. A frantic foray as the jittery rodents ran over the first golden brown leaves in search of forage. Oak, maple, spruce, cedar, and pine trees graced the canopy above, making the abundance of life a possibility.

Bella was entranced by the melodies of nature around her when Godwin whispered just loud enough for the mounted party to hear, "We are being watched." The haunting tone broke Bella's train of thought and she felt a shiver race down her spine. Both she and Blythe twisted around in the saddle, searching for the culprit of their new troubles. Godfrey and Godwin moved slowly, nearly stoic in their movements, their gaze methodical in its stalwart scan of their surroundings. The deft grace with which Godfrey moved lent a more fearsome bent to the man, who—up to this point—had been nothing but a comedian. The revelation made Bella tilt her head as she looked at the elderly soldier. His grey beard and tousled hair shone slightly as a small film of oil reflected the sun's rays.

He held his hand up towards her, as if recognizing her gaze upon him. "The boy has got a sixth sense about these things. If it says it, it's probably true," Godfrey said matter-of-factly. He turned towards Godwin. "Are yer hairs standing up?"

Godwin sighed. "Yes, but you know that that is not a part of this."

"Maybe so lad, but it's been a sure sign so far," Godfrey said prompting a scoff from Godwin. Regardless, Bella could now feel something was awry, even though the forest felt so alive. Whatever was following them was used to these trees.

After a minute, Godwin and Godfrey both urged their mounts forward, the voyeur choosing to remain unseen. Another kilometer-and-a-half and the group remained in a state of vigilance beyond what they had achieved previously. Bella could feel eyes on her. Once or twice the sound of a twig snapping would induce a spasm from the party, and the horses tugged on their reins, desperate to be out in the open again.

"Blythe, take Precious here. I am going to find something out." She handed the reins to Blythe and drifted behind the party. Godfrey and Godwin were at the lead of the pack, alert and ready for action. Bella looked once more at Godwin's tousled dirty blonde hair and couldn't help but notice the scruff that lined his muscular jawbone. She snapped her sight quickly away from Godwin, cursing inwardly at her lack of focus.

Bella was about ten paces behind Blythe, and she fell into a stalker's gait. Her steps were methodical, her breathing shallow and without noise, and her profile as low as possible. Blythe surrendered some of Bella's ruse by constantly glancing back at her in worry. The surrounding brush made it difficult to see further than a few meters in front or behind, but she followed in their steps which gave an avenue between them. A small window of sight surrounded them. The tall grass and weeds made up the bottom sill while the thick upper foliage of the trees made up the upper sill. Bella scanned constantly through the grass stalks, looking for the specter of threat that could so easily hide in this forest.

In the five years that Elgion existed, Eukarian forest had already claimed the lives of three people. Four including Gilneas. It was wise to stay alert in such a place, and Bella's heart rate mimicked her thoughts. She tried not to imagine an ogre or troll bursting through the trees, and after several minutes she realized that they had fallen off human-made trails altogether.

Bella heard Precious whinny as if she could feel her master's anticipation. Step after step; breath after breath; pulses of the more fanciful fears flashed in her mind. The deep forest was an easy way to lose yourself in fear and the whole group was gripped in that intangible web of fright.

She glanced frequently around as she navigated through tall stalks of grass and the occasional stands of rag, horse, and catchweed. Branches hanging from fir, spruce, and cedar trees were frequently crossing the path in front of them, and Blythe, more than once, had to help Godfrey coax the horses past the obstacles. For nearly an hour the group had travelled in fear of an ambush. Bella tried to stay under the grass and hidden from sight whilst Godfrey and Godwin forged the path forward. All the while, the hairs of Godwin's arm had not gone down, and the feeling of being watched never left Bella's mind. When her muscles ached from the constant crouch walk, she finally relented.

She stopped and waved to an anxious-looking Blythe to continue forward. Bella remained still in the tall grass for several heartbeats, straining to hear if any footfalls besides their own were present. The forest sounds continued unimpeded. Birds and squirrels chittered away happily as small rays of golden light pierced the forest canopy. Bella breathed in slowly, taking in her surroundings. Saurians. The unmistakable reptilian scent hit her nostrils.

The hunters had not known she was there or did not know how truly pungent they could be, but all the same. An oily aroma of reptilian design caught the air. Bella slowly rose from her crouch, the muscles in her legs coiled and taut; ready for action.

She barely poked her head above the grass she had been using for camouflage, and there fifteen meters behind them in a cluster of fir trees, she spotted one of their hunters. A subdued red and orange-colored beast that resembled a chameleon in its face. A long pole firmly gripped between two massive hands that had long spindly fingers capped with small suction cups. The hands looked clumsy, but she watched as the chameleon-like figure gracefully transferred the two-handed pole to one hand and held it behind itself to not disturb more foliage than necessary. She realized the creature was about to be on the move again and she was alarmingly equidistant from her party and this new threat. The implicit danger forced her to grab one of her trusty daggers from its bootstrap. Slowly she unsheathed the vicious blade all while walking carefully backwards towards her group, her eyes never leaving the hunter.

With awe, she watched the saurian taste the air around itself, clearly on the hunt. She watched it twitch its head back and forth abruptly, darting its eyes around, each eyeball independently searching for new threats during its hunt. Its tongue was constantly licking the scaly lips in front of it and when it did finally move again its whole body snaked side to side as if swimming through the undergrowth. The creature held the pole behind them in a rigid line, creating a second tail

For a time, Bella just observed the pursuer, and she alternated between a faster forward crouch walk and the slow backward movements in order to catch back up with the group. She spotted the bulbous chameleon head poking above the grass and then disappeared a minute or so later only to reappear somewhere closer a few seconds later.

Bella kept up this game with the chameleon for a few minutes, before it spotted her. On one resurfacing occasion, the creature had tilted its head to the side, focusing its rather large eyes on her location. She sat perfectly still, peering at the reptilian face through the grass, when a flash from her dagger in a small ray of piercing sunlight gave away her mistake.

Her cover blown; Bella's mind raced as she thought of what to do. This maneuver carried an inherent risk, because, if they were ambushed, she would be vulnerable for a short time. However, if the ambushers were unaware of her, it would pay dividends. Now she could not reap any of the reward and now was only bait.

She stood baring her teeth and holding the dagger in a reverse grip, the blade pointing menacingly towards the saurian. She yelled out to the pursuer, challenging it to either flee or make the mistake of a foolhardy charge. Instead, the saurian froze in its tracks, clearly not expecting such a brazen move. Slowly it moved the two-handed pole back into both hands. The Chameleon fixed her in a stony glare, and the sounds of the forest stopped. The air suddenly felt still; unnervingly so. For one long uncomfortable minute, the strangers did not move or back down, until, without warning, the chameleon leaped backward, clearing a few meters with the powerful hop. Branches and foliage bent or snapped as the saurian did so. The grass on which it landed was now flattened, and a lone branch that had snapped during the maneuver now dangled in between their line of sight. The creature stood, raising the pole above its head and bellowing into the air, an odd croaking sound emanating from its maw. Its scaly skin covered most of the teeth inside of its mouth save for two clusters of jagged fangs that hung off its upper mouth. The beast bellowed the inhuman sound for three turns of its head, blanketing the forest with its call.

Three other saurians appeared from the brush, all three bipedal and seemingly intelligent. They all wore some form of garb or dress that varied in shape, but all carried the same style, indicating more than just mimicry of something they had seen in another intelligent species. Two of the saurians slid on their bellies but held a strong torso upright as they did so. They had four arms a piece and their heads were crowned with a scaly hood, akin to the cobras of the Kos'Ragan badlands. The last one appeared to be crocodilian in appearance and its head was capped with the most ornate-looking headgear of the group. The four saurians stood together in a line all staring in defiance at her.

Godfrey and Godwin, axe and sword respectively drawn, came to Bella's aid and now flanked her. Blythe kept the now frightened horses from bolting.

"What's this then?" Godfrey whispered in Bella's ear.

"No idea, but I ain't ever seen them so *organized*," Bella said in response. Stepping back a couple paces, hoping to defuse the tense situation.

"They look like a scouting party, and I may not be a genius but them fellas is talking to one another," Godfrey said pointing the head of his ax towards one of the snakelike fellows and the crocodilian saurian. True enough, they seemed to be moving their mouths along with hand gestures, a clear sign of some form of speech, although Bella could not hear them speaking due to distance or because they whispered, "Didn't I tell you the boy's arm hairs never lie?"

Godwin shook his head at that and simply said, "We need to get out of here. Each one of them looks formidable."

"Agreed," Bella stepped back some more, but before they could continue their methodical retreat the crocodilian leader stepped forward and held a massive stone mace into the air. He called out in some sort of speech then slammed the ground forcefully with the mace. Bella anticipated an attack, but instead, the party of saurians turned back into the thicker forest and disappeared.

"Well, that was … strange," Godfrey said a few moments after the beasts had left.

# Chapter Eleven

## Bella

Three days had passed since the encounter with the saurians. Bella felt uneasy since that day, but as Godfrey rightfully pointed out, everyone's arm hair lay perfectly flat. Still, it felt odd. She no longer got the sense that they were being followed as closely as before, but that didn't mean they weren't being watched. The journey had not been easy, and the members of their group were battered and bruised from many hours of travelling through heavy foliage and forest cover. Blythe appeared miserable in his silent travels. Head bowed, staring at the ground as he forced himself forward. In some way, she pitied the man, but now was not the time for softness and she told herself that he would just have to endure.

Godfrey and Godwin endured the trek with slightly more grace than Blythe, and from their lack of complaints altogether, better than herself. The two men strode through the brush with a rather stoic persona. Godfrey's normal talkative manner was subdued to only light conversation around the fire they lit at night for their meals. His lack of conversation may be the only indication he suffered.

She had come to miss the old man's constant chatter, especially since it was the sort of comforting speech only those of long military service knew how to deliver. The horses trudged alongside the crew, annoyed to be forced through branches and bushes. Fortunately, Bella had brought a sack of Barnabus's oats from the stables to entice Precious, Scout, Kedwin, and Lilith when their stubbornness battled with their obedience.

On the second day after the saurian encounter, they found some reprieve when they entered a large swath of pine forest. They made their way slowly upwards and now found themselves on the side of a slope that had been carved by the Farney River. The pine trees dominated the higher altitude and hillside conditions where rain couldn't accumulate as heavily. The thicker foliage of the lower forests gave way to scrub and pine needles that blanketed the forest floor, and in many spots, the sun beamed down at them through the much more open canopy above. The spirits of the group rose with the frequency of the sunlit patches, and besides a few stretches in which they had to 'side-hill' they were able to ride their horses, a welcome rest to weary feet. Godfrey had taken up his usual mannerisms and they had ended their day feasting on honey with bread, some huckleberries that they had stumbled upon, and a few fat grouse that Godwin and Blythe had taken down with bow and sling.

The following day they arrived at a small lake at the top of a mountain. Their surroundings were of spruce and pine and upon request Bella allowed Godfrey to fish out a few fat bass from the clear waters.

The man pulled fish free from the water. "Look at the size of this one! We are gonna be eating good tonight lads!" Bella smiled warmly at the now-beaming Godfrey, and he responded with a gentle nod. Godfrey danced off towards his horse to secure his haul while Blythe and Godwin both gawked at the fat fish.

"Come on all, this is the end of the Farney River. By day's end, we will be on the plains north of Mossgrave." Bella's tone was gentle. True to her word, they quickly came upon a downslope of the Eukarian hills, and two hours after leaving the crystal-clear lake they arrived at a clearing devoid of tall foliage or trees. The view that spanned in front of them took Bella's breath away. She could see for kilometers in the distance, piercing past the plains stretched before them.

Godwin whistled softly, "Now that there is a sight." Bella glanced at Godfrey half expecting a reply from the enthusiastic man, but he just stood mouth agape. She could hardly blame him. The land before them was relatively unexplored. A dry plain that stretched far to the north into a boundless horizon. Little rainfall landed in that place, and only a few glimmers of water could be seen, shimmering like jewels in a sea of golden grass. Huge flocks of birds peppered the sky and tiny brown specks could be seen moving through the sea of grass.

"Mum, look there," Blythe called out, pointing down to the left of their gaze. At the base of the hills, she could just make out a large protrusion of dark brown and grey. The ugly formations did not look natural, and Bella could make out a clear separation between a couple of the masses, even from their vantage point on the hills. "What do you think it is?" Blythe queried, a tinge of nervousness souring his voice.

"I don't know, but it doesn't quite belong there," Bella replied. She was holding her hand over her eyes, shielding them from the sun's glare. Her other hand was clenching and unclenching as she bounced slightly up and down with restless energy. Her horse gently nudged her with her snout. "Quit that," she snapped, but Precious continued her pestering. Bella turned round on the horse and fixed it with angry eyes. "What is it!?" Precious shook her head from side to side and blew air gently. Bella stood there angrily, but slowly her eyes softened. "Oh, alright but I am not sure the others would agree." Bella spoke seriously to the horse.

"Agree with what?" Godwin asked.

Bella half turned to the young man and smiled. "Agree that we should get close to that eye sore at night." She patted Precious on the side of his jaw, cooing at the horse gently.

"You can understand that thing," Godfrey called out incredulously.

"Well, I listen, and sometimes what I hear just so happens to align with what I may have already thought of," Bella smiled wryly at Godwin and Godfrey. Without warning, she mounted Precious, rocking the eager horse backwards a few steps. "Precious here just knows when to nudge me towards action." She grinned at the dumbstruck fellows as her hands deftly found the reins to her mount. She clicked her tongue and started off down the hill towards the unnatural outcrop.

Bella couldn't help but smile as she heard Blythe call out. "Don't worry boys, you will get used to it!"

*

Darkness had settled over the plains, and the moon cast a pale light on the surrounding landscape. Bushes and trees—so radiant in the day—were just varying shades of black or grey in that weak moonlight. The cries of nocturnal predators could be heard piercing the night and the yelps of their prey complemented the eerie chorus of sound. Yet the loudest noise in that area was the undeniable sound of an encampment. A smell like vinegar and sickly rot punctuated the air, brought downwind from that offender of the natural noises of the night.

Bella remembered how Godfrey exclaimed when they first tasted that acrid smell on the breeze, "Damn! What in the stones is that!" His face had slowly turned from disgust to horror. "Mum, I think we better get ready. I have smelt this before in the badlands of Kos'Raga." He dipped his head in reflection, bitter memories swallowing him up. "There is no denying it, that's the smell of an orc."

That statement prompted the party to hole up in a nearby thicket about three kilometers from the encampment. They were careful to remain upwind and away from the brutes on the plain. Bella and Godwin, selected for nighttime scouting, had stripped down to their tunics, breeches, and a dagger apiece. Lightened of their armor and kit, the pair had crept their way towards the flickering torches of the camp.

The orcs had set up their shelters at the edge of the forest, nestled between a hill that stretched for another three-quarter-kilometer to their north and a small draw to their south. In the weak moonlight, Bella could barely pick out the contrast between brush and open terrain. Yet in front of her, a slightly darker shade of black betrayed the presence of a significant-sized bush.

They were about two hundred meters away from the farthest torch, and Bella figured that the inky black bush would serve as a decent enough observation post. Already she could see shadowy figures walking between the structures that ringed the outer edge, orange torch light giving them a menacing corona. With a light touch on Godwin's arm, she signaled to him that they should make their way into the bush. The pair crept, making only the slightest of noises as the leaves rustled from disturbance. Bella was impressed by Godwin's agility and found herself staring after him in the dark, only the faintest moonlight illuminating his face. A pale glow revealed his strong jaw studded with stubble, reflecting off his dirty-blonde hair and wide blue eyes. Before she could allow her desire for the strapping warrior to take further hold, she wrenched her gaze towards the stinking encampment, angry at herself for the lapse in concentration.

The camp was a crude thing. There was a cleared area where cages and torches were strewn about all stretched out in a semi-circle. Behind that clearing, in a pattern like concentric rings, about ten ramshackle wooden shelters studded with bone and hide loomed in the darkness. Bella could make out some sort of totem behind them, central to the whole camp and visible through a gap in the huts, and behind that effigy lay three larger shelters, which appeared to be made with sturdier stuff than everything else. Yet what kept Bella's gaze was the effigy. A towering construction that was well-lit by many torches, and to Bella's astonishment draped in what appeared to be corpses. Although she did not see any human-sized corpses strung on that monstrosity, she doubted that these brutes would hesitate in decorating this dour totem with her own corpse.

Yet for now, the spikes that protruded at thirty-degree angles along the central spire of the effigy were adorned with saurian, deer, and even iktomid corpses. Even from this distance, Bella could tell that many were old and desiccated. Their skin, what was left of it, looked like it had cured into leather after many hours in the sun and elements. Others must have been of fresher procurement, for bright red patches slickened the spire behind them. The light of the torches reflected off the still-wet surface, which gave the effigy a rather menacing sheen. A red glow bathed the remaining offal and organs that still hung from the freshly dead. This horrific sight was given more weight once Bella noticed that the whole of the spire was stained in dried blood, giving the structure a sickly rust color.

The effigy was nearly twelve meters tall with a wider base at the bottom to support the weights of the dead, and the whole construction lay on a raised wooden platform that lorded over some sort of trench-like pit that appeared to run around the effigy itself. Bella counted about two dozen corpses on its sinister design, which consisted of three to four spikes every meter. Each one meant to hold the carrion of their victories. Although it was difficult to make out, it looked as if the spire was modular.

She continued her investigation of the spire and saw two orcs, more brightly lit than the rest. She couldn't make out fine details, but they wore heavy garments on their shoulders and were both carrying some form of staff in their hands. Tiny glints of reflection indicated that the whole of their bodies were studded with bits of metal. She could tell they were praying to the structure. Loud growls and barks pierced the night air; a cacophony of rage offered to whatever twisted god listened to their insanity.

"There has got to be one … maybe two hundred orcs here," Godwin whispered, anxiety poisoning his voice. Bella squinted in concentration, recounting the number of structures she saw. She nodded gently, agreeing with Godwin's rough approximation. This news would need to be brought back to Elgion. After all, a warband of orcs that rivaled the size of their own settlement could not be tolerated this close. There was no sign this foe knew that a village ripe for plunder lay just one hundred kilometers or so to the south, but there were obvious signs that they were plundering the Eukarian forest. It was only a matter of time until they ran into a human.

Bella heard a loud crunch to her left and froze in place. One of the brutes must have been out as an exterior patrol, and in their haste, they had not noticed him. Another crack immediately after the first warned that the beast approached their position quickly. Every step was loud and ponderous, the volume rising with each successive thud. Bella reflected briefly on the stories she had heard about orc sizes. Some were known to reach heights of three meters and weigh upwards of five hundred pounds. This was a smaller variant, but its lumbering gait alluded to a large barbaric creature. She grasped Godwin's wrist, holding him tightly as both a warning to a compatriot and a comfort against the fear.

That fear rose quickly as the orc stopped near their position and sniffed loudly. Bella's mind raced. *Could he smell them? Could they outrun the brute? Could they kill him before he raised the alarm?*

None of these thoughts brought solace because the answers to each were not in her favor. She knew that this thing would sniff them out soon, and whatever type of alarm it raised would be sounded in response to their discovery. The creature sniffed again; this time even closer. The audibility of his moist, mucus-filled, nostrils swung from side to side, as if the creature was some sort of bloodhound searching for prey. Bella changed her crouch to one capable of a quick vertical leap and dropped her hands down to the daggers strapped to her thighs. The grunts and snorts were zeroing in on them, and their pitch and tone changed to something of a finale. Its breaths were long and loud as they pinpointed their target. Then just as furiously as the snorting had begun—it stopped. An inhuman bellow that felt as if it were going to rend the veil of reality in twain wailed from the creature.

Bella was unnerved but nevertheless drove herself out of the bush and towards her porcine foe. He fixed his gaze on Bella, but her speed outmatched his reflexes, and before he could respond she had wrapped her legs around his torso and was plunging her deadly daggers in between his clavicle and shoulder muscle. She hoped to drop him quickly with the over-whelming maneuver, but the beast still stood as she plunged the pair of blades three times into a growing gash in its shoulder. Godwin came into view from the right, plunging his sword into the orc's side with an adren-aline-soaked grunt. A small sprinkle of fear tainting his voice. The orc bel-lowed again, not in alarm but in pain.

Yet, the brute still did not fall. Bella was about to plant her blades for a fourth time when a meaty hand grabbed her from behind, and, with in-human strength, flung her back into the bush.

Dazed, her vision blurred. She could hear Godwin yelling as his blade clashed against something metal. She reached up to grab hold of a branch, using it as leverage to pull herself back into the fight. She heard two more clashes of metal on metal and a sudden truncated squeal that sounded like a pig who had finally met the butcher. As she dragged herself out of the bush, she saw a victorious Godwin standing over a headless orc. Yet she did not revel in his victory, for behind him the amber light of several torches danced. The bobbing amber glow was a sure sign that more orcs were on their way. Godwin could see in Bella's face that something was amiss, and ever so slowly he turned around.

Godwin stood frozen in place. Bella cried out to the dumbstruck man, "Run!" but he did not move. She dashed out of the bush and grabbed him by his bicep, yanking him out of his stupor. He looked at her and his eyes narrowed in focus.

Together, they sprinted away from the oncoming foe. They crashed through the brush that had, just moments ago, given them refuge, and in the not far-off distance, Bella could make out two torchlights bobbing up and down, held by mounted men. She could just make out the gangly fea-tures of Blythe and three mounts below him, and just to his right the ter-rible horsemanship of Godfrey. Her muscles strained as she pushed herself hard away from the enemy. She heard the orcs now; a cacophony of hoots, grunts, snorts, and howls that filled the night with dread. She could also hear whistling noises darting through the air around them, as projectiles were thrown, shot, or launched at them. A few of which were lit and cast a faint amber glow that blanketed the surrounding landscape. They were in a long clearing; the surrounding—now spent—projectiles cast a reddish glow on them, making them obvious to all outside observers

Bella heard Godwin's heavy breathing behind her, making her conscious of her own gasping breaths. Pushing the pain of the frantic sprint away, she hauled herself towards the now prominent figures of Godfrey and Blythe. Just ten seconds more. Yet, ten seconds could feel like a lifetime in situations like this. Suddenly, A great whooshing noise pierced the air. A sound like boat rowers splitting the waves rang out, but only it sounded like these rowers were going at a pace and frequency of uncanny proportions. It was almost in the aftermath did Bella finally register this new noise. The heavy chopping sound grew in frequency until it was nearly all-consuming. *Fwop fwop fwop fwop fwop FWOP FWOP FWOP!* Something massive cut through the air behind them, but before anyone could respond it was too late.

Godwin cried out in pain. He fell to his knees, and his torso soon followed suit. His remaining momentum skidded him a final few centimeters so that his prone body lay right in front of Bella's feet, an oversized ax embedded deep into his back; his spine severed. She crouched towards the fallen warrior, examining him for signs of life. She brushed his hair aside exposing an eye; its skin stretched from being rubbed against the hard ground. She saw no signs of movement and … no signs of life. Godwin's face made her feel numb inside, as if the events unfolding around her were not real. One minute, she had heard his rich deep breaths as they tried to escape and the next, he was just … gone. There was nothing there in his eyes. A sudden rise in yells from the orc line galvanized Bella to sprint once again towards Godfrey and Blythe.

"No!!!" Godfrey bellowed as he saw his nephew's corpse lying on the ground. Bella looked at Godfrey's face and saw utter dismay. The near-constant humorous grin was replaced with deep sorrowful lines of pain. Godfrey, in his torment, did not look back at her. The old warrior re-mained mounted, for the danger was still prevalent.

Blythe skidded to a halt next to Bella and pulled Precious's reins to-wards her, desperately urging her to mount and ride off. She was about to reach for the reins when a smaller orc burst from a copse of trees to their left. The beast closed the distance rapidly, running on all fours like a bear. Bella could see a crude blade in one of his hands, bouncing off the ground dangerously as the monster loped towards them. Before she could mount a response to the threat, Godfrey came charging at the orc via horseback. He yelled loudly into the night, his anger frothing from the sight of his dead nephew. With mighty fury, he swung his war axe and took the orc's head clean off. The effort of the charge nearly unseated him, but he man-aged to curb back towards the group.

The chaos of the night accelerated in cadence, and those few seconds that had stalled the group increased the density of orcs approaching them. Already, Bella could see a line of four massive orc warriors approaching them through the clearing. The details of their hide-and-bone-bound ar-mor were plainly visible. Flaps of thick hide were daubed with congealed blood and held together with sinew and a rather malevolent-looking red weave. Most of the orc's bodies were covered in a lattice of bone, and crude metal. Bella had taken in these details in a split second knowing that to delay any longer was to bring the already too close enemy closer.

She leaped into her saddle, turning to Godfrey. "Come on, we got to get into the woods," she yelled out to him. His face was marked by sav-agery, and Bella knew the old man wanted to wet his ax blade more. Yet to give into that savagery now would spell certain doom, and Bella pleaded with the man to ride clear of the meadow. Godfrey very slightly dipped his head, indicating his ascent to ride clear.

Bella blew out a quick sigh of relief, and yelled to Precious, "Come on girl let's hope the Maiden is with us!"

The air was thick with the sound of buzzing projectiles, and the roars of bloodthirsty orcs. Bella found herself crouching low in the saddle instinctively, trying desperately to not meet Godwin's fate. She felt a slash against her right thigh as something screamed past her. She could hear Blythe grunt in pain as another crude weapon found some purchase on him. Twenty meters in front of them there was a maw of blackness which opened into the forest surrounding them. She steered Precious towards the hole and patted the horse's neck, praying that no roots or holes would snap her mount's legs.

Without warning Bella was flung forward out of her saddle. A bolus wrapped itself around Precious's back legs snapping one of them instantly. The horse used to hard riding and danger, did not cry out as it fell face-first into the dirt. Bella rolled overhead three times before her momentum finally stalled. As she came back to her senses, she heard Precious whinny in agony.

Finding her feet, Bella saw Precious who was turned completely around, having flipped herself when she hit the dirt. Her broken back leg hung uselessly at a disturbing angle, and the other three scrambled in panic trying to find grip on the slick ground. Through the dizziness and pain of her—most likely concussed—head, she looked on at the horse she had trained and loved since they had arrived in Elgion; broken in the dirt.

Even though death stalked close by, she tried to calm her beloved mount. "Shhh, it's alright," she said as she patted the air in a calming motion. And just as abruptly as the horse had begun flailing did it stop. An orcish spear now jutted out of Precious's head, a sickening thunk reverberating in Bella's ears. The horse was killed instantly, and it slumped to the ground. Three arrows poked out of the horse's flank; their feathers flecked with blood.

"Ember's breath, we got to go!" Godfrey screamed as he pushed his horse into Bella's shoulder.

Clearly, she had been out of it for too long, since Godfrey was not just using his horse to rouse her from her confusion, but he was also using it to fight off yet another small orc. He swung his ax wildly behind her, meeting crude iron in return. Bella shook her head and looked at the blood-amber vignette of the old veteran, fighting desperately to keep her alive. Blythe had already pulled Scout and Lilith alongside her.

"I'm sorry mum," Blythe yelled into the chaos of the night. He dismounted to help her back into the saddle. "She was a good horse," he said as he kneeled, holding his hands splayed out as a stepping stool for Bella. Bella looked on at Blythe, tears threatening to overwhelm her. Yet he did not look back with empathy; instead, fear stole across his face.

Sinking into a state of combat readiness she noticed the dip in light behind her. She wrenched the smaller dagger, that adorned her chest, free and spun to greet the newcomer. A massive orc loomed over her with a club raised high above its head. Out of instinct, she lunged the small blade towards the throat of the beast, but it was deflected by a shard of bone. Her hand, pushed to the side, was resting on the orc's shoulder when it brought the club down, bellowing in rage as it did so. Her lunge had brought her in close enough to take the power from the blow, but she was still dazed by the orc's meaty hands falling onto her skull. She dropped the dagger low and slashed it into the orc's side. The beast grunted softly, seeming to be mildly annoyed more than hurt.

With malevolent eyes, the orc stared down at her over its massive fangs and grinned. Before Bella could respond, she was pushed to the ground by one oversized hand. The sudden shock of the blow did little to stymie the fear she felt for what was coming next. For the beast reared the massive club over its head once again and swung.

# Chapter Twelve

## Alexa

The light patter of footsteps; tiny taps reverberating through blankets of moss; sounds barely noticeable. An unwelcome sensation that forced more beads of sweat to soak through Alexa's body, dousing her tunic in the briny liquid. An impossibly thick forest loomed overhead with dense green foliage. She tried to steady her breaths, forcing her eyes shut.

*Chit chit chit*, a sinister clicking noise emanated from the trees; closer than she would have thought possible. Her eyes shot open, the whites of her sclera exposed and filling with dread.

*Chit chit chit*, another series of clicks behind her. She spun around quickly and paced backward slowly, moving away from the unwelcome noise.

*Chit chit chit*, the sound clawed its way through the dense brush in front of her, yet she saw nothing. She reached behind herself for her bow, but it simply wasn't there. Instead, she was left with an empty grasping hand. Her heart pounded in her chest now and she increased her backward retreat.

*CHIT CHIT CHIT*, the scraping gnawing sound of iktomid feet, accompanied by booming clicks raked the trees and branches nearby. The sounds portrayed the threat as being right on top of her, but still, there was only foliage.

Without warning, the choking vegetation shot up and up and *up* into the air. The trees and brush grew to an impossible length, consuming everything in their path. They grew until the light from the sun was extinguished. In the new darkness, only her breath could be heard, and it was trembling with fear. In that damnable silence, her ragged exhalations were accompanied by a slowly growing light. A red orb pulsing in intensity, mirroring her breath. As she hyperventilated in response to the strange—unnerving—light, more and more of the red orbs flickered to life. They took form, and she could see that they clustered in groups of eight. They surrounded her now, and she spun to take in their full scale. There must have been hundreds of them!

*CHIT CHIT CHIT!* The iktomids all cried out at once before the largest of the red orbs stepped in front of her. She sank to the ground, frozen with terror. A light from some unknown source illuminated the monstrosity in front of her. Fangs as tall as herself, and a maw of unfathomable hunger opened. She gasped in horror as the mouth came down upon her, swallowing her whole …

*

She shot up to a sitting position, her body tense with fear. Her breaths came quick and shallow as if she had been drowning. Sweat flicked off her as she torqued her body out of sleep. A sudden rush of air hit her as the blankets fell away, allowing the sickly sweat to rapidly cool her. The heavy chill gave Alexa's mind back a modicum of control, and she urged her breaths to a slower—calmer—pace. It was still dark out, and the chill air from the open window whipped through the apothecary treatment room. She pulled the blanket back over her shoulders and reflected on the nightmare that had woken her so many times.

Sophia had said that the intensity and frequency of the nightmares would fade in time. "Time heals all wounds," echoed in her mind even now. Although Alexa couldn't tell if Sophia truly believed that or not. After all, they had both seen their share of armless or legless veterans in the streets of Augustia who year after year never got better. Regardless, Alexa prayed that she was right. Minutes passed as she regained her faculties, and with steady movement, she laid back down to rest. Yet, as usual with this nightmare, sleep would not come. Realizing the futility of her situation, she resigned to wait in silence for the rising of the sun.

By the time Sophia had opened the door to bring Alexa her breakfast, madness had nearly claimed the ranger.

"You have been dreaming again," Sophia said, her lips pursed in a matronly fashion. The Keeper crossed the room gracefully and placed the wooden tray in front of Alexa. "*And* it looks like those dreams are interrupting your sleep again." The Keeper handed her a spoon, nearly shoving it into her grasp. Sophia stood over Alexa until she spooned a gob of the still-hot porridge into her mouth. She swallowed the heavy meal, feeling its weight plunge into her stomach.

Sophia never wasted time with flavor. Nevertheless, and with no small amount of will, Alexa swallowed the tasteless food. Satisfied with her sister's performance, Sophia retreated to the little writing desk that now lay in the corner of the room. The all-too-familiar copy of *Hyclepius's Teachings* sat open in the middle of the desk. Its well-worn pages were yellow around the edges and its spine looked as if the book had been opened thousands of times.

Alexa stomached another bite of the heavy oats, noting how that book had remained a near-constant companion for Sophia as they combated the iktomid's sickness. In fact, that dusty old tome may have very well saved her life.

"A bit heavy on Maidenstone use, but it has many useful tidbits," Sophia had told Alexa on one of the many days that they sat together in the cramped observation room. One of the few interesting occasions that had happened over the two weeks since Alexa had regained consciousness. Two weeks of grueling trials as she tried to regain her strength. Two weeks in which they pushed the limits of her body, testing to see if she was fit enough to be removed from observation. So far, she would always reach a point at which waves of weakness or nausea would take over, and a disappointed Sophia would be forced to carry her sister back to bed. Day in and day out continued like this until the duo became quite terse with one another, and bitter memories of the past were dredged back to the surface. Although the sisters shared a close relationship, those familial bonds were strained at present. Alexa's bonds were particularly strained; Necrostone was not something you used on family. There was more than one story about Mosyneta continually replaying the memory that was asked for within the mind of the remembrancer.

A cruel fate that might last her whole damn life. Surges of anger would build whenever it crossed her thoughts, and she struggled not to place some of the blame for her recurrent nightmares on Sophia. After she scraped the last of the porridge into her mouth, she gazed at her sister. She felt one of those waves of anger wash over her. She tried clenching and unclenching her fists, hoping that the action would allow the rage to wash away, but the thought of those damn vapors violating her would not go away.

Vapors that had robbed her of her senses; like being possessed. She hardly remembered the use of the stone at all. All the same, it *had* been used and only in the telling did Alexa learn what she had disclosed during her near zombified story. It seemed that everyone had been present during that retelling, save herself, and in forcing her cooperation without her consent they had stolen the liberty of disclosure in the pursuit of truth.

Although Alexa was grateful to Sophia for saving her life, her anger only seemed to grow after every occurrence of the nightmare. This anger mounted upon all the other frustrations of the last two weeks.

Unable to contain herself any longer she finally burst. "Why did you have to use a stone!?"

Sophia looked up from *Hyclepius's Teachings* a small furrow on her brow developing, "All Keepers use stones … that is what we do. Well besides making sure they keep safe," Sophia said with a relish of mirth in her voice. She continued more thoughtfully, "And besides, no sane healer would avoid the use of Maidenstone. Especially with a case as is bad as yours."

Sophia brought her cupped hand to her mouth in contemplation. Alexa noticed a slight movement beneath Sophia's outer vest, a methodic rubbing. The Keeper's left hand was still cupped to her mouth until she slowly brought the fingers together at the apex of her chin and pulled them straight away as if she were pulling an invisible string. "Ah, you mean the Necrostone?"

"Of course, I mean the Necrostone!"

Sophia's head rocked back, shocked at the furious tone of her sister. "Well, I am not sure what you are so upset abo—"

"You stole my memories! Of course, I would be upset! You act as if you did nothing wrong, but … but. Bu—"

"Sister, I don't understand why you are so upset," Sophia repeated.

Alexa had her head bowed to the floor slightly after she had trailed off, but she now locked her gaze onto Sophia once more. She felt the fury in her eyes and Sophia dropped eye contact under the weight of the stare.

A moment of strained silence passed before Sophia clicked her cheek. Gently Sophia spoke, "I didn't mean to hurt you, sister, but I can see why you would be angry. The Necrostone can feel … like your own memories were sold to the highest bidder. Yet, I assure you, Bella and I took precautions to avoid you divulging the more personal details of your journey. Ember's breath, I mean I don't even know the full telling of your story."

"You could have just asked me! You didn't have to make me the plaything of some god."

"You are not a plaything. You do not understand what you are talking about!" Sophia sprung out of her chair unexpectedly, rising to the barb, and upsetting the desk in front of her. The desk did not fall over but instead slammed back to the ground making a rather alarming racket in the small room.

Sophia now stood; her autumnal red ponytail whipped over her shoulder, and her Keeper's cloak, its amber folds seeming more weighted than usual, hung heavily on her shoulders. Her outfit was exposing the skin of her neck more readily than if it were properly adjusted. Alexa steadily threw her legs over the side of the bed and found her footing. Sophia held a small azure stone in her right palm, which was emanating a small purple glow within.

"You done then?" Alexa asked with scorn in her voice. "If that's all, I would like to return to my Hall." She crossed the room to her now flustered sister. Sophia breathed heavily a few more times, expelling some of the wroth that had spilled out so explosively.

Eventually, Sophia nodded slightly. "I have some medicine you should take, but in the last few days, you have made good progress. Our last incident saw you only requiring a minor sit down." Sophia pulled her cloak over her shoulders, its red trim highlighting her grim countenance, and tucked the azure stone away as she spoke. "I was going to recommend you return to duties today anyways."

Alexa scoffed. "Oh, were you? Well, thank you so much for your *recommendation*." Sophia winced at the words but produced a small vial from her vest and handed it to Alexa. She snatched the vial forcefully, stopping centimeters from Sophia's face. "You know, you Keepers aren't the only ones with knowledge of the stones! As a Ranger, we are to gather knowledge of all things, and the one thing I learned about Keepers and their *Stones* was that not all those fragments have your best interests at heart." She paused making a show of nodding where azure stone had been. "You best reflect on your relationship with the Stones *sister*."

Alexa grabbed her coat and charged out the door.

# Chapter Thirteen

## Erin

Rangemaster Erin Apararius had seen Alexa approach up Hook Street from her second-story office. She had watched in amusement as Alexa had stomped with every step of the way towards the Hall; anger souring her gait and posture. The Rangemaster knew Alexa well enough to surmise that a fight had occurred between her and her sister.

Not surprising seeing how the Keeper had used Necrostone on her. If anyone used that damned stone on her, she would be furious. Thoughts of the broken ranger coursed through her mind. A recollection of the blackened constellation of corruption resting upon Alexa's shoulder, and a weak and fragile soul lying helpless as her red-haired sisters dashed to and fro, desperate to save her. The resilience required to make the journey home after such a wound was not inconsequential, she figured as she bit the inside of her cheek.

The Rangemaster couldn't help but place feelings on Alexa's potential in the higher echelons of her mind, a thought that had occurred many times during her command of the Elgion Ranger's Hall. Regardless, and as impressive as the feat may be, the Rangemaster now saw an impetuous youth storming toward her, and the best thing to do with a storm is to get out of the way.

Not wanting to endure the oncoming weather, Erin Apararius concluded that it would be best to give the young soldier time to calm down and reflect on what had troubled her. The wizened warrior did not greet Alexa in the main hall. After a few minutes of contemplation, the Rangemaster made their way down to the training grounds, knowing that her chances of finding Alexa there were the highest. After all, its calming solitude would be something highly sought by someone of Alexa's demeanor, especially someone who had just fought with their Keeper-sister.

The training ground's courtyard may have been outside, but it was still flanked by three walls of the building. It lay nestled in between the open-ended square design of the building; like a box that had been opened and had the contents of an archery range, pugilist's pit, gymnasium, and sparring arena stuffed inside. The neat design of the space made it one of the more secluded areas in the village of Elgion, especially since the open end faced into the rarely occupied fields west of town, a condition exacerbated by the putrid work of the nearby tannery. There in the center of the courtyard stood Alexa, preparing to take a practice shot at one of many straw dummies.

"I see that you are feeling better," Erin Apararius called out, her words truncated by the whistle and thud of an arrow striking home. Alexa did not slow in stringing her next shot, pretending to not have heard the Rangemaster's words. The shot had gone wide and Alexa's cheeks grew red with a turbulent flurry. She saw the muscles in Alexa's jaw tighten, an evident pain response from her recently injured shoulder. Erin Apararius saw the ranger take a deep breath and steady her aim, intense focus on Alexa's face, and she saw the relief the ranger felt as she released the shot. *Thunk!* The arrow once again hit—left of center, and Alexa threw her bow down in frustration. She sat on one of the wooden benches that flanked the courtyard; her head tucked into her hands.

The Rangemaster sighed but still made her way down the steps of the deck that surrounded the courtyard. She had grown to like the tall, brown-haired, and brown-eyed ranger, knowing her for a strong, athletic, and serious sort. Not the type to be taken down easily. Yet, Rangemaster Apararius also knew that Alexa was unsure of herself, and whether that uncertainty was rooted in fear or another malady she wasn't sure. A stoic combination that could forge the best of humanity or drag out the worst of it.

Yet she was here; training, which meant the very best may still be in the lead.

The Rangemaster stopped a couple of meters away from the downcast warrior, took a deep breath, and spoke, "You know, I remember once, when you and Gilneas smelled up my entire Hall with onions."

Erin paused a moment, judging the mood of her audience, but Alexa just stayed motionless, which Erin took as a sign of consent in and of itself. "Yeah, you both came back from a ranging loaded with onions, onions on your breath, onions in your packs, and even onions on your sweat. For weeks after you came back, I couldn't get away from the smell of onions." Erin stepped closer to Alexa tilting her head down, "The two of you were quite literally pissing onions for days."

Erin heard a muffled chuckle emanate from the downcast ranger, who chose to sit upright and take her head out of her hands. Erin saw a glimmer of interest in those brown eyes, so she continued with a little more relish, "It was your first year as range-mates together and I don't know how you all got so many onions, but the rest of the rangers were furious with you two."

"If I recall, we ran into a whole meadow loaded with them," Alexa stated.

The Rangemaster nodded at the explanation and continued. "Well color us lucky, because it seemed that for two weeks, we had nothing but onions for breakfast, lunch, and dinner. Ember's breath! We even ended up with pickled onions on occasion for the rest of the year."

Erin motioned for Alexa to make room for her and sat down next to the ranger. "Food is food, but I got to say I was worried about you two. Some of the things I heard the other rangers say. There was quite a level of discontent at your onion escapades," Erin stated. Alexa looked at her, puzzlement furrowing her brows, but just then she slapped Alexa's leg and let out a quick bark of laughter.

"Oh, come now Alexa, you yourself were tired of onions after the first few days!"

"Maybe …" Alexa stated with a hint of mischief.

"But you know who never seemed tired of those damned onions?" Erin raised an eyebrow at Alexa, prompting her response.

"Gilneas," Alexa murmured, her warming mood suddenly chilled by the mention of his name.

"That's right, that sodding onion lover never let his optimism dim. He was like a beacon in the dark. Even I found myself looking for his light on my days of greatest doubt …" Rangemaster Apararius let the last words trail off. A subtle trick she had learned from a life spent in or around roles of leadership. A trick that almost always hooked her audience, either with concern or morbid curiosity, and in the corner of her eye she could see Alexa's curiosity had peaked.

Time to hook her catch, "I know you feel doubt. Maybe you doubt yourself? Still, you are not the only one to feel this way, and the best way to honor Gilneas is to carry on. To push forward and honor his memory with the skill and determination I know you have inside of you."

Alexa sat up straighter.

Erin added, "I understand … Rangemaster."

Alexa's eyes widened after she had said the word Rangemaster, and as if she suddenly realized that she was speaking to her commander shot up and stood at attention. "I am sorry for my anger, Rangemaster."

Erin Apararius stayed seated and stared at Alexa for several moments, allowing for any cracks in the resolve of the ranger to widen. In that gulf of time, she reflected on the many soldiers she had commanded. From the stalwart to the foolhardy and everything in between, she had been leading men and women for twelve years. And in those twelve years, she learned how important it could be to redirect a grieving soldier's attention, to reaffirm their efforts in soldiery at the critical moment.

If authority was applied correctly, Rangemaster Erin Apararius knew, then anyone could be made to endure. Alexa, a stalwart and promising ranger, needed only a little of that pressure applied and she would continue to be an exemplary soldier. In time shedding any doubts she had placed on herself. A full minute passed before she allowed—unbeknownst to Alexa—a hollow smile cross her lips, "There is no need to apologize." She stood and placed a calming hand on the shoulder of her charge, "Instead, let us speak the words of our order in honor of Gilneas. Would you like that?"

Alexa looked at her and nodded, a look of desperate appeal within her eyes.

Erin pursed her lips, closed her eyes, and nodded at the ranger. "He goes now to that Far Range. That place where we all must go. He was our brother, our companion. He was a Warden of the Wilds. He was a guardian against the unknown. He was a watcher in the woods. Here we remember him, but here is not where he stays. We *will* see him again on that Far Range … goodbye." The Rangemaster finished, allowing a moment of silence to fall.

Alexa reopened her eyes, tears threatening to drop, and looked up at the Rangemaster, "Thank you, mum."

Rangemaster Erin Apararius smiled at the stalwart soldier and spoke again, "There is need for you to become the Ranger you are meant to be." Erin grabbed Alexa by both shoulders, fixing her head just centimeters from Alexa in an attempt to solidify her words. "There is a need for you to continue, despite the loss of brave Gilneas. And finally, there is need for you to help me figure out what in Ember's breath is going on to our north."

Alexa grinned at the use of the common curse, obvious tension ebbing away from her. Slowly the ranger replied to Erin, "Well … I know my sister has absconded with some of the citizenry and ventured up there."

"That she has," Erin replied with the inflection of a teacher who is disappointed in their pupil.

Alexa dipped her head. "As foolish as her actions are and trust me, I have spent many an hour grinding my teeth at her idiocy, she was brave to do so. After all, the rangers were going to do the same thing, but just with more … preparation."

"And an actual plan." The Rangemaster interrupted. "Your sister could very well have endangered the whole of Elgion."

"I know Rangemaster, but I know Bella and I know that's not what she intended. She is just … impatient."

"Impatience is a hallmark of fools," Erin Apararius said, her tone stern. The commander could see the twitch of anger on Alexa's lips. She could see the rebellion rise within her pupil, and she watched in satisfaction as the student overcame their temporary anger at the insult to her kin

Alexa replied, struggling to contain her wrath. "Of course, Rangemaster, regardless she has forced our hand. So, what will we do now?"

"Now, that is the right question," Erin said feeling a more genuine smile cross her lips. "First, we will have to get you back into fighting shape!" She slammed a hand against her chest and then began to walk towards the Great Hall. Alexa, unprepared for her commander's sudden movement, needed to be guided by one of Erin's hands that still lay clasped over her shoulder. "Of course, you will be without a range-mate until another group of recruits comes in the spring, but no matter. You will stay by my side and learn a thing or two."

Alexa paused at this, forcing the Rangemaster to stop. Her gloved hand was pulled back by the sudden immobile shoulder. "Y-you honor me, Rangemaster." Alexa bowed her head in appreciation, stunned by the commander's words. Erin let a warmth blossom across her face.

Although the smile was genuine, it was a rare sight to see your commander smile so. The expression the commander saw in return told her that she had brought the ranger back around to the fold.

"Ah, it is no matter. Now let's see if we can get you debriefed and re-equipped."

With that, the commander and the ranger walked side-by-side discussing myriad details of recent ranging events and together disappeared into the Great Hall.

# Chapter Fourteen

## Alexa

Early morning jog, random herb identification, strength exercise, break-fast, combat tactics, combat drills (spear, shield, and axe), strength exercise, lunch, afternoon jog, strength exercise, campcraft, dinner, evening patrol, archery drills, rest. *Blessed rest.* Three days in a row Alexa endured an intense routine set forth by the Rangemaster. She had been ecstatic at first by the prospect of training alongside her commander, but she soon realized that the old woman had taken it as an opportunity to push Alexa and herself to the limit. Excruciating and exhaustive mental and physical exercise was implemented and acted upon with enthusiasm, and they had not relented for three … straight … days.

The first morning Alexa had taken it as a challenge to try and outdo her impromptu partner; to demonstrate her value. During their first exercise outing, an endurance jog, Alexa had sprinted the last hundred yards or so of what she thought was the finish line. Only to discover that the front of the Ranger's Hall was *not* the finish line. Commander Apararius had just kept going, without even glancing at her, even though they had already jogged all the way to the Farney River crossing, back to the stables, and around the Hook Street loop. Three laps had come and gone, and Alexa realized that this was not going to be an easy training regimen. Immediately after their intense jog, they had settled into the lifting of heavy clay jars loaded with grain.

"One must never forget to exercise the legs," Rangemaster Erin Apararius intoned to Alexa after they had completed their third set of grain-assisted squats. Alexa had forced a smile at the inane comment, not knowing what else lay in front of them. They drilled only to break the sessions with intense breakdowns of varying topics of ranger craft. From squad and army tactics to such esoteric inquiries as the consistency of various animal feces. A mental and physical load that pushed her capacities to the brink. Every time Alexa thought she was going to break and every time she wanted to surrender to her body's whims, she was instead shamed into continuing. Shamed just by looking at the unfazed expression of her— quickly becoming disliked—commander. She had hoped to see some sign that the older woman faltered; that Alexa need only endure a step more or a rep more, but never did she see a single sign of that tough old soldier weakening.

Alexa was woken before sunrise on the fourth day of her assignment to the Rangemaster. Her entire body was on fire, and she could barely move. The pain and strain she had felt from her wound had been overridden by her absolute mental and physical exhaustion. She could barely lift her feet from the ground by the third morning, and now, once again, prepared for another day of grueling exercise. At any minute she knew that the Rangemaster would burst in, all jolly and rested, ready to seize the day. Yet as those minutes ticked by in silence no one entered the room. Laying there in the quiet, she contemplated her pains and delayed the inevitable.

*

Some time had passed in meditative silence, before a morning dove called through the open window. The peaceful melody soothed Alexa's mind, and she smiled at the blissful reprieve. Yet, she could not shake the feeling that something wasn't right. Some fundamental flaw was affecting her current circumstances, and with dawning horror, Alexa realized that she had dozed off.

She leapt out of bed, ignoring her complaining muscles as she pulled her tunic and trousers on. She zipped out of the door and made her way down the stairs with abandon.

Nearly falling on the last few steps, Alexa rounded the corner at the base of the stairs, only to almost run headfirst into a pair of rangers freshly back from patrol. She skidded on her right leg as she tried to maintain her balance and dart around the rangers.

"Damn Alexa! You in a hurry?" yelled Elira, a ranger who had arrived at Elgion on the same boat as Alexa and her sisters. She was as experienced as her and as such always felt like a sort of competitor. Elira smiled when she said the words. It felt like an olive branch and Alexa reckoned that with Gilneas's fall and the weird mannerisms of a tight-knit group like the Rangers, Elira was indeed *trying* to make friends.

"Sorry, just ... busy," Alexa replied, her hands held in placation, as she regained her footing on the opposite side of the hallway to them. She raced off without another word, leaving the ranger pair confused by her demeanor. She dashed towards the front entrance, hoping that the Rangemaster had not already returned from her morning jog. She burst open the double doors, expecting to see that dour old veteran, with crossed arms, waiting on her tardy student. Instead, she saw the stern commander in deep conversation with the Guard-Captain and a rather worse-for-wear-looking Blythe, standing awkwardly to the side.

From her vantage at the top of the stairs, she saw the two commanders speak softly to one another. Their manner was relaxed, and Alexa recognized the ease of conversation that the two shared, a certain closeness only achieved through long association. Before long, the Rangemaster spotted Alexa. Commander Apararius held her hand up towards Guard-Captain Alexander Vitrusian pausing him from further conversation. She nodded over to Alexa and beckoned for her to approach. The Guard-Captain fixed her with his stare; grey eyes peeked out from under thick grey eyebrows. She felt a shudder spasm up her back as the two commanders looked upon her, but she hurried to answer the beckon all the same.

Before the Rangemaster could say anything, Alexa dropped to a knee. "Rangemaster, forgive me for my tardiness, I did not realize the time."

Alexa sat there on her knee, head bowed, for what felt like forever, trembling in fear of the unknown consequences.

"It is forgiven, ranger. Please stand, greet our Guard-Captain," the Rangemaster beckoned. As Alexa came to attention, the grey light of mid-morning kissed her face, the blue and gold radiance showing the world that it would be another beautiful fall day.

Commander Apararius elaborated, "It seems that even more news has been brought to our doorstep." Alexa saw the Rangemaster look uncertainly at the Guard-Captain and frowned at the possible implications.

"Blythe, where is my sister?" Alexa asked the huge man, a hint of fear in her voice.

"I told you she is perceptive, Alexander," the Rangemaster said as she smacked the Guard-Captain playfully on his forearm with the back of her hand. Blythe was about to speak when the Rangemaster silenced him with a raised hand. "Alexa, this may be hard to hear," the commander said with a gentler tone than usual.

She jerked her head back, "Doesn't matter Rangemaster. I … uh, I need to hear. Wh-where is my sister?"

Guard-Captain Vitrusian spoke. His deep voice slicing through the air. "Bella's party that fled in the night some days back were attacked by a rather sizeable host of orcs. This attack came whilst they were trying to scout their encampment." Alexander held his hand out towards Blythe, "This man here escaped on the prompting of one of my own *errant* men in order to bring word to us. From what we have been told, she was last seen being taken captive by the foul pigmen." Alexa couldn't help but quiver under the weight of the words. The fear of losing the sister who just days prior had sat so lovingly at her side felt heavy in her soul. She closed her eyes trying to hold back tears.

"Yes, it's a damned mess," the Rangemaster said.

Heat rose in Alexa's chest. Vitriolic anger at her commanders' harsh words boiled in her chest, but before it could manifest into full-fledged rage the Rangemaster spoke again.

"We are preparing an expeditionary force to confront this new menace to the north, and if we are lucky, rescue the two stolen souls." This statement helped ease Alexa off the oncoming rage, and she was thankful for that. She knew that the wrong words here against her commander could lead to more dire consequences later. However, she had just become curious. "Only two? I thought she left with three men?" she inquired. Blythe's head bowed downwards, almost as if in mourning.

A heavy pause stole the air from the four of them. Alexa glanced around at their faces, eager to hear the news. Eager to know the full truth, the Guard-Captain spoke in somber tones, "Godwin … did not survive the attack. That much is confirmed. Blythe here watched the poor boy die."

Alexa looked at Blythe with empathy. She had known the big man for almost three years now. Ever since Bella and Blythe had teamed up and used their skills to keep what few livestock they had alive during the ocean crossing to Elgion, they had been close companions. Blythe was almost like a brother, and there in that moment, she saw in his eyes nothing but sorrow.

"Don't worry Blythe, we will find them. We will find her," Alexa said before she could even think about it, as if on instinct.

Rangemaster Apararius tilted her head up, a look of curiosity and, to Alexa's astonishment, pride on her face. The Guard-Captain nodded, and Alexa swore she could see the left side of his mouth rise, an almost imperceptible smile stealing over his normally dour features.

"Yes, yes, we will, but first! We need to plan," Captain Vitrusian said.

"Ah, that's right." Commander Apararius snapped her fingers as if to snap herself out of the distractions around her. The Rangemaster continued, "Alexa, can you take Blythe here to get some food within our hall? After he has eaten his fill, have him help you round up some decent mounts from the stables."

A cart trundled behind them, temporarily making conversation difficult. The commander used the time to look at the Guard-Captain and the duo seemed to share a knowing glance. Based on their expressions, Alexa felt as if the two had just shared some secret conversation within their minds. The outcome of which must have been disappointing. After the cart had passed out of earshot, the Rangemaster clicked her cheek and continued, a sense of disappointment in her voice. "We are gonna need all the help we can get. And, to save the war-trained horses for future defense, all the other mounts we can get from the stables."

Alexa knew that the guard, The Warriors of August, kept a contingent of mounts themselves all trained for war. She figured that diving into the civilian stables for a martial matter was the cause for the unspoken words amongst her commanders.

The Rangemaster continued, "Meet us back at the hall with what horses and supplies you can gather. Once you have those secure. Place them in our holds along with our own mounts."

Alexa nodded, knowing that the Rangemaster meant the small corral in which the Ranger's Hall kept livestock or other beasts temporarily. Either for butchery or for other curiosities was dealer's choice.

Erin Apararius nodded back at Alexa. "If we are lucky, we can get the governor on our side. And if we are luckier still, we can get a group of us moving out by dawn tomorrow. Come! We have much to prepare!"

With her commander's orders finished, Alexa slammed her fist to her chest in salute and moved off at a brisk pace, grabbing the dazed Blythe so he would follow. Blythe and Alexa worked in silence as they gathered up the supplies and horses requested by the Rangemaster. The short walk to the stables was punctuated only by the sounds of the blacksmith's hammer ringing through the village streets. Alexa felt the tension between the pair as a palpable mass. Both remained quiet, preferring to leave the unspoken as is. So instead, they made haste to the stables and immediately set to work. They gathered six horses in total, two of which were old and preparing to leave their work life behind.

*Bella always had a soft spot for these beasts,* Alexa thought, knowing that many stablemasters would 'dispose' of a no longer functioning horse. Yet here they were loading two solemn and aging horses with saddlebags filled with what little provisions Blythe and the other stable hands could scrounge up. Salted mutton, grain rations, and some old cabbage bunches made up most of the foodstuffs. The remaining four horses consisted of two work stallions and two young mares that Blythe said were, "Nearly ready for heavy riding. Up to and including combat capable riding."

Together the duo of Alexa and Blythe led the horses loaded with saddlebags out of the stable gates. At the threshold, one of the old stallions reared in protest, whinnying in tandem with his rebellion. Blythe pulled gently against the reins of the horse, but it refused to move past the gate opening. Alexa watched as the bulky man attempted to soothe the horse and lead it out again; and again … to no avail. The large paws of Blythe had even produced a small crabapple at one point for bribery's sake, but the bribe fell short of its goal and the old nag did not budge. Blythe let out a large sigh and turned to Alexa. She saw that his dark brown eyes were glistening almost as if he were about to cry.

"You go on ahead. I … I need to take care of ol' Patches here," Blythe said. Alexa saw him produce a knife from his tunic and he held it up, informing her, without words, that Patches would be soon under the knife. "I know mum wouldn't want this, but we don't have the time. And well, we will need the meat. All these people out in the wild without making food? I don't want any hungry bellies when the snows become a half-a-meter deep."

"I understand ..." She looked at Blythe like one who is remembering a loved one lost.

Blythe turned away with Patches and called over to one of the stable boys, "Kynos, help this ranger with the horses." Kynos leapt into action and grabbed the reins of the other old stallion as well as the two remaining pack horses. As Alexa pulled away from the stable gate with the two mares, she looked at the big man. She couldn't help but feel approval for the unique person known as Blythe. Ever since they had been introduced to the nearly two-meter-tall behemoth, he had been a constant companion to Bella, and at first, he appeared quite simple. Yet the truth was that he just didn't want to be in charge, and he always preferred to follow. It was like he was afraid that his size would consume and harm those around him. So, he tried to stay hidden, and he tried to stay away from confrontation. There, in that moment of raw practicality, Alexa saw, and not for the first time, that Blythe showed a quality few could match. She smiled at the back of the man and quietly whispered to herself, "Good luck Blythe."

Kynos and herself had stabled the horses within the corral of the Ranger's Hall and had carted the saddlebags inside the main foyer of the entrance. Already a stock of supplies was taking shape and rangers, including Elira and her partner, Matthias, scurried about preparing for the journey to come. Shortly after she had delivered the requested supplies, the Rangemaster appeared on the second floor of the guild building. Alexa noticed the commander stand and watch her company work. Her hands clasped behind her back. Alexa busied herself by unloading the saddlebags, which was entirely unnecessary, but was an excuse to watch the enigmatic ranger captain. Three whole minutes passed before the Rangemaster finally changed her position. She moved to a more prominent position on the banister above the foyer. Yet still, the Rangemaster did not speak, instead, she just waited for her proteges to notice her, and something in her demeanor told what rangers noticed her to stop and listen.

"Hey! Stop that, commanders waiting," Elira called out to Matthias after he continued to move without perception whilst everyone else grew suddenly silent and still. The dumbfounded ranger stopped; his anger apparent at the interruption before he noticed the Rangemaster. His head twitched around as it dawned on him that he was the last to notice the figure above them. Quickly, he stood to attention, trying to hide his embarrassment.

It dawned on her that the silence was to see who would notice her first. Alexa hoped the Rangemaster had known she'd spotted her right away.

"As some of you may know, two of our citizens have been captured by orcs," the Rangemaster called out over the heads of her assembled company. Her voice was rich and authoritative, carrying easily through the open building, "The Governor, the Guard-Captain, and *I* just finished discussing our response to this threat, and let me be the first to tell you." She paused at these words grinning at the rangers below her. "We will be traveling out to meet those stinking brutes not in pairs, but as a company!" Commander Erin Apararius nodded approvingly as the rangers let out a small cheer at the news. "Before us lies a great challenge. Before us lies a foe that is merciless and strong. No, this will not be easy and do not doubt for a second that we will face grave danger. The orcs are fearsome foes, and we *will* be tested. Rangers!" She barked the last word, snapping many to attention. "This will be the first time that we have marched as a company. This will be the first time many of you have seen combat. Do not fear, for *I* will be with you!" Many of the company nodded their heads, the room feeling alive as it was swept up by the commander's inspirational words.

"I will be with you. And, let me tell you this! As brutish and harrowing as our foe is! There is one thing that the orcs do not have, and do you know what that is?" The Rangemaster held the crowd with an inquisitive look, as if she was requesting a response. Yet, before anyone could respond, she yelled out whilst thrusting a closed fist into the air, "Us! The Wardens of the Wilds!"

The crowd suddenly erupted into vigorous cheers, pumping their fists into the air. Thirteen rangers, not including herself, Blythe, and some various locals cried up into the rafters of the hall. Roused quickly to pandemonium by Rangemaster Erin Apararius.

Alexa looked at her commander, awestruck at the power and leadership that she wielded. Using words and movements with such deft grace. Alexa felt herself caught up in the excitement of the crowd, and she felt adrenaline surge through her as she yearned to fulfill her commander's orders.

Sill her leader continued her speech, "I do not wish to lie to you, and because of that let me be the one that bears the cold truth." The commander paused, waiting for the excitement of the crowd to ebb. She bowed, "Some of you may die." The crowd once so raucous now fell deathly silent at the grim warning. "But in that crucible of death and daring some of you will rise ... to glory!" the Rangemaster looked straight at Alexa, a near imperceptible squinting of her brows followed by an even less perceptible nod.

Alexa froze. She could not fathom why the Rangemaster singled her out, but the moment of exhilaration continued forward.

"Yet, there is nothing to fear in death, for you will be able to join your brothers and sisters on the Far Range. That beautiful green land of verdant majesty. So," the commander paused making her body twist to and fro as if she was inspecting the whole assembly. "Who here is ready to fight!?" A roar of assent rose to the ceiling. "Who here is ready to save our people!?" The crowd roared louder, and Alexa, amid her own roar, swore she felt the force of the reverberations from the rafters hit her. "Are you with me, Rangers?!"

In unison, the rangers responded, "Yes, Rangemaster!" A response Alexa had called out many times during her early years of training. The tumult of the gathered crowd was like a dam burst, and the air buzzed with adrenaline, excitement, and a tinge of fear. In a small pocket of time, Alexa was sure, that group would have dared to face the gods themselves.

"Now! Company, we have until dawn tomorrow to prepare for our journey. I want all this gear sorted and doled out into each pack. I want our mounts fed, watered, and prepped for a hard ride. I want any non-rangers going with us to be shown a weapon and which way to point it. Are there any questions!?" The Rangemaster looked over the group, but no response came. "Well then, get to it." The crowd cheered again as she walked away from the banister and disappeared. Alexa dove to help Blythe, who inspired himself, was already loading one of the packs with needed provisions.

# Chapter Fifteen

## Alexa

Thirteen rangers, seven horses, one Rangemaster, and Blythe set out from Elgion before the sun rose. They were loaded with provisions, weapons, armor, and supplies for a two-week journey, opting to journey on foot so that the horses they took could carry supplies instead of people. The Rangemaster even went so far as to keep one mount unburdened in case a fast rider was warranted, and though Alexa struggled with sore feet she found the journey to be rather cathartic: time ticking by without her really noticing. The crossing at the Farney River ford was marked by her finishing off a hunk of fresh bread from one of the three loaves each ranger carried. The sound of the running water made her feel thirsty and she—along with a few others—refilled their skins at the riverside, drinking deeply from the cool waters as they did so.

The company marched on through the plains north of Elgion, passing rather unremarkable groves and thickets along the way. The Farney River slowly disappeared as its bends took it ever eastwards. Alexa found the brisk march to be much easier than she anticipated. Inwardly she had groaned when the realization of a company march into the wilds became a reality, for she had been unsure if she was up to full fighting shape. Nonetheless, the steps kept coming with little to no complaints from her muscles, and her energy was more resilient than anything she had known in the last couple of harrowing weeks.

This near miracle made her reflect on the recent training regimen she had conducted with the Rangemaster; like that old veteran knew something was coming and needed everyone ready. Once again, she recognized the foresight of her commander and wondered if all leaders were constantly moving the pieces of their command as the Rangemaster did. A few times during the march Alexa was broken from her revelry by the Range-master issuing fresh scouting orders to a pair of rangers. The commander maintained a constant forward vigil ahead of the company and swapped these groups every couple of hours. Alexa was fortunate enough to avoid the more exhausting scouting duty, but not because the commander was taking pity on her. Instead, Alexa knew that no ranger ventured alone, and to send her out without a range mate would be cruel and to send her with a trio would be wasteful. So, she occupied herself with the sights surrounding her, the Rangemaster's uncanny knack for leadership, and thoughts of her Bella … and the now dead Gilneas.

Although they had only made it about two-thirds the distance a group of rangers travel in a day, mostly because of the preparations that were needed before departure, Alexa's mood had become somber. After all, a sixteen-kilometer hike through the northern plains gave her plenty of time to digest recent events, and in her mind's wanderings, she had gained some new resolve.

She reflected on a tenant of the Ranger's Creed, *all those who fall are not lost. For the Far Range awaits us all, and it is glorious.*

Gilneas was at that Far Range now, and Alexa hoped that he would keep up on his almost annoying level of positivity. She reflected on her first lucid moments after her iktomid bite, and how Bella had been there, a thought that threatened tears as she saw her compact sister just sitting there in that little apothecary. Bella was as hard as nails, but beneath that rough exterior was a heart of gold.

Laying down that night beneath the stars, she swore that she would find Bella again. She hoped that she would be up to the task as she drifted off to sleep.

The next day turned into more dreary weather and the morning was crisp and windy. Many of the rangers started by rubbing sore muscles and joints. Alexa was not immune to this and her muscles, especially her left shoulder, ached in the morning cold. She looked over at the Rangemaster who was rubbing an ointment on her calves.

The old woman spotted Alexa observing the near ritualistic procedure. "Ginger and willow bark. Does wonders for the pain." Erin Apararius held a small tincture of the stuff to Alexa, and she rubbed a small amount of the proffered ointment on her shoulder. Instantly, relief washed over her, and, in gratitude, she smiled at the Rangemaster.

Who in turn smiled back warmly, "You keep that bit there." The Rangemaster held up another tincture. "Besides I have got plenty, thanks to your sister. So, the least I can do is give some to you." The tincture disappeared back into its sack and a serious pall fell on the commander's face. "In fact, don't forget to use that. I haven't heard of many people getting over phantom pain from a wound such as yours …"

The company legged the next sixteen kilometers to Elger's Landing at a much faster pace than yesterday. Alexa couldn't gauge whether it was the desire to get off the windswept plain, or as the Guard-Captain liked to say, "The fat had been burnt off."

Regardless, the group arrived at the landing in the late afternoon. In urgency, the Rangemaster pushed them up the hill so that they could reach the nearest lumber camp before dark, and they stumbled to a stop as the last of the light faded. Alexa was so exhausted that she hardly remembered being shown the small cabin that housed her for the night.

The next morning, the sound of wrens whistling their bubbly tune into the forest greeted the company. After applying the tincture given to her by the Rangemaster, more liberally this time due to an even more sore disposition, she headed out into the camp proper. The Rangemaster was speaking with an obviously distraught man, and Alexa approached the interaction warily, cautious of the man due to his frantic, grief-stricken, behavior. Several rangers were already taking stances that would put them within arm's reach of the man within seconds but far enough away so as to not offend either the man or the Rangemaster.

"You have got to help me," he cried out.

"I can't help you if you don't calmly tell me what you know," Rangemaster Erin Apararius replied.

"Look, I don't know what else ya need to know but muh boy is missing damnit!"

"You have mentioned that already, but I know little of the details." The Rangemaster maintained a relaxed posture. "When did you last see your boy? Where did he like to venture to? Have you seen anything strange lately? These are all questions that will help me. So, if you could just take a moment and collect yourself, we can get to the bottom of this *disappearance*."

The man, a rather surly looking fellow with forearms that Alexa thought resembled small trees, looked slightly offended at the Rangemaster's reproof but, nonetheless, he made a concerted effort to calm himself, breathing in and out slowly. After a moment, the man replied, his voice still shaken but far less frantic than before. "Sorry, master just frustrated is all."

Alexa noticed the more formal 'master,' a term usually reserved for members of The Chosen's Wisdom back in Augustia. She also realized that the Rangemaster had not corrected him. *Another tactic perhaps.*

"Muh boy's name is Hareth and we come from that there camp to the northeast. It edges the territory, and … well, my boy liked to go out and see the wilder parts of them woods. 'Specially when I was out working. I told him *so* many times to stay close to home, but he never listened. He's got his mother's spirit I tell ya."

A forlorn smile crossed his lips at the comparison of mother and son. "He would come back with all kinds of things." The man paused, a memory suddenly hitting him, and his eyes watered. With some reluctance, he continued, "He came home with a little hunk of wood once." His breath caught but he forced the next words out, "that he swore was a gnome." The man wiped away a tear hurriedly. "Ember's breath, it kinda did look like one. With a tiny-pointed head an' everything. So, I helped him shape it to look more like it … he took that thing everywhere."

The Rangemaster approached him and put a calming hand on his shoulder. "He sounds like a good boy, and we will do our best to find him." The man looked up at the Rangemaster, a glimmer of hope twinkling in his eye. The commander pressed home her advantage. "What else can you tell us? Did you see anything strange lately? When was the last time you saw him?"

The man furrowed his brows. "As a matter of fact, there was something strange master. Four folks, all on horses, came through camp naught but ten days ago. They came from Elgion, but they kept to themselves. One of their lot played with muh boy, but I didn't trust him." He shook his head like someone who had seen a troubling development, emphasizing the strangeness of the visitors. The lumberjack stopped the eccentric gesture and then looked up at the company, noticing the many members surrounding him. Eventually, his eyes landed on Blythe and the man's chest puffed slightly. He stretched out a finger towards Blythe. "In fact, I see one of them right there."

"That there is Blythe, and without his speedy return from that group's ill-fated journey, we would not be here. And regardless of the circumstance of our arrival, we would not be here to help you … without *him*," the commander said almost chidingly.

The man stared at Blythe for a moment longer but decided not to pursue. "Other than that. We have been hearing strange noises at night. Animals and the like hooping and hollerin'." The man narrowed his eyes and with a touch of dread in his voice, he began again, "Something is afoot. Something has got everything on the move."

"How long has your boy been missing?" inquired the Rangemaster.

"A day and a night now," said the lumberjack, "He didn't come home, and after we searched for him all last night, we picked it up again this morning. When it looked like all hope was lost, I rushed here to see if anyone had heard anything."

The Rangemaster nodded at the man and then at her assembled company. An approving look crossed her face. "Lead us to your camp, and we will look for your boy from there. If he is out there, we will find him."

The ranger company set off with the lumberjack who they discovered was named Hora. A pang of sadness crept through Alexa as she thought of a young boy lost in the woods, knowing that if all came to naught, they would at least be helping these people. Fantasies of saving the young lad swirled about in her mind as they traveled along a dirt path that edged the Eukarian cliffs. After a time, they passed the falls above Elger's Landing and headed north along an even narrower dirt track, leading into the forest.

The company hurried past these sights of majesty and grace, only stopping briefly to gather water at a clear pool at the falls top. Venison rolls—warmed at the previous camp—were their lunch, preserving their strength as well as their speed. Hora looked exhausted by the time they reached his camp, drained by the emotional and physical toll he had been through. As he approached the small cabins within the camp, his wife, equally distraught-looking, hugged him tightly. The rangers camped around the small cabins that night, being brought warm stew and fresh bread from a reserved old man and the grateful mother of Hareth.

The commander ordered the company to spread their sleeping furs around a campfire in the center of the cabins and posted a guard detail to be carried out through the night. As the moon rose, the forlorn cries of nocturnal creatures whistled through the trees. Yet, there was something else, a distinctive croaking noise more akin to an amphibian. Alexa pondered as to where a large enough body of water resided near the camp to warrant such noises.

The symphony stayed the sleep of many of the rangers, and all but a few were restless under the spell of the forest's mysteries. Alexa just listened to the disturbances in the forest and after a time Elira, along with her range mate Matthias, crouched next to Alexa's sleeping fur. Elira as was her custom spoke without any pleasantries, "I know you hear it too. What in all the gods is going on out there?"

Alexa turned to the watcher of the pair, Elira, and replied, "I don't know but I am just glad it's not skittering."

Elira's teeth reflected in the firelight, "After your tussle with those spider bastards, I don't blame ya. But I didn't see any ponds or pools nearby. Nor did I see any of these folk get water from anything but that well they got. So, why frogs? Ember's breath, half our job is knowing animals, and I guarantee those out-of-place noises have got us all in a fright. Probably even the commander." As if on cue the Rangemaster appeared by their side, gliding in from the darkness behind them, forcing Elira to jump slightly at the surprise appearance.

"What you are hearing, ranger, is the sound of a saurian hunting party. The very person we are going to save has on a few occasions told me of her unsuccessful attempts to capture one of the beasts. Alexa, your sister, usually referenced an out-of-place click or croak just before she would spring her ambush. My guess is that those croaks we hear now are to direct the hunt, as would fit the reptilian nature of these animals." The Rangemaster held up a hand signaling for quiet.

An explosion of noise erupted from the trees, and the sound of a few dying boars erupted from its epicenter. The rangers were now all up and preparing for combat, but slowly the noises faded as the death cries dripped away to nothing. For a few brief seconds, the rangers could hear the vigorous sounds of a predator feasting before another croak sounded.

A final flurry of activity as the dead boars were dragged off into the night, and the forest fell to near silence save the call of an owl.

"A successful hunt," the Rangemaster stated. "To risk being so close to us fits with what Hora said. I think the orcs are driving these hunting parties, the iktomids, and every other damnable thing of this forest south … to us." The commander looked around at the now-gathering rangers, "We are not in danger tonight rangers. Get some sleep, we have a long day ahead of us tomorrow."

# Chapter Sixteen

## Alexa

The next morning Hora and his wife—desperate to assist—led the ranger company to the edge of the lumber camp, pointing out the various directions the boy liked to travel. The Rangemaster thanked Hora and his wife for their hospitality, promising them that they would return with the boy or with evidence of his whereabouts.

With the hospitality of civilization behind them, they entered a realm unbent by the scythe or the hammer, a place still free of humanity's spread. Rangemaster Erin Apararius spread her company out in a line with twenty-five-meter intervals between each pair of rangers. Alexa and Blythe were commanded to stay with her in the center. The rangers moved in their infamous combat stance, which consisted of one ranger who stood tall looking at the horizon and up for threats. This ranger, the watcher of the pair, carried the impressive eighty-pound war bow, whilst the other ranger, the guardian, crouched low holding a one-and-a-half-meter ash wood spear. Every bow-wielding ranger held their string at the ready, knowing that in an instant they may be embroiled in a fight. The forest held little of its normal music and the company felt a sense of dread fall upon them.

The trees rustled in the light breeze and save for the sound of leaves blowing in the wind, the forest was quiet. For a group of individuals highly attuned to the behaviors of the natural world, a tangible chill rippled through the company. The ranger pairs frequently passed commands back and forth, using simple hand gestures universalized throughout the Ranger order. The nearest guardian signaled that it was all clear to their left, his movements shaky, underlining his nervousness.

Alexa's group consisted of Blythe, the Rangemaster, and herself, and for that odd trio, she took on the role of watcher, not only because she was trained in that manner but also because her commander was busy scanning back and forth between the troop, maintaining a strict command and control. Blythe tried desperately to wield the spear given to him without stumbling through the undergrowth, and slowly they combed through trees, hillocks, and thick brush looking for any sign of the boy that had been lost, yet with little luck. Wherever he had gone or whatever had befallen him was leaving little trace save for tracks far too old to coincide with Hora's timeframe. After a kilometer of arduous stalking through cedar, spruce, and thickets of brush, the company came to a staggered halt, prompted by the hand signal of the far-right ranger group.

"Looks like we found something," the Rangemaster whispered. The center trio moved towards the ranger group who had signaled.

Once they had arrived, Elira, the one who called the halt, pointed at a bush. Alexa strained, and just when she began to think that Elira was seeing ghosts, she noticed it. A small spattering of blood on a leaf that was near the base of the bush. Begrudging admiration of Elira's skill took root.

The commander must have spotted it too because she moved to touch the stained leaf, testing to see if it was still wet. "This is a few hours old. Whoever put it here could be long gone. Still, good work Elira."

Elira flashed her bright white teeth. The group of rangers looked around trying to see if any clues would present themselves. Alexa noticed something strange about the track laid before them. The inner workings of her mind, the years of training, and the raw instinct that had carved her into a ranger pressed a question forward that formed in her brain, something was wrong with this track. She dropped closer to the leaf laying on her stomach and bringing her eyes to within a few centimeters of the purported leaf.

"What are you doing," queried Elira, but Alexa simply held up a hand.

With a moment of silent concentration did the strangeness—the wrongness—of the track come to fruition. The 'spatter' was not all going in the same direction. The blood droplets had a pattern indicating that they were dropped from above; not sprayed onto the leaf from the side. Alexa looked above her and saw no overhanging branches.

Even if this had come from the trees, and the wind caught it, there would be some spread to the droplets; some indication that they didn't just drop straight down. The smallness of the individual droplets made it difficult to perceive at first, but now it was clear that someone or something had placed this blood on the leaves intentionally. Something *wanted* them to find this and follow its false trail.

"Commander," Alexa said. "This was placed here on purpose."

"And what makes you think that?" Questioned the commander.

"These droplets came straight from above." Alexa pointed upwards, "And if you notice there are no branches above us."

The commander looked up and then looked down at the leaf, opening her eyes wider with each repetition as she took in the truth of it.

Alexa continued, capitalizing her points while she had them engaged. "If it were a passing animal, who would be running mind you, or the wind caught the blood from an animal on a branch further down, there would be spread indicating that. There isn't"

The Rangemaster looked up and down another time and studied the leaf closely before finally speaking, "Maiden's blessings, I think you are right."

Elira stood behind the Rangemaster, annoyed at Alexa's attempt to shoehorn herself in, but was now looking quite amazed at her competition's perceptive skills.

"My guess is that we are gonna find a false trail, leading us all the way to an ambush," Alexa said triumphantly while pointing northwards into the forest where that potential trail might lie.

"That's very likely ranger," the commander cautioned. "But we could also be looking for the signs."

Alexa nodded at the commander's caution, recognizing the old Augustian saying 'looking for the signs.' The cautionary phrase simply implies that when you are investigating something, more often than not you will find evidence proving what you wanted to find in the beginning.

The commander, upon seeing the understanding on Alexa's face, continued, "Regardless, we must move forward with caution. Elira; Matthias come with us. We are gonna close ranks and try to get the jump on this ambush, if it exists." The commander paused a moment before smiling at Alexa, "Good job, ranger."

Alexa blushed slightly as she smiled in return. Elira and Matthias followed the false trail as bait, while the remainder of the company held fifty meters to their left. Using the high ground to hopefully spring the trap that had been set for them.

"Let's hope we can ambush the ambushers," the commander said as she organized the rest of the company into a twenty-five-meter horn that took on a very shallow angle. A strong tactic for catching prey whilst maintaining a strong defense. For several minutes they moved forward until they came upon a relatively open patch of forest that consisted of birch and maple trees.

The mat of decaying leaves and wood below their feet made the ground look like a big, connected carpet. For about three-quarters of a kilometer they stalked through the open forest, studded with irregular bushes, using clear lines of sight in all directions as useful aides in their hunt. The clearer air whipped through the trunks and as Alexa caught a fresh scent, she whispered to the Rangemaster, "Mum, I smell something."

Erin Apararius, now loaded with an abundance of caution, stopped, holding up her hand to signal a halt to the rest of the company. She sniffed the air deeply, allowing the fragrance of the forest to soak into her. She released a deep breath and replied, "I smell it to *orcs*."

Alexa felt the hairs on her arm rise at the proclamation, and her heart quickened its pace. She tried to stay calm. "Wha-what do we do?" Her voice trembled slightly, and a worm of doubt raced into her gut.

The Rangemaster fixed her with her gaze and simply mimicked taking a breath whilst bringing her hands palm-up and then palm-down. Alexa quickly understood and caught her breath, steadying her nerves. The attempt to spring the trap had not worked, but they were fortunate enough to sus out the enemy before the enemy found them. The Rangemaster signaled to all her rangers to come to her, and when they had all circled their leader, she spoke.

"Alright lads and ladies, this is what we get paid for," the commander began, "Stella pick a tree on our left flank and get up into it with your bow. I need you to take out as many threats as possible from a distance. Dillon do the same on our right. Blythe, you stay back with our mounts, and if this goes sideways—which it won't, ride back to Elgion. The rest of you standard formation … here." She pointed to a small grove in which the bows would have the best line of sight.

"Are there any questions?" When the rangers did not voice any, the commander finished, "Alright then, let's get to it."

The company hurried to fulfill their leader's orders. When they had spread out to their assigned positions, bows were strung, blades were tested for sharpness, and kit was adjusted. But before long, they found themselves waiting in restless silence between two clumps of maple trees. Birch trees were interspersed ahead of them, but any archer with some skill could find an angle to fire from. Time crawled ahead of her as they waited for any sign of their quarry. Uncertainty gripped her and she hoped the porcine fiends would make their way back up their own false trail.

Alexa's mind swung between wild spikes of exhilaration to frightful fits that hoped the orcs had not wanted to fight. Yet, inside of herself, she knew that the cursed foe, who apparently even defiled this new land, would not let a good fight pass it by. She knew that they wanted to ambush them for easy slaughter and—failing that—gladly fight them head-to-head. After all, they were well known for their love of battle and rarely did one hear of an orc lacking courage. She hoped that her *own* courage would not fail her.

Several minutes passed with little to engage the mind. Whisps of wind whipped through the relatively open alleys between the birch trees, pushing dead leaves into flurries of flight. The rich aroma of earth and decay filled the air, a panoply of scent common to the forest. Yet, it was the only thing normal in those trees for no bird or animal calls could be heard. Tension rose inside of herself as she imagined the approaching enemy drawing near.

As if on cue, Alexa spotted the first of their foe. A two-meter tall green-skinned-monster side stepped from behind a one-hundred-meter distant clump of maple. It wore little clothing on its torso save for a scrap of cloth that served to hold a few trinkets, and its legs were covered with a roughly hewn hide skirt. Even from here, Alexa could see its tusks jutting from its mouth, a feature exclusive to the males of their species.

"Steady now, don't fire unless I say. It's unlikely, but sometimes these … lovely people, will talk," the Rangemaster said to apprehensive chuckles. More of the foe appeared, and she continued, "Plus I don't want any of you geniuses missing and giving the enemy the wrong idea."

Alexa smiled at the bit of humor in such a dark time. It was possible for them to hit a target at this distance, but that was at a stationary object; on a nice day with the knowledge that one wouldn't die if they missed. Thirty seconds had passed before an array of twenty orcs stood in front of them, their formation loose—but not disorganized.

Alexa spotted individual characteristics between the monstrosities. The orcs varied from a slenderer light green with youthful-looking skin to hulking dark green monstrosities with bolted hunks of bone and metal attached to random locations of their body. The whole of the group had no uniform features save for their tusks.

As the orcs fanned out, she gripped the flexible wood of her bow. It was a slight consolation for the absolute turbulence she felt inside. Her mind raced as fear wormed its way into her heart. A flash of iktomid fangs came unexpectedly to the forefront of her mind and she trembled, cursing herself as some small part of her wondered if she could run away.

Her mind sapped her resolve as one of the beasts, a tall dark-green orc with circular arrays of blood-flecked bone stepped forward. It looked older than the others and its clothing seemed more complete, a full patch-work hide skirt and the macabre tunic, studded with small bits of a dark red stone, adorned him. The other beasts roared piggish oaths as the monster took the fore.

"Be ready," the commander called out. As if in reply, the bone-riddled orc roared a blood-curdling oath into the forest and swung a hideous-look-ing machete down toward the rangers. The call to arms was laid, but to Alexa's surprise, only six of the orcs charged forward. The lightest green orcs burst into a sprint towards the company, let loose by the crude ma-chete and its owner. "Fire well, rangers!" Yelled the commander, giving permission for them to engage as they saw fit.

In the time it took them to knock their arrows and fire their first vol-ley, three of the enemy number were halfway to them. Seven arrows flew out to the sprinting orcs, three of which missed their mark, skidding use-lessly off into the dirt. Dillon's arrow from high took one in the throat, felling it instantly. While Alexa, Elira, and another's arrow took the closest beast across the chest and shoulders. It ran on for a few paces before grind-ing to a stop.

As Alexa prepared her second arrow, she saw the spears of the guard-ians thrust forward, their shafts held up in between the windows left by the rangers. She felt a moment of pride at seeing her company mimic the tales of old that surrounded her ancient order. Another tale would be woven today.

Alexa drew her bow, focusing on one of the front runners, who was now only twenty meters away. A gangly-looking fiend who used all four of its limbs to push itself forward, a hunk of wood held in one hand. Alexa stepped back, fear taking root as the inhuman monster raced towards her.

"Brace for charge," the commander called whilst drawing her sword. Alexa fired, but fear had powered the shot. The shaft went over the beast's shoulder, spoiled by her poor posture. She cursed inwardly, and her heart raced as a nearly insurmountable desire to flee threatened to overwhelm her. As she felt the tug of flight pull her around, the beast leapt into the air. The young orc bellowed in rage as its impressive frame barreled towards her. It had propelled its one-hundred-and-fifteen kilograms of muscle into a full leap, the club stretched in front of it, ready to crush Alexa underfoot. Only seconds had passed since the battle had started and now, she felt frozen in time. It happened again. She had wanted to flee; she wanted to run. But it was too late; instead, she just stood, mouth agape, awaiting her doom.

To her surprise, a glint of steel impaled the hideous orc. A fountain of hot blood sprayed across her face.

She shuddered involuntarily and exhaled in an almost reverential release. The guardians had stepped forward to brace for the charge at the perfect moment, and her savior, a young man named Roderick, nodded at her as she stared at him wide-eyed. The bath of blood served to remind her of her strength, and she felt her resolve return. Her fear melted down into a ball, as she underwent her baptism of blood. And now she would reap revenge on those who had stolen her sister and help cleanse the whole of this forest of her enemies. As the revelation took hold of her once scared heart, she saw an orc make it to their lines and roll at the last second underneath a guardian's spear thrust.

It came out of the roll with a savage blade, uppercutting the metal into the unfortunate guardian's groin. The man was a newcomer like Alexa, Tyrin was his name, and he screamed in sheer terror and agony as the orc gutted him. Rangemaster Erin Apararius roared as she brought her sword down, severing the orc's limbs at the forearm, cutting the offending blade away from its grasp. She returned her sword with a backswing, severing its neck as she did so. The orc slowly crumpled to the ground as Tyrin fell, his screams falling to dying whimpers. Alexa recovered her senses, and she watched as the last two younger orcs were felled by arrows to the neck by both Stella and Dillon. Alexa recognized why the Rangemaster had chosen those two to take the high ground.

The company had held their ground … for now. Alexa took in a few heavy breaths to fully recover. As she did so, she heard something from a nightmare. The apparent leader of the orcs now called out, loud enough for all to hear, in deep guttural tones. The foul mockery of speech seemed amplified on the air like it was being repeated by something even more sinister than its creator. Behind the echoing speech came more grunts and utterances of foulness unbeknownst to Alexa. The wailing lamentations of the orc leader—this beast who seemed to be communing with the gods— reached a crescendo, and the trees themselves were lashed by a sudden gust of wind.

The rangers steadied themselves against the sudden and strange manner of this creature, but Alexa could see and feel within herself something wrong in the air. A foulness unknown, a dark malevolence that was summoned forth.

Maybe this thing really talked to a god. During the company's fretting, the beast beckoned for one of his kin to come forward, and there, to the company's horror, was a small boy. *Hareth,* Alexa gasped.

The boy was alive, but it was obvious that he had been abused. He trembled visibly even from this distance. The boy couched his head in fear as he approached the leader; *The God-Talker.*

"Ember's breath," Alexa heard the commander whisper. Yet the oath did not stop the monster from continuing its ritual. It raised its crude cleaver into the sky, yelling with even more vigor than before. He called upon something, or *someone,* to bless them. As the cursed words faded, he brought the cleaver down. She closed her eyes, not wanting to see, and she heard the boy yelp.

The sound made her wince, and she could barely bring herself to look once more. When she did so, it was not a great sight but a might better than what she believed had happened. The boy, Hareth, had lost his arm, severed at the elbow. The shock of the blow had forced him unconscious, and he fell to the ground at the God-Talker's feet. The perpetrator pointed the now bloodied cleaver at the company and bellowed once more. This time it could physically be felt, a reverberation brought on by supernatural assistance. The larger variants of orc charged, somehow faster than their lighter kin.

"Kill the bastards," the Rangemaster snarled.

With vicious intent, Alexa knocked another arrow. She felt like an angel of vengeance. A deliverer of justice on those of foul and corrupt demeanor, and with her face caked in quickly drying blood, her visage matched her intent. The final fourteen large brutes, including the God-Talker, were devouring the leaf-strewn ground, and the company responded.

Alexa pointed her arrow at one orc directly in front of her, breathed in, adjusted her aim to match the distance, and fired. Years of training yielded seven arrows fired in virtual simultaneity. She watched her shaft sink deep into an orc's torso, hitting right where the heart should have been. The orc bucked back from the blow but did not stop. Quickly, she knocked another arrow, aimed, and fired again. The beast rocked back as the second arrow took him in the chest, just centimeters from the first shot. Once again, the orc was rocked back. It took two more steps, grasped at the shafts uselessly, and fell heavily to the ground.

With her first victim slain, she refocused on the next closest foe. In her quick survey, she saw that the enemy contingent had eaten up fifty meters of distance and would be on them in seconds. She also saw an impossibly large throwing ax hurl towards Stella, her scream rendering the verdict of the throwing weapons success. Alexa gritted her teeth at the loss. She breathed in, and time slowed to a trickle. The orcish threat came on, but Alexa felt in charge; she felt ready; she felt warrior-born. All the years of training and all the doubts faded away. A surge coursed through her muscles, and she tuned herself towards slaughter. She targeted her next victim, knocked her arrow, aimed, and fired. Her target was taken in the neck, and it fell to the ground, its momentum forcing it to skid through the dirt. The shaft of her arrow splintered upon the beast's fall and spun wildly into the air.

"Guardians, forward!" Yelled the commander. The spear-wielders once again stepped in between the windows left by the rangers. Alexa refocused on a third orc, which was now a breath's distance away. She did not waste that breath and fired quickly, the shot connected with one of the enemy's bone plates, and the arrow spun away into the foliage. She had twisted to the side to make the shot, thus making her unaware of the enemy's charge hitting home in front of her. Hot breath and foul-smelling spittle smacked her face as one of the brutes roared into her ear. She turned to the deafening sound and saw a vicious maw of yellowed teeth and tusks. She rolled back and to her left on instinct, trying to maintain distance.

The two guardians in front of her had thrust their spears forward to meet the particularly large orc. However, the beast leapt into the air just before the charge and one of the weapons only skimmed along the orc's left flank, fouled by a hunk of metal and bone. The second spear hit home, but the momentum of the beast had pushed the guardian back far enough for it to be within striking distance of Alexa. The orc swung a heavy cleaver in a vicious downward stroke towards her, but her evasive roll spoiled the blow. The guardian whose spear had missed, took the initiative and planted his blade deep into the vulnerable area under the orc's armpit. The beast bellowed in anger and pain; its hideous, piggish, face swiveled at this newest offense. With its right arm still raised, hindered by the spear shaft, it grabbed the cleaver with its left hand, carrying the blade down on the guardian ranger. The cleaver bit deep into the man's shoulder, deep enough to expose meaty bits of viscera to the air. The guardian—wide-eyed with horrific realization—held the spear firm in his dying moments.

Alexa regained her balance from the roll, and rushed forward, bringing an arrow to bear. She aimed directly at the beast's eye, and as the orc grinned malevolently at the wounded guardian, she fired the arrow directly into its brain. Instantly, the grunts were cut off, and the weight from the cleaver fell loose. Without the attempts to bury the blade straight through the guardian, the man teetered over, his cruel stabilizer now gone. In poetic justice, both man and orc fell simultaneously. As they crashed to the ground, Rangemaster Erin Apararius roared in challenge on Alexa's left. Roderick, the surviving guardian, and her both realized that no threats remained in front of them and thus spun to the sound of this newest challenge.

Rangemaster Erin Apararius's sword clanged against a heavy metal club, deflecting the blow. Three orcs, including the God-Talker, had hit the company's center. One of the brutes slumped, impaled by three guardian spears. Further down the line, Alexa could see not only the bodies of her fallen kinsmen but also two more orcs engaged on the far left. Roderick stepped in to assist his commander.

The God-Talker took the head from one guardian, and her two companions tried desperately to revenge their decapitated brethren. But the orc leader dodged quicker than Alexa thought his size would allow.

The Rangemaster deflected another blow from a different beast, and the opening allowed Roderick to capitalize on the surprise advantage. Roderick impaled the orc straight through the throat whilst the commander brought her blade back around to cleave into the orc's skull. A spurt of blood jetted forth, and past that stream, Alexa could see one of the two orcs that had been on the left rounding on the commander.

A spear, which was snapped in half, was jutting from its torso—a guardian and a ranger dead at his feet. Alexa charged the beast, tossing her bow to the side. It would no longer be useful in this close of a fight.

She rolled under a wild swing from the orc and sprang up near the spear. She grasped the shaft with both hands and ripped the pole out, twisting it as she did so. A gout of thick blood poured forth from the wound, and the beast staggered; its life force draining away. Although not her weapon of choice, all rangers trained with the whole arsenal, and she put that training to the test. She stepped in thrusting the weapon hard toward the orc's face. The shaft broke a tusk as it pierced through the creature's maw and buried itself into the back of its neck. She ripped the spear back out, blood streaming after the spear tip.

The orc fell to its knees, a pathetic sucking noise emanating from its throat. Its hands grasped uselessly; the breath stolen away. Her own breath came fast and heavy now. Exertion took its toll, but the fight was not yet over. A scream cried out to her right. She turned to see a blood-red mist being blown into the faces of the two guardians who were—to this point— engaged with the God-Talker.

The guardians screamed and clawed at their faces, steam rising from the mist. Alexa did not understand how such a thing was possible, but within seconds she noticed the likely culprit. There, on the God-Talker's chest, lay a red stone that now glowed almost as if it was a ball of heated iron ready for forging. The air had gotten thick, and she had the distinct sensation of fury, almost as if she could taste her rage; taste iron-rich blood. The God-Talker had called forth the power of a stone, and whatever god that aligned itself with this foul creature made her bloodlust palpable.

The blood-stricken guardians fell away before the God-Talker, his mouth open in a malevolent grin. His teeth were stained red from the mist he had called forth, and a look of victory crossed those coal-black eyes. The rangers stood in shock around the beast, each in turn piecing together the magic that had helped their foe. The Rangemaster seemed particularly troubled by the development, and the God-Talker did not hesitate to take his advantage.

Alexa was too far away to stop the coming savagery. The orc leader stepped in whilst the blood mist was still settling, the screams of the blood-burned rangers heralding his movements. With two great strides, it closed the gap between himself and the Rangemaster. Commander of the Elgion Ranger's Hall, a veteran of the Harrowing of Creos, and holder of the title Rangemaster raised her blade too slowly to stop the massive cleaver; her movements appearing sluggish after watching her rangers be burned by blood magic. The cruel blade rent the commander's armor at the apex of her sternum and laid a gash across the breadth of her chest.

The Rangemaster sucked in a shocked breath. Her face melted into a look of confusion and horror. All the steely confidence that had been her hallmark now broken down to something of a much baser form. Alexa's heart sank as she watched her stalwart leader take what was surely a mortal blow. The God-Talker grinned, blood dripping from its mouth just centimeters from the Rangemaster's face. Dillon, no longer engaged, fired upon the God-Talker. A shaft from his post sailed through the air and struck the orc just behind his collarbone. The arrow buried itself so deep into the monster that only the feathers remained visible, blood already soaking the white fletching. The orc's expression shifted instantly. From malicious victory to confusion. Alexa and Roderick, who remained uninjured, lunged. Roderick's spear pierced deep into the left side of the orc and Alexa's own weapon quickly followed suit, slicing underneath the orc's ribs on his right side.

Roderick roared as he pushed his spear tip deeper into the God-Talker. Suddenly, his confused expression dissipated, and he threw his head back and looked up into the sky. Alexa could see his eyes turn white as they rolled back into his head. A strange buzzing noise grew in intensity. The God-Talker opened his mouth, and a guttural droning issued forth. The buzzing noise continued to increase in intensity, making Alexa want to drop the embedded spear shaft and cover her ears. Yet curiosity as well as a desire for revenge held her in place.

Within a matter of seconds, the buzzing and droning came to a crescendo and then without warning … stopped. The God-Talker's body convulsed momentarily and then went rigid. A stream of blood shot straight into the air from the orc's mouth, turning into a macabre beam of light. The beam congealed into a ball and Alexa heard—NO—felt a whisper scythe through the air. Voices—hard and malevolent—appeared and disappeared all around the dying orc. She had seen plenty of communes with the gods and knew that this was one of them, but this felt different somehow. Like they conveyed with something far more sinister than any god she had encountered. As the voices converged on a repeating phrase that she could not understand, the ball of blood writhed, expanding and contracting violently.

The God-talker convulsed again. He twitched and thrashed so violently that Alexa released her grip on the broken spear shaft, electing for more distance from the commotion. As she stepped away, the God-Talker fell to the ground away from the dying Rangemaster. Rivulets of blood streamed away from the orc towards the growing ball of blood, and his color quickly drained.

When it appeared that all the blood had been drained, the ball suddenly stopped its writhing and one word boomed loud into the forest, "MAGDRIS!" She knew then who it was, who this bloody god that aided the orcs. Magdris, The Crimson King; the one you told stories about to keep children from misbehaving. With that, the ball jetted off northwards and quickly traveled out of their sight. Alexa felt a chill crawl up her spine …

"Commander!" She was pulled back into the moment by a cry from Roderick, who ran to the Rangemaster's side as she fell. Alexa sprang into action and quickly knelt next to her dying commander, helping Roderick pull the machete free from her torso. The commander coughed and sputtered as the cleaver finally fell away from her wound and blood formed at her mouth.

Feebly, she grabbed Alexa's shoulder. "You … you did well." The commander smiled weakly at Alexa, and all she could do was return the gesture.

Tears threatened to burst forth. She could do nothing but busy herself with some cloth in a vain attempt to clean the grievous wound.

"There is no point," the commander said with great effort. "You, Roderick, and the others need to go." She smiled at Roderick, as she said his name.

The remaining rangers now gathered around them, and what Alexa saw was not heartening. Of the thirteen rangers they had started with only four stood around them. A total of five including Blythe now circled around Alexa, Roderick, and the dying Rangemaster. Elira, Matthias, and Blythe Alexa knew well. The other two were a pair of veterans known as Dillon, one of the steel-eyed killers in the maple, and Tilde, yet after seeing their commander struck down, they appeared as no more than husks shaking in the breeze. The other survivor, Roderick, simply known as Ro, was a young recruit like Alexa. His 'ranger', William, lay dead on the forest floor along with so many others. He was the guardian who had fought next to Alexa throughout the battle, and he seemed steady but was covered in dirt and blood. A veteran now, although a veterancy hard-earned.

"You all must head back to Elgion," the commander said, "you must prepare for more of these … savages." She coughed again, more blood spurting forth from her lips.

Roderick wiped away the blood. "Commander you are coming back with us," he said, desperation in his voice.

"Oh, be quiet now," the Rangemaster said with the reproachful tone of a loving parent. "I know when I am spent." She paused at this moment and placed her bloody hand on Roderick's cheek. "It's going to be alright," she said simply.

Roderick cried, the dam of tears finally breaking forth, forcing a stutter. "No! We must head-he-hea-head ba—"

"Quiet!" He was quickly cut off by the commander's stern voice. The Rangemaster mustered what strength she had left to fix each of the rangers in turn within her gaze, silently saying goodbye to them. She ended with her, "Alexa."

It was like a call to action. Alexa straightened at the summons.

"You have the stren—" her voice was failing her now and the blood poured freely from her lips, "You have the strength, t-to, lead. But you must *earn it!*" The commander said, raising her fist with great effort and punching Alexa in the chest.

The impact of the words hit Alexa like a hammer. She looked around at the others, at Dillon and Tilde, who had fought in many more battles than her. The commander saw her unsure expression and her glances at her companions and simply smiled. "Prove it to them; prove it to yourself." she reached her hand out to Alexa, urging the young ranger to take it. Alexa grasped the open palm, wrapping her hand around the commanders, the grasp of brotherhood. The commander looked once more into Alexa's eyes before they slowly glazed over, a long piercing breath exhaled. Rangemaster Erin Apararius's chest rose once more and fell; never to rise again, and Alexa wept.

# Chapter Seventeen

## Alexa

The beleaguered company returned to the logging camp with Hareth in tow. Hareth's parents were waiting at the edge of the encampment eager for their return, and when they saw Ro, cradling the small boy in his arms, they ran. At first, the parents were overcome with emotion. Many minutes were spent sobbing and taking turns holding their boy, wrenched between joy at his return and horror at the bandaged bloody stump that was his arm. Eventually, their worrying forced Ro to lower the child to the ground, and when the parents felt safe that the boy would survive, Hora looked around.

Alexa could visibly see him counting the remaining rangers and when he ended at five, she saw his eyes widen. His mouth opened and closed in hesitation until he found his voice. "You all look like you have seen the worst of it. What, uh, what did you find out there?"

"Orcs," was Elira's simple reply.

"I see …" he said distantly.

"They won't trouble us now, but we will need some help with our wounded and our … dead," Elira finished. Alexa chewed her lip at the mention of the dead and feeling conscious of the Rangemaster's dying words simply nodded in agreement.

"Of course. Of course. Hannah," Hora said as he grasped his wife's cheek. "Let me see to these folks." She nodded with closed eyes; tears streaming freely down her cheeks. Hora looked upon her and opened his mouth as if he was going to say more but evidently thought better of it. Quickly, he dashed back to the camp and returned with the remaining loggers who came rushing to help. Looks of shock and sorrow were abundant, stunned by the change in the company's condition. The other camp wife,

Malissa, was the first to act and ordered her husband to fetch some buckets of water from the well.

The rest of the logging camp quickly followed her lead. The rangers sat on tree logs and stumps—really, wherever they could. Flinging down their kit; glad to be free of its burden. Alexa sat heavily on a nearby stump, placing her bow next to her. Slowly, she unlaced the straps binding her leather jerkin together. As it fell away from her left shoulder, she twitched in pain.

"Here, let me help you with that," Malissa said as she knelt next to Alexa. The camp wife hesitated as she looked up at Alexa's face, a face so covered in blood that her skin looked like the scales of some red reptilian creature. Malissa swallowed and, with firm lines weaving across her face, pressed on. Slowly pulling away the armor, its material crusted to the skin from sweat and freshly opened scabs.

"Don't worry, you will be alright," Malissa said with a wince as she lightly bathed the wound. All around them, people set about helping the downtrodden rangers unburden themselves of the toil they had endured. A clearing in the trees had turned into a bathhouse.

After the rangers had been cleaned and their wounds tended, they went to the battleground and buried their dead. No customs amongst the Augustian peoples nor the Ranger's Order prevented them from being buried in such a place. In fact, Alexa knew some rangers preferred to be buried out amongst the ranges and hills of the wilds. This forest, Mossgrave, would be a fine burial hall for those who spent their lives in the wilds.

So, with the help of the encampment, the rangers buried their dead. It took the rest of the day, and twilight lay heavy in the trees by the time they had finished. Some of the loggers grabbed torches and placed them strategically around the burial site, casting a rather somber light on the scene.

For a time, they, along with the loggers and Blythe, all stood in silence, unsure of what to do next. With just the crackling of the torches, minute glances from Ro, Dillon, and Tilde were the only sign of change in that makeshift funerary wake. She knew that they must speak the words. Still, no one did, not even Dillon, the oldest and most experienced ranger. She looked at the downcast faces of the surviving company, hoping for someone to take up the mantle of leadership. The loggers, knowing this was a moment reserved for the ancient order of the rangers, shuffled nervously. Still, no one even raised their head.

Even Elira, who had spoken first to Hora upon their return to the camp seemed cowed in this moment. Alexa stared for a few seconds at the ranger, and Elira, sensing eyes upon her, looked up. They shared a moment; eyes locked with something of a mutual understanding coming to light in that glance. Elira dipped her head once as if to affirm the choice. The unspoken choice of the company.

The Rangemaster's final words apparently had not gone unnoticed. With a lump in her throat, she concluded that—just for now—she would take up the mantle, but when they got back to Elgion they would sort it out. They would find someone more worthy, perhaps an appointee from the Governor. Yet, in the here and now, she knew that these defeated warriors needed her help; needed her to lead them. So, in the flickering torchlight, Alexa swallowed hard; ready to speak for the first time—and hopefully last time—as the leader.

"They go now to that Far Range," her voice was quiet at first but increased in volume as she found her confidence. "Where we all must go. They were our brothers … our sisters … our companions."

Slowly, the downcast faces looked up.

"They were the Wardens of the Wilds. They were the guardians against the unknown. They were the Watchers in the Woods. Here we remember them, but here is not where they stay. We will see you again on that Far Range … goodbye."

Tears broke free from some of the assembly, most of which from Blythe who actively cuffed them away. Upon seeing the gentle giant so open with his emotions, Alexa recalled Elira telling her how Blythe had saved the commander from an even earlier demise at the beginning of the orc charge.

Blythe, the simple stable hand who continued to surprise all, had counter-charged a brazen orc who had broken past the guardian spears. Although he had not killed it, he had pushed it back.

Alexa allowed them time to grieve after she had spoken and, in that space, she had locked eyes with Dillon and Tilde, who although shattered from losing someone they had fought with for so long, nodded at her. A sign of their acceptance of her speaking the funerary hymn, and—she hoped—a sign that they would follow until a replacement was found.

After the nighttime ritual, the group gathered up the Rangemaster's sword, the few unbroken arrow shafts, two still usable guardian spears, two bags of golden figurines of unknown origin, which were on the God-Talker, and what few orc weapons that could be reasonably carried. Although they knew that they could not use them, the metal would be highly prized by the smith back in Elgion. When they had gathered what they could from the dead, the group headed back to the logging camp, where they had an uneasy sleep. At dawn, Alexa woke the company, and with very little reluctance she convinced the loggers to come with them back to Elgion.

Alexa took a moment to stare out through the trees to the north at the edge of the encampment. "I will find you Bella", she said into the empty forest, swearing an oath to her lost sister. Grief at the loss of her Rangemaster, at the loss of so many of her company, and now grief at her inability to strike out into Mossgrave in search of Bella hit her like a tidal wave. Slowly, tears came to her eyes and she allowed herself to weep silently. In that grief, she sent a prayer to Ember, to the Maiden, and even to Mosyneta to keep Bella safe.

"She is out there ya know," Elira said. Alexa did not hear the ranger sneak up on her and started at the sound of her voice. "I mean ... she *is* alive out there. If anyone can reckon with this damnable forest, it's your sister. I have never seen a stablemaster—Ember's breath—anyone so fierce as that little firebrand," she finished, placing a hand on Alexa's shoulder.

Alexa grasped the proffered hand and allowed her tears to fall freely. "I know ... I know. I just wish we could find her now."

"We *will* but you and I both know that we won't find anyone like this." Elira looked around and waved her free hand back and forth as if to show the weakness of their position. "We *have* to regroup. And when we are back to strength, we will come out here and—" Elira paused. Her voice suddenly hard and full of malevolence. "We will burn the lot of those piggish *bastards* to the ground!"

Alexa closed her eyes, nodding along with the solemn vow of vengeance. She clasped Elira's hand tightly and with matched intensity. "Yes ... We .... Will."

They finished their preparations for the return journey, but before they left, Alexa sent Ro along with Hora out to the more secluded logging camp. She instructed them to meet them at Elger's Landing. After all, she figured there was no choice now. They had to pull back to Elgion and prepare for a fight, and these loggers were far too vulnerable to be left out here.

The pragmatic nature of her frontier spirit knew that Augustia would be displeased with the lack of timber, but Augustia would be even more displeased if they returned to a settlement of fire and ash. So, with as much haste as they could muster the ranger company, Blythe, the loggers of

Eukarian Forest, and all those humans who lived in that cursed place returned to Elgion, and Alexa swore she would return. She swore she would find Bella and make the orcs who had done this pay.

# Part Two

# Chapter One
## Sophia

"I already told you! We don't have goat cheese!" Sophia exclaimed. Her words rang back at her, bouncing off the brass horn she spoke into. A staccato vibration buzzing through the air, serving only to annoy the embattled Keeper even more. Her voice, as she always thought when hearing it, did not sound as pleasant as she would have hoped, and her focus waned under her own interminable scrutiny. Yet, she had to press on. She *had* to press this negotiation forward.

A tinny voice barked back, slightly above a whisper, "Who doesn't have goat cheese? Are you sure there isn't someone else we could talk to?"

"I'm afraid that I am your only avenue of rapprochement at this juncture, and I can assure you that any other individual from here to Augustia will tell you that there are no goats here in Elgion." Sophia could see the tiny leader—no taller than her index finger—move away from the embouchure. His oversized conical hat, which made him twice as tall, bobbed up and down as he jaunted over to a group of his comrades. She watched the group of frustrating gnomes discuss their next sarcastic rebuttal and couldn't help but reflect on how she ended up in this absurd situation.

Earlier that day she had been approached by a cabbage farmer from the eastern fields. The poor man had held up a half-eaten cabbage to her as he had stumbled into her apothecary. "It's all chewed up ya sees," tears threatening to burst from his droopy eyes. "Rats mum … they have gotten to the stores. I tried to kill the buggers, but they keep coming back." His voice was pleading, like a man at the end of his rope. A man who—Sophia thought—had rightfully come to find help in his plight.

"And *where* are these rats getting into?" Sophia inquired.

"Into the eastern cellar mum," he paused a moment, his head tilting upwards at a slant, as if he wished to express what he was thinking. "The one to the south with the single door mum, not the big'un with them fancy double doors." The man furrowed his brows, and then, apparently satisfied with his description, nodded.

Sophia, although she did not show it, felt alarm at this revelation. Many folk would go hungry come the winter if the communal cellars were being ravaged by rats. She would have to look at the numbers later but decided that—at the moment—action was required.

"Thank you for bringing this to my attention. I will address it right away," she replied cordially.

The farmer, pleased with the response, nodded his head egregiously, backing away slowly out of the apothecary. The revelation that he had spoken to a person of means, let alone a Keeper, and achieved his goal without ill effect dawning on the man.

He stuttered nearly incomprehensibly, "th-th-thank you mum." He quickly turned to leave but banged heavily against the apothecary door. Sophia heard the man grunt, and she swore she saw him hit the door nose first. *That is going to hurt,* Sophia thought to herself, alarmed at the man's injury but—she had to admit—a little bemused.

"Are you … are you alright?" She asked after the man.

Now, thoroughly embarrassed, the farmer turned back to Sophia once and then twice; seemingly unsure of what to do, and then abruptly nodded once again, opened the door, and jolted out into the street, bits of his cabbage chasing him as it fell to the ground.

Upon that farmer's guidance, and after she could quit grinning at the near comedic exit she had witnessed, she went straight to that eastern cellar. Not the one with the fancy double doors, but instead the humbler single-doored burrow. It was one of the eight cellars that dotted the surrounding countryside and would serve as important stores for the coming winter.

*One of the few things that buffoon of a governor got right,* Sophia thought as her mind came back into the present. The gnomish ambassador had still not formulated a reply and Sophia waited patiently, looking around at the quaint burrow. The cellar's walls were buttressed by heavy timbers with patches of slightly damp soil woven between the gaps of the strong braces. These timber braces served to hold up a series of wooden rafters, which in turn supported a heavily sodded roof. The floor beneath her was dirt scraped to a flat surface. All around her were crates and shelves filled with the bounty of Elgion's vegetable industry. Potatoes, cabbages, turnips, and even some carrots were the primary foodstuffs, but she did see some pickled vegetables and even a small crate of blackberry and huckleberry jam all stored in small clay jars covered with meshed cloth. The sight of the jams made her mouth water, thinking of the delectable treat known as huckleberry pie. *No god or man has ever made anything as good as that again,* she mused to herself in hyperbolic fashion.

Sophia's revelry was interrupted by the rather vigorous bobbing of a red-hatted fellow within the circle of gnomes, apparently thoroughly invested in their argument. Truly, this species was a marvelous denizen of Telaea, albeit an annoying one.

When she had entered the cellar, she had been immediately bombarded by a stone, no larger than the palm of her hand, from a tiny catapult. Luckily, or more likely intentionally, it had only bounced harmlessly off her heavy Keeper's cloak. When she had turned to face the threat, she saw a rat, strung up by its hind paws, a multitude of tiny cuts laced its body. She quickly realized that it was all a display. A display of this gnomish clan's prowess, and now they were trying to court her favor.

The forethought to plan this performance showed great ingenuity on the gnome's part. Even the idea that the gnomes were able to decipher that this particular cellar would be the first to have a leader arrive and address the rodent problem demonstrated a capacity for reconnaissance and spy craft. How such tiny creatures traveled so fast and so far, to accomplish these goals, was yet another marvel. Sophia had heard murmurings during her studies that some of the small folk could use the stones to greater effect than any human could. Either from the sheer volume of consumption, due to their size, or from some unknown magical capacity of the gnomish race.

She still remembered one lecture, on the races of the world, where the professor discussed how some people believed that the gnomes could teleport via heavy consumption of Quickstone. Now, this wasn't a stone Sophia had invested much scholarship into, but she did know that, when consumed by either beast or man, the consumer would enjoy unnatural agility and speed. The unfortunate side effect was that the body of the consumer was still constrained by its natural capacity. Many athletes were known to have 'blown' their hearts out or tear their muscles using the stone during their competitions. Yet maybe these little folk did not need to strain their muscles to travel; instead, they made their way through some hidden passageway in the fabric of the universe?

A universe in which these ancient gnomes—from her understanding—always existed. Although her knowledge of the species was limited, she had on a few separate occasions delved into their mysteries. Keeper Kaldin's book: *Keeper's Stones and Living Things*: had dedicated an entire chapter to the gnomish kind. It discussed such things as the uncertainty of where the gnomes came from, and how there had been instances of the rowdy breed since humans had been storing foodstuffs. They, alongside their rodent cousins, occupied places anywhere that humans dwelled, looking to profit from the bounty of the stored goods. *Unlike* their rodent cousins, however, the gnomes were amenable and willing to work for their share of food.

Which Sophia thought was a paltry sum compared to their worth. As it stood, the gnomes had consistently struck deals with humans to defend their food stores. Often in exchange for a share of the food and, on occasion, trinkets. The price for their defense was never high, a couple of heads of cabbage, a jar of pickled carrots, or—their favorite—a wheel of cheese. Apparently, this clan was particularly fond of goat cheese.

"What cheeses do you have?" the gnomish leader interrupted Sophia's revelry. His bright, green-colored, hat was all that was visible behind the brass horn that the gnomes had erected.

She smiled broadly, giving herself a split second to carefully craft a response. "My lord," she began, giving the probably unearned moniker to the gnomish leader. "Although we *do not* have goat cheese. We do have cow and ox cheese of the finest quality. Quality that will befit the value of your people's help."

After a moment of contemplation, the gnomish leader once again bounced away from the brass horn towards his comrades. She could see him speaking to a group of gnomes, gesturing wildly as he did so, and what she saw made her smile softly. Their conical hats shook vigorously up and down, a sign of agreement, and she marveled at the tiny rainbow of colors she saw. Every individual wearing a different colored hat, some may share a red, green, or blue, but she noticed they were never quite the same hue or shade. A mark of individuality amongst their kind.

"We will take some ox cheese," the leader called out, and just as Sophia was going to reply in agreement he continued, "*but* we want two wheels!" He said this loudly; so loud that Sophia could hear him as if he were a small child in the room instead of a finger-sized man talking through a horn.

His nervousness was plain, but still she knew if she didn't haggle, they would think her weak. She crossed her arms, allowing silence to settle. She could see the gnomes begin to fidget, their little hats jittering to and fro. Sophia allowed the nervous tension to rise, and as she did so she rubbed her Embershard amulet. It glowed faintly, demonstrating a fraction of its power.

Just when she thought the leader's hat was going to fly off his head from all the nervous vibration, she spoke, "One *tiny* rat doesn't show me that you are worth two wheels of ox cheese." She paused again, knowing that they hung to her every word. "Instead, I will provide your clan with one wheel of ox cheese, and if your people prove to be … sufficient for the guarding of our stores then we will provide you with another."

The gnomish leader managed to squeak out a reply, "Ye-yes, yes! That sounds like a good plan! Wh-when can we expect the ch-cheese?"

"I will have it brought here by the end of the day."

"Good, good," the gnome leader replied. Then, rapidly, as if the words would not be blamed on him, he added, "You better."

Sophia struggled not to smirk at the little creature's defiance. Even afraid, they can't resist the barb. Probably a good quality for people who fight rodents that are three to four times their size, she thought. "Now is there anything else you need, lord?"

His confidence was re-bolstered after his jibe, "Not right now, but let us know when you heathens finally get some goat cheese."

Sophia allowed herself to smile at this comment, but it was a smile laced with danger. She stared down at the gnomes and sprinkled a hint of malevolence over her disposition as she loomed over them. Then she turned to leave the cellar.

Before she reached the doors, she half turned back towards the gnomes. "Oh, I will," with a sudden flurry, she rubbed the Embershard amulet. "Ember … light my way," and in an instant, her hand was filled with a small flame. It hovered over her palm, casting no heat on her, even though it was so close. The amulet itself protected her, and her Keeper's knowledge allowed her to harness the fiery spirit of the dragon. Although this was for a simple demonstration of power, Sophia always tried to use the Embershard sparingly, afraid of its power, afraid of the god's vengeance should she ask for too much.

After allowing the gnomes to witness the magic fire, she gently blew the flame onto a nearby candle. *This ought to make them think twice about scampering off with our cheese and not holding up their end of the bargain*, Sophia thought. The flame, reddish-orange, glowed, seemingly overpowering the natural light that cascaded from a couple of overhead windows.

In that unnerving light, she ended the negotiation, "I will see you in a week to monitor your progress and judge whether your clan is worthy of a second cheese wheel." She smiled once again, taking note of the near-petrified attitude of her new partners, and turned to the door. Her business concluded she opened the cellar door and headed out into the light.

# Chapter Two

## Sophia

In the light of day, and after the comical effects the gnomish behaviors had on her psyche, Sophia was reminded of their seemingly untenable position.

Three days ago, the rangers had returned, and Sophia could not think of a bleaker picture. The hallowed rangers, masters of many a battleground, had been badly wounded—NO—nearly beaten. Their vaunted commander now lay dead, buried in the very forest that claimed her life. The memory of their gloomy return was still fresh, and she remembered how, in the immediate aftermath, fear had gripped the townsfolk. Sophia felt that palpable fear pollute the air until it threatened to boil over into a riot. She remembered how she craved the effects of the Magi Stone just to escape the terror.

In her own state of paralysis, she watched as the tumult threatened to spill over into an even worse calamity. She, as a Keeper, should have been a bulwark against that calamity. Yet instead—and somewhat surprisingly—Alexa, who now appeared to be the impromptu leader of the rangers, helped calm that panic.

"People of Elgion, I need your help. My people need rest and recovery. Who among you can take count of our weapons and provisions?" Alexa had asked in a calm but authoritative manner. In the request, she had given those worried folk something to occupy their mind.

She had even reminded Sophia of her own duties. At first, only a few shaky hands had risen to complete Alexa's task. After she continued to dole out minor duties, most of those shaky hands were put to work. Now, three days after her moment of unfettered leadership, Alexa had whole work gangs helping to fashion defenses, ranging from the construction of a new wooden palisade along with weapons to man it to the simple preparation of foodstuffs and medical supplies for the coming conflict. She had rallied groups of new recruits to train with shields, spears, and whatever other weapons they could find. Alexa had marched the perimeter of Elgion ensuring guards were sufficient and their discipline was sharp. All of this had happened without so much as a questioning remark towards Alexa's authority. Her and Elira, the apparent 'right-hand man' of Alexa, had simply went to work. And in their work, they had led the people towards an objective. Sophia could see those people, including the governor, the Guard-Captain, and—Ember's breath—even herself looking to them for some sort of beacon against the coming storm.

A storm that people kept from their minds with occupied hands. The blacksmith had not stopped working since that day. Every night she heard the cling-clang of the smith's hammer late into the night as he forged away his fears. People had taken to gathering there, using the light of the fires and the company of their fellow townsfolk to stave away their anxieties. It didn't help that the days were becoming increasingly short and even Sophia felt the strain of the approaching darkness brought on by winter's coming gloom.

Not wanting to be left out of the comfort of company, Sophia had ventured down to the forge after her evening meal the last few nights. On the second such evening, Alexa and her finally got a chance to talk. A conversation that should have happened immediately upon Alexa's return, but after the harsh words exchanged in their last interaction, both sisters had avoided one another. Yet there in the warmth of the forge, they had tentatively approached one another.

Alexa had started the conversation. "I could not save her ... I'm sorry."

Sophia, seeing the pain in her sister's eyes, felt a swell of sympathy wash over her.

"Sister, no, it is not your fault," she said emphasizing each word so as to punctuate her point. "No one could have gotten all the way to her. And the fact that you and some of your companions are here today, is because you are you; *you* are rangers." Sophia pointed at Alexa. "By the stones! You fought an orcish warband and won, a warband that from your own accounting was using the bloody magic of Magdris."

Sophia looked into her sister's eyes, wondering if Alexa knew how close she had come to death. How close Sophia had been too having not only lost one sister but also have another irrefutably dead. After all, very few could have taken the full brunt of an orc berserker charge and survived. Now she was in the flesh, trying to apologize for failing. Sophia wrestled with a twitch of anger, brought on by her sister's overzealous sense of duty. A sense of duty that at times made Sophia want to scream.

Alexa tried to hold the gaze but suddenly broke away, staring at the firelit ground instead. Sophia pressed on, wanting her sister to know it was ok, "You did your best, sister. And knowing you, that best was more than *any* of us could have asked for …" Sophia trailed off.

Then, as if the words brought the memory back, she reflected upon their last encounter together. They had left on a sour note, and only through Alexa's skill in combat were they given a chance to mend that rift. "You were right you know? You were right to chastise me for using the Necrostone on you. And … you were right to call me out on the Magi Stone." Sophia allowed the ramshackle apology time to suffuse the air, she nervously pulled at her fingertips while she waited.

Not until after Alexa looked back up from her self-imposed exile, did Sophia speak again. "It's only been a few days, but I have not touched that *particular* stone since you said something. Maybe I was abusing its … Power!" She clenched her fist raising it towards Alexa in small celebration at finding the right way to describe her misguided use of such an artifact.

"That's good, sister," Alexa said with warmth in her voice. "Honestly, I felt terrible after our last conversation, and … I'm sorry for how angry I was," Alexa now looked back into Sophia's eyes. "It was—I guess—unnecessary."

"You said what you felt was right in the moment, and … you said the truth," Sophia replied earnestly.

"Maybe so, but I could have been a little easier on you," Alexa said with a hint of amusement.

"What are sisters for but to beat each other up once in a while?" Sophia joked back, and she stretched her arms out, as if to welcome her sister back. Alexa, as stoic as they come, could not help but smile at the jest and she rushed over to hug her sister.

Muffled within her Keeper's cloak, Sophia heard Alexa whisper, "I hope she is alright, but I worry."

"I'm sure she is."

"How do you know?" Alexa asked, hope in her voice.

"If anyone could survive with savage beasts it would be Bella."

Alexa laughed unexpectedly and pulling away slightly from the embrace, called out, "You are not the first person to say that!"

"Because it is true," Sophia said as she grabbed Alexa by the shoulders and pulled her away just far enough so that she could look into her eyes. The two sisters' unable to contain their happiness burst into laughter. Their mirth echoed around the forge that night, and the people of Elgion felt a little hope stir, seeing two of their leaders so embroiled in laughter.

*

In the few days after that reunion, Sophia found herself trying her best to help the settlement prepare wherever she could. It had been a few years since she had last been this exhilarated with work. She was absolutely overloaded with matters of logistics and academics that she barely had time to worry. It was just the way she liked it.

One of her primary goals was to take a greater interest in the duties of the quartermaster, who was inundated with paperwork. Supplies and provisions were being doled out at an unprecedented rate, and the poor old quartermaster was woefully unprepared for a wartime environment. Sophia, knowing how important the logistics of warfare were, had taken it as her personal responsibility to ensure that no Elgion citizen would go hungry or cold. She wanted to make damn sure that they at least made it to the battlefield.

When she wasn't pouring over poorly transcribed quartermaster's reports and half-maintained ledgers, she was drowning herself in every book she could find that mentioned the Orcish race. She had already known of their god, Magdris, who was believed to inhabit the crimson stone also known as Bloodstone. In her studies, she had learned, or perhaps relearned, that the bloody god was a mercenary who had fought in the many conflicts between the gods. The Crimson King, as he (or it) was also called, was a god that only cared for death and bloodshed and would serve whichever side offered them the greatest chance to kill. Very few of the human race worshipped this malevolent god and only a select few of the other races even considered calling Magdris as their patron. The orcs were the only major group of peoples in all Telaea to have any form of worship to the Crimson King, and even then, that worship was crude at best.

Magdris had apparently fought a thousand battles across the stars, shedding droplets of himself all across the universe in the process. Some postulate it was never enough to coalesce into a stone, but it was just enough to curse the races of Telaea and beyond—if there was a beyond—with the occasional desire to perform wanton acts of cruel destruction and malevolent slaughter. Which didn't explain why there were literal Bloodstones in their world, Sophia had thought, cursing that theory for its inadequacies.

Others believed that it was only the proximity of a race, sufficiently versed in hatred and bloodshed, that allowed the stone to coalesce into any viable form. Which explained the orcs being the only primary users of Bloodstone.

Unfortunately, there were only a handful of accounts of a non-orc, let alone a human, trying to use the stone, and those accounts almost always ended in madness for the user. In an even more curious manuscript, Sophia had found a small nearly disregarded theory. That theory postulated that Magdris sought out the orcs *and* that Magdris had only ever 'showed' those usable pieces of himself to the orcish race. The few that believed in *Magdris's Choice*—as it was called by its believers—thought that somewhere within the orcish mind there was a place for empathy and compassion, and that only through the actions of the bloodthirsty god were they so far cursed to live a life of wanton cruelty and warfare. It was a beautiful theory, but until they stopped trying to kill everyone, she would leave that theory for the lovers and the dreamers.

Instead, she had focused on priority information and insights, especially since her late evening reads were seriously burning into her already low supply of candle wax. So, she had learned that Bloodstone only ever naturally occurred within the wastes of Kos'Raga, the ancestral home of the orcs. She had also learned that—on rare occasions—the stone of the bloodiest god on record had been found growing at the sights of large and particularly bloody battles. Regardless of its origins, whenever someone … non-orc, had attempted to harness the crimson stone, it had either ended in the absolute destruction of the user's psyche, or it had turned the intended target into a bloodthirsty berserker that only ended when they died. Alexa's description of the battle further reinforced those accounts with her own description of a *palpable* rage. So, in all her studies she could deduce one thing. The Stone of Magdris, The Crimson King, whatever *they* were called, was not beneficial to the denizens of Telaea.

So, to try and stave off the dangers of Magdris, who she had no idea how to fight, Sophia tried to find employment that could strengthen their position and keep her mind off her fears. And thus, she found herself, fresh out of the cellar where she had just parlayed with the gnomish clan, making her way through a landscape of browns, reds, and oranges. Colors of an autumn that was in its late stages. The oak and elm trees that were dotted around the field were bare of leaves save a few hardy stragglers, and the grass had long since turned to a light brown. The cabbage field she trudged through still had small patches of green, although those were from the detritus of the cabbage harvest and were quickly turning into a sicklier blackish green. The whole scene felt in line with the future of Elgion, and the crisp chill of the midday air served only to reinforce the dour thought.

"Mum," she was interrupted from her thoughts by a shout. Lumbering across the cabbage field she saw Blythe, slipping with every other step as his feet tried to gain purchase on the recently harvested field.

She sighed deeply as she laid eyes on the giant. The big man had latched himself to both Alexa and Sophia, desperate to be of use, or— Sophia figured—to keep his mind off the missing stablemaster. Apparently, that desperation had turned him into a messenger for the day.

A pang of sadness hit her as she looked at him, a cruel reminder that Bella was still out there—or worse … dead. Her sigh was also born from the knowledge that the most likely contents of his message were more dire tidings of the future or orders of the more stressful variety. Sophia halted upon his yell and waited patiently as the giant tried—too little success—to maintain his dignity whilst running in the muddy field.

She crossed her arms and was settling in to watch the display when suddenly she felt a tug, a pull on her periphery; like a whisper of light passing behind her perception. Her hand twitched and spasmed, sending spasmodic signals that warned her it was suddenly cold and empty. Sophia swore she heard a whisper, a faint hushed tone that beckoned her.

Something tugged from the shadows of her subconscious and was desperately trying to pierce the veil of her autonomy, a rogue hoping to hijack her mind. She tried to fight that shadowy presence but then her head started to ache. A fog fell over her thoughts, and the ache morphed into a throbbing overwhelming sensation, not solely of pain but of such force that it was impossible to focus on anything other than the throb. As her thoughts slowly tried to coalesce out of that maelstrom, she felt a wave of anxiety wash over her, and, as sudden as the onset of the mental attack had been, did she realize what was missing. What had caused her turmoil.

Since the days of Alexa's departure, she had been battling with waves of desire and despair. Many nights she would sit up late, her mind circling around and around that blue gem. On one occasion she had broken, she had sat there sweating in her room until she could take no more. She had succumbed to the stone's allure and had felt pure ecstasy for a few moments. She had sat there fondling the stone, listening to its whispers for nearly two hours that night. The next morning, she had woken with a face covered in dried blood, on the floor, and feeling like her mind had been split in two. From either luck or divine intervention, the stone—thankfully—had rolled out of her hand sometime in the night, leaving her near death on the wooden floor.

Now, that deceptive rock, that *Sorrowstone*, called to her once again. Not yet in a literal sense, but more in an overriding desire to eliminate its absence. Her whole body was being lashed with one torment or another. Her mind had been commandeered and from a thousand different nerves, a signal was sent for her to just feel it once more. To embrace the stone without its protective leather satchel and to just let herself go once more. She recognized that on many occasions the sensation of the stone underneath its little leather pouch could abate the cravings, but those cravings had become so monstrous that only the raw feeling of the blue gem's devilish faces could satisfy her. With what little foresight she had left she strained, forcing her thoughts to the forefront, figuring that Blythe's appearance may have brought this curse back.

That's what it was, a curse, one that she had held off for the last few days primarily due to the sheer workload she had dove into. She did not have the time to be distracted, and now in this freshly harvested cabbage field, amongst the decaying debris of that bountiful harvest, she felt the pull of desire once more. A pull that had brought her hand inside of her vest to rest on the pocket that contained the stone.

"Why do I have this with me," she said to herself, but she knew the answer. She may have been able to abstain—save for that one night—from its use since Alexa had called her out, but she could never bring herself to part from it completely. Now, she could feel its cool surface through the leather pouch. Its smooth oval shape called out to her, and her mind screamed at her to hold it once again. Her brain slammed against the walls of her defense and urged her to succumb to the release. She couldn't allow her consciousness, even for a moment, to slip into the thought of using the Sorrowstone. A message that repeated over and over of pure ecstasy and joy if she would just allow herself to use the stone once more.

"Just once", Dolocius called, echoing her thoughts. "Just … once … more."

"I can always recover; I can always quit again later. After all, I have been doing well," she reasoned. Her hand crept into the pouch, and the last vestiges of her mental defense fell. Her mind slipped into the mire of desire, and she felt that surge of joy and relief that her body had been craving. For a few seconds, she felt a wave of numbing; relaxing; unfettered bliss wash over her.

"Mum," Blythe shouted again, but this time it was from just a couple of meters away. Sophia had been standing still, gazing into nothingness for several seconds after his arrival. Now, startled from her mental battle she yanked her hand free from the clutches of the stone.

"WHAT!?" Sophia yelled in pure anger at Blythe. The big man recoiled at her sudden fury. She immediately felt regret at her response. "Sorry, Blythe I-I-don't know what came over me," she said softly, hoping to ameliorate the relationship between her and the ever-loyal Blythe.

Slowly, he recovered from his guarded stance, clenching his jaw as he mustered the courage to mutter his unnecessary apology, "Sorry, mum. It-it's just that your sister wanted to know if you were going to join them."

"No need for apologies, Blythe. I am the one at fault here, but what do you mean *them*?" Sophia inquired.

"Uh, well your sister, the governor, the Rangemaster, an—"

"Alright, alright I get the picture. The whole lot of *them* are there." She silenced the man by calmly patting at the air. Yet another meeting, Sophia sighed inwardly. She had already attended two separate such meetings and found that she was unable to contribute anything of value to the leadership of Elgion. The current state of things required defensive preparation, which was not her forte, and she had sequestered herself for logistical assistance. Her contributions hardly required her to report on her progress as frequently as the current regularity of meetings. What she had reported on in those meetings seemed to be respectfully glossed over. So, she had found ways of being conveniently busy for the last three such conventions, including the one that Blythe was currently asking her about.

"Unfortunately, I will not be able to make it. Inform my sister that I have obtained some food security and that I will inform her of the details later."

"Yes, mum." Blythe nodded. He turned to head back to deliver the message. Instead, he stopped, seemingly unsure of himself, and jolted back towards Sophia in a rather clumsy half-turn-half-slip in the mud. "Mum, the Guard-Captain wanted you to have this," he said, holding out a book that had a beautiful vellum cover. Its front was colored red with gold trim and looked to be worth a fortune. Sophia reached out and grabbed the book, noticing its lack of mud in comparison to its most recent bearer.

*Strategos Dante Stelios's Observations of War.* Sophia tried to hide her astonishment. Blythe, as nervous as he was, cleared his throat to hurry the interaction along. Obviously, she had failed at hiding her admiration.

Sophia jolted out of her reverie, replied in the distant tone of one awed by magnificence, "Tell the Guard-Captain that his gift will go far in our preparations." She turned the beautiful book over at least three times, admiring the intricate patterns scrawled into the cover. Surely, there was knowledge of the Orcish race; maybe, if she dared, first-hand accounts of encounters. Her heart fluttered like a child who had just eaten a honeyed treat. She looked at Blythe, a warm smile on her face, which he returned.

"I must be going mum," Blythe said his face now beaming because of Sophia's happiness.

"No … wait," Sophia said, reaching her hand out to the big man, "I need you to come with me. I have a deal to keep." With that, the unlikely duo, one Keeper and one stable hand, made their way through the mud-slicked field back to Sophia's apothecary.

*

It was already late afternoon before they had kicked off their muddy boots and sat in the foyer of the apothecary. Both were exhausted from the trip. Sophia was resting in a feather-cushioned armchair that she had spent a fortune on, and Blythe sat on a large wooden bench she had near the front door. The bench seemed to be swallowing him up because he slowly sank into a position parallel to the ground. Seeing Blythe get more comfortable made her regret that the day's work was not done.

She allowed a few more minutes to pass, giving herself and Blythe a well-deserved break. Then, with great reluctance, she broke the blissful calm that had befallen the room. "Blythe, I am sorry my friend, but I have one more task for you."

Sophia pulled herself up from the inviting comfort of her chair. She went to her pantry and pulled out one of two wheels of cheese, the other being half-eaten, from an upper shelf. She handed the cheese to the reluctant Blythe. "I need this brought to the southeastern cellar," she rested her hand on his shoulder and, because he was still sitting, stooped slightly to look into his eyes, "You know the one?"

Blythe nodded his head, his eyes somewhat bloodshot from the sheer exhaustion of the last few days. As Sophia looked into his eyes, she pondered whether there was anyone more loyal. "Just leave it on the main table in there, and the people looking for it will come get it. No reason to stay," she ordered him, smiling gently as she did so.

Blythe simply nodded once again slowly pulling himself up to a more upright position.

"If you do this for me, I will see about getting you some better shoes, so you don't have to slide your way through the muddier parts of the year," she said with a wink.

Blythe's face lit up at this, recognizing the humor. "Thank you, mum." Sophia pulled away from the man, and he slowly rose to his feet. "Mum?" he asked gently.

"Yes," Sophia replied.

"You think she is alright?"

Sophia was stunned, and before she could speak, she had to summon her courage. There in his eyes, she saw a glimmer of hope. She saw the desire to hear words of comfort. Not the truth which was, unfortunately, that she just did not know. With what grace and composure she could muster, she replied, "Yes, my sister … my sister is as strong as they come; As you know. No little orc is gonna stop her."

The pair smiled at one another and before Blythe left with the cheese, he looked one more time at the Keeper. "Thank you," he said nodding before he ducked out the doorway.

# Chapter Three

## Sophia

Sophia spent a few moments reflecting on the nature of Blythe. His stalwart and amiable nature made him an irreplaceable companion in these dark times. Times that would require companions of the best stock, and Sophia had a suspicion that Blythe was of the best stock; despite his attempts to hide his quality. She also suspected—for quite some time—that the big man was not as brutish and simple as his outward appearance would convey. She had noticed small inconsistencies that gave glimpses into his hidden talents.

Firstly, he had been glued to Bella since the founding of Elgion, and on more than one occasion he was able to predict what Bella wanted before even she did. Such a quality did not come easily to one slow of mind. Secondly, he was ever watchful, he always seemed to be observing and absorbing, and he always made sure to do it in such a way that his observations didn't seem intrusive. For a man of his stature, remaining unobtrusive was no easy task. Finally, she reflected on how valuable he made himself. No matter the occasion, whether messenger, brute, or otherwise, Blythe was always there to assist.

So, why was his manner so fidgety; so coarse? The thought guided her mental image to that of Bella, and her almost comical barks and yelps at the big man. As soon as those images had made her smile in memory, they had in turn brought on a pang of sadness. She hoped beyond hope that her sister was alright

In her musings over the qualities of Blythe and her longing to see her sister, her hand had drifted ever so slightly, subconsciously, to once again find itself resting on her pocket. The Magi Stone's smooth polished edges could be felt through the wool lining of the pouch. *One use wouldn't hurt.*

She looked at the book Blythe had delivered from the Guard-Captain, its golden trim reflecting the last rays of sunlight piercing through her windows. After all, she needed the focus to dive into such a treasure.

She inhaled heavily through her nose, and as if to purge all external pressure she exhaled just as heavily. Her eyes closed and she allowed her mind to go blank, savoring the moment that mind and soul had craved. With reckless abandon, she clutched the stone in her palm.

Time flew by in a flurry as she delved into the tome. *Strategos Dante Stelios's Observations of War* had more than just information about orcs, but insights into many facets of not only the races that inhabited Telaea but also life itself. Sophia was enthralled, and she plunged into Dante's prose with a scholar's relish. She devoured his tales on the bandits of the Golden Highway and his exploits in the War of the Five Points. "Never expect an enemy to behave, behaving in war is never successful," Sophia read to herself as she went over a particularly juicy section on the strategos' attempts to break the 'three-year siege,' as commander of the Argolonian effort to capture that city.

The 'three-year siege' was a series of conflicts over the rich port town of Argentios. This town was originally held by the Vidrosiites at the beginning of the war, but within a few months, it was captured via a seaborne invasion by the Xelandeer navy. The Xelandeers, as the strategos put, "were effective, efficient, eccentric, and the best damn sailors on the seas." The Augustians, holding the largest army and wealth, prepared a besieging army to arrive at the city to capture it for themselves. There the Augustians stayed for nearly a year before logistical failings and disease forced them to abandon the siege. As Dante put it, "the Augustians are masters of industry, but amateurs at logistics."

Sophia felt pride at the author's respect for Augustian prowess but did take note of the fact that although the Augustians started the war with the largest chance of success they did not end the war with the city of

Argentios. Sophia wondered if Augustia—Ember's breath—even just Elgion, should incorporate some of the strategos's thoughts into their own stratagems.

As if to answer her request, she saw a tiny scrawl in the margins, apparent notes laid out by what appeared to be the Guard-Captain's hand. She chuckled internally, recognizing—as she had suspected—that the Guard-Captain most assuredly knew more than he let on.

She continued the history of the 'three-year siege.' The Argolonians, a city-state that never had much wealth, relied on the quality of troops and superior tactics. Thus, they were renowned for having the best-trained soldiers in the old world, the author being one of them. Sophia rubbed the Magi Stone faster, now diving delightfully into Dante's retelling of his company's capture of Argentios. Starting with the capture of the Ivory Tower.

The Ivory Tower was the northernmost bastion of the city and was thought to be impregnable without at first being inside the walls proper. The cliff it rested on was an escarpment that steeply inclined from inside the city to a sheer drop nearly thirty meters down at the edge. The Ivory Tower was placed atop that escarpment, and the walls of the city ran along the cliff face. With a troop of only thirty men, Dante had scaled the cliff, mounted the subsequent wall along that cliff, and then had captured the tower itself without so much as making a sound. From there they were able to ferry soldiers and supplies up the escarpment all night until a small but significant force of Argolonians had gathered. In the dawn light of the next day the Xelandeers were faced by a determined enemy inside their walls, and within a matter of hours were slaughtered by the battle-savage Argolonians. What few Xelanders survived escaped via ship. For the remaining months of the war, Dante held onto the city whilst facing yet another siege by Sophia's countrymen.

Wrapped up in the 'three-year siege' of Argentios, she did not notice her candles spluttering, and her reading was interrupted by the nearest of them burning out.

She touched her face and felt no warm blood or other ill effects. She reassured herself. The knowledge gleaned from the fascinating read felt crucial to their upcoming conflict. Yet deep inside she knew that she was only pursuing her own scholarly hunger. Still, she pressed on, trying not to think of how long it would have taken for a candle to completely burn out. The wicks of a new batch of candles were lit with a touch of her Ember-shard amulet. *Surely, it was a candle that was nearly burnt out already.*

She forced herself onto her original study goal, and opened a section entitled "Beasts of the Land." There she found sections on myriad creatures that the strategos had encountered. Mountains of information on anything from centaurs to trolls were packed into its pages. Sophia, already chastened by her previous distraction, quickly skipped past several exciting bits until she found a section on orcs. The strategos had dedicated a substantial amount of time and parchment to writing about the porcine fiends. He even went so far as to dedicate the first page of the orcish section to an amateur illustration of one. Undoubtedly the illustration was done by the strategos himself, but its details were sufficient to prove useful.

There was no sense of scale on the page, so it was impossible to tell how big or small any of the drawing's contents were. Still, she combed over the details of the image. Two massive toes split themselves unevenly on the orcish foot and that divide carried on for three-quarters of the length of the foot. At the end of each massive toe was an ungainly nail. There was no way that that foot was more efficient at running.

Sophia reckoned that their feet were probably geared more towards carrying heavier weights or other such burdens. Regardless, the ill-designed foot could prove to be useful information to the people of Elgion. So, her first useful information in tow, she started a missive of facts regarding orcs.

She combed through the rest of the image of the orc, paying particular attention to the bone and scrap armor, adding to the missive along the way.

Before long, she had dived deep into the strategos's knowledge of orcs, and Sophia had jotted down a rather lengthy brief. In its scrawling, she had written how the younger orcs are generally 'blooded' in battle, having to charge into an impossible foe before being given the right to warriorhood. She had described the typical weapons; clubs, cleavers, and axes, that the orcs were known to use and that they always preferred weight over agility. She had noted the patterns of armor the orcish race were known to wear, a series of bone, hide, and metal patches that were slapped onto their host seemingly at random. She had described bits of their culture, which included the dichotomy of male and female orcs within their society, truly one of utter tyranny against the females of the species. She had also dived into excerpts from survivors that described the orcs' sheer obsession with blood, particularly the blood of their captives. And finally, she had written a stark warning against the power and the typical mannerisms of the 'God-Talkers', a phrase Alexa had used, and Sophia had taken a liking to.

With her missive nearing completion, she pushed on hoping to find as many revelations and facts as she could from the writing. She hoped that she could divulge the information to Alexa in the morning. "Orcs need blood to use their magic? This is why they—" a single bloody droplet flecked the page, stopping her dead in her tracks.

Her whole thought process unfolded as she realized her nose was bleeding. Sophia scrambled to think of how long it had been. Panic crept in because she truly could not tell. "Ember's breath!" She cursed.

Most stones when used too heavily could be lethal and some were believed to bring on fates worse than death. A stone occasionally referred to as the Sorrowstone could only be of the latter disposition.

It's ok. It couldn't have been more than an hour or so. Sophia tried to reassure herself between increasing anxious breaths. Yet she knew better, she had dived into the reading with relish and had gone until her candles had burned down. She knew that she hadn't rubbed the stone consistently for the whole time, but several hours must have passed with infrequent use.

The powerful cry of a barred owl suddenly reverberated through the otherwise quiet night, and Sophia realized that it was well into the evening. It was well past the normal waking hours of Elgion, and now the normal hustle and bustle of the street and the surrounding homes had died away. However long she had utilized the stone, she would regret it.

She hastily wiped the blood spatter up with a nearby cloth, but the futility of the task became apparent when a cascade of droplets fell onto the page. She cursed inwardly at the desecration of the text and quickly backed away from the tome. The Keeper tried to stifle the blood flow with the cloth, banging into the central table that normally held food and drink. The table was at waist height and her rapid backward egress into it forced her into a sitting position. She grasped around herself as she held the cloth to her nose, trying not to lower her head for fear of making the bleeding worse.

She felt one of her clay cups and by luck felt the cistern she kept water in nearby. She blindly poured from the cistern into the clay cup. The sound of water drizzling onto her wooden floor added misery to an already miserable situation.

A sudden wave of dizziness slammed into Sophia, and in response she shot down what cooling liquid made it into the cup, trying to stave off the rapidly accelerating dizziness. Her focus turned to a candle holder in a vain attempt to steady her blurring vision, but the holder spun. Nausea washed over her, and she braced herself on the table.

As her head was forced into a bow, her nose opened like a spout, blood gushing forth. Her head, now hanging slumped between her shoulders, swollen with pressure, and she gazed blurrily at the growing puddle of blood. With an almost nonchalant action, she opened her mouth, and a fountain of vomit issued forth, adding to the blood puddle on the table. She saw the disgusting mess in front of her and moaned. The cistern and cup she had used to drink from were now tainted with reddish-orange chunks of half-digested food, and splatters of rapidly drying blood. *At least she hadn't hit another book.*

Yet her optimism rapidly dwindled as the nausea returned. With desperation, she tried to find something to hold the oncoming vomit. In the corner, she saw a wicker basket where she held trash. She raced across the room towards the basket. Unfortunately, all the grace she had cultivated during her time as Keeper was lost in an instant as she rushed toward her salvation. A salvation that became too far to reach as the hem of her cloak, having fallen loosely off her shoulders, got caught underfoot. The hindrance tripped her next step, and she fell face-first towards the ground. Her mind went blank as she slammed into the wooden floor.

# Chapter Four

## Sophia

Rays of golden light slowly migrated across the floor, moving with the rising sun. As the light drifted across the wooden floorboards, it reflected off a rather substantial bloodstain. The warm amber rays transformed the crimson colors of the dried ichor. What appeared to be a smattering of cherry jam, with little globules of substance, splayed out around the still unconscious Keeper's face. She had fallen face-first into the sturdy floorboards and had instantly been knocked out. The Magi Stone, the late night, the lack of food and water, and finally the heavy fall had all mixed to make a potent concoction to steal the senses. Now, breathing shallowly, her face felt the first flickers of that warming light caress her face. The commotion of a village day had been well into its third hour before the first ray had made its way to her resting place.

It was slow at first, but the light marched up onto her cheek and continued onto her eye. There, with the dazzling radiance of the sun's light did Sophia's mind stir. At first, an involuntary slap at the disturbance and then a groan of agony. Her brain took stock of the damage that had been wrought to her physicality. She felt dried blood caked to her face, and her mind throbbed with a headache beyond reckoning. Her throat felt cracked and her belly sour. Her vision swam back into existence, and she slowly lifted her head off the ground. Old vomit and crusted blood tugged gently at her cheek as it was ripped from its mooring on the floor. She managed to lift her head a couple of centimeters off the ground, looking across the floor to try and gain her bearings.

"Where am I?" She asked herself groggily. Her brain still struggled to process, especially as it fought waves of immense—throbbing—pain. She turned her head slightly and caught a glimpse of a tipped-over wicker basket, chunks of half-digested cheese and cabbage splattered around it. Her brain pieced her leaky conscious back together. Slowly, the thought of being; the thought of herself came to fruition.

I am a Keeper, I am Sophia, and I passed out here on the floor last night. She almost spoke her name aloud as she recounted herself. The triumph of knowing won, she pushed herself up from the floor and managed to pull her knees towards her chest, using the nearest wall as a backrest. She looked around the room slowly, her head throbbing in complaint as she did so. Eventually, her gaze fixed on the bloody stain on the floor, which could have been produced by no one other than herself. The horrific realization of her overuse sapped her spirit. A tug of doubt and self-loathing gripped at her insides, clawing its way into her self-confidence.

*What is wrong with me!* She screamed internally. She struck her forehead in frustration. The flagellation led to a new wave of nausea and agony. The urge to vomit came on like a tidal wave, and with no ability to prepare, she projected bile across the room. The unwarranted memetic response forced her onto her hands and knees, and she clutched her stomach as the acidity of her own insides burned. She groaned at the discomfort.

"I need to—" her thoughts were interrupted, and she vomited again. This time straight onto the floor, the force causing much of the vomit to splatter onto her clothing. She retched several more times as she desperately tried to keep herself from collapsing, and after what felt like a lifetime, her breathing and her stomach settled.

She needed to see Alexa and tell her what she had learned. For if the rangers' descriptions were accurate, and she had no reason to doubt they were, they were dealing with a horde of orcs that were intimately connected with the god of blood, more so than other clans within the records she studied. A revelation that became only more horrible when she reflected on Dante Stelios's final words in his writings on the orcish breed, "Their ties to that god of blood, that Crimson King, are as much a marker of their capacity in warfare as dark clouds in the sky are a marker of rain to come."

She stood slowly upright, allowing her thoughts to strengthen her resolve. Although she felt terrible, she leaned on her secret physicality and her discipline to push her through. She thanked the stones that she had kept a daily painful regimen. The regimen in question, just a basic exercise routine, was unknown to the townsfolk, and now it helped her body purge the toxins more effectively. She had never wanted people to see her exercise, wanting the mysticism and superstition surrounding Keepers to be fortified. She had thought—rightfully—that if someone were to see her, say, jogging like a common soldier it would only serve to break that carefully crafted illusion. So, nearly every morning, save this one and a few others, she underwent a series of high intensity but basic bodyweight exercises. Those exercises gave her the strength to push past her affliction and cross into her bedroom.

There she found the basin of water she kept for hygienic purposes. Sophia splashed the tepid water on her face. The liquid was less than refreshing but still served to give her the jolt she needed. "Gods, I look like laepous shit", she said to herself as she looked down at her puke-stained clothes.

She pulled off her old vest, being careful to extract the many vials and stones she held in its pockets and replaced it with her only spare. With whimsy, she recognized the luxury of having a spare in these parts. She also donned a new cloak. One that had been recently retrieved from the launderers and had the smell of lavender and soap still fresh in its golden folds. She also decided that a good spot scrub on the exposed parts of her blouse would suffice. With the worst evidence of her terrible night disguised, she stepped out the door. Immediately, she was dazzled by the sun's brilliance, forcing her to shield her eyes with her outstretched hand. As her bloodshot eyes adjusted to the discomfort, she gauged the height of the sun. It was nearly midday. She cursed as she realized she had missed half of it already.

It was cold, and the ground was glistening with moisture, but since there was nary a cloud in the sky nor a puddle on the ground Sophia realized that it must have been from frost melt. Winter had arrived and as if to cement the seasonal change a group of three men were goading a horse-drawn cart of firewood through the mud-slicked Hook Street. The oldest amongst them called out a greeting, "Hey there, Keeper."

Sophia did not speak but waved in response, she couldn't be bothered. The three men glanced at her, but after realizing the Keeper was not in the mood to talk, carried on. The oldest amongst them sparking back up what seemed to be a conversation they were having prior to her arrival. Sophia took a deep breath and bounded up the street, going towards the Ranger's Hall.

After navigating the treacherous mud-slicked Hook Street, Sophia stopped at the crossroads where the well, market, and warehouse were conjoined. There in the open space behind the town well was a group of twenty men and women all holding bows, and at the head of the motley group was Alexa.

"The most important thing I can teach you in this small amount of time is simple," Alexa bellowed out to the crowd. "If your target is small," she held onto the last word, pacing back and forth in front of the crowd before she spoke again. "Your misses are small!" Alexa made her way behind the group, "Now, show me what you can do!" The makeshift soldiery faced a set of four straw targets with a simple splash of white in the middle of each target. Without any discipline and in ragtag order, the individuals drew back their bows and fired at the targets.

Sophia noticed that the bows were a mixture of hunting and training bows. Bows that would struggle to pierce any armored target but could be lethal to exposed skin if used properly. Many of the shots did indeed strike the straw target. A truth that would only be found in these hardy pioneers. However, Sophia did notice that although the strikes mostly rang true, they did not hit with much impact.

"Good, good. That was a fine strike, Joshua!" Alexa called out as she paced behind the motley group. "We will make a warrior of you yet, Ella," the de facto Rangemaster said as she tapped a girl on her shoulder.

Ella couldn't be any more than fifteen years old, a product of the dire circumstances they found themselves in. Sophia hoped that this encouragement would not push Ella to the front when the battle came.

Suddenly, Dunkeath, the miller's oldest son, called out to Alexa but loud enough for all to hear, "What 'bout the rest of us? We good enough for ya?"

Alexa's smile vanished and she slowly pulled her hand away from Ella's shoulder. She stepped over to Dunkeath, who was just a few centimeters taller than the ranger. Alexa stood in front of the young man, staring into his eyes showing off her implacable nature, and just as the tension felt like it was going to explode Alexa grinned.

"Let's make it a contest then. Three of my shots against three of yours," Alexa said whilst she produced a bow string from a satchel on her hip. "Elira," Alexa yelled out to her de facto second in command.

"Yeah!?"

"You mind fetching my war bow so that I can show this *recruit* how to shoot," Alexa said while looking at Dunkeath. The tiniest hint of disgust veiled within the stare.

Sophia couldn't help but feel proud of her sister, thinking how well she was adapting to her new responsibilities

Elira grinned almost malevolently, "With pleasure." Elira reached down between her and her partner, Matthias, and grabbed Alexa's heavy war bow. The ranger walked a few paces towards Alexa and tossed the mighty weapon. Alexa caught it with deft grace and immediately unfurled the string. She dropped the bottom of the bow to the ground and proceeded to step on the bottom horn. She reached down, hooking the string around the bottom horn, and with a fluid motion she pulled the string hard whilst holding the bow in place and hooked its loop around the upper horn of the bow.

She made it look easy, which made Sophia laugh, especially since she knew that the eighty-pound draw of that bow would be near impossible for most of the folks present to string with such ease. Bow strung; Alexa calmly paced over to a set of arrows that were stuck in the ground. The new Rangemaster plucked one from the ground, strung it, aimed, and shot all within a matter of seconds. Her arrow hit the furthest target square in the crude white circle that dotted each target. Sophia reckoned it was a thirty or so meter shot, and it was done with such fluidity that the watching militia was stunned to silence.

Dunkeath, his face red as a tomato with embarrassment or anger, laughed nervously. "Just you watch," he said with uncertainty.

Slowly, he approached the same spot as Alexa had shot from. Alexa stood, her hands resting on the top of her bow, a look of amusement blessing her face. Dunkeath held his gaze on the new Rangemaster as he approached, and as he reached the arrows he nodded to her as if out of nervousness. He grabbed his arrow, strung it, and aimed, but he did not shoot with the rapidity that Alexa did.

"What's the matter? Sun in your eyes," Elira called out mockingly, issuing a chorus of laughter from the group.

Dunkeath, lowered the bow for a second, turned to the mockery, laughed again nervously, and turned back. Once again, he drew back his bow and aimed, and with several seconds of aim time, he finally fired. Sophia grimaced as she watched the shot scrape the top of the target and fly harmlessly away from the straw. The whole crowd—save Sophia—burst into laughter. Dunkeath, now glowing so red Sophia thought he would ignite, threw down his bow in frustration but, unsure of what to do next, stood awkwardly with his hands clenched at his side. Sophia decided to approach Alexa, knowing that any training cohesion would be lost for several moments. This opportunity gave her the perfect time to speak to her sister.

"Alexa," Sophia called out. Alexa, still chortling, turned to see Sophia. Her face was a warm smile at first but slowly devolved into a look of neutrality bordering on a frown. Sophia quickly closed the distance, pushing through a few of the still laughing militia. "Alexa, I have much to tell you," Sophia said excitedly.

"You gonna explain why you look like that," Alexa replied, crossing her arms as she did so. Sophia noticed Elira's approach, apparently there to support her new leader.

The two had to of come to an agreement sometime back, for Sophia had never known Elira to be so submissive. Sophia chuckled nervously at the response of her sister as well as Elira's approach. "Look, I was busy all-night reading this." Sophia said, holding up *Strategos Dante Stelios's Observations of War* for Alexa to see.

Alexa narrowed her eyes as if to discern some mystery, and Sophia could see Alexa's eyes darting up and down her frame.

She felt like she was being inspected—almost interrogated—but she pressed forward. "You see that sphere of blood you observed in the forest, it's connected," Sophia said, her voice rising with enthusiasm.

"The only thing that abomination is connected to is death," Elira said. She had stopped a few paces away just after Sophia had displayed the book. Alexa held up a hand, checking Elira from further speech. Elira took the command readily enough.

"Well, that's actually quite accurate. You see that sphere of blood that the-uh-um-God-Talker summoned," Sophia stuttered as she used the phrase Alexa had used to describe the beast. "Well, it's connected to the magic of the stones. One in particular, Magdris, which you and your rangers stated was the name of the god that echoed through the forest just before the ball disappeared. Anyways, the strategos, the one that wrote this book, noted on his journey that orcish clans innately attuned with Magdris tend to be more … successful," Sophia said, unsure of how to describe the connection. Seeing that she still held her sister's attention she laid back into her speech, "I think that this clan, that God Talker, was an orcish Keeper!" Sophia paused at this revelation, and after a moment decided to clarify, "Well the closest thing to a Keeper the orcs would get. You, see? These orcs are not only attuned with Magdris but are actively communicating with him!"

Alexa nodded to show she understood and then asked, "But how does that information help us?"

"Wel-well I—" Sophia mumbled, taken aback by the response.

"Sister, I think that you need some rest," Alexa said irritably.

"No!" Sophia shouted too loudly, and the crowd turned to look at them. "I don't need rest. Look, those bastard orcs are using bloodstone, and since we now know that. We can counter them!"

"With what though?" Alexa asked shrewdly.

"We know Magdris, the patron of the bloodstone, wants more blood to be shed. So, if we can prevent that they lose power," Sophia said her tone becoming exasperated.

"So, and let me get this straight—" Elira said grabbing at her mouth and then pointing to Sophia with her whole hand. The gesture a mockery of a lawyer's more formal gestures in a debate hall back in Augustia. "Your solution to the orcs is to … not let them kill us? Man, I wish we would have thought of that," Elira said with outstretched arms.

"That's enough!" Alexa cut Elira off whilst giving her a look of admonition. "Come on, sister, why don't you walk with me for a bit, and we can discuss your … discoveries." Alexa grabbed onto Sophia's shoulder, spinning her away from the crowd and guiding her back down Hook Street. Yet, before they had made it even a few paces, a voice called out.

"What's the matter, *Rangemaster*? Afraid you can't pull that shot off again?"

Sophia turned to see a defiant Dunkeath standing tall.

The crowd parted from the man who dared challenge both their Rangemaster and their Keeper. Alexa turned and sighed heavily. Dunkeath used the pause to continue his attack, "The apple doesn't fall from the tree I see."

Sophia thought that phrase odd but couldn't dwell on it for long because Dunkeath glowered at her as if she was a demon come to Telaea. He approached the pair, continuing his monologue, "Oh, what's the matter, Keeper? Ya' don't 'member me? Ya' don't 'member bullying my family; my father? Is that why you are so pale, you run out of innocents to push about?"

Sophia was dumbfounded, her mind was still ravaged from the morning's sickness and her overindulgence into the Magi Stone. Yet for the life of her, she could not think of why Dunkeath would say such a thing.

"Well, let me remind you, *Keeper*," Dunkeath's voice was loud, strong, and full of scorn. A voice raised to rally people to his side, and to Sophia's astonishment, a few faces looked genuinely interested in what Dunkeath had to say. "This here patron of peace, this here Keeper of rocks—" he grinned at Sophia, gaps within his smile of slightly yellow teeth, and dared her to rise to the insult.

When she did not, he continued, "This here Keeper of rocks defiled my family's home with an au-audacious," he stumbled over the large word. But beamed when he spit it out, "Act of blackmail and terror." Dunkeath pointed at the Keeper as he finished his opening denouncement. As he did so, a tremor of mumbles rumbled through the crowd.

"I … I did?" Sophia was cut off abruptly by Dunkeath, who felt emboldened by the crowd's response.

"You did!" Dunkeath's voice was at its peak now. "Ya' took yer sister and her brute, and ya showed up to our door in the middle of the night so that ya could steal our winter stores."

With sudden clarity, she remembered this scornful youth. The boy who glowered at them as she had forced his family to return the wheat they had stolen. Dunkeath, the son of Gareth the miller, was apparently not over the supposed insult and had found his time to enact his revenge.

"Your father was stealing! Stealing from all of us, and you know it," Sophia exclaimed after the recognition gave her the use of her voice once more. She stepped away from Alexa, who in turn reached out to Sophia to try and hold her back. It was too late, Dunkeath had angered her. And to make it worse he was attempting to embarrass her in front of the townspeople. She would not have it. She stepped forward to meet the rabble-rouser, nearly bumping her chest against his own.

"Stop," Alexa called out, but neither Dunkeath nor the Keeper paid her any heed.

"Ya thinks just because you have some fancy rocks that you can do whatever ya want? Not anymore; we won't have it," Dunkeath yelled, turning in a circle whilst raising his hands. A clear attempt to garner support from the crowd, and Sophia noted a marked display of showmanship. "We are tired of being afraid of ya, and why should we be afraid of ya? You smell of vomit and regret."

"You do not know what you are saying! You do not speak to a Keeper this way!" Sophia yelled in response. Her blood boiled. Her head throbbed again, a tremor of the morning illness. Yet she gritted her teeth and carried on, her wrath pushing her body past the anguish.

"And why not!?" he asked derisively.

"Because I am your Keeper, and you do not speak to your betters this way!" Sophia yelled. Silencing everyone in sight. She regretted her choice of words, but her anger had spilled over.

The silence hung heavily, and Alexa tugged at her elbow. "Come on, sister. Let's go."

Sophia—flushed with embarrassment—turned away, knowing that no resolution would come in its immediacy. She had been a fool, and her sister was giving her an escape route. She had to follow, but Dunkeath would not let her leave so easily.

"Ya see? Ya see what they think of us." Dunkeath's voice was incredulous. He now held both hands out towards the sisters. The open space around him became his podium from which he could harangue Sophia and Alexa, and he used it to maximum effectiveness. Some of the people were nodding in agreement, and a few yelled in ascension. "They don't care for us. They only care for their own. Even our glorious Rangemaster allows for this abuse to continue. Ember's breath, if it weren't for their sister, we wouldn't even have to worry 'bout the damned orcs."

Sophia could not contain it any longer. Her rage had been boiling already, and Dunkeath's display, his pure disrespect of authority, and now his insult to his sisters, forced her to the brink. "Ember, take you!"

It happened much too fast to comprehend. So fast that time for logic and reason were nonexistent. In the blink of an eye, Sophia had turned towards Dunkeath, grabbed her Embershard, ignited a halo of righteous fire around her, and blasted the poor man with a projectile of searing fire. Alexa had been pushed back as the Embershard worked its magic, unable to stop Sophia for fear of being incinerated. Sophia's incantation and her years as a Keeper gave her the power—whether desired or not—to ignite its magic with ease. And with that ease she had conjured a searing fireball that lanced from her hand without a thought, slamming into Dunkeath's shoulder. The man spun ninety degrees, falling to the ground as he twirled.

Her victim vanquished; she stood engulfed in flame with a hefty chunk of the village staring at her in horror. "Well, shit," she murmured to herself.

# Chapter Five

## Gal'Tsus

Gal'Tsus enjoyed watching the sows feast on flesh. He loved watching them squabble over the scraps that were thrown from the effigy. One sow, a particular favorite of his, punched another sow square in the jaw, knocking her away from a severed arm. The arm, which had belonged to a puny human, was the first hunk of meat that had been served to the sows for over a week. Gal'Tsus had been in the mood for some entertainment and had decided to feed his hungry harem. Eager to watch them pathetically fight for scraps. It was an orgy of carnage that gave him a warm feeling inside. *Everything was going great.*

With a smile on his face, or at least the closest thing to a smile for an orc, Gal'Tsus watched his favorite sow hold off another competitor with one hand whilst using the other to hold the vile flesh near her gnashing maw. Just as she looked like she was going to be overwhelmed, a crudely butchered leg came flying end-over-end from the effigy. Another prize now occupied the stinking sow pit, and the pressure on the arm-holding sow relented. She was free to gorge herself on the flesh. Gal'Tsus watched her snout dig in; he watched her mouth become slathered with congealed blood. The sight was enough to excite the war chief, and he decided it might be time to add more warriors to the clan.

He started towards the steps that led to the sow pit. There at the bottom stair was a smaller sow who, upon seeing him approach, prostrated herself in an attempt to win his favor. Favor that would grant her more chances at survival.

Gal'Tsus chuckled at the pathetic move, deciding to kill that one at the first sign of hunger. For now, he would leave her alone. After all, she was swollen with child from one of his warriors. That child could grow into a warrior itself, or in desperate times another source of food.

His mercy did not extend to his foot, however, and he booted the small sow square in the shoulder. She squealed in fear, reeling back from the war chief. He laughed harder, a throaty bellow that overshadowed the sounds of feasting. The injured sow now hunkered at the edge of the sow pit, trying to disappear in the muddy embankment. Gal'Tsus moved down the trench towards his desired mate, shoving another pregnant sow to the ground who was too slow to move out of his way. More body parts were being flung into the pits, and the sows were too hungry and too distracted to notice their war chief amongst them, including his target. He placed a massive hand on the sow's shoulder, frightening the female orc.

She tried to cower away, half-covering the now eviscerated arm, but Gal'Tsus was even more excited by the fear. He forcefully turned the sow around and bellowed in her face. She, a veteran of Gal'Tsus's overlordship, did not make eye contact with the war chief. She just hung her head in defeat, accepting the tyrant's rough grasp.

"Boss," a gravelly voice cried out. The speech was indecipherable to human ears, but there in the orc's encampment, the grunts and guttural growling of the tusked brutes passed for speech. Gal'Tsus interrupted from his conquest, angrily turned towards the voice.

"What!" Gal'Tsus bellowed in reply.

"Magdris speaks again," the gravelly voice replied. The voice belonged to Bur'Yari, a Blood Thrall of the warband, and the orc who had been flinging body parts into the pit. As Gal'Tsus knew, the act of butchery tended to bring out the Crimson King, and when the lord of blood spoke it was best to listen. Gal'Tsus did not bow to anyone, in fact, he had subdued many bands of orcs in the badlands of Kos'Raga. Those acts of subjugation were made easier by his size. He was a behemoth, even for orc standards. A size attributed to age. No one knew if orcs ever stopped growing, but everyone knew orcs did not live long. Gal'Tsus reckoned he was at least fifty-six or maybe fifty-eight years old, and reckoned he was one of the lucky few who got to live that long. Due to his unnatural lifespan, he had become a giant amongst his kin and an utter monstrosity to the other races of Telaea.

Gal'Tsus was scarred all over his dark green skin and his right tusk was shorn in half slantwise down the middle where a human sword had landed in a battle long ago. Gal'Tsus had hands the size of boulders even with two of the fingers on the left hand and one on the right missing. His legs were like tree trunks, and his chest was the size of one of their effigies where they hung their prey. All of this hid a deceptively quick frame, and as Gal'Tsus often said, "a bloody heart ready to win victory for all orcs." Yet even with all that immense strength and skill, even Gal'Tsus did not ignore the Blood Thralls when they said they had a message from Magdris.

Already one such message had come, one hour before his *entertainment*, in the form of a sphere of blood. The sphere flew, dripping ichor and vitriol in its wake, and eventually rested above the encampment's central effigy. There, hovering above the spiked wooden trunk, the bloodsphere whispered, or at least that's the closest thing Gal'Tsus could attribute to the awful emanation that came from it. He remembered the living offerings wailing as if they had gone through some incomprehensible torment. A torment that was exacerbated by a constant stream of blood and ichor that was disgorged from the sphere. Gal'Tsus himself had felt on edge from the display, and it wasn't until Bur'Yari came to his side that any answers were provided.

"It has a message," Bur'Yari said plaintively. "And for a bloodsphere of 'dat size, this message could've only been bought wit' death."

Gal'Tsus had grunted in appreciation at his blood mage's explanation. Bur'Yari then had taken the liberty to convene with the sphere. As soon as the Blood Thrall had begun his séance to interact with the blood-soaked orb, a new more prodigious cascade of blood issued forth from the sphere. The blood poured like a waterfall, soaking the effigy and its ill-fated inhabitants, who—in exhausted agony—whimpered. Sounds of terrible wroth bellowed out of the sphere, lashing the onlookers with a sense of utter dread and woe. A near imperceptible droning, like the sound of a multitudinous hive of insects, whirred in between the wailing emanations of the sphere and the Blood Thrall. An aura of uneasiness pervaded the air and Gal'Tsus felt sick, his head throbbing, until finally the sphere divulged its last ounce of blood.

The last slop sluiced down the effigy's face, which had been followed by an ominous silence. Everyone there, including the effigy-impaled prisoners, remained in stunned silence until Bur'Yari finally spoke.

"Dus'Mek is dead. 'long with our scouting party … it's like ya feared, boss. Da humans are here," Bur'Yari said slowly, evidently afraid of his lord's reprisal. When that did not come, he continued nervously, "Dus'Mek used da last of 'imself to send us this *message*."

Gal'Tsus was taken aback by the revelation, knowing that it was no easy feat to take down Dus'Mek. An orc who was no young 'thing', and who had not only slain his fair share of foes but had also been one of the most prolific Blood Thralls in Kos'Raga. It was nearly unbelievable, but although Magdris was many things, he was not a liar. Any message carried *solely* by the magic of Magdris, the magic of the Crimson King, was unlikely to allow a lie-tainted message to be carried forth. And they didn't commune with other gods.

Gal'Tsus had stewed over the message, choosing to entertain himself with the feast he had given to his sows. Now, it seemed that Magdris had more to say, and Gal'Tsus's mind reeled back to the present as Bur'Yari conveyed another—final—message from their patron god, "Magdris isn't happy." Bur'Yari's eyes were in the back of his skull and his head was flung back facing the sky. "He wants more blood, our effigy is too small," the Blood Thrall said.

A moment passed and Bur'Yari coughed violently, so much so that even Gal'Tsus thought that the Blood Thrall was going to die. Yet, just as Gal'Tsus began to approach the afflicted shaman, Bur'Yari doubled over, hacked one huge gobbet of spittle, and then vomited out a small spasm of blood. Gal'Tsus had seen it before with the Blood Thralls and knew that their magic, their ability to talk to the lord of blood, required copious amounts of vitriol. Whether that vitriol came from the Blood Thrall or not didn't matter.

With the blood evacuated, the Blood Thrall spoke, "Humans. Those humans to our south. Those plague-ridden savages who have slain one of my loyal followers would do well as a source of food for your clan," Bur'Yari said, but as if his voice was not his own. Bur'Yari, the blood-red ruby on his chest glowing like fire, spoke again, but with what could only be described as the voice of Magdris, "This feasting would let us become strong enough to build a massive warband. A warband to rival those cursed scale-skins that have humiliated you since you arrived here."

Gal'Tsus roared in anger at the mention of the cursed lizardfolk. Many months ago, Gal'Tsus had led over four hundred warriors, young and old, along with a complement of sows across the salty water, and for many months he had lost warrior after warrior to lizardmen ambushes. The scale-skins, as his warband had taken to calling them, would appear out of nowhere, kill one or two warriors, drag off the bodies, and disappear all before anyone could respond. Until the last few weeks, his warriors had not killed or captured a single enemy. Now the effigy was hung with two of the smaller scaly skinned foes, which reminded Gal'Tsus of the small skinks that lived in Kos'Raga.

It was a small pittance for what they had done. It was not enough. Gal'Tsus, the warband, and Magdris demanded more. More blood, more slaughter, and more feasting would be the only way to assuage the anger.

His clan, upon the whispers of Magdris, left the old world many moons ago. Those whispers had led them to a human settlement on the coast of the old world somewhere far north of the badlands. There they slaughtered the village, burned it to the ground, and took four of the big wooden rafts the humans liked to float around on. Although the warband, much like all orcs, was terrified of the big water. He recalled the pitiful sight of not one but several of his warriors as they tried to swim back to land never to be seen again. What was worse was that one of the big rafts had simply disappeared in the night. Yet, Gal'Tsus at the word of his Blood Thralls—Bur'Yari and the now dead Dus'Mek—persisted, and his clan floated on the salt water for many sunrises and sunsets. They had persisted on what rotten food and provisions the humans had stored on the boats, and with their crude faith in their bloodthirsty god, they eventually crashed into land once again.

Now here they were being led by the blood god again. Led to a juicy human settlement, Gal'Tsus mused wolfishly.

He vowed that he would give Magdris all the blood he would ever need. In the open space past the sow pits and in front of the smaller orc huts, two youngbloods were fighting. Gal'Tsus knew exactly what to do to inspire his clan. He leapt out of the pit, forgetting his earlier desire to mate, and began to stride confidently toward the brawl. Naught but ten meters away, he stopped and observed the fight, the youngbloods were unaware their chieftain watched them. They were no more than four years old, just starting their journey to becoming warriors, and—Gal'Tsus's reckoned— no larger than one of the human fighters.

A savage lunge managed to knock one youngblood off balance, but he quickly recovered and darted to one side as another lunge came for his

face. The lunging youngblood overreached and now his side was dangerously exposed. Taking advantage of the situation, the elusive youngblood
grappled around his enemy's torso, lifted him clean off the ground, and
performed a nasty suplex on the off-balance orc. The suplexed orc looked
dazed, and Gal'Tsus swore he heard something break during the fall. As it
became clear that the dazed orc was alive but not willing to rise and fight
again, Gal'Tsus made his decision.

He approached the two youngbloods. Other orcs had gathered not
only to witness the brawl but also because they had noticed their war chief
taking an interest in the fight. Now, those orcs cleared space for their massive leader, many of whom knew all too well what was about to happen.
The currently victorious youngblood was tossed aside by one massive hand
from Gal'Tsus, who threw the considerably sized youngster like he
weighed no more than a small stone. The dazed orc realized his fate and
tried to scurry away. *Too late.*

Gal'Tsus reached down with both hands, slapping them on the orc's
exposed shoulders. He hauled the youngblood up into the air with a tug,
grabbed the orc's legs with one massive hand, and heaved his victim in a
vise-like grip over his head. The orc squealed and squirmed but could not
escape. Gal'Tsus roared at the watching orcs, and, with one deft motion,
dropped the youngblood on an outstretched knee. A loud crack splintered
the air and instantly the squealing orc fell silent. His spine was severed, and
his life was spent.

"Magdris!" Gal'Tsus yelled. "Magdris, I give you this boon!" He beseeched the heavens, searching the sky for his Crimson King.

He roared a deafening bellow into the sky, and after a reverential
pause, he carried the corpse to the effigy. Seeing an empty spike on a lower
tier, he flung the corpse with one hand, impaling the body onto the massive
wooden trunk. Blood welled around the hole made by the spike and the

corpse slid down slowly, making a macabre sucking noise. Bur'Yari moved to stand beside the war chief, careful to be out of arms reach.

"'Dat should keep our lord happy for now," Bur'Yari spoke gently.

"'Dat youngblood wouldn't 'ave made it," Gal'Tsus said.

"Yes, boss," Bur'Yari paused giving time for his honorific to do its appeasement. "Yet, I wonder if'n the humans we captured would know more 'bout Magdris's vision." Bur'Yari bowed in placation.

Gal'Tsus looked at the Blood Thrall with pure malice. "Ya think I don't know that? You're lucky ya can speak to Magdris! I should impale ya right 'ere for your insolence!"

His anger was frothing, already at a boiling point from the day's events. He clenched his fists in rage, wondering how stupid the Blood Thrall thought he was. The foolish Bur'Yari must have thought he was just some dog to be led. Still, he knew that going south was the best option and that he would probably discover the most about the humans straight from the two pathetic flesh bags they had recently captured. Besides, it was always a good time to torment something.

A wicked smile crossed his face, and Gal'Tsus looked at the cowed Blood Thrall. "Chop 'dat pathetic youngblood up and feed 'em to the warriors. I will talk to the *humans*."

"Yes, boss," Bur'Yari said, hurrying away to do his master's bidding and avoid his wrath.

Yet before he could, Gal'Tsus—with lightning speed—snapped his hand outwards, grabbing the Blood Thrall's shoulder. He spun the orc around, forcing him to face his master. "If'n you ever t'ink to make a suggestion to me 'dat ain't a message from Magdris 'gain, I'll gut you like a fish," Gal'Tsus said malevolently.

Bur'Yari squealed inadvertently, "Ye-Ye-Yes boss, never again."

"Good … Now go!" Gal'Tsus said pushing the Blood Thrall away. He watched Bur'Yari stumble away, grabbing his crude butcher's blade as he did so. The hunk of crudely sharpened iron made a sickening thwacking noise as it sliced off huge chunks of flesh, which were then thrown into the rapidly gathering crowd of orcs. Gal'Tsus, still on the raised wooden platform that held the effigy, turned to his warband. He roared, raising his hands as he did so. The gathering orcs roared back, their blood now up at the display they just witnessed. Even the youngblood who had been spared was jumping with delight, his face now stained with blood from a hunk of flesh that had been tossed near him.

"Magdris has spoken! Our lord of blood wants us to go deal with soft human runts to our south. Blood Thrall says that there is an encampment of weaklings 'der! Well ..." Gal'Tsus paused for a moment, lowering his hands, and surveying the watching crowd. He began again after he was satisfied with the apprehensive silence, "Magdris don't like that those filthy ingrates are here. So, we fix that, we burn da puny human village to da ground!" He yelled as he raised his fist into the air, prompting another roar of approval.

"Get ready! We move soon. And when we get 'der, I promise that all bellies will be full of flesh! Juicy ... human ... flesh!" he roared accentuating each word with relish.

Now his clan was in a frenzy, ecstatic at the prospect of loot and fresh meat. Gal'Tsus lowered his fist and smiled wryly at the watching crowd. *Surely, the blood lord would approve of that!* After a moment's pause, basking in the glory of his warband's admiration, he headed off towards the iron-wrought cages used to keep prisoners.

# Chapter Six

## Gal'Tsus

Gal'Tsus made his way past ramshackle huts that were in a crude semi-circle around the southern portion of the effigy. Here the warriors who were newly blooded or had not yet risen to a higher standing within the clan lived. Orcs with an inkling of respect amongst others and thus were afforded the luxury of a roof over their heads. A roof they generally shared with ten or fifteen other warriors. As the war chief made his way past the huts, he came to a clearing that spanned outwards roughly one hundred meters and ringed the ramshackle huts, in the same manner, those huts ringed the effigy. Here the lowest rungs of orc society, the youngbloods and the crippled, lived, having to share the space with the prisoners.

Gal'Tsus grunted in disgust. The prisoners here had been spared the spikes of the effigy but that was not necessarily a better fate. Unbeknownst to them they usually were only kept alive so that their meat would stay fresher. Plus, Gal'Tsus always enjoyed it when the victims of the spiked effigy would scream. You could never get a good scream from a dead prisoner.

Although this area had its vision obscured by the warrior's ramshackle bone and wood huts, orc society ensured that everyone could see some portion of that glorious central spire. A spire that consisted of a large wooden totem, generally formed from a large oak or ash trunk, was barbed with malicious metal spikes and studded with small chunks of ruby-colored stone. Stones that the Blood Thralls long ago learned helped them commune with Magdris. This was always the epicenter of any encampment he had ever known, and the orcs devoted everything to its upkeep.

An ambitious youngblood could at any time—day or night—look to the center and see the splendor of the orcish race and, of course, the glory that was the Crimson King. Gal'Tsus noted that on occasion the prisoner's proximity to the edge of the encampment had invited some to escape, but that was just how it was. Although he was known to be a rather smart orc for his kind, he was not one to fly in the face of tradition. Especially if that flight would only grant him a slightly better hold onto prisoners he frankly did not care about. The youngbloods and the cripples were meant to take care of the prisoners, whether that meant keeping them alive or using them as practice did not matter. Also, the thought of anything other than an orc next to his sows *or* his effigy—unless they were being impaled on it—made him sick. So, Gal'Tsus found his way to this land of misfits, and there spotted a stack of cages with two frightened-looking humans huddled together in the corner.

There were five of the ramshackle cages stacked haphazardly together, and none of them seemed to have been made by the same craftsmanship. Gal'Tsus knew that the few orcs that were gifted with metalworking, the only artisanal skill of value, tended to completely forget how they made an object. Only to have to relearn it in its entirety when they needed it again. It was prime orcish behavior, and to Gal'Tsus made much more sense. No need to load his head up with some nonsense he may never use again. Instead, fill his head with thoughts of a fresh kill hung on the effigy, a young sow, and something to fight.

The shadows were beginning to lengthen and a particularly bold youngblood came racing over to his war chief with a lit torch in hand. Gal'Tsus, in a better mood due to seeing the puny humans cower before him and seeing as how the torch gave him the light he needed to see the pathetic humans cower in fear, decided not to rip the youngblood's head off.

"Where's yer filthy little city at?" Gal'Tsus asked the pair of humans. Both of which were now shaking visibly in fear. The larger one, a male by Gal'Tsus's reckoning, looked downtrodden and beaten. His eye was swollen, and it looked as if his arm hung more limply, that is more limply than a normal human arm. The other human, a fiery-haired female, still looked as defiant as ever. Even by human female standards, this one was small. She looked wiry though, like some of the more agile youngbloods, and Gal'Tsus could see cords of muscle on her slender frame. Gal'Tsus had already noted her defiance and told himself that when he finally threw her on the effigy, he would make it quick. A small token of honor to an enemy that showed courage.

Even now the red-haired human was obstinate and stared directly at Gal'Tsus. There was challenge in her eyes, even in her weakened and vulnerable state, but as Gal'Tsus learned long ago any sign of a threat to his authority would grow and fester. Without warning, he charged the cage, lifting its end into the air at a forty-five-degree angle. The humans shrieked involuntarily and held one another at the side of the cage still on the ground. Gal'Tsus roared at them through the bars. His bellow finally cowed the female, and she looked away from his *magnificence*. She understood. He let go of the cage, allowing it to drop heavily to the ground.

With his authority sufficiently secured, he decided to begin his interrogation. He knew that he stood to gain little from this interaction, but he loved to look at his enemies, to taunt them, and to gauge their resolve. Gal'Tsus had dealt with enough humans to know they couldn't understand the *superior* orc dialect, but nevertheless, he liked talking to his prisoners. He found that when he did speak to them, most looked more afraid and even *more* apprehensive. Even now he could tell that both humans were more wide-eyed—more afraid—his speech prompting some sort of instinctual response.

"Well … ya gonna speak? Ya, ingrates," he queried them again, and he watched as they visibly recoiled from his words. The female simply shook her head, indicating that she did not understand. The male was holding his limp arm, whimpering as he did so.

Then an idea struck him, an idea that relied on the very minimal knowledge he had of the human language. An idea that would make his torture of the humans worth more than just pure satisfaction. *Hu-Hu-Human that's what they call themselves.* As the terrified humans looked at him, he suddenly smiled. A toothy grin that made both of his victims recoil, "Human … wh-where," Gal'Tsus said with difficulty.

He had to say each syllable slowly and deliberately, and as he did so, he looked around with his hands out. Gal'Tsus had survived long enough and had captured enough of the puny folk to have picked up some of their speech and communication, but those two small words and the gesture were reaching the extent of his knowledge. He was not the first orc to speak human words, but there couldn't have been more than a few. It was obvious these humans had never heard an orc speak their filthy tongue.

Gal'Tsus waited a few heartbeats, and when they just looked at him dumbfounded, he repeated the question louder. "HUMAN WHERE," he shouted the words, garbling the annunciation into a near incomprehensible mess. He paused once again after yelling, hoping for a response. When the humans just glanced at one another, seemingly uncertain of what to do, he reached out to lift the cage once more.

"Wait!" the fiery redhead spoke. The word was foreign to him, but he had sworn he heard it before. A whisper of memories in which terrified humans held up their hands, using that word before he landed the killing blow.

"Humans are gone," she said again, and with a look of sorrow, she shook her head. "We are the only ones." Gal'Tsus didn't understand a word she said, but he understood that she was trying to indicate that there were no humans. *She lied! What 'bout Dus'Mek!?*

Suddenly he grabbed the cage, lifted it, and bellowed again. "HUMAN WHERE," he roared at them as he let the cage slam down again. This time the humans did not have time to respond to him lifting the cage and both fell face first. A cry of pain was heard from the male. He reveled in their agony, choosing to lower himself to the now-prone female. He savored her defeat; her dazed expression as she tried to recover herself. He brought his massive head within centimeters of hers. The shadows created by the youngblood's torch gave his already malevolent face an even more sinister appeal, and as she raised her head—still stunned—Gal'Tsus could see the effect his visage had.

Her eyes, at first glazed by the sudden jolt from the crashing cage, bolted open. White orbs dominated her face, and after the initial facial movements her body stayed motionless; paralyzed. Gal'Tsus could smell the fear, and he knew that her resolve was nearly broken. "Human … where?" He asked again, but this time in the gentler tone he had used originally.

He could see the conflict in her face, the twitching muscles, the near imperceptible tremors in her brows. All of it indecision. That age old debate on whether she should save herself by betraying her own or whether she should lie and risk herself. In the end, he knew she would save herself; they always did.

She pointed past him, pointed south, and said in a tremulous near whisper, "South."

Gal'Tsus smiled and reached out one massive finger, which was nearly the size of her forearm, and gently touched her cheek. In his language, he crooned to his prisoner, "Good."

She closed her eyes at his touch, and wet, warm, liquid coursed down her cheeks. A few drops of which touched Gal'Tsus's finger. He recoiled in disgust. The human female seized the opportunity of his distraction to flee to the back of the cage. Gal'Tsus flicked the disgusting fluid from his finger and roared once again. As he watched the female grasp onto her companion, trying desperately to find comfort, he felt a surge of joy, which quickly replaced the disgust from the warm salty liquid.

Gal'Tsus was no fool, and he knew that the human might try to mislead him. Yet, in that moment—as he already knew—the human had indicated and spoken true. The humans were south, and he had hardly needed her confirmation to know that. Gal'Tsus knew that he had planted the seeds of thralldom into the once defiant female, and that seed would continue to grow into a more and more competent slave guide. Gal'Tsus had hoped, with some *motivation* of course, that by the time they had reached her settlement, she would be betraying everything she knew about her filthy kin.

In the beginning, like many other humans, she may try to deceive them, but daily reminders of Gal'Tsus's prowess would serve well to prevent the worst excesses of that. Magdris's teeth, even if she were not to guide them, Gal'Tsus would scour the land in front of them as they marched south until they found a trace of humanity. That would only serve to slow them by a few days. For now, she would remain alive but enthralled by him.

As for the male, he would impale him on the effigy tomorrow, using his death as another lesson to the female to not resist his power. He sighed, thinking of the work ahead. He stared at the indigent humans. All of it could wait until tomorrow. For now, he had sows to breed and an army to gather. He turned back towards the effigy *and* the sow pit.

# Chapter Seven

## Bella

*Zip … zip … zip.* Bella paused, waiting for a response. Her arms burned with the motion, and her hand felt hot from the constant friction. *Zip … zip … zip.* She paused again, listening for the sound of her jailors or a sign from her cellmate. She continued to saw away at the crude but rather reluctant piece of metal that held her prison closed. *Zip … zip … zip.* What little light she had to guide herself came from the silver of a waning crescent moon. Her breathing grew heavy, and she struggled to keep herself motivated enough to keep working. *Zip … zip … zip.* She looked back at her cellmate, Godfrey, who had a broken arm, a battered face, and torn mail and clothes. His once chipper demeanor now replaced by an exuberance of despair. *Zip … zip … zip.* She knew she must press on; she knew that they had to escape … tonight. *Zip … zip … zip.*

She could hardly gauge the passage of time. It felt like at least three hours since their encounter with the hulking monstrosity that could only be the leader of their imprisoners. Three hours since the brute—in his fury—had dislodged a small hunk of metal from the ramshackle cage that held them. Three hours since Godfrey had pointed to a metal pin that upon closer inspection appeared to be the only thing holding the cage door in place. Bella remembered thinking how that would be preposterous, *surely the door would be affixed with more security?*

Yet, as she had thought of the discrepancy, she had glanced at the cages around her. They all were of different designs, all for the same purpose of course, but no two cages were alike. After seeing the sheer crudity of orc design, the concept became less and less ludicrous. She had dared to hope that if she could only saw through that pin, they could reach freedom. After all, she dared not imagine what would happen to her and Godfrey if they remained prisoners. *Zip … zip … zip.*

The big orc who had slammed their heavy cage like it was a toy would surely increase his sadistic torments as time passed. She still remembered the sheer glee, or what could only be mistaken as glee from an orc, as he had stared into her face. As he had looked into her eyes—full of terror— she knew he had wrought pleasure from the exchange. She had also seen intelligence. Not the intelligence that one would expect from a scholar, like Sophia, but the unmistakable intelligence of a sentient being. A being capable of warfare, capable of slaughter, and capable of torture. There, in that beast's eyes, Bella could see that the orc planned *something* for her. Just like how he had broken her resolve and forced her to point towards Elgion. Well, where she thought Elgion was. No, he would continue to subjugate her to barbarity. Barbarity that would force her to do what she was loathed to do, guide him and his warband to Elgion, to the pioneers, to Alexa and Sophia, and beyond. *Zip … zip … zip.*

That could not happen. She would rather die. *Zip … zip … zip.* Before she allowed herself to become an orcish thrall, she would stab herself with the metal she was now using to try and purchase freedom. Yet, deep inside herself, she felt uncertain. Uncertain that she could face death or that brute and resist the fear; resist the desire to survive. *Zip … zip … zip.*

"Psst," Godfrey whispered.

Immediately, Bella halted her sawing, fear omnipotent. She dared to look over her shoulder at her sentry. His good arm was raised, an artifact from his soldiery, an artifact that would normally warn his followers of danger. He glanced to and fro, and, before long, a smaller orc came stumbling by with a lit torch in hand. The beast grunted profusely, as was common in their kind, and clumsily traipsed past the cage. Bella and Godfrey were stone still, fearing any reprisal from their captors, yet none came. After several minutes, Godfrey gently nudged Bella with his boot, indicating the 'all clear'. *Zip ... zip ... zip.* It had been more than three hours now, and for those three hours, they had kept up this charade. They had pretended to be cowed, to be defeated, and to be utterly despondent. Yet at the same moment, they continued to fight for their freedom. *Zip ... zip ... zip.* Bella could see the pin was nearly severed. Her arms quaked with pain. Bones and sinew were being forced to continue past exhaustion. Muscles and tendons were being forced to endure when they had screamed for a break an hour and a half before.

*Zip ... zip ... zip,* she couldn't quit, giving in was not an option. Whenever her own will faltered, she just glanced back at Godfrey. A man who had been through a hellish plethora of pain, and he *still* kept guard. He *still* kept fighting, and if he kept fighting ... so would she. *Zip ... zip ... zip.*

Suddenly, the metal gave way, leaving Bella stunned. One moment she felt nothing but resistance, nothing but the hot metal in her hands, and nothing but the absolute agony of what seemed like an insurmountable task. The next moment all she felt was her iron grip holding the makeshift file; all of which hung loosely at her side. She just stared at the metal door, and behind her, she heard a slight intake of breath from Godfrey. The moment they had been fighting for was there, and both were stunned by their victory. Yet, just as she began to feel elation, the consequence of sawing a linchpin from its mooring came true. The crude metal door tipped— slowly at first—and Bella, stiff from exhaustion and stunned by her accomplishment, just watched.

As the contraption made its descent, her reflexes finally kicked in where her mind would not. Years of training with animal and blade forced her muscle memory into action. Impulsively, she reached out to slow the descent of the cage, but her hand still gripped the makeshift file, and the contact of metal on metal rang out. She cringed at the sound, but nothing besides preventing the crash of the door could be done now. She kicked her heels back, trying to heave it upright, but the weight of the orcish monstrosity pulled her down.

No matter her resistance, she couldn't stop it. In a sudden flurry, the metal bars came crashing to the ground with her in tow. As it landed—with a much too loud crash—it flung Bella. She flipped in the air, landing a few meters from the cage itself. She skidded on her backside for a couple painful meters.

She groaned, both from the sudden jolt of pain but also from the surety that the whole enterprise was jeopardized. She groaned because she knew that at any minute a stream of angry bloodthirsty orcs would come running at them from the dark. Yet, lying there waiting for her demise, nothing happened.

No sounds of scuffling footsteps, no howls of rage, or even any cries from the creatures of the night could be heard. It was as if Sophia herself had blessed them with some spell of illusion, some trick of the night. If Bella could believe her luck, the only two who had noticed the tremendous cacophony were herself and Godfrey.

"Come on, mum, we best get going," Godfrey said as he shuffled over to her side. Bella smiled up at him, hardly believing their luck. Godfrey returned the gesture and, with a playful tone, spoke again, "Well, I know I'm a handsome bastard, but we can't just stare at each other."

Bella couldn't help but chuckle, and the two risked a small laugh in the dark. After all, *if the crashing metal didn't alert anyone what could a small laugh do?* She grabbed Godfrey's good arm which he offered to her in assistance. As he pulled her up, she grunted, "How in all of the Maiden's blessings did they not hear that?"

"Gods know, mum, but I'll be damned if I'm gonna stay and find out," Godfrey said. Bella could see Godfrey's laugh turn into a grimace as he brought her upright. She could see the pain course through him.

She'd brought them to this. Her impulsive charge had brought them here.

She shook her head, both to knock the intrusive thought out and to clear her mind. They were in near darkness, save for some faint moonlight and the red cast of torchlight dotted throughout the orcish encampment. Knowing that Godfrey was seriously injured, she wrapped her arm around his torso and threw his good arm around her shoulder to take his weight. "I know yer a handsome bastard, but don't get any ideas."

"Just when I thought we were starting to like one another," Godfrey chuckled. Immediately a groan emanated from him, echoing his regret at the laugh. The sudden move to help her and his effort to pull her upright had taken its toll, and Bella knew she would have to carry him free of this wretched place. Free from the death that haunted them here.

*You killed Godwin.* The voice in her head intruded again. *You brought him here to die.*

"Shut up," she said aloud. The wane torchlight showed astonishment gleaning on Godfrey's face.

"Sorry … still just shook," Bella apologized weakly. She tried to lighten the mood again, "Now let's get your broken self out of here."

Together they shuffled southwards, away from the torches, and away from the cursed encampment. As they walked out of the torchlight, they heard the unmistakable grunts of the orc patrols. Bella continued to pull Godfrey along, hurrying him faster than she would under better circumstances.

"They are sniffing around, I guess someone heard us after all," Godfrey said with effort. Both had heard the unmistakable sound of their piggish snorts.

It was only a matter of time. Together, stumbling in the dark, they passed the first stand of trees that ringed the encampment, and, as they passed under the boughs, Bella felt a small measure of security.

"We ain't outta the woods yet," Godfrey said with forced humor.

The escape must have rekindled the more affable nature of the stalwart soldier, even in light of the pain he must be feeling. She pushed him on until they had trudged about one hundred meters into the dark forest. She pushed him until the thickening trees blotted out what little light had illuminated the night. There she placed him down, and he settled his back heavily onto a thick fir tree. "How are you feeling?" she asked gently.

"Right as rain mum, right as rain," he replied, and Bella decided his affirmation was most decidedly a lie.

"You have a broken arm, several broken ribs, a bruised face, and despite earlier opinions one ugly … ugly face. So no, you ain't right as rain," she said in a light but reproachful manner.

"Alright, maybe a smidge less than well. But it ain't gonna matter once those dumb brutes figure us out. I'm surprised their guard hasn't sniffed us already." Godfrey grunted, the pain coursing through his body.

He turned gingerly, twisting his torso against the tree to look behind him and back towards the orc encampment. From here it looked like no more than a dark lump in the ground with one massive candle in the center. The memory of Godwin was still fresh in Bella's mind, his corpse being impaled onto that center spire. The spire that the orcs obviously revered, a spire that seemed to be visible from all areas of the encampment. She likened it to a temple, and she shuddered at the thought of what mad gods the orcs must worship if their temples required such macabre offerings.

"Alright, let's see what we can do here," Godfrey said as he twisted back around. He tore a piece of his tunic off and fashioned a sling from the scrap of cloth.

"I figure if we can get back up this hill *and* if the wind is in our favor we can clear out from these bastards before dawn," Bella said with conviction.

"Yes, *mum*," Godfrey replied with some mock sternness. He stood, testing the makeshift sling he had made for his broken arm, and to demonstrate his readiness he nodded stiffly to Bella.

The pair set off into the dark. No torch could guide them, because they could not risk the light. They could not risk being caught again, especially after the brutality of being imprisoned the first time. Most of Godfrey's injuries had been sustained in that tumultuous time. Bella had been fortunate enough to be knocked unconscious and thus was no more than a piece of cargo to the orcs. Albeit their care for cargo was not much better than it would be for a living being.

Godfrey—unfortunately for him—had been conscious during the whole process, and as humans are prone to do … resisted the whole time. His resistance had been rewarded with several blows to his face and torso, earning him several broken ribs and a bruised face. His broken arm was a gift granted to him after he lashed out at one of the orcs for tossing Bella's unconscious body carelessly against the back of the cage.

Of course, Bella only knew of this from what Godfrey had told her when she had come too. A daze of pain and a swirl of confusion had greeted her when she had finally woken. The debilitating blow she had received now was just a harsh headache and a solid lump on her skull. Godfrey had been the only thing there that had made sense at first, and he had helped her gain her bearings.

In the broad daylight of the orc encampment, they had huddled together as far to the back of the cage as possible. Like scared rabbits, they had cowered away from the multitude of big and small orcs that had passed them by. Most did not even pay them attention, but a select few came by either growling, rattling the cage, or a combination of both in order to frighten them. Their reactions—no matter how stoic—always rendered a laugh or chuckle from the grizzly brutes, and Bella knew that they would die or wish they were dead if they had stayed.

Now, they stumbled on root and branch as they made their way up the hillside forest. Already, she felt like they had made it one-thousand-meters away from their prison. She looked back at Godfrey just in time to see him catch his foot in a root, falter, and begin to fall. She was too far to help him, and she saw him instinctually trying to reach out with his broken arm. The sliver of moonlight illuminated the grimace of pain he felt from the movement, and she watched as he stiffened and collapsed to the hillside.

"Uggh," Godfrey grunted, loud enough to make Bella wince. She rushed down the hillside to him, immediately trying to lift him back to his feet.

"Are you hurt?"

As he gained his feet, and as he made a hyperbolic cascade of grunts and groans, he replied, "No, no. I ain't dead yet." Together they stood, looking at one another, and for a moment their eyes shared a moment of consolation. A memory and a recognition of shared pain and for a moment … of haunting agony. Then those eyes widened to expose sheer terror. Terror brought on by a lone orcish war horn.

"Let's go!" Bella shouted, and she yanked on Godfrey's good arm. They still had no light and were forced to scramble over obstacles that only appeared suddenly from the shadows. Yet, there was no time for caution, already Bella could hear a plethora of piggish squeals. She stole a quick glance back as she helped Godfrey over a fallen tree trunk and saw the plain light up with torches. She hefted the wounded man over the trunk and pushed on his backside, urging him up a particularly onerous stretch of hill. Together they stumbled over a rock that capped the embankment they climbed, and together they collapsed at the beginning of a small stretch of hillside meadow.

"Ditch some of your clothes," she said to Godfrey. She tore off an already torn sleeve and tossed it into some bushes to her right. Godfrey, seeing that she was trying to create a false trail, took off a crusty sweatband from his scalp and tossed it. "Now let's hope they aren't just sniffing for fun," she said as they darted off sharply to the left.

They crashed over another embankment. Bella knew that the trail they were leaving would be so obvious that a child could follow it, but she was clinging to hope. The stinking bits of clothes may delay them for a second or two, but a second or two might be all they need to find a river or other such salvation. The orcs were howling now, enthralled by the nighttime hunt.

She could see that the horizon was being kissed by the first taste of daybreak, and a purplish haze was lifting the veil of night. They had worked through the small hours to secure their release, and neither she nor Godfrey had rested much since their capture. One would think that their captors would have gotten significant rest, but Bella had never seen them stop moving, and she knew they couldn't have slept much the night before. After all, they had been busy subduing Bella, Godfrey, Godwin, and Blythe. *Gods know where he is, if he even made it out.* And now these brutes were up and about at full tilt. She couldn't help but feel that orcs operated at levels well above that of human endurance. Their only saving grace was the cloven hoof design of the orcish foot, an organ designed to carry immense weight—not for speedy travel. Yet still, the beasts were gaining on the two.

They crashed into another grove of trees that was about fifty meters away from the flat meadow. "Back uphill," Bella said, her breath shallow due to the exhaustion.

Godfrey did not respond, but just lunged up the hill, his breath labored. They climbed another steep embankment, using brush and saplings as makeshift rungs to a hillside ladder. Bella's heart was racing now, and she knew that they would have to stop soon; however, she could not see the crest of the hill. Godfrey's foot slid downhill after a poorly placed footfall. He righted himself clumsily, and after looking up the hill he hung his head in despair.

Bella, not wanting to continue either, used the moment for a small slice of respite, and together they stole a few breaths. A few seconds passed and another horn, this one much closer now, prompting them to move again. Neither had to speak; instead, they trudged up the hill in desperation. Another agonizing minute passed as the pair pushed themselves, sucking in massive breaths between exertions. Both were near collapse and just as Bella felt like she was going to give up, they reached another flattened meadow.

This time, with the aid of the grey wolf light of dawn, Bella could see for at least one hundred meters. A flat open space with sparsely dotted trees lay before them. As she surveyed the open terrain, an earth-shattering roar sounded just down the hill. Bella knew that that must be the massive tyrant that had forced her into submission. Her blood curdled as fear embraced her.

"Let's go," Godfrey said, a modicum of his breath recaptured. Together they set off at a jog, covering the open ground quickly. Strands of tall foxtail grass were gaining their first touch of golden brown; a color they would wear all winter. The splash of color made navigating the terrain easier, and Godfrey and Bella had both regained their breath by the time they reached the end of the clearing.

Bella glanced behind them, and she could just see the tips of torchlight cresting the hill. The enemy was hot on their trail, and she hoped the torchlight would keep them night blind.

Godfrey was already pulling himself up the hill, ready for another bout with the physical torment they had just endured.

Bella pushed up the slope. Her thighs felt like fire and her calves were reaching the point of cramping. Still, they pushed on. She could taste blood and metal in her ragged breath. The metallic tinge accompanied her inability to speak. For minutes, the duo strained their physicality to the limit. Their heads bowed and tongues silent as they endured their trek. The early dawn was pierced by heavy breaths and by piggish grunts. An occasional whoop or holler piercing the rhythmic breathing, like a discordant instrument in an orchestra of exertion. Bella knew they were getting closer, that the orcs were closing the gap, and in a few minutes, they would be overtaken. But they *could not* give up. She knew that she *must not* give up.

They scratched and clawed their way up the slope which was dominated by dormant grass, rocks, and patches of fir and pine trees. Every step was agony, and the passage of time felt like a crawl for Bella, as was common when pain was the domineering emotion. All of her focus was dedicated to her breath; dedicated to putting her next step forward. An exercise in will and endurance that required immense fortitude just to push for that next upward step.

Her foot slipped slightly on the loose soil, and the recoiling action gave her time to look behind her. There she saw three orcs, illuminated by torchlight on the hillside they climbed. With tremendous effort, she forced her voice between ragged breaths, "We ... must ... hurry."

"Hilltop," Godfrey replied in a hoarse ragged breath. He managed to lift his good hand slightly and pointed up the damnable slope they were on.

Bella could see rays of morning sunshine piercing through a line of pine trees. With what energy she had left she pushed herself off to the right of Godfrey and bear-climbed up the remaining steps. It was still one hundred meters or so off, and Bella's pace—quick at first—turned into the desperate clawing of the doomed. The orcs, once a distant braying, were now whooping with delight. They could taste their prey, and before long they would. She pushed herself past the point of reason, into that abyss of survival that overrides any logical thought and turns the body into a weapon.

A weapon honed on a unified goal, and her goal lay within just a few more bounding steps. With a final breath, she hurled herself up to the top of the hill, cresting its slope and collapsing onto the relatively flat surface. It still rose, but very gently now, and pine trees were in thick droves. Enough space lay between each tree to allow the morning sunlight through.

That morning light, so blinding in its brilliance, illuminated her. She lay now on her back, sucking in huge mouthfuls of air and grimacing against the pain of muscle fatigue. A few seconds later she heard Godfrey collapse not far from her. The two of them both gasping in the cold mountain air; both of them bathed in the morning sun. She lay there on the grass recovering for several seconds, unconcerned with her pursuers. Her body had given her the last of its strength, and in doing so it had also given her the feeling of victory when she had crossed that hilltop. Now as her senses swirled back into normalcy, she realized that that victory would be very short-lived.

She rolled onto her side, still gasping for air but in between mouthfuls she managed to croak, "Godfrey." He didn't reply, nor did he move at first. He was too focused on his own recovery to care. "Godfrey!" she yelled now with what strength her voice could muster. "Godfrey, w-we gotta move," she stuttered.

He flung his arm up as if to indicate he heard her, but his obeisance was that of heavy reluctance. With excruciating slowness, the pair rose once again. The sound of orcish war cries could be heard halfway up the slope they had just conquered. Judging the distance of the sounds, Bella figured that within thirty seconds they would be within missile range, and in forty-five seconds they would be dead. With a nod of grim determination, Godfrey and Bella started off at a jog across the gentle hilltop.

They jogged about two hundred meters before Bella looked behind her. She could just see the first of the smaller orcs crest the hilltop. She could see their piggish faces—a faint tint of green in the morning—light up at the sight of their prey. Nearing resignation she turned back to her jog, her body past caring at this point, and a numb state of mental apathy had taken over. *It was almost ironic.*

To her left was a beautiful pink sky, touched by the golden rays of the sun. Clouds that were dark just moments prior were now reflecting the rising sun's rays, making the sky look as if Ember had graced the horizon. It truly was beautiful, and that beauty was juxtaposed by some of the foulest creatures to inhabit Telaea naught but a couple hundred meters behind her. Breaking from her small reverie, she noticed an outcropping of rocks coming up on their left. The dull grey of boulders now fully shone in the morning sun. She brought herself alongside Godfrey and simply pointed towards the feature.

It was the beginning of a precipitous slope that dropped off into a steep-sided valley. Pine and fir trees blocked their view to the bottom. Scree and boulders clung loosely to the embankment, making for a rather treacherous-looking decent. She looked over to Godfrey, who like her was resigned to their doom *and* like her must have been thinking the same thing. A violent roar broke her glance as it boomed from their left, a herald of their impending capture—or death. A capture that at best would be an exhortation of the worst misery. A plethora of pain was all that lay in store for them, and so—with little reluctance—she simply turned back to Godfrey and said, "Jump."

Not surprisingly, he simply nodded his head. They both turned towards the slope. It would be impossible to navigate it carefully, and besides, from where they stood, they would need to start their descent by dropping down from a boulder. From there, scree funneled down towards the bottom until it disappeared behind thickening trees. There was no way of knowing if a cliff or other such dangerous obstacle would confront them after that first hurdle, but there *was* a way of knowing what fate would confront them if they did not commit. Bella could sense Godfrey looking back at her, and with another turn of her cheek, she looked at him. They shared in a moment of pain, in a moment of fear, and in a look that served to soothe the nerves. Together they would jump, and together they would discover the fate that lay in wait for them.

With legs feeling like concrete, she urged herself to the edge, and subconsciously she reached out for Godfrey's hand. It, of course, was not there since it still lay in its sling, but Godfrey noticed the gesture and with a hint of his old jovial nature said, "Well, stablemaster. Let's go for a ride."

He jumped. The veteran managed to keep his feet for a few seconds while he slid down the scree, but his lack of balance from the broken arm toppled him. Bella watched the old soldier careen down the hillside for a couple seconds before finally leaping herself. Her timing could not have been better, for just as she dropped, she heard—and felt—the now familiar sound of a throwing axe gliding centimeters from where she had stood. *Fwop fwop fwop!*

She crashed to the ground. Her balance was immediately ripped away by a hidden boulder lying under the scree. She managed to rip her foot free just in time to catch the ground with her next stride, but her momentum was carrying her top half toward the ground faster than her bottom half. She tucked in, trying to land on her shoulder so that she would roll in the combat style that Alexa had shown her. Before she plunged to the ground, she saw Godfrey—rolling haphazardly—disappear behind a stand of pine.

Her first two rolls, although done out of necessity, were relatively controlled. Yet on the third rotation, she rolled faster than she could respond. She came out of her third tuck and attempted to slow her descent by planting her feet down. The angle of the hill and the conserved momentum were too much for her to overcome, and she was catapulted forward— face first. She managed to tuck her head and angle her body slightly to the side. Now, rolling like a log down a hill, she caught every bump and jolt onto her vulnerable body. Her legs slammed into a tree trunk which spun her wildly off course. The sudden loss of control put her in a panic state. A state in which she became solely focused on protecting her head to prevent injury. A multitude of brush and rocks tried to pry her free from the fetal position she had adopted, and, at times, they succeeded.

At times she would sail through the air for a few heartbeats only to slam back into the ground at bone-breaking speed. Nature buffeted her to and fro as she careened down the hill and that unforgiving tempest knocked her limbs astray. Her exposed parts were quickly slammed or raked by nature's claws before she could retract them. Tumbling once again, she rolled off a score of branches and launched into the air. The suspension from pain, for even that split second, felt almost cathartic as she managed to grasp back onto her conscious mind.

That catharsis ended suddenly when she slammed back to Telaea, all control lost. Her limbs splayed out around her as her breath was knocked clear. She felt stunned, her concussed head swelling for a second as it tried to make sense of it all. Fortunately for Bella, her journey down the hill, as sudden as it had begun, now ended in a whirl of pain and confusion.

# Chapter Eight

## Bella

Her senses swam. Her ears rang with a high-pitched whine. Her vision was blurred, and she could not focus on the swirling images before her. Her smell was gone. She wasn't even sure who or what she was at first, her brain in a fog of concussive reality. An involuntary groan escaped her lips, and an involuntary spasm caused her to arch her back. The sudden pain served to stitch her semblance of self back together. With reluctant optimism, she celebrated her ability to still move.

She flexed her fingers gingerly, testing their operation, and once satisfied with that, she felt around her abused body. All over felt like one massive bruise, her legs felt like she had ripped or strained some muscles. Her arms burned from the myriad scrapes and cuts she had sustained. Sudden pain splintered her skull, and she cupped her forehead in her palm as if to take the burden of its weight away. She was in utter agony.

"Godfrey!" she managed to yell out. Then rolled onto her side. The pain was immense, but she managed to roll herself over far enough to more easily right her body. As she sat up, she saw that she was in a dense thicket of pine trees with several moss-covered stones and branches covering the forest floor. The ground, in comparison to the slope she just crashed down, was relatively flat. She hoped this was the end of that slope, unsure she could bear another ounce of downhill as agony ripped through her bruised body.

"Where are you?" she questioned; her voice timorous in the trees. She managed to scoot herself backward into a more comfortable sitting position. Her body ached all over, but no sharp pains, typical of broken bones, ailed her.

"Godfrey!" she yelled out again. A reply came in the form of a rustling bush. She reached down to her right thigh where one of her trusty daggers would have been and was greeted with an empty hand.

Never without a blade, the absence of one made her feel inadequate, especially now. She crossed one of her legs under her buttocks, allowing herself to be able to spring up at a moment's notice. The brush did not rustle again, and the forest was quiet. The disturbance to its domain had not gone unnoticed and something within those thick boughs held its breath. Her neck prickled in anticipation, the unassailable feeling of being watched loomed over her. Almost inadvertently, she called out once more but this time in a whisper, "Godfrey, where in Ember's breath are you?"

"Ughhh," a weak voice replied.

She couldn't pinpoint where the sound came from, but it was off to her left, just out of sight. She forced her worn muscles into action and crouch-walked towards the noise, wincing at the pain with every rickety step. She still held her arm in front of her, as if she held the dagger, knowing that even without a blade it was better to parry a surprise with an arm than with your face.

"Godfrey," she whispered again, but this time from the protection of a large pine tree. There was a stand of rowan berry brush—its bounty near depleted—which blocked her view forward.

"Ughhh … mu-mu-mum," the voice called out slowly, words escaping in a stutter of pain.

The voice was clearly just past the berry brush. Bella pushed through, abandoning caution for the sense of security her comrade would provide. As she cleared it, she saw Godfrey lying on the ground just past a fallen log. His broken arm was a disheveled mess, and one of his legs was twisted at an unnatural angle. He was conscious, writhing what functioning limbs he had in pain. She hurried to his side, kneeling near his torso, her hand caressing his forehead

They had defied death together, and it broke her heart to see him so torn and broken. This man, who had supported her seemingly out of nowhere, had endured alongside her with little more than faith in her abilities to guide him.

With tears threatening her cheeks, she spoke, "It's alright; it's alright." A drop broke free, coursing down her cheek, and her hand brushed over his scalp. She smiled at him, remembering his humor, "Old man."

Slowly, he reached his good hand up, clearly to embrace her, but his strength was failing, and it only managed to breach slightly above his torso. She grasped the hand in hers, knowing he reached out for comfort. A shimmer of a smile crossed his lips, and with great effort, she saw his cracked lips part to speak, "I-it-it's just a—" he paused to let a wave of pain pass. "Just a scratch."

She burst into laughter at his response, his humor a light in the dark as always. Her laughter was contagious, and as he caught the viral mirth he was instead rewarded with pain.

He coughed nastily, and, through gritted teeth, spoke again, "You really should think next time. Before you act."

His voice was calm, and the chiding was more humorous than serious, but in those words, she felt their truth. She knew she had been brash. Not only on this expedition but many in the past as well. She could have scouted more cautiously instead of trying to sneak right up to the front door of the orcish camp. She knew she should have never left Elgion without the support of its leaders. She knew she had been headstrong, and she knew that this was not the first time she had been reckless.

Bella replied through tears and laughter, "Well … you shouldn't encourage me." For a moment he just looked at her, expressionless, and then suddenly he grinned mightily and laughed once again at the expense of his broken ribs.

Behind them something scurried through the brush and, heightened to fear, Bella spun quickly to challenge the threat. She still was kneeling but prepared to spring up and bite, kick, and claw whatever decided to test her. Adrenaline pumped through her veins, her tired muscles—young and strong—coiled in preparation for action.

Godfrey groaned behind her, "Gods damned orcs. Just kill us already."

"Shhh," she silenced him without looking. Her focus was on the brush, listening and waiting for the culprit to give away their position. An orcish bellow could be heard outside of the forest, and Bella knew that their pursuers would be making their way down the hill. She could only hope that the orcs, knowing victory was at hand, wouldn't risk the tumble she and Godfrey had taken and thus wouldn't benefit from the speed. She did not look towards the sounds of the orcs, for she could sense that something was there. Something stronger, smarter, and much more deadly than the normal forest denizens. The hairs on her neck, still taut from her previous instinct, felt like they were going to jump right off her skin. A burst of lime green moved into sight, its owner moving too fast to make out who or *what* it was.

Bella tensed, preparing to greet this attacker. A saurian, its gecko-faced snout snarling, landed not but three meters from her. It had landed on the fallen log, which was near the rowan berries. Now, short spear in hand, croaked at her in challenge. She bared her teeth and placed her legs back ready to leap at the newcomer. Once again, she tensed her hands as if to grip her daggers, her fists curling around nothing.

The gecko-faced saurian was about one-and-a-half meters tall, but with a pronounced stoop that accommodated its large head. Truly, Bella struggled to tell where the lizard's torso began and the head ended, for there was little in the way of a neck. The saurian's whole frame was propped forward, like a coiled spring ready to unwind, and the animals' front legs, nearly as large as the hind legs, held four digits in which dexterous actions could be performed. Dexterous actions like wielding a spear, a spear that could gut her if she made a wrong move.

Her life and Godfrey's were hanging by a thread, but whether she would be bludgeoned by orcs or stabbed by lizards was up for debate. The saurian stayed planted on the log, pointing his short spear at Bella, and, without moving from that spot, it barked three times in quick succession.

The barks were proceeded by two snakelike saurians slithering out from the brush behind Bella, flanking her on both sides. She twirled around trying to face the new opponents, and when she realized she was surrounded, her instinct forced her to turn rapidly, facing each enemy in kind. The newcomers held menacing-looking daggers in short arms. Their legs, although currently in use, looked like nothing more than props to hold a long snakelike torso upright. These particular beasts were capped with a heavy dark green cloak.

After her cursory glance at the serpentine sauroids, she couldn't help but think of rogues—whether a mockery or not was up for debate. Her excitement quickly dwindled. She recognized that the apparent leader of the group had exposed their allies in a show of force. A strategy used by someone wanting to talk. As she turned once again towards the leader, she lowered her arms. She struggled against instinct and lowered her guard to demonstrate peace. She spoke slowly and calmly hoping to assuage the ambushers, "We mean no harm."

The gecko-faced saurian replied with a series of rapid clicks, pointing at their comrades as they did so. Then as their face rapidly twitched back and forth between her and their friends, they suddenly stopped, fixing her with their reptilian eyes. There was intelligence there.

The creature pointed the spear, not with malice, but as if to demonstrate that it was talking to her. Slowly, it rattled off what Bella could only describe as words, but they did not make sense. The syntax of speech was apparent and was deliberately being spoken slowly, but Bella could not make sense of it.

She shook her head to show that she did not understand. The saurian's snout furled in annoyance, and they dropped the spear point towards the ground, a clear sign of frustration.

A roar broke the peace of the parlay between human and saurian, and with rapid decisiveness, the saurian leader clicked to their companions. They pointed at Godfrey and with their free hand made a sign that looked like a human walking. Their eyebrows, or what looked like eyebrows, raised as if in question.

Bella, almost stunned at the clear communication, shook her head. Without delay, the saurian clicked whilst pointing their spear at one of the serpentine sauroids. The snake-like lizard quickly moved towards Godfrey. Before anyone could react, Godfrey was hoisted into the air by a coiled loop of the snake's tail. Godfrey, not seeing the interaction between Bella and the gecko-faced lizard, yelped in alarm.

"It's alright Godfrey … I think they want to help," Bella managed to say as she kept the leader fixed in her sights. The leader narrowed their eyes at Bella, then looking out towards the sound of the orcish roar, beckoned at their companions. They all moved off, further away from the slope, and Bella, not wanting to be left to the devices of the orcs, quickly followed.

The saurians navigated the brush with extreme ease, and Bella struggled to keep up. Even with her agile nature, she had on three separate occasions, warranted looks of loathing when she stumbled on a branch or scraped too loudly across a trunk. Yet to her, she was being pushed to her limit just to keep up the pace the saurians set, not to mention the level of exhaustion she was already at. Nevertheless, the saurians tolerated her presence and Godfreys, who lay in the snake-like lizard's tail dumbstruck.

He tried to speak once but his words came out in a jumble and trailed off into wonderment. Primarily because the serpent who held him, stared at him as he tried to speak. Bella knew that the old soldier was questioning everything he ever knew at that moment. To be fair most other 'smart' creatures humans had ever run across throughout the world had wanted to kill people, not help them.

The roars of the orcs died away as the saurians turned and twisted through the brambles and trees. Two different creeks were crossed, and on two occasions Bella noticed obvious attempts at masking the trail behind them.

They were experts at this. *How many times had she been the pursuer, and they'd used the same tactics on her?* She decided that in the end, it was what would keep her alive and keep her away from the brutality of the orcs. The brutality of that monster, whose mockery of a smile still haunted her vision. Bella, exhilarated by her near-death experience and the knowledge that she would indeed not be killed that morning, managed to push on, even though every step felt like gravel.

And those steps only felt heavier as the looming threat of the orcish warband dissipated. She no longer could hear their war cries, and she suspected that they had lost them some minutes ago. She slung herself over a tangle of roots and with ill-grace tripped and fell against a fallen trunk covered with moss. The soft growth felt almost like a blanket against her ravaged body, and she slumped against the mock bed sighing heavily with exhaustion. The gecko-faced lizard, who had been constantly scanning their surroundings, quickly noticed Bella's halt and came to her side. For a moment they looked at her, glancing up and down her frame. Apparently, they decided that she could not carry herself anymore. They called out to the other snake-like lizard with a series of rapid clicks. Just as fast as they had done with Godfrey, Bella found herself wrapped up in the loop of the serpent's tail.

At first, she squirmed uncomfortably against the grip, but as the snake carried her fluidly and gently through obstacle after obstacle she relaxed more and more. Her torn muscles unwound as they slithered over fallen logs and branches, her bruised skin swelled with healing fluids as they crossed mist-strewn creeks and streams, and her heart beat more slowly as they glided through the moss-covered forest—like a bird in flight.

Bella was mesmerized as these saurians navigated the wilds. She had only ever known this place as one of great peril and here they were just marching through it like they were taking a stroll through the back fields of a homestead. She knew better than most that the dangers of the Eukarian forest were not so hard to overcome

Still, these saurians navigated with ease, an accomplishment that could only be possible if you were one with the trees. During their trek, the snake-like saurian carried Bella with a surprising gentleness, using its hind legs to support more of its weight and using its pendulous tail to swing her past obstacles. Bella was awestruck by the experience and with the sense of tension dying away, relaxed. Before long she felt the weight of her eyelids droop down on her dead-tired face, and with little reluctance she let sleep claim her.

# Chapter Nine

## Bella

She woke to the sound of gentle rustling nearby. A fire cracked as a fresh log was tossed upon it. The sounds of forest birds and beasts thrummed gently in the distance, and Bella felt a cold breeze brush past her face. The coldness made her realize that she was wrapped in a heavy fur blanket upon a leafy mattress. The fire she heard was illuminating the room, and through the dancing shadows on the wall, she could just make out the room's dimensions.

A simple wooden hut. A wooden frame that supported a mixture of dry leaves and needles woven together with some type of rope. It appeared to be hemp but she couldn't be sure, as her eyes adjusted to the firelight and her mind tried to recognize where she was. It was not fuzzy enough, but she reckoned it was some simulacra of hemp. The entire construction was wide enough to comfortably fit her mattress, the fire, and an opposing wall with an accouterment of pots and vials she was not familiar with. Then she saw it, a saurian that had the face of a chameleon, stirring some sort of brew in a cauldron over the fire.

The sauroid, much akin to the one that tracked them on their journey northwards, simply fixed her with one of its cone-shaped eyes, never stopping the stirring action it performed on the earthy-smelling brew. Bella sat up slightly, a wave of pain that washed over her abdomen made her regret the move. She felt bruised all over, and her body was stiff with soreness. The wave of pain was mitigated by her curiosity, and she slowly reached up a hand to wave at the strange lizard.

*These saurians are a whole people in of themselves.* The chameleon did not alter anything but just continued to stir. One eye fixed on Bella whilst she could see the other telescoping around at a disconcerting frequency. Was it nervous?

She felt some sort of bandage wrap that swathed her torso, and as she craned her neck to look at her side, she felt some sort of lotion or oil slide underneath the wrap. She lifted the heavy fur blanket and was about to touch the bandage when the chameleon's tail gingerly pushed the blanket back down on her body. Not in a way to harm her, but to dissuade her from messing with the bandage. Bella noted that the rest of the chameleon did not move. Like a machine, it's one eye stayed fixed on her, its arm continued to stir in a robotic motion, and its other eye telescoped around frantically all while it moved its tail independently.

She was fascinated by it all. In a matter of what felt like a few hours, she had seen so much of saurian culture. The people of Elgion had already determined that the saurians were more intelligent than the average beast, but most believed they were more akin to a pack of wolves. Savage and fierce but full of cunning. Yet, here they were, this conglomeration of species aptly named the saurians, at a level of civilization not many years removed from their own. After all, it had only been a few hundred years since Augustia was founded and to this day many people lived in huts of equal or worse standing than the one she found herself in now.

There must have been a concept of ownership, and a concept of complex toolmaking and craftsmanship. For no race could have just stumbled upon the workmanship required to forge the pot that the chameleon sauroid was stirring. Nor could any race just stumble upon the complex weave and lattice that made up the wall that surrounded them. Bella also reckoned that this hut must have been owned by this chameleon who watched her, and individual property tended to carry the weight of civilization.

As she lay looking at her host, she recognized the similarities between this saurian and the one that had tracked them in the brush some days ago. A covenant of species bound to a similar purpose. The thought of that crocodillian-like beast beating the ground with its massive cudgel flashed through her mind. It had cried out then with a loud croak, a unique cry that she now noticed shared some similarities with the rapid clicking the gecko had used earlier. All these creatures, it seemed, were using a common language. A language Bella figured would be impossible to speak due to the biological differences between humans and saurians, but maybe a language that had enough commonality that she could learn to understand it.

If she could understand a language, she could reply to that language. A flurry of exciting thoughts raced through her head, as she fantasized about communication between her and the saurian peoples. *Maybe*, she could finally get them to let her approach one of those raptors.

Her reverie was cut short by a sudden burst of cold air from outside. A hide flap hanging over the entranceway was flung open, and through the threshold came the gecko-faced lizard she had encountered in the woods. The chameleon host's head twitched slightly and was now cocked so that she could look more easily at both the entrance and Bella with its telescopic eyes. Bella noticed that the beast still did not stop stirring the pot nor did it stand.

The gecko quickly made way for another and for a moment Bella did not breathe, for what crossed through that entrance next was a sight to behold. A monolithic beast now blocked the doorframe, its bulky frame accentuated by strips of scaly corded muscle. Shimmers of emerald green and muted orange flashed in response to the firelight. Legs the size of tree trunks held the saurian upright, and the beast crouched; not from a natural stoop but from the desire not to crash its head into the ceiling.

Bella reckoned the beast stood a little over two meters tall, and from its girth must have weighed a substantial amount too. It looked like the leader they had met in the brush days ago, but it was *massive*. She had scanned the creature from its feet to its head and there at the apex of the form lay a crocodilian head, akin to the massive reptiles that trawled Deinos Bay. Its snout, although long, was not as elongated as its more natural cousins, but Bella could still see razor-sharp teeth protruding from its closed jaw. The upper portion of the head also appeared to be larger than a crocodile and the eyes were more pronounced; any sign of bestial stupidity entirely absent.

She noticed that the chameleon host finally changed its rhythm, an ever-slight pause in the stirring of the pot could be heard and a fractional second was spent with both eyes fixed on the crocodilian sauroid. He, or she—Bella couldn't be too sure—was someone of importance.

Bella tried to sit up again, as much out of reverence as respect. The chameleon's tail gently whipped around to grab the fur that now slid from her skin and pushed her back down into the bed. Yet, as the tail began to push, the crocodilian sauroid snapped with a hiss. A hiss that somehow conveyed a message and not just a threat.

Immediately, the tail was retracted, and Bella was free from constraint. For a moment the bipedal crocodile just stared at Bella, and she stared right back. A moment of recognition crossed between them; recognition of intelligence; recognition of emotion; recognition of pain.

The crocodilian broke eye contact with Bella, perhaps shying away from the reality of connecting with another species. Then, as if it did not care about the moment they had shared, it nonchalantly raised its hand upwards to communicate that she should stand. Bella noted that its hand were scaly, and like the other saurians, it had opposable digits that must have allowed it to manipulate tools. Bella obeyed the command and slowly swung her legs off the mattress, allowing the fur covering to fall completely off her torso.

Thankfully, the saurians had respected her modesty and left enough clothing on her to cover most of her skin, save her abdomen and her right calf which were wrapped in thick bandages. She loathed to think of the chameleon saurian undressing her to check for wounds but took comfort in the fact that the lizard replaced what clothing it could.

As she mused to herself, she braced for the pain she knew she would feel. With a final glance at the crocodilian, who—like the gecko—looked at her with expectant eyes. She slipped to the floor. The pain was present but remarkably *bearable*. Whatever these saurians had done to assuage the damage done to her was working and working well. She gingerly tested each leg with her full weight and then twisted her torso slightly to ensure that she had a good range of motion. Beyond some general soreness, she felt ready to move. She looked up and nodded at the saurians.

The crocodilian made some sort of facial gesture that Bella assumed was a smile and then spoke to its companion in a series of clicks. Clicks that were much slower than how the gecko had used them, but definitely of the same language. The gecko-lizard replied with a few quick barks, nodded its head, and then promptly left the hut.

The crocodilian, seeing that his follower obeyed its command, gestured at Bella to follow; its large—scaled—hand waving towards its chest. Slowly, the beast turned around to exit the hut, and as it did so a massive spiky tail swept behind it. Bella could see the crocodilian was trying to be gentle, but nevertheless, its girth accidentally upset one of the vases against the far wall. The chameleon snapped out its own tail to stabilize the vase, but not without contention. Bella heard the chameleon host bark out a series of rapid clicks and croaks; obvious syntax apparent in the communication. She rushed after the crocodilian, and the chameleon made a noise that could not have been any closer to a curse. Trying not to smile at the similarity to a crotchety old housekeeper and the chameleon host, Bella walked into the cold outside air.

She was greeted by a wash of muted sunlight, and before her eyes could fully adjust, another gecko-like saurian was behind her with an ill-fitting cloak. She felt the material, deer hide … yet another commonality.

Her eyes filtered the sunlight quickly, helped by the thick tree cover, a trait of the deep forest. Thick pine and cedar trees surrounded them, their trunks heavy with moss. The land around her was not flattened like a human settlement would be; in fact, it did not even appear to be a village at all. Before her eyes could realize the trick that was played on them, she thought she had walked out into yet another stretch of the dark forest of Mossgrave. Yet, hidden in the boughs and branches were huts and lean-tos. A veritable village of structures surrounded them. All of which matched the color of their natural surroundings and all of which were built into—not on top of—the landscape that they occupied.

In between it all was a path that at first glance was invisible. One that her 'guide' strode down without pausing to ensure she was following. Bella hurried after the saurian, and, as she did so, saurian villagers popped out. At first, it was startling, because to Bella's untrained eye, they appeared out of nowhere. But as they continued past hut after hut, the sheer number of saurians popping out took away from the fright. Geckos, chameleons, snakes, crocodilians, and some form of skink-like lizards looked on at her, all of which seemed utterly in awe at the sight of her.

Three smaller geckos ran in front of her and made a noise that could easily be mistaken for laughter. Their parent—at least she thought it was a parent—chittered in a rapid— irritated—tone followed by a swift cuff around the head. It was all so surreal, like a mimicry of the villages from our old stories, but just with a splash more of scales and forked tongues.

As she followed the crocodilian, A flurry of cold wind whipped down the path. On that breeze tiny whisps of snow danced past Bella's face. She tried not to shiver as the cold hit her and she tried not to think how long she had been away from Elgion, or how long it had been since she'd seen Sophia or Alexa.

A pang of regret coursed through her, welling up in her throat as a lump of sorrow. She swallowed hard as the leader stopped, brushed a hide flap to another hut aside, and then moved to the side whilst looking back at her. It gestured for her to enter the hut, and, for a brief moment, she felt afraid of what lay in store for her past the dark threshold.

*Why would they have healed me first?* Without further hesitation, she ducked inside the hut and was greeted by a pleasant warmth. Before her eyes could adjust, her nose picked up the smell of herbs. Witch hazel and chamomile, and something else …

The foreign smell reminded her of Sophia's apothecary as she had stood vigil for Alexa, and that memory ignited her recognition of the scent. It was the stench of fever sweat and the vapors of healing that so often permeated a sick room. A sickly-sweet smell that Bella was becoming too familiar with for her liking. Before she could take in her surroundings a voice called out, "Hello, mum."

"G-Godfrey!" Bella exclaimed.

"In the flesh … well, most of it anyways," he said, and Bella could hear the weakness in him. Slowly, the gloom faded and was replaced by the sight of Godfrey, draped in furs much like she had been, lying on a mattress. "I see our lizard friends finally got you awake," Godfrey said. "I would wave but um—" he held up a nub where his left arm used to be. "That's kind of difficult at the moment."

He sat up and she could see that he was laced with bandages around his torso. *A miracle that these saurians were able to heal him.*

Godfrey smiled as he saw her look at the bandages, "Yeah, these beasties worked some wonders. They even managed to keep from chopping muh leg off." He said as he knocked on his right leg, the hollow sound of wood echoing back. He pulled the fur back to show the splint that lay astride the broken leg.

It was then that Bella noticed another occupant of the hovel. Another chameleon-like lizard that sat in the dark recesses of the far wall. The chameleon rewarded Godfrey's wrap on the splint with a flick of her tail to his knuckles.

"Ow!" Godfrey exclaimed, pulling back his hand from the leg. "This ol' bag never minds herself."

Bella couldn't help but wonder if the chameleons were the healers of the sauroids. *Did the different breeds have specialties?* Before she could follow that train of thought, the chameleon caretaker croaked in what could only be taken as a chastisement.

Godfrey in turn replied with a hiss of his own, "Sssss … you ol' windbag. I was just trying to show the mistress that you hadn't chopped off muh leg." The caretaker made a motion towards its own leg and then made a big 'X' with its arms, a clear sign that Godfrey was not allowed to mess with his healing appendage. "Fine, fine."

Bella could hear a sort of odd comradery in the words. Almost like Godfrey had developed something akin to a friendship with this caretaker. If anyone could develop friendship with this species—so far removed from them—it would be Godfrey.

Bella chuckled, "Are you alright? What … what happened?"

Godfrey just looked at her thoughtfully before he finally beckoned with his good arm to come closer. He scooted some small distance to make room for her to sit on the mattress, which was rewarded by another chiding hiss from his lizard caretaker.

Godfrey held up his arm to show compliance, not in the manner of someone afraid, but in the manner that a troublesome son would to their mother. "Woah … relax there scale-face, I'm just making some room for our guest."

Bella moved to sit down, now noticing how tired she was from even the short trek through the village. Her body was still incredibly sore, and she was sure that her healing process was still well underway. She sat next to him, and, with the awkwardness that proximity can bring, she cleared her throat; unsure of what to say.

Godfrey spoke gently, "Mum … we made it. I don't know by what luck or by what twist of the god's fate, but we made it. Sure, I'm missing my arm, and I feel like I got run over by every horse from here to the sea, but Ember's breath I'm still breathing."

"I know, but how; *why*?" Bella asked incredulously.

"I don't know why these folks have helped us exactly, but from what I can gather they ain't too friendly with the orcs. And … it seems they are mighty keen on our enmity of those pig-faced bastards." Godfrey said matter-of-factly. "In fact, before you were awake, that other lizard guy." Frustration broiled within him born by the struggle of remarking on individuals not of your own species. "Ya know, the one that came and helped us?"

Bella nodded.

Godfrey continued, "Well, he—at least I think it's a he—came in here, and although I couldn't understand a lick of what he—or I suppose I should say *they*, made it very clear that they did *not* like the orcs. He—sorry … *they*, also asked if we came from Elgion."

Bella smiled at the man's naivete and recognized her own in that regard.

Godfrey paused a moment to think and then continued. "Well, they asked with their hands. At least I think that's what they was asking and not wanting to upset our hosts I answered truthfully. I mean … they *did* save my life."

Bella bowed her head, soaking in the information. She looked back at Godfrey who was backlit by the central hearth and felt a swell of sorrow. A swell of regret at leading this good man astray.

"Godfrey … I'm sorry," was all she could say. Godfrey looked at her earnestly and nodded his head in acceptance. Bella continued, sorrow heavy in her voice, "I-I'm sorry about Godwin. I'm sorry about the orcs. I'm sorry about your arm. I'm sorry about this whole mess."

Interrupting her from her torrent of apologies, Godfrey chimed in, "Ahhh, come now. It ain't all your fault." He smiled at her ruefully. "I mean ... Maiden's blessings, a *lot* of it is, but not all of it."

She laughed unexpectedly, and the sudden noise startled the chameleon caretaker who stood defensively.

"Woah there, Grace. It's alright," Godfrey said, waving his hand downwards to steady them. "I have taken to calling her after my momma because she sure acts like mine did," he said to Bella. Grace, the caretaker of this particular hut, slowly stood down from its defensive posture.

Godfrey added, "I mean, if she's in fact a she. I haven't quite figured out how to tell that apart. Maybe it ain't quite as obvious as it is with us. Not like I have seen them getting frisky or anything."

Frankly, it didn't quite matter to her, or, she suspected, to Godfrey. After all, Grace—the it, he, or she—was part of a group that had helped them survive an ordeal. Without them Godfrey and herself would most likely be lashed to that horrific totem the orcs had so proudly displayed in their camp. A shudder rippled through her.

"Well, however you look at it. I *am* responsible for leading us here, and that means I *am* responsible for Godwin's death," She closed her eyes, summoning the courage to look at that man's uncle. To tell him once again that she was sorry for what she had done, and instead, silence stretched into that musty hovel. The only sound was the crackling of the fire, as the pause between words loomed. "I ... I am sorry that I rushed in. I was a fool."

Godfrey bit his lip, heavy in thought as he drummed up his own response, "Look ... mum. We ain't always gonna get it right, and I know that in hindsight what happened paints you in the wrong light. But, why you think I am here? Why did you think I came with you?"

Bella was slightly taken aback by this question and furrowed her brows in response.

He carried on, "Well, it's quite simple really. The Keeper … well, your sister I mean, and my boss had a little chat. And the Keeper … your sister I mean, asked the captain to send someone with you. So, the captain agreed and sent me along to help you."

"The Gu-Guard-Captain?" Bella stammered.

"That's the one," Godfrey said pointedly. "You see, your sister figured you were gonna charge headfirst into the fray. And well the captain agreed and figured that you and your sisters are some of Elgion's best hopes for a bright future. Ember's breath, yer gonna make mistakes. Yer gonna stumble. Yer gonna fall. But if you keep that dogged determination that you show so fiercely, the orcs, the frontier, and anything else the gods—or nature—throws at us ain't gotta a chance to beat us."

The words hit Bella like a gut punch. Full of meaning, emotion, and wisdom all at once. She had liked this man from the very beginning, but she was starting to wonder if Ember, the Maiden, or some other god had sent him to watch out for her.

"Of course, I was mad at you," Godfrey said. "Mad at you for being a damn fool, but Godwin wasn't ordered by you to follow. He followed you gladly, and let's be honest. That was an orc blade in his back, not yours, and fate decided that it was him, *not* you that would have that blade buried in your back." He smiled but with a somber tone. "So, don't keep on beating yourself up over it; instead, you find a way to make it right."

Bella firmed her jaw. "I will." She shifted her weight on the mattress, the soreness creeping into her bones. She was still stunned that Captain Vitrusian and her sister had sent someone after her. "So, how did you and the captain go about it?"

"Well, you see, Captain Vitrusian came to me shortly before your little pow-wow and told me to keep an eye on you."

"Wait? Was that the captain the night we left?" Bella asked, shocking Godfrey with the suddenness of her words.

"Yup, that's the one." He produced a tattered piece of vellum from inside his vest. Bella grabbed it gently and unrolled the scroll, reading the parts that weren't smudged or torn asunder.

*Keep an -e on her an- keep - safe. -n to something. Report -ith news of -rcs. Maiden's Ble -*

The letter ended abruptly due to being smudged. Still, next to the seal of the Warriors of August, there was a nearly illegible mark. One that the captain called his signature.

Godfrey, rightfully figuring she had finished reading, spoke, "He left that for me and Godwin before we left. Dropped it right outside of the paddock. He knew that you would go charging off into the dark, and he needed to make sure we knew that he still wanted us to go with you. I am glad he did because me and Godwin were mighty worried about being accused of desertion. This mark gave us proof otherwise like he knew that it would," Godfrey said as he pointed to the torn vellum.

Bella soaked in the story and felt a sort of relief. Relief that her sister, along with the Guard-Captain, had understood her frustration that day.

"Well, I am glad they sent you," Bella said. She felt grateful to the Guard-Captain, to Sophia, and most of all to Godfrey. A moment passed in silence, and she cleared her throat, uncomfortable at the awkward pause between conversations. Not able to handle that pause any longer, she spoke abruptly, "I can't believe we're still alive."

Godfrey smiled, perhaps entertained by her nervous behavior, and, in reply, added, "Speak for yerself!" He raised his nub of a left arm again. "I think next time I go with you anywhere; I would like to come back with all my limbs."

Bella laughed suddenly. It was a booming laugh, one that would have embarrassed her if not for the multiple near-death experiences that she had recently experienced. She could not help but release her emotions, and those emotions came out in a torrent of mirth. A mirth that seemed to permeate the surroundings and infect all who could sense it. For a few seconds, Bella laughed alone, but as she continued with no signs of stopping, Godfrey joined in.

The two brought themselves to tears as they laughed, even going so far as to force Grace to smile, or at least what Bella thought was a smile. For a moment, they allowed each other to release their tension. The horror of nearly dying pouring out into a comedy of near maniacal laughter. Slowly, the laughter died, and the two friends sighed contentedly.

Basking in the silence, Bella moved the conversation forward, "Well, whatever these lizards have planned for us. I don't see you going anywhere anytime soon."

"Aye, I think you got that right," Godfrey said.

"The gecko-looking one. I think I can speak to them. They seem … receptive," Bella said.

"You think you can get 'em to bring us to Elgion?" Godfrey asked.

"Oh, I think I can get them to do more than that," Bella said almost mischievously. "You see, why would they bring us here? Why would they save us from the orcs? I think these guys and gals may want to team up."

"Team up?" Godfrey asked in disbelief. "Like an alliance?"

"*Exactly* like that. We already have used hand gestures to communicate *simply*. Now, we just need to communicate some slightly more complex hand signals, and we could have that big croc chomping down that gods-awful totem the orcs had." A tinge of malevolence in her voice.

Godfrey smiled in kind, the violence of a lifelong soldier overriding any illusions of calm. "Sounds like a plan to me, boss."

Bella chewed her cheek for a minute and then slapped her knees as she stood, "Well, Godfrey. I promise you I will get you out of here, but first I gotta figure out where in Ember's breath we are and *why* we are there."

"I understand, mum," Godfrey said as he dipped his head in respect. "Don't you worry about me. Grace and I are getting along famously." He winked at the chameleon. Grace did not respond save for a slight twitch of their eyeball.

She had her work cut out for her. But perhaps Elgion and these saurians could help one another; could benefit from one another. She would have to convince them of that first. Bella looked at Grace, so alien, so strange. Yet, there was intelligence there, and, frankly, there was a debt there now. Bella resolved that she would do this. For Godwin, for Godfrey, and Elgion. She rapped the side of the mattress in a goodbye salute and headed for the door.

"I will brief you on what's happening as much as I can," Bella said as she looked back at the veteran.

"I wouldn't expect any less," he replied, and with that, she walked out the door and back into the cold.

# Chapter Ten

## Bella

Bella shivered as a cold breeze whipped past her. The crocodilian leader was standing—unmoving—like a statue, and Bella assumed that the lizard had adopted that posture for the whole time she had been with Godfrey.

It looked as if it was conserving energy, and she figured that a sentient bipedal race of lizard people would struggle in cold weather. Yet, here they were, seemingly accepting what surely sapped the energy of their cold-blooded nature. *Something gives them strength in the cold, unlike their more ... animal cousins.* She decided to ask Sophia to look into it as she gazed upon the massive crocodilian.

The saurian must have felt her gaze because they snorted irritably and gestured with their head for her to look elsewhere. When Bella followed their guidance, she saw an approaching spectacle. The gecko-like lizard, who had been sent off earlier, was approaching; three raptors in tow. A trickle of fear pricked up her spine as the fearsome beasts charged headlong at her, their razor-sharp teeth protruding from their extended maws. The beasts moved fluidly—even with a rider. A comparison that was easy to make since one of the three beasts was unburdened. The gecko stopped a few paces away and hopped from the back of the raptor. They used no saddles. Bella recalled the few chases she had conducted in pursuit of the elusive creatures, noting that they had no saddles either.

While Bella pondered the vagaries of raptor captivity, the gecko-like lizard walked a couple of paces towards her and then stopped. He looked at her with inquisitive eyes and slowly moved its hand towards its chest.

The beast spoke, "Hissslocke." A moment passed in which it seemed the whole of the village just stared at Bella expectantly. The beast repeated the word, "Hissslocke." Then she understood. *This creature tried to convey its name to her!*

Bella brought her own hand to her chest and replied, "Bella."

The saurian tried the unfamiliar words on its tongue, "ahhLLLAA."

Bella tried her luck, "Hislock?" A burst of snickering and hisses erupted from the watching crowds. Obvious mockery of her failed attempt at its name. The crocodilian hissed loudly, silencing them all, and Hislock continued.

Hislock pointed to the crocodilian, "ToaaTaaa." Bella just nodded, not wanting to prompt another round of mockery. Then the two—gecko and human—just stared at each other, not sure of how to proceed. Toata, or at least that's how Bella would refer to them, broke the silence by speaking to Hislock in their strange tongue.

Hislock responded excitedly and ran to a satchel that was held by the other mounted companion. The saurian brought the satchel eagerly over to Bella, and without hesitation pulled a severed orc's head out of the bag. Bella, stunned at first, reacted in a way that made Hislock recoil. The gecko snickered in apparent disgust, evidently thinking she was afraid of the gore, but the saurian did not let that sour the diplomacy overly much.

Hislock took the head and made a gesture that looked like a knife slicing a throat. It then pointed at itself and then in turn at the rest of its tribe. The gecko raised its fists which prompted a series of grunts from the onlookers. The gecko then pointed at Bella and made the same gesture whilst nodding at the head. They knew that she was an enemy of the orcs as well, that she had killed them when she could.

In response, Bella smiled, walked toward the severed orc head, grabbed it by its ears, and promptly spat in the dead orc's face. There was a moment of silence before a sudden chorus of cheers. At least, what went for cheering for a covenant of lizards. When the cheering had died down,

Hislock handed the orc head off to a waiting chameleon who shuffled off with it towards a campfire.

*Were they eating them?* She couldn't satiate her curiosity, because Hislock put one of its scaly arms around her and led her towards the unmounted raptor. Hislock grabbed the steed's bottom jaw and pulled it towards them. The raptor stopped in front of her, and she could feel its hot breath flowing across her face as its powerful frame lay just centimeters away. Hislock gestured for her to mount. She stood with her mouth agape for a moment and then glanced at the leader. The big saurian just dipped its massive jaw with permission.

Disbelief gripped her heart as a childish squeal of glee threatened to burst from her.

She approached the awesome lizard slowly, using her years of animal knowledge to try and keep the creature calm. She made sure that every movement was visible, and she approached its side. She gently pressed her hand on the crest of its head. It bucked slightly, resisting her at first, but like a well-trained steed, it relented to her touch. She got to the side of the raptor, and, without a saddle, did not know what to do next.

Hislock looked at her from over the beast's back. The gecko hissed out some indecipherable instructions, then, aware that those instructions weren't understood, demonstrated how to mount. They leapt up onto their own raptor by grabbing the opposing shoulder and heaving themselves up. The saurian looked back at her.

She reached her arm around the back of the raptor, grabbing the left shoulder of the beast. She felt its cool scaly skin under her palm, and with a couple of preparatory hops, she sprung up onto the back of the beast. She used her years of horsemanship and husbandry to deftly swing her leg over and, with just a slight teetering off to one side, steadied herself. The raptor—obviously a tamed beast—shifted at her weight but did not buck or move in protest. Bella managed to secure the reins, the only control implements available to her, and, after shifting herself into as comfortable a position as she could find, looked up at Hislock. The gecko was staring at her, its face appeared to be amused and astonished at the same time.

Hislock must have thought she would fail at this. Yet, here she was, mounted and ready to ride. Bella nodded. The gecko shook its head and turned to Toata.

Toata clicked roughly a few times speaking in their strange language. Hislock nodded vigorously and then let out a wailing croak that was echoed by many of the surrounding villagers. The raptor bucked backward and with an almost chivalric prestige, Hislock bolted forward on their steed. The other mounted gecko bolted off after its leader, and Bella was quickly being left behind. Toata grinned with its malign teeth, taking obvious pleasure in her confusion. Toata nodded towards the departing raptor riders, suggesting that she should get a move on.

Bella understanding the prompt yelled out, "Hyah!" The beast did not budge. Nor did the raptor move even after she flicked the reins. It still didn't move after she dug her heels into its side. Her only reward for her efforts was an angry hiss. At a loss for how to command the raptor, she looked around in mute appeal. The villagers were all in different stages of amusement, some hissing delightedly, some bent over, and others wearing the wry smile that Toata now wore.

Toata, with their bemused look, was apparently happy to let her suffer for the amusement of their tribe. Until with reluctance, the crocodilian made a strange whooping noise. She'd heard that noise before, back in Elgion when she'd tried to catch these raptors.

With a jolt, the raptor took off into the trees, nearly unseating her as it accelerated. She lurched forward, grabbing around the raptor's neck in a desperate attempt to cling on. Brush and branches whizzed by her head, and at first, she could do no more than crouch in fear.

On a horse, such a rapid ride through the woods would end in injury—or worse—and Bella was content to just let her unorthodox mount pick its own path. They leaped over roots and brush, dodged tree and limb, and they seemed to glide through the trees. Bella realized that these mounts—these creatures—were at home here and that no amount of her own guidance would help them succeed. She was just a passenger on this forest ride.

Through that verdant growth came the two other raptor riders, apparently waiting in a mock ambush for her. They deftly took place in a small 'V' around her mount, and when Bella looked back at Hislock, the gecko held up a small spear and croaked in triumph.

*They are having the time of their life*, and, for a moment, Bella felt freedom. She felt the cold air whip by her face, scouring her cheeks with its brisk temperament. All around her were pine, cedar, and spruce trees. Alongside the hardy brush of the forest, the scenery was a vibrant green, even amongst this cold breeze. There were some barren trees, hardy oaks, and elms that had pioneered their way here, but they were so sparse that the forest still held onto its emerald luster. She breathed in deeply, allowing the raptor to guide itself, content to sail the tides of fate for a moment. It was simply bliss.

"Ooof," she called out as she was flung from her mount by a low-hanging branch. The blow hit straight to her upper abdomen and as she had feared originally, she was unhorsed—or unraptored—in a painful fashion. With ill grace, she tumbled into the moss-strewn undergrowth, and, much like her tumble down the hill, did not feel anything break. Her heart that had just moments ago slowed with the near meditative stance she had taken was now racing with adrenaline.

After being struck back into reality by the unforgiving ground rocking her body, she rolled backward to gain a more advantageous position. There, kneeling in that forest, surrounded by the thick pine trees she laughed. She had survived so much, she had thwarted death *over and over*, and she could not help but laugh at her unbelievable luck.

How could she be so lucky when she had made so many mistakes? What fate; what gods; what Stones had she pleased to survive? Or was she just plain lucky? She did not know, nor did she think she would discover that truth. But as the laughter took over, she resolved not to leave so much to fate. She would take better care not to risk so much, to not put good people like Godwin and Godfrey in so much danger again, but most of all, not squander the gift that had been bought by so many lucky chances.

She resolved to make it right as she imagined a return to Elgion with a new sense of self. A sense that allowed for risk when necessary and caution when caution was due. For now, she would laugh, because the gods smiled on her.

Hislock and its companion had returned to check on her, and Bella could see that the gecko leader was about to scorn her. To pour its chastisement on her carelessness, but instead, it was taken aback. Apparently, the shock of seeing a frail-looking human just laugh after such a painful-looking dismount was enough to halt any reproachment.

Bella stood—still in hysterics—and knowing that Hislock could not understand her decided to speak anyways, "The gods love me Hislock!"

The saurian just cocked its head. Hislock called back to the errant raptor, a whooping croak into the brush. Like a dog to a whistle, the raptor came storming back, tearing through the trees to heed its master's call. Paces away from Bella the unmounted raptor stopped, its bestial eyes not recognizing the predicament it had placed its rider in. Bella, knowing that this animal had only done what it knew, and that she, in her flippant approach to this forest ride, was responsible for her dismounting, called to the beast.

"It's alright there, bud. You didn't know." She placed her hand on its jaw, an action she had performed a thousand times with horses. She could feel the muscles in the raptor's jaw tense as if it were a spring ready to flip away, but as she hummed soothingly while petting the beast, it slowly relaxed. She felt exuberant after the spurt of adrenaline and moved to the raptor's side. As Hislock had shown her, she mounted. This time she executed the procedure with much more grace and quickly gained control of herself—and the mount. Hislock looked at her in a form of disbelief, and then, as quickly as the branch had knocked her away, Hislock's shocked expression turned to a smile. The gecko recognized her spirit and welcomed it as a friend. The saurian roared to the heavens, holding its small spear aloft. Bella in turn punched up into the air, yelling with her new ally in kind.

*

For the next three days, Bella and her gecko companions rode the forest highways. Learning the idiosyncrasies of one another and determining each other's capacities. It was an exhilarating time, and Bella struggled to remember that she was on a mission from Elgion.

They spent hours riding through the brush, stopping along the way at various beautiful locales. Stops that were punctuated by little morsels of saurian life. Bella would see Hislock and their companion either gather some rare herb, notice some animal tracks, or just attune to the wild. They hunted, gathered, and scouted all in one, and Bella soaked up as much as she could. It was clear to her that Hislock had been tasked with guiding her in the ways of their people.

A people who had taken them in and cared for them. At night, they would return to the village in the trees, and Bella would communicate with Hislock or on a few occasions the sterner—taciturn—Toata. She learned that they were fervent enemies of the orcs and that the saurians had watched Elgion since its founding. She learned that there were many villages of saurians in the forest and that Toata was taking a risk by caring for her and Godfrey. It was made clear that the saurians were not fond of humans, an animosity born of fear, fear of the unknown strangers to their lands. *A rational response.*

She had wondered if Augustia would hold true to its claim. "No land will be taken from those who dwell there. We go in peace and exploration. We go to—if unclaimed—make a vanguard outpost from which we can explore this new world. We go for all of Augustia and for all of the human race." Strong words for a city-state that had on more than one occasion acted in their own best interests.

Whether the fear of humanity was deserved or not, did not dissuade Hislock, for that gecko had convinced Toata to help them. Hislock had seen the potential of humanity and wanted to ally with Elgion. They also had apparently wished to satiate their curiosity towards this newly found sentient species. Hislock had been the catalyst that led Toata to save Bella and Godfrey. *And*, it was Hislock that had finally managed to convince Toata to try and secure an alliance that would see the saurians and the people of Elgion scouring the orcish threat from the land.

She had learned all that from the hefty use of sign language, dramatic motions that would only be seen on a theatre stage, and small words that were shared. Their languages did not mesh well—at all, and Bella knew neither race would be able to communicate fully with speech for the foreseeable future. Yet still, some words were easy enough—or novel enough—that they *could* be shared. *Orc, human, Elgion*, and more struggled on the lizard tongue, but through the crudity, Bella could decipher those small words and in turn the saurians could do the same with her. They now called her Bella consistently, albeit with a heavy emphasis on the stronger consonants, and she had built some small rapport with many members of the tribe.

When she wasn't with Hislock or the saurian people, she would sit with Godfrey, who mended well. The old soldier had got Grace to fashion him with a walking stick and with obvious pain, he managed to limp around the village. The smaller saurians had taken a liking to Godfrey, and he, although he pretended he didn't, had taken a liking to them. The little reptiles would run to him, hissing in what Bella only thought was laughter and run off with his stick.

He would hop after them roaring, "I am gonna get you! You little brats!" They of course would drop the stick and run off laughing the whole way. At night, Godfrey would tell fantastic stories, that not a soul—save Bella—could understand. Yet, such was his charisma and enthusiasm at the telling, that the saurians would sit enraptured at his tale. The children huddled around his feet and the adults, pretending not to crane their serpentine necks to hear better, would all crowd around the campfire at night to watch this strange visitor regale them with age-old nursery rhymes and mythical legends. Bella had heard them all as a child, but she had to admit, his language and hand signals did those fairy tales justice. Ember's breath, even with just one arm, she could tell just from his body what the stories were about.

They did all this in a torrent of activity over the few days, and, as the third night was coming to a close, Hislock, at the prompting of Toata, beckoned for Bella and Godfrey to come with them to Toata's hut. They entered the crocodile's abode, who growled softly at one of its children to leave the tent.

When they were alone, Toata said slowly and deliberately, "... Orcsss." Toata's tongue struggled to let go of the 'S', and as the syllable still lisped on its tongue, Toata slammed its fist into its opposing hand. Toata pointed at Bella and then Godfrey and with even more slowness struggled to say, "... Fr-friend."

Bella, shocked at the obvious use of human speech, looked at Toata with her mouth agape.

It was Godfrey who replied, smiling as he did so, "That's right! We are—" he paused to point at himself. "Friends." Godfrey then pointed at

Hislock and Toata and, with as much ambassadorial regality he could muster, said, "Friends."

The two sides smiled and nodded at one another, and satisfied with the pleasantries, Toata produced a small roll of parchment. There was a map on the elegantly crafted paper. An artisanal craft that not only rivaled the best paper found in the old world but also had writing and sketch work that would be the envy of Minollo, the god now entombed within the Artstones.

There on that beautifully crafted map, she could see the Eukarian forest, the rich farmlands southwest of Elgion, Deinos Bay, the orcish encampment, and of course the village of Elgion.

Toata pointed at a spot on the northeast corner of the Eukarian forest and then pointed to the ground, indicating where they were on the map. They then pointed to the orcish encampment and slowly said, "Orc." It was like Toata invoked some ancient evil when he spoke their name. They wanted all to know the gravity of the threat. Toata then drew a line with its finger all the way south to Elgion with careful slowness. Toata then looked up at them to gauge their response.

Bella nodded at Toata. *They were saying that Elgion would be attacked by the orcs.*

Toata then grabbed Hislock's arm and, pointing at Bella with an outstretched hand, said, "Friend." They then made a hand signal that looked like a person riding a mount. Toata then pointed at both Bella and Hislock with open palms, and with sudden violence slammed the hands together. What was left was a spear point formed from the scaled hands. Showing them all, Hislock and Bella would ride together, as an implement of war. Then Toata clenched a fist, and, with careful slowness, moved it down to the symbol for the orcish encampment on the map. It was as if the crocodilian were squashing a bug. Toata looked around at them all and when it was clear that they were to attack the orcs, the leader grinned malevolently. With malice in their hissing tongue, they spoke once more, "Orc."

Bella couldn't help but grin at the saurian leader. She saw the offer of friendship and the warrior's spirit within the noble. She would not squander this opportunity, and she knew that to not take this risk would be to risk losing all of Elgion.

Yet, she knew that this was one risk that was worth it. Besides, these reptiles seemed more than capable of dealing with those repulsive orcs.

"Friend," Bella said, and she looked earnestly at them both. Standing as tall as she could, she slammed her fist into her chest. Toata and Hislock looked at her with curiosity, and as they did so, she reached out her arm.

Hislock, understanding the gesture, clasped her hand in its own. Toata in turn did the same as Hislock and Godfrey embraced. Within that hut, they had cemented an alliance, and now Bella knew that with Hislock and the saurian raptor riders, they would move to reinforce Elgion. *May the gods help the orcs from the fury that's coming.*

# Chapter Eleven

## Alexa

A cold breeze blasted across the plain, and Alexa's breath misted in the morning air. Like little clouds, her exhalations floated up past the riverbank. Wind whipped the multitude of cattail stalks that peaked over the bank's top, which gave way to a newly blanketed field of near-endless white. Small patches of brown poked out of that blanket at irregular patterns; reminders of where stands of trees or brush stood tall. Alexa strained her eyes and flickers of light danced along the pristine surface, dazzling her vision.

The shimmering lights made it difficult to maintain a vigil for their prey. A long and thankless task that served to dull the senses and strain the wits. Suddenly, another squelch of near-frozen water seeped into her already-soaked boot, *Ember's breath, not again*! She had a tenuous hold on the side of the riverbank, which was in a constant state of sinking. The small patch of mud she stood on inexorably caved to her weight.

Alexa couldn't imagine that Elira or Matthias had it much better, and she could only hope that their quarry appeared soon. For if it did not, she would be forced to give her and her small crew a rest. A rest to warm frozen joints, aching bones, and muscles. She had realized very early on that the ability to stay static in an uncomfortable location was a skill not many possessed, but a skill that was quite necessary to hunt or trap prey. These tasks are vital to the ranger cadre, and tasks that these three rangers had completed many times before. Yet, regardless of their ranger's fortitude, hours of exposure to subpar conditions would dull their senses, and she needed Matthias, Elira, and herself to be ready for the action to come.

Already it had been two hours since Matthias had come charging back down the river with news of a small orcish scouting party.

"Three of the beasts. The small ones they used on us at first in the forest," Matthias had said.

Alexa knew that he was referring to the battle in Mossgrave where more than half of the ranger company had perished, A presage of a coming storm. A storm that would include a fight for the very survival of Elgion and everyone who lived there. They had been given weeks to prepare after that battle, and thanks in large part to Alexa, they had not squandered those weeks. Yet, no manner of preparation could forestall the coming conflict.

All along the Farney River, she had dispatched the remaining rangers. The six—including herself—were split into groups of three, and much like the group she was now with, ranged up and down the river. They knew that the orcs would have no choice but to cross the stream, and she hoped to lure the foe into a singular crossing. One that would give her and her defenders plenty of time to inflict grievous wounds on the orcish menace.

*For every step they took towards Elgion they would suffer.* "We will keep the enemy blind and deaf to our movements," she had promised the war council just four days ago.

Now on this stark frozen plain, it was time for her to make good on that promise. The rangers had set out just after that council meeting and, within a day, they had spotted the orcish warband. A host of nearly two hundred fifty warriors, old and young, at Elger's Landing. Alexa, with the help of the three best scouts within the town guard, had immediately set about blinding that host. They used what few horses the village had to send her scouts out around the warband in groups of three. They had made short work of the orc scouts, who were all comprised of the smaller younger variety of orc. Foolhardy youths, who wore little armor and had little sense as they charged at any foe, desperate for glory. Yet, their victories were short-lived because the host pressed on in a relentless march towards Elgion. The orc leaders had used the signs and markings of Elgion's citizenry as guides toward their home. Markers that guided the foresters and rangers to and from the Eukarian forest were now used as a beacon for their enemies. Nevertheless, the orcish warband had been slowed, and—fortunately—the orcs had lost several young warriors to the arrows of her rangers. Now, they were about to lose more.

Her thoughts came swirling back to the present as hazy shapes jostled across her field of view.

"There," Matthias said excitedly as he pointed to the distant specks on the horizon. A group of three figures were clumsily trudging through the pristine snow. Alexa and her companions had chosen their place well, knowing that the orcs would be tempted by the massive mill that towered over the surrounding countryside. An obvious landmark and an obvious place for an easy fording of the river. A muddy track on either side of the river showed where the people had crossed the river. Crossings that were made to fish, hunt, or help move resources from the northern reaches of Elgion's industry. The mill was just upstream of that ford, acting as a miniature dam for the crossing so that even when the river became bloated with ice melt it was still a manageable ford.

Now, at the beginning of what was shaping up to be a harsh winter, Alexa and her team were on the opposing bank of the mill and were crouched just upstream of the ford. Their presence would be virtually invisible to anyone approaching from the north, and they would use that to lay a deadly trap.

"Remember," Alexa whispered to her companions. "I want *one* of them alive."

Elira responded, licking her teeth as she did so, "Let's give them a message for their masters,".

Alexa grinned back at her companion. "A message—" she paused to emphasize the point, "—that should lead them here." Alexa pointed back to the crossing, "And hopefully to die there."

Elira snickered in uncanny glee. "Oh … we will make 'em suffer boss."

Alexa smiled once again at her companions and with little pleasantries commanded, "Alright let's get ready. You take the leader," Alexa nodded at Elira. "I will take the straggler, and Matthias—" Alexa said as she glanced down at his spear. "Be ready in case we royally screw this up."

Matthias nodded in his normal—serious—fashion, "Yes, Rangemaster." Alexa was only slightly taken aback by the title. After all, it had only been a few weeks since she had taken on the vaunted responsibilities of the leader of the rangers. She also recognized that the title was not formalized, but only an interim title for a tumultuous time. She smiled slightly at the stoic warrior and using his discipline as courage she strung her bow. *They were ready for a fight.*

She peeked over the riverbank and saw the three figures now grown into human-shaped silhouettes. Silhouettes that easily betrayed the fact that they belonged to orcs. Their gait was clumsy, and they trudged through the snow as if nature would just give way. Instead of using any form of grace or agility, they barreled forward using brute force to overcome the obstacle. Even from here, Alexa could see their breath in the air, huge plumes of it saturating the air. *Wasteful.* She looked back into the shallow water of the ford. The caps of large boulders were just visible.

The cold water, which lazily floated past the conglomeration of shallow rocks, reminded her of the chill she had felt all morning. She and Elira had been waiting at the water's edge since dawn, and now her limbs felt numb. She flexed her fingers to try and force some blood, some warmth, back into her digits. She would need the dexterity soon. The three companions, knowing the time was close, looked at one another for a slice of comfort before the storm. A series of rapidly approaching grunts sent a shiver of tension through the rangers. *Any minute now.* Alexa placed an arrow on her bowstring. Out of the corner of her eye, she saw Elira do the same. One of the orcs hooted loudly, calling some inane command to its comrades. Alexa gripped the rear of the arrow between her fingers, the familiar sensation calming her nerves.

She gripped onto that calm feeling and forced a slow exhalation through her nose. Time dilated, a moment's respite before the storm. A sensation that Alexa was rapidly becoming familiar with. She breathed in again, filling her lungs, preparing for that doldrum between breaths.

Her peripheral vision caught sight of the first orc dropping into view, its oversized legs supported on cloven—hoof-like—appendages, splashing into the ford. More of an instinct than a reason forced her to rise, drawing the bow as she pivoted into a firing stance. By the time the second orc had touched the water's edge, Alexa was ready to fire. She could see Elira's arrow poised just to the right of her; months of training together had put these rangers into near synchronicity.

The orcs were now fully in view, trudging left to right through the shallow water. Alexa sighted in on her target; sighted in on the orc's exposed throat. *Small targets make for small misses.* Slowly, she exhaled. Allowing her heart to slow. Allowing her mind to purge itself of doubt. *Two thumbs length to the right, pace fast, breathe and ... loose.* She fired, tracking her arrow as it flew towards her target.

Her aim was true, and the orc was struck on the side of its throat. A sickening thunk and a splash of red on the orc's green skin was her reward. Her target collapsed almost immediately; dead before it even hit the water. Elira's target was also struck in the throat, but it slumped to its knees. It gave out one final cry of defiance before it succumbed to the wound, its body crumbling to fall beneath the waves. The middle orc, the one Alexa and they had hoped to use as a messenger, was utterly baffled by its companions' deaths. The young orc turned around to look at its companion behind them, but when they saw nothing the beast's face morphed into a mask of utter confusion.

To the eyes of that orc, it must have seemed like its friends had just … vanished. Both Elira and Alexa had re-knocked their bows; ready to strike the beast in non-lethal ways. They had to bring it down but not cripple it so badly it couldn't walk. The orc swiveled left and right once more, trying to make sense of the death that just befallen his group. With an almost annoying slowness, he finally noticed Alexa and Elira standing; bows drawn.

The orc's face curled into a rictus of malice, and a roar of pure anger issued from its short-fanged maw. With a crude cleaver, it charged at them, but it was hopelessly far away. Alexa fired her second arrow, striking the orc on the upper right shoulder. The force of the blow spun the beast's torso, nearly severing its grip on their weapon. Stumbling through the shallow water the orc continued to press forward. Matthias seeing an opportunity charged forward swinging the back end of his spear like a club. The heavy pommel of the weapon cracked against the skull. The orc, its eyes glazed, took a few more involuntary steps forward and then crashed face-first into the river. Alexa, fearing that he would drown, ran to their side. Matthias, who stood victorious over his victim, finally realized the predicament and helped Alexa drag their victim to the riverbank.

She flung the orc over on its back and with practiced grace gained a dominant position. Matthias and Elira were groping at the tattered strips of cloth the orc wore, checking for any small sliver of weaponry. Alexa, after handing her bow to Elira, slapped the orc hard across the face. "Why are you here!?"

His only response was to cough and splutter as cold river water gushed from his mouth.

She slapped him again, allowing her anger to guide her, "Where is my sister!?"

"Al—" Elira began to speak.

"Quiet!" Alexa yelled back, but with too much force. Still holding onto the orc with both arms, she turned to look back at Elira. "Sorry," she mumbled and then quickly turned away. *She mustn't let her anger win.* She shook the creature again, forcing its eyes open so that consciousness was apparent on its piggish face. "Where are your friends?" Her voice was still curdled with anger but recognizing her emotional outburst she forced a more menacing—measured—wroth.

The orc laughed. There was no way it understood her speech, but it must have implied meaning from her impromptu questioning. The laughter was stopped by Matthias quickly jabbing the pommel of his spear onto the orc's skull. The beast's eyes went blank for a  moment, and its face betrayed the pain it felt from the blow.

"Yeah! You aint so tough, are you?" Alexa asked as she smiled at the orc. She pulled his face close to her own, grinning malevolently. "I am going to rip out your miserable guts." She slammed the orc back down, and as it recovered from the blow, she pulled a dagger from her thigh sheath and held the blade to the orc's throat.

The beast went still as a stone, immediately recognizing the threat. Alexa could see the fear creeping into its face, the specter of death was calling to it, and the looming thought of torture—of pain—weaseled its way into his foul heart. Of course, she would never *actually* use torture, but for their mission this *thing* did not need to know that. "Good boy," she eerily crooned. Without pulling her gaze from the orc she called out, "Elira."

"Yes, boss," her second-in-command replied.

"Can we give our new friend here a trophy to take back to its masters?" Alexa asked, still grinning at the orc.

"Oh, I got just the thing."

Alexa heard Elira sawing at something and figured that an ear or a finger would be produced. She petted the orc's head whilst still holding the dagger to its throat, "Just you wait friend." Alexa heard flesh give way and the sound of sinew being torn, causing the orc to flinch. Alexa jerked the orc's head towards her so it would not break her gaze, "Shhhh, it's gonna be alright." The orc was now utterly terrified, and Alexa could feel its muscles tensed; ready to spring from its position at the slightest opportunity. She could only hope that this cretin would crawl back to its master.

"Will this do boss?" Elira asked as a wet morsel landed on the riverbank. Alexa sat back up, removing the dagger from the orc's neck. This gave the orc just enough leeway to raise their head and see the 'prize'. She heard the beast whimper. To be fair, even she was taken aback.

Sitting just centimeters away was an orc head, severed crudely at the neck. She could not delay though, and frankly, she knew that this would only hasten the beast's return. They needed fear to drive the orc back to its warband. They needed that warband to abandon caution. They needed that warband to charge headlong at this ford, seeking vengeance. She grabbed the severed head and slammed it into the orc's chest. Involuntarily, the beast grabbed at the head, and as he did so he made a pathetic mewing noise. Whilst he was still recovering from the shock of holding his comrade's decapitated dome she leapt up from her dominant position.

"Now, run along," Alexa said pointing with the dagger back up the riverbank; back towards their warband. The orc scrabbled backward a few paces, using his hooves to push himself frantically away. He was unsure of his safety and looked back and forth with panicked jerking motions between the menacing rangers. Then—whether through fear or logic—they scrambled upright and sprinted back up the bank.

Panic and the act of holding the bloody prize made them clumsy and his ponderous hooves scarred the riverbank as he tried to make the climb. Eventually, he mounted the obstacle and there looked back at the rangers. Elira waved, smiling like she was an old friend. Alexa saw the orc shudder then sprint away at a full tilt.

After he became just a silhouette on the plain, they turned to the next part of their plan. The rangers moved the corpses free of the ford, allowing their bodies to drift downstream. They then moved to the mill where their horses had been hobbled. The beasts—some of Elgion's finest stock—had remained quiet during the ambush, and Alexa thanked Bella for training such diligent mounts. "I should return by tomorrow," Alexa said to Matthias and Elira.

"We will be here," Elira said, a hint of sarcasm in her voice.

Alexa swung herself up into her saddle. "We will make them suffer here," she clenched her fist.

Matthias nodded; his brows furrowed in the stern manner that she was accustomed to. Elira grinned at her, and Alexa silently thanked the gods for giving her such stalwart companions. Elira had been her second ever since the fall of the former Rangemaster; ever since the fall of their leader. A leader that Alexa doubted she could match, but in Rangemaster Apararius's honor she would try. For if she failed, they would all be lost, and at that prospect of leaving her beloved company leaderless, she had taken on the mantle of responsibility. She had taken on that solemn duty, and she had resolved to keep the candle lit. Elira—who must have felt something similar—had been a faithful companion for the last few weeks. From assertion of authority to kind words, Elira and Matthias had bolstered her, and, in no small part, helped her maintain her new position as Rangemaster.

"Remember—"

"We know, we know," Elira interrupted her, "we have the spikes ready, and we will make sure those stupid bastards don't see them." Elira paused and then smiled warmly. "We will do this."

Alexa couldn't help but smile at the simple words and with little ceremony turned her mount back towards Elgion. "Good luck friends, and I will see you tomorrow morning with the guard." She cantered off on her steed, waving back at Matthias and Elira.

*

Upon her return to the city, she found the community bustling with activity, and as she stabled her horse, she was immediately assaulted by her newly assigned clark. "Mistress, I have the reports on the food and weapon stores. If you coul—"

She snatched the parchment from his hands before he could finish speaking.

- *Approximately 11,850 lbs of flour*
- *Approximately 10,000 lbs cabbage*
- *Approximately 5,000 lbs carrots*
- *Approximately 2,000 lbs berries, nuts, and other edibles*
- *2,000 lbs dried fish and 1,000 lbs dried meat. Estimates weak; fish and meat used heavily by vendors. Unreliable.*
  *Note: Winter and Spring stores at or above acceptable levels. Eastern cellar full too bursting—gnomish magic? Need to thank the Keeper.*

"This, this is apparently a gift from the um … gnomes," the clark said holding a dead rat by its tail. Alexa looked at the proffered gift. The man was miserable as he held out the rat, trying to keep it as far from himself as possible. She couldn't help but laugh.

"Thank you," she said as she grabbed the rat by the tail. With no more delays, she walked toward the city center.

On her way, she could see the industry of her people. For weeks now they had prepared for the coming invasion. They had built a rough palisade that lay just past the stables and kilnmaster's hut, straddling the road that stretched to the north. When they ran out of timbers, they dug a ditch around the remaining perimeter of Elgion. A momentous construction that was only made possible by the resilience of pioneering folk, and by the imminent threat of death. They had left a causeway leading west out of the city and towards the port, betting that the orcish host would not attack from that direction. They had not built the best of fortifications, but, instead, the most efficient with the time they had been given.

Any advance from the north would be checked by the newly built palisade and when the enemy tried to get around that timber blockade, they would be forced to cross a steep ditch. Across that ditch, they would be greeted by the Warriors of August. That illustrious order, who served as the town guard, and who would be bolstered by the newly trained militia. Although they couldn't put much hope into raw recruits, it was more of a benefit than a hindrance.

Yet, if they did make it over the ditch and past the guard, the city itself had tiers of crude blockades set up. Anything that could be used as a barrier had been strung up along Main Street. There were three constructions, and their dimensions made travel over the wide road difficult. Difficult enough that if you tried to mount the various crates, chairs, and tables you would have to expose yourself to the weapons of the defenders; all on unstable footing. Alexa had managed to secure small perches near each blockade, and, if any rangers still lived at that stage of the defense, they would be able to rain arrows on the enemy from above. Yes, it had been a busy few weeks and now, holding a treasured gift from their only allies, she went to finalize the defense.

She walked to the first blockade, the clark still in tow.

The governor hurried over to her. "Rangemaster!" he called out. His voice was already strained, an attribute that had stayed with him since the first grim reports had been returned from her scouts.

She sighed inwardly, bracing for the coming flurry of questions and demands. She knew that he was not trying to agitate her, but the man had a particular talent for grating her nerves. A mutual feeling towards the portly man that she shared with Sophia, who, on many occasions, expressed her dislike of the governor to Alexa. Considering the utter chaos of organizing a village's defense with limited resources, Alexa had all the more trouble maintaining her composure around the man. Yet, in the last week, she still had had more meetings with him than she could remember.

It had been a tumultuous time, and, with meeting after meeting, the remaining leadership of Elgion had pondered over the defense of the city. Decisions that had led to the fortifications she now saw, decisions that had recently placed her in the ambush she had just conducted, and decisions that led her back here to gather a contingent of the guard. The guard, or as they preferred to be called, The Warriors of August, were by far their strongest tool, soldiers that had trained with sword, spear, ax, and shield for years. Outfitted with mail, helmets, and grim discipline, the guard would be the first line of defense.

Alexa had found an unexpected ally in the leader of those warriors, Guard-Captain Alexander Vitrusian, who to her surprise supported most of her decisions.

She remembered Captain Vitrusian simply saying, "No, you should take sixteen of my warriors for that." An argument in her favor, as she had proposed her ambush at the ford.

He had also readily given her his best scouts to aid her efforts on the plains north and east of Elgion. She had expected the Guard-Captain to be recalcitrant to her request, but he had not only given her more soldiers than she had originally asked for in the ambush, but he had also quietly been supportive of her. Alexa, after one of the many meetings with the leadership of Elgion, had asked the captain why he was so amiable.

His reply was simple but serious in tone, "You are a new leader, a leader that is desperately trying to keep a beleaguered company afloat. You need confidence; your people need confidence and so, if your plans aren't completely stupid, why not support them?" He had asked with a smile and Alexa could see the wisdom of the words. "Of course, it helps that your ideas are lock in step with my own," he said with a final relish.

She smiled at the memory. The governor—on the other hand—served to criticize or worry over every detail of everyone's plan. It took some time, but Alexa had realized that his constant nitpicking served to uncover the flaws in their plans, and reluctantly Alexa had learned to appreciate the man's contributions. Yet, through all that counsel, there was one person she wished she could hear—Sophia, and here on the brink of doom that sister of hers remained reclusive.

She had withdrawn from the community and although the fruits of her labors: gnomish food defense, ample healing ointments and salves, and missives on orc behavior, were used heavily in their defensive preparations, her presence was sorely missed.

"Rangemaster! Any word from your sister yet?" The hefty man with his balding pate wheezed as he spoke, his breath rapidly deflating as he tried to match pace with Alexa.

She was in no mood for this conversation, so she did not show mercy by slowing her pace. She only wished to oversee the final touches of the defense and to speak with the Guard-Captain, not to go over what Alexa already knew the man wanted.

The governor fell behind, obviously expecting her to stop to talk to him, but, when she kept walking, he just stood there, mouth agape. Flabbergasted by her impertinence, he shook his head and with some effort, he sprinted back up to her side. He managed to wheeze, "We need her for what's coming."

She felt the rage begin to boil as she skipped over a newly made rut in the road, one of many from the frantic preparations they had undergone.

"There will be a time for punishment, but for now we need her to do her job!" the governor said. He shouted this last sentence; not for necessity, but because his breath was mismanaged and, like a runner at the end of a sprint, he could only speak at the height of his inhalation. It was apparent that the governor was unused to such circumstances, and his voice came out louder than he expected. He clasped a hand to his mouth, embarrassed at his unnecessary shouting. The words galled her, and—unable to maintain her composure—she abruptly stopped, spinning to face the overweight man.

The sudden stop nearly caused the governor to tip over. The man, unused to such a brisk pace, had trouble getting his legs to cooperate. He slipped in the mud and his right leg jutted forward. He managed to catch himself, and, with ill grace, rubbed the front of his elaborate vest to maintain some dignity. The governor cleared his throat and tried to regain a more regal posture.

Alexa replied with barely subdued venom, "*Governor*, I am well aware of what my sister has done, and I have spoken to her. Yet, she is more vexed by this than *you* know, and for all my trying I have never been able to get her to budge. On this matter or any other."

The governor only half-listened because he was now desperately trying to control his breath and only wheezed in response.

Alexa felt her cheeks heat up. She felt the rage broil inside of her, and she knew that she was just a step away from exploding into a torrent of outrage at the pomposity of it all. Yet, she also knew that he was right, and, like him or hate him, he had a point. That didn't stop her from plying another barbed comment towards the out-of-shape man, "If you *need* her so bad, then why don't you—"

"I believe the governor is trying to say that we would all like to see more of the Keeper's presence, even under the circumstances." Guard-Captain Vitrusian—who had snuck up on the pair—interrupted. The captain winked at Alexa and then placed a calming hand on her arm. His tone was much lighter than the governor; soothing. "This is a difficult time for all of us, and we know how much family means. Yet, our town needs its Keeper."

The governor was right, and whether she wanted to or not she needed to get her sister on board. Alexa placed her hands on her hips, looked up towards the cloudy sky, and blew out a huge sigh. "Very well, I will speak to her again … But I can't promise anything."

"That's all we ask. Right, governor?" Vitrusian asked with a leading inflection.

The governor, trained in diplomacy, caught onto the guidance. His large jowls oscillated as he made a sort of grumbling noise. It was a common feature of the man whenever he formulated a new reply. He would shake his head very slightly and grumble like he was priming his voice for action. "Yes, we simply wish for us to put our best foot forward. We are more than happy with what you have done as the new Rangemaster." He was now holding the upper portions of his vest, a normal pose for people in the debate halls back in Augustia, and, to show comradery, he punched at Alexa. "Surely, if one of you sisters can accomplish this—" he said as he used his opposing arm to gesture to their surroundings. "Then I can't imagine what all of you combined could achieve."

*It's going to snow*, she thought as she continued to hold her head towards the heavens. She had closed her eyes, barely listening to the governor. The last words, which included the term 'sisters', were not exactly the right one. Alexa looked down at the governor, narrowing her eyes as she did so.

Silence fell over the trio, and the governor, knowing he misspoke, vibrated nervously. He made the grumbling noises he was so known for, and his face turned beet red. He grasped the top lapels of his vest tightly, in a form of protective response.

*He may be a fool, but he meant no harm.* To everyone's surprise, she smiled at the governor, "Yes, we would amaze you."

"Umm, oh yes … quite," the governor managed to stutter.

"Now, *governor* me and the Guard-Captain need to discuss the particulars of the ambush we are to lay. Remember?" Alexa asked.

"Ah, yes-uh-very well. I will be off. Um, I need to make sure we have—we have—*cheese!*" his volume like a person who just remembered what they were going to say. After recognizing that he had just shouted cheese in the middle of the street, he grumbled some more, abruptly turned on his foot, and made his way in the opposite direction of any food storage.

Alexa and the Guard-Captain watched the man saunter away, wry smiles on both of their faces.

It was several paces before the governor found a victim in which he could recover his dignity. With extravagant gesturing, he called out to the quartermaster, who—unfortunate for him—was just returning from the palisade, "You there, where are the reports on our boats!"

"He is a strange one, *but* he means well," Guard-Captain Vitrusian said.

"I know," Alexa said, and the two turned to face one another.

"The soldiers are ready. How did it go?" the captain asked with anticipation.

"Good, we killed two and put the fear of Ember into a third. The hook has been baited, and all we can do now is pray to the gods that our *fish* will bite."

"Good, good … While you were gone one of your ranger groups returned *victorious*. It seems that every attempt the enemy has made to gain sight has been thwarted by your troops," he said proudly.

Alexa merely smiled at the compliment, not knowing how to reply.

The Guard-Captain sensed her lack of words, "Come, we have much to do. After you speak with your sister, meet me in front of the hall. I will show you the men who are going to help you. For now, I will leave you to the business of family."

With that, the pair set off down the road and when Alexa came to the crossroads that led down Hook Street she waved to the Guard-Captain and set off to see the Keeper.

The apothecary stank of old herbs and sweat. A rather pungent smell that constantly evoked Alexa's desire to gag.

"It's good that you have come sister," Sophia said, but with no emotion; distant. The Keeper moved a folded rag from the chair in the waiting room and gestured for her to sit.

Not wanting to enter the hovel further, but compelled to help her sister, Alexa reluctantly took the offered seat.

"How goes the preparations?" Sophia asked.

Alexa cleared her throat, trying to expel the sour taste that pervaded the air. "Good … The palisade is complete."

Sophia nodded in acceptance, taking a seat behind the desk she used for when she received townsfolk. Her face was sunken, and she was dressed in the Keeper's robe, an uncommon choice for her. She usually preferred the lighter Keeper's vest and cloak with its multitude of pockets, preferring the agility it offered. Like its wearer it usually reflected the more lighthearted nature of Sophia in comparison to her dourer comrades.

Yet, even with that new garment, Alexa could see in the dimly lit room that the robe was dirty. From her unkempt hair to her untrimmed fingernails, Sophia's appearance was far below the standard that she normally maintained. The two sisters looked at each other, one behind their desk trying to maintain their composure and the other sitting awkwardly in a chair trying not to gag from the stench.

Alexa, not able to endure the silence, spoke, "Sister … this-this isn't like you." She gestured around the room, her hand eventually ending with an open-palmed gesture towards Sophia herself.

Sophia did not respond at first and simply breathed heavily through her nose.

"We need you; I need you," Alexa said turning her hands towards herself; emotion rich within her voice. Still, Sophia did not speak. "What happened to the miller's boy was unfortunate. I don't know what we need to do to get you back to who you are … but it ain't this." Silence.

Sophia bowed in contemplation. The air was heavy and tiny dust motes floated lazily in what minuscule sunlight there was. Distant shouting could be heard, the only sign that a war was approaching.

"Say something!" Alexa shouted.

Sophia jerked her head up abruptly, anger and sadness apparent. "What do you want me to say? I nearly killed someone, and *now* you all want me to just … get back to it?" Sophia's voice was tremulous. "I know that I am needed, and I have sent reports, missives, and what healing items I have to you all, but I just can't—" Sophia trailed off; emotion taking over. The Keeper closed her eyes briefly and finished but with the sound of a sob threatening to break free. "I can't face them again."

Alexa saw the pained pleading in Sophia's eyes and responded with all the empathy she could muster, "You can do it; you can do it with me."

"It's not that simple. Yes, I could walk the streets, and be allowed, but my own head would haunt me." A single finger tapped Sophia's temple.

"Have you used the stones? Is there anything to help you there?" Alexa inquired.

Sophia bit her lip, "I fear it was the stones that caused this." An azure gem suddenly gleamed in the dim light, produced somewhere deep within Sophia's robes.

Alexa felt unease penetrating the heavy air and shifted uncomfortably in her seat.

Sophia, looking even more pained, quickly shoved the stone back into the recesses of her robes. "You see, sister, I might not have heeded some very specific warnings." A weak smile cracked dry lips.

Alexa did not know how to respond; she could only smile back in similar fashion. Another awkward moment passed in silence. "What would

Bella say?" she finally asked; more from the desire to break the silence than actual curiosity at what Bella would say.

"That Dunkeath was a right bastard," Sophia replied brusquely.

*Did she … did she just say that?*

Sophia returned the gaze, and, slowly, they smiled. Once that smile formed so did the laughter. A heavy laugh that ended in a hearty boom. Slowly—organically—it ended.

"Yes, yes she would," Alexa said as soon as her last fit of laughter faded.

"She's still out there … somewhere," Sophia replied.

"You think so?" Alexa asked eagerly.

"I know so; I asked the stones," Sophia said tapping her temple again.

Alexa knew that the Keepers could speak to the stones, and she had even heard the Maiden reply to Sophia on some particularly difficult occasions. Occasions in which Sophia was performing a difficult surgery or trying to expel a deadly disease, and, in those moments, Alexa had heard something in the air reply to Sophia. It was like whispers in your dreams. Whispers that were clearly something trying to communicate with them.

Sophia continued, interrupting Alexa's thoughts, "I asked Ember, and nothing I have heard indicates that she is dead or gone. In fact, well, you know it's all interpretation—" Sophia said qualifying what she was about to say. "But from what I have gathered *she* is on her way back to us!" She said the last bit with enthusiasm.

Alexa raised her brows, knowing that the magic of the stones was elusive. After all, Keepers occasionally got the interpretations wrong, but something in Sophia's voice, something in Alexa's gut, told her that this interpretation was right.

She couldn't help but smile, "I believe you, sister." Tears welled in Sophia's eyes, and it appeared to her that the kind words helped thaw—albeit just slightly—the cold depression that had gripped her sister. "Look,

I know what you did was wrong, and I know that you are sitting in here beating yourself up over it." Sophia looked abashed and Alexa knew she had struck a chord. "Yet, this isn't the way."

Sophia twisted her head from side to side, pain evident in her movements. "I know—" She whispered.

"Then, come with me," she held out her hand. "If Bella is out there, I am going to need your help."

With a cold and distant tone, Sophia replied, "I can't … not that you don't speak the truth, but because I have a battle to win."

"What battle? We are already *going* to fight a battle."

"One of the mind; one with the gods themselves," Sophia said, holding up the azure stone, which now had a faint purple glow to it *again*.

It dawned on her, Sophia was calling out for help. Her warning to her weeks earlier had been a prelude to her demise. Now, she has fallen too far into the power of the stones. "Oh, sister," Alexa said sympathetically.

Sophia's lips curled slightly in recognition of the sympathy. "And there is little you can do to help me. But I will promise you this. I will make my presence felt by the people. I will calm the fears of those who have doubts. I will be there when the orcs arrive."

"Thank you," Alexa replied.

"But know this," Sophia said, her voice hardening like ice. "What I face *may* consume me. May consume all that *I* am. And know this—" Sophia paused, her words hanging heavy in the air. "I will not let *this* consume you or anyone else." Suddenly, her voice was filled with anger. "Not again!" She slammed the table abruptly. The erratic motion made Alexa jump, and she knew that Sophia was remembering her outburst at the well.

"I know, sister, I know … we will get through this," Alexa said soothingly.

Sophia looked at the stone for a millisecond longer, and as if to bury the object, she shoved it back into her robes.

"This place stinks though," Alexa said in the manner of a sibling teasing their own.

Sophia chuckled, "I know."

Alexa stood, "So, with that, I must be going. I can't have the townsfolk keeling over from whatever stench I have picked up. Not before the orcs arrive." For a moment, they just stared at one another. A familial bond—a tugging—urged Alexa to hold out her arms in an offer to hug.

Sophia looked shocked at first, but not able to contain herself, stood abruptly, upsetting her desk as she did so. The sisters embraced one another, and tears sprang freely.

"I love you, sister," Alexa said.

"I love you too," Sophia replied. For a minute they embraced, lost in the love of family. The two—for the briefest of time—escaped the horror and gravity of what responsibility had wrought. They found shelter in a bastion of love and comfort. Then, as quickly as it began, Alexa grabbed Sophia's shoulders and held her at arm's length so she could look into her eyes.

"We *will* get through this."

"I know," Sophia replied with a smile.

Alexa turned away and made her way out to the exit. She paused at the door, "Oh and get rid of those robes. You've always looked better in the vest."

Sophia laughed, heartily this time, and, with fresh tears, replied, "I know."

# Chapter Twelve

## Alexa

Alexa and her cadre rode with all the remaining horses that Elgion could muster. Beasts of burden and war all rallied in common purpose. Twenty mounts in total. Ranging from the larger pack horses to lithe riding mounts.

Amongst all those fine mounts, a tinge of sadness gripped her heart. A memory flashed, and an image of Bella riding her mount—Precious—amongst the paddocks of Elgion's stables, faded in and out of her mind's eye. Her mount, who had carried her to and from the mill on three occasions now, was one of the few riding mounts that Bella had so meticulously trained and cared for.

It was not that Bella had ignored the pack beasts. In fact, she had on many occasions chastised Blythe, who was the primary caretaker of the pack horses, on some form of treatment or care he provided. Memory gripped her again and she recalled one such chastisement, "Hey! They ain't as nerve-dead as your overgrown self. You got to be gentle!"

Alexa smiled at the thought and wondered how Blythe remained so loyal to her ruthless sister. Yet, she could not dwell on memory because she and nineteen others were riding to war. Riding to a battle she did not know the outcome of. The remaining three rangers, Ro, Dillon, and Tilde and the sixteen-strong guard platoon that had been so graciously given to her by the Guard-Captain made up her warband. All her group stared forward; faces grim and determined. Some smiled or nodded at her as she looked at them, but others simply stared forward. Their minds were set to the dark purpose they knew was awaiting them. *Warriors all.*

Warriors who she hoped would be enough to cause grievous damage to the orcish host, and she dared to hope that it would deter that menace entirely. Yet, she also feared—after seeing the warband whilst scouting—that Elgion would not stand against such a foe. The militia, no matter how stalwart they seemed, would break quickly at the first sign of trouble. A likely possibility once the larger orc warriors charged their lines.

So, she had planned and schemed a way to spoil that outcome, and she had come to an idea. A trap which would be lain in the river's shallow water. She would place the guard contingent in the streambed at the center of the ford and entice the orcs to attack a clearly inferior force. Hoping the bloodlust of her enemy would stir them to incaution, she would force the enemy to impale, trip, and bloody themselves on traps laid just under the waterline. When the enemy was confused and in disarray, she hoped that she and the rangers could lay waste to the enemy. Shattering them with spears and arrows as they desperately tried to survive a grim onslaught by the shield wall of the Warriors of August.

She went over and over the plan in her mind on the ride to the mill, and, in the fashion of someone obsessed, she was shocked to find that they had arrived at their destination. The time had flown by.

Elira and Matthias, who had stayed at the mill overnight to keep an eye out for the approaching horde, had quickly greeted them and the group. The whole lot—knowing what to do—set off to their tasks with only a curt nod from Alexa.

The guard, along with Dillon and Tilde, set spikes and boulders in the streambed to trip or maim the foe as they charged.

Ro, Elira, and Matthias set about carrying spears, and arrows, and even throwing stones at two small vantage points on the riverbank. Each point flanked the ford and had been fortified with crates and rocks by Elira and Matthias the day prior. Small points on which her rangers would wait until their moment to strike.

Alexa had worried that the enemy would see the obvious construc-tions and sense a trap, but when she viewed the approach from the other side, she noted that Elira had cleverly covered the front of each bastion with some brush, camouflaging the truth.

The company finished their grim labors and now wallowed in the fear that comes before battle. The soldiers busied themselves by sharpening weapons or ensuring traps were hidden and secure when finally, as the weak winter sun was near setting, Ro called out, "Enemy approaching!"

Alexa had been down in the water testing the knots on a bundle of sharpened stakes when she heard her ranger's call. Quickly, she raced to the riverbank, unworried by the foe spotting her. She clambered up the slope and there in the distance she saw the unmistakable sight of a host approaching. A thin black line arrayed across the frozen plain. A sight that—for a moment—gripped her in fear.

"Your orders, Rangemaster," the sergeant of the guard said. She had been staring at the host for a minute and when he spoke it had startled her.

The sergeant was a burly man with a thick beard that came to a point. His hair was gray, and his arms were thick with a mat of grey hair as well. He was a fine specimen of a warrior, tall and strong.

She looked into his eyes, which, by contrast of his hair, appeared grey as well. Alexa smiled at Sergeant Prinius, a veteran of many campaigns, knowing what help he had just rendered; knowing that he had saved her from the embarrassment of looking afraid in front of her command.

"Right," she replied. "Let's get you and some of the guards on this side of the bank. I want our friends to see us and … hopefully come running."

Prinius nodded and set off down the bank. "You three with me! The rest of you, shove off to the far bank. Make it look like you aren't ready for a fight."

The host was approaching fast, and she looked back across the river to her rangers. She called out to Elira, "stay hidden until the moment's right."

Elira, popping out from behind her barricade lifted her thumb and replied, "We know!"

Alexa smiled at the sarcasm and was glad to hear her friend's humorous tone in the face of such a force. "I will be with you shortly, but first … I have a beast to trap!" She heard Prinius and his three guardsmen clambering up the riverbank and she pulled her bowstring out of the satchel on her hip.

"Looks like they are ready for it," Prinius said, noting the running gait that was now apparent all along the enemy's line. In typical orc fashion, the war host was running full tilt into whatever lay ahead of them. *They are even more hasty for blood than Sophia said they would be.* Alexa's mind raced across the missives that Sophia had dutifully sent out to all Elgion's leaders. Missives that contained knowledge of orcs and ways to beat them.

*The orc is known to be a reckless foe. Whether it is bloodlust or bravery does not matter when it comes to their charge. For every force that has faced them, has lamented the fury of their charge.* Sophia had written.

Her tone, always so matter of fact—so *nonchalant*—even when talking about the potential methods by which their enemy might kill them. Yet, the knowledge *was* helpful no matter how frightening it may be.

"Yes, but so are we," she replied to Prinius. She turned to face the guards down in the riverbed, knowing that they still had minutes left before the enemy would arrive. Alexa girded herself. "Warriors of August! Rangers of the wilds!"

The guard, some of whom sat on their shields trying to look like they were resting, now looked up at her.

She spoke strong, hoping her words would carry faithfully to her hidden rangers, "We all know what faces us today. We all know that the orc is a deadly foe. Yes … my heart has been gripped by fear." She paused, holding her chest, and she noticed Prinius furrow his brows in confusion as he stepped towards her. Obviously, unhappy with what she had just said. He opened his mouth but she interrupted him, "Yet what is fear, but the knowledge that action is required!?"

Her sudden change in tone, a forcefulness of voice, inspired a few of the guards to stand.

"Action that may very well take your life, but action that is needed to save all we hold dear … all we love!"

Some of the now standing guard were nodding at her words.

"Today we may face that uncertain future, that Far Range on the hills; those plains of Elysium, but today we also face the certain future of our people! Today we will tell the foes of humanity that we are not to be trifled with! That we are not simply going to fall to their demands! Today, we tell them that we are the Warriors of August! That we are the Wardens of the Wilds! That *we are Elgion*!" She raised her fists to the sky as she yelled; loud and long.

one of the guards were sitting anymore, echoing her cry with their own yells of defiance. Defiance against the coming death, and to Alexa's delight she heard Ro yell from behind his barricade, "For Elgion!" She turned to Prinius, who, grinning from ear to ear, nodded at her.

"For Elgion, Rangemaster," Prinius said before he slipped his helmet over his head. He unsheathed his sword and held it aloft, which prompted another cheer from his men.

*For Elgion.* Alexa turned to face the charging foe. The enemy was between two and three hundred meters away now. She could hear them roaring their own challenges and see the younger orcs pulling ahead of the rest. She could see the bloodlust in them, and she knew that they would charge straight into her trap. She and Prinius shared a glance, and—without speaking—both knew that it was time to lead the beast to the slaughter.

With a healthy dose of adrenaline and years of training, she quickly strung her massive war bow and fired an arrow towards the approaching host. *One last goad to the bull.* She watched the shaft disappear uselessly into the snow in front of the orcs. With that, Prinius held his sword in challenge towards the orcs, and, after a moment, reversed the direction of the blade and called out, "Back. Back to your positions!"

The apparent retreat emboldened the orcish young, and Alexa could hear them bellow in unison as she fled down the bank. Prinius and his three men were now picking their way carefully through the underwater traps, trying to cross before the orcs had reached the river's edge. Alexa dreaded the real possibility of some smarter-than-average foe discerning the trap that lay in wait. From her vantage in the water, passing a bundle of sharpened stakes, it was difficult to imagine anyone not noticing the danger. Yet, Prinius and herself checked again and again from the top of the bank for the visibility of the ambush, and each time they had been satisfied with the result. Now all they could do was enact the plan and pray to all the gods it worked.

"Warriors! You know what to do," Prinius barked. He had suggested to Alexa that the guard look disorganized in the ford. "That way the enemy will sense an easy slaughter," he had said with the sort of psychopathic relish only a veteran of battle could perfect. "Of course, when the first scent of defeat enters their profaned nostrils. We will close ranks and make them see how foolish they are."

Now those guards were ambling about, trying to look helpless, but Alexa saw that everyone was armed with a shield, spear, and blade. A group that couldn't hide their training from a trained eye no matter how hard they tried, and—much like the traps in the water—the guard's strength was hidden behind a thin veil of deceit.

The first orcs appeared at the riverbank and paused there. As reckless as they were, they did have *some* strategy and sense. Even the foolish young ones would wait for numbers to gather before they initiated a charge. That did not stop them from bellowing insults and challenges towards the Warriors of August, and it did not stop them from nudging closer. The orcs tasted blood, and seeing the guard in disarray made their desire for slaughter even greater. Alexa noted the more vocal orcs taking steps forward, almost involuntarily, until some were slipping down the river's edge. A gathering of approximately thirty amassed on the bank when a bellow—more commanding than the rest—was issued, and the thirty orcs lopped down the slope towards the ford. Alexa primarily saw the unarmored and smaller young orc variety, but within their number were some warriors. Perhaps, the newly anointed; glints of metal reflected off ramshackle armor pieces.

Prinius made a good show of looking like he was trying to get the men in order but failing. He flailed his arms around and cried out in an intentionally shriller voice, "let-le-let's go! Get together!" His stutter was a manufacture, a manufacture that served its purpose well. The first orcs hit the water, splashing into the cold stream at a near gallop. She could see their faces now; maws open in bellowing rage. Their porcine faces betrayed nothing but contempt for the foe they charged, and Alexa watched as one of those faces turned from utter rage to surprise. A young orc, his skin the color of moldy peaches, a sign of the truly young amongst their number, suddenly stopped in the stream. One minute he had been brandishing a metal cleaver above his head, running headlong at the guard, and the next he was halted. Alexa could see a wooden pole protruding from behind his leg. The stake had gone clean through his shin and now buried itself so deeply into his flesh that it pierced the backside of their thigh. Alexa watched the orc's face and saw confusion, almost like they had been betrayed. Then the confusion gave way to pain, but not before other orcs also met the same fate. The entire leading group slammed into some sort of obstacle, either tripping on boulders or impaling their legs and feet onto sharpened stakes.

"Form up," Prinius called, his voice suddenly firm. The guards, as if they had never been lost, suddenly locked shields with the discipline of years. The sound of wood knocking together was a comfort to Alexa, as she waited safely behind their group. She had wanted to be at the top of the ridge, but her presence there too early could give away the next part of their plan. If any orc saw her up there, they could discern that enemies were waiting at the top of the riverbank and caution would become the orcish approach, an approach that could not occur.

Now she simply waited for the right moment to retreat up the bank, desperately wishing to shoot at the ambling horde. First they needed to goad as many orcs into the ford as possible.

"Forward. Three steps now," Prinius called, and the guard marched staunchly forward. More orcs were pouring down the river's slope now. Many warriors were amongst their number, and upon seeing their vanguard balk at the face of the human shield wall, they bellowed in rage.

Alexa relished the perfection of the plan as the newcomers pressed the charge forward, refusing to see the predicament that their fellow orcs had fallen into.

"Brace now," Prinius roared as the first orc warrior, to not fall victim to a trap, closed on their line. The orc did not hear the cries of pain from his entrapped comrades, for they charged virtually alone at the shields. Unaware that those it had charged with just moments before had been waylaid.

Alexa watched them leap the last couple of meters. Their massive frame hurled forward, and they slammed their cleaver into the center of the line. Prinius crouched slightly and took the massive blow on his kite shield. She watched splinters of wood fly away, but the shield remained strong. As the orcs' cleaver ricocheted uselessly to the side, the man to the left of Prinius stabbed forward with his short sword into the orc's belly. A spear from the second rank bit deep into the orc's shoulder. Both blades plunging deep. The beast raised their cleaver above their head for another strike, but Prinius—now recovered—buried his blade into the orc's throat.

One minute so fierce, the orc now looked almost helpless as the strength drained from them. The cleaver fell away from their grip, toppling down their back. Then as the orc slumped to the ground, she heard a whimper, one that almost invoked pity, cry forth from the orc's dying breath.

Yet, there was no time to feel for either orc or man because in the few seconds it had taken to dispatch the lone orc, more survivors of the treacherous ford were charging the line. *Now.* Alexa saw at least sixty or seventy orcs crowded into the water. The next wave of attackers stalled at the river's edge, piecing together the ambush that had been placed.

"Now," she yelled at the top of her lungs, and, like a spring, the rangers burst from their cover. Ro, eager as always, threw a spear almost immediately which impaled itself into a charging orc young. The spear hurled the orc back, who disappeared beneath the water. Alexa scrambled up the bank to join her fellow rangers, and as she did so she heard blades slamming against shields. Cries of human defiance were loud in the air as they took the charge head-on.

"Kill them! Kill them all," Prinius roared.

She managed to get to the hilltop, and there she turned to look down at the carnage. The guard held firm, their number undiminished, and she watched as another orc warrior took an axe blow to the shoulder. The orc fell to its knees and there the surrounding guards impaled him with sword and spear. Alexa, recovering from her frantic uphill climb, watched the guard step forward again. Their wall became a herald of death for the trapped orcs.

Arrows and spears flew from the ranger's vantage points, almost all the projectiles, striking true into orc flesh. The bellows of rage turned into squeals of fear as the orc morale faltered. Alexa knocked her second arrow in the battle and aimed at a rearward orc. She saw the enemy beginning to creep backward, but she shot at a particularly large foe who was halfway down the bank and struck him straight in the neck. The massive beast toppled down the slope, crashing into other orcs.

The makeshift boulder pushed foes forward—willingly or not. Every small push forward brought them closer to the waiting blades of the human shield wall. The water was turning red now, and the bodies of the dead were piling up so that the ford had the appearance of a makeshift wall.

"Shoot the rear ranks!" Alexa cried out after she loosed her third arrow, striking an orc who had ventured too close to the river's edge. He toppled down the bank and splashed into the water below. Two more arrows flew into the orcish rear, striking true. Some of the orcs, wise to the ambush they had stumbled into, were now desperately trying to clamber back up the bank. Those who had not made it down the slope were being pulled back. A few—foolish as they were—still attacked the guard's shield wall, but those courageous few were batted away and fell into the blood-soaked ford. A reluctant retreat now rippling across the orcish line from a foe they had thought—just moments ago—to be easy prey.

"Forward," Prinius cried again, and now his guard were halfway across the ford. Up to their thighs in the water, they impaled any unlucky orc who remained; the orcish resistance now gone. The foe was driven into a panicked mass at the muddy bank's edge with only about twenty of their number remaining. Many having fallen to not only traps but also the blades and bows of the human warriors. Yet still the guard pushed forward. The traps they had lain now hindered their progress, but they managed to hold a ragged line of shields, menacing the surviving orcs with death.

Alexa shot one orc in the back as it tried to claw its way up the hill, unable to find purchase as its paws slipped uselessly away; full of mud clods every time it tried to gain a hold. Its muddy body fell away, an arrow in its back; a splash of brown and red diluting the river.

Alexa strung another arrow ready to fire, and as she did so she saw a massive orc crest the short ridge of the river's edge. The beast roared a defiant cry that, in its intensity, stopped orc and human alike. The beast then hefted a spear in its hand and with herculean force hurled the javelin down into the guard's ranks. The projectile slammed into the shoulder of one man. The force with which he was hit flung him backward. From Alexa's point of view, it looked as if the spear had shaken the very ground, for the men around the unfortunate guardsmen were hurled back as well. The one who was struck fell beneath the water, not to rise again.

"Prinius! Get your men back here," Alexa cried out as she shot her next arrow toward the spear-throwing hulk of an orc. The orc dodged the shaft and as suddenly as they recovered, they stared across the stream at Alexa, and with deliberate slowness raised a massive hand to point at her. The beast grinned, with a smile that curved unnaturally high. His face turning half-white with the starkness of his tusks, one of which was shorn down its middle. She felt a very real shiver quake down her spine as she tried to maintain control.

The orcs were beginning to amass on the river's edge again, spears and javelins in their hands, and the few remaining orcs still in the river were now regaining their composure, their leader inspiring them to fight back.

"Keep shooting, keep them from charging!" Alexa shouted to her rangers, pointing at the few remaining orcs who could still charge and threaten the guard. The soldiers of Elgion could easily take the six or seven remaining orc warriors, but with spears and javelins being thrown at them their losses would be grievous—or even total.

"Back … back. Stay in line now!" Prinius yelled as his guard slowly crept backward, their shields still aloft. A spear thunked into one of the kite shields burying itself into the arm of the man holding it.

Alexa heard him cry out, but he maintained his discipline and continued to retreat in order.

A woman tripped on a boulder and fell backward. Her shield temporarily splayed out away from her body, an orc took the opportunity, hurling a spear square into her chest. A short cry of pain and then she went still.

"Keep going," Prinius yelled.

Alexa pierced an arrow into the eye of one orc warrior who had regained his courage. She saw him begin to charge and she loosed the shot with calm precision, impaling the beast. He fell forward without a trace of life remaining. Only two orcs now remained at the bottom of the riverbed and those two cowered behind their fallen comrades.

"Now, keep those other bastards pinned!" she shouted as she pointed at the spear-wielding menaces. "Ro; Dillon help the guard back up the slope!"

Ro and Dillon moved out from cover, and both grabbed two large wooden sheets tossing them onto the slope's edge. Alexa was all the more grateful to her second-in-command for suggesting they use the sheets, especially after watching how grievous the casualties were on the opposing riverbank.

Prinius's forces were nearly out of the water and he, realizing that they cleared any obstacles, called out, "Alright lads! Back up the slope!" The guard, who were so close to catastrophe, retreated. Spears and javelins pierced the ground behind them as they quickly clambered up the wooden ramps. With no more losses, the guard made it to the top, pulling the wooden sheets up behind them. As quickly as the battle had begun, it fell into a lull. No arrow or projectile was thrown or shot, and the two forces just faced one another. They faced one another over the bloody ruin that lay in the ford below, and almost as if they agreed upon it, the two groups fell silent.

The massive orcish leader held up his hand to silence what few jeers remained on his horde's lips, and as that host fell silent, he looked at Alexa again. Slowly, he brought his massive hand down to point at her once again. When it was clear he pointed at her, he brought the finger back to his throat, mocking a slicing action. This time he did not smile. Suddenly, he roared, making her jump in fright, and she felt fear trickle into her soul.

"Oh, shove it … you overgrown lump!" Ro yelled back. The guard, the rangers, and even Alexa were so taken aback by Ro's retort that they laughed, and she watched the orcish leader's face turn from menace to anger.  The brute's attempt to threaten her having fallen flat. He roared again at them; impotent in his rage. In reply, she stared back at him and laughed into his face; laughed at his failure. The rest laughed, for they had achieved victory. They laughed because they had survived. They laughed because no matter how scary the orcish leader may have been, they had defied him. Yet, most of all, they laughed because little Ro had watched the largest orc any of them had ever seen and told him to shove it.

Alexa not wanting to linger any longer called out, "quickly now. To the horses. Let's get out of here before they make a ramp to cross that ford with their dead." The group set off to their mounts, and although they retreated from the battlefield, they left lighter of heart, knowing they had inflicted grievous casualties on their enemy. They had lost two soldiers, but the time to grieve them would come later. For now, as they rode away, Alexa heard only one emotion. That emotion was elation, and that elation was reflected in a singular cry. A cry for a leader who had brought them to success. A leader of men and women, a leader who faced her fear and won, and a leader who had brought them victory.

"Alexa! Alexa! Alexa," they cried. The shouts flew on the wind as they raced away on their mounts. Even the man with a pierced forearm managed to shout for her. Prinius—loudest of all—punched at the air as he cried her name. Alexa, slightly embarrassed by the praise, only rode in silence, thinking of what was next. Thinking that no matter what fate had in store for them she had and would bring the people of Elgion to a defense that would defy any foe … no matter how terrifying.

# Chapter Thirteen

## Sophia

"You need me", the sibilant voice beckoned. "You will need me when they come. One … more … time,"it promised. "One more time and then you can be done. You are a good person. You *deserve* to use *me*," the hissing voice hung on the last word; almost savoring it.

Sophia did not know for how long she had been staring at the azure-encrusted stone with its faint purple glow. She held the stone in front of her in a fold of cloth, afraid that the slightest touch would send her spiraling. Even now the stone appeared more radiant; even more vibrant than she remembered. A beckoning glow that was luminescent in the darkening room. It's azure casing seemed to be sloughing away the longer she stared at it. It was so beautiful especially when she slowly swirled the stone, making the colors dance.

Sophia had not wished to use the stone. She had wished to race outside and celebrate her sister's return along with all the other villagers; nevertheless, she found herself locked in the stone's sinister embrace. Ever since Alexa and her had reunited on better terms, she had fretted over the very thing the villagers now celebrated, the ambush. An ambush that Sophia had worried would claim her sister's life and maybe—in its failing—doom them all to a grisly death at the hands of the orcish threat.

She had managed to keep herself occupied for a whole day and night, but slowly the worry crept in. A sensation that forced her to sit at her desk, a place normally meant for quiet contemplation. There as she sat pondering her sister's fate, ruminating over the myriad outcomes, she had subconsciously begun to rub the Sorrowstone. The soothing action of the stone assuaged the anxiety she had felt, until it was too late, and its malignant tendrils had hold of her. She had cursed aloud as she recognized her folly and had flung the cursed object across the room.

Yet, there as the light slowly faded and the candles gutted out, she heard the stone call to her. She heard its malevolent pull, "Come to me. Once more won't hurt. Come to me." It had called to her as she crouched against the wall of her room, and slowly she had convinced herself to pick it up once more.

She figured, NO, she knew that from what little was written on the Sorrowstone, that its power stemmed from the god Dolocius. A god known for his cunning and deception. The god that had betrayed Ember and his allies to a fate that ultimately allowed for the fracturing of all the gods. Now as the echoes of the cheers continued outside, she found herself sitting in her desk chair holding this cursed thing, this 'Magi Stone', thinking on a lifetime of decisions.

She did not know how long she had sat at her desk just staring at the stone, but a spark of life, brought on by a new wave of cheers, reignited her resistance. She stood, mirroring her conviction, and the action made her breath come rapid and unsteady like she had been exercising. She needed to get out there. She *needed* to see Alexa. Yet, as she reached for the door, she paused—stone in hand. No matter what her resilience to the stone's wiles, she knew—deep down—that she was going to use it again. She knew that she would want to embrace it again, and even with her resolution to abstain in the here and now, she knew she would falter later.

So, not knowing where she would be over the next few days, she subconsciously was planning for its usage, setting contingencies in place. Giving her fragile psyche that sliver of hope that she would resist, that she would overcome, but also giving way to the uglier truth; that she would fail. In that failure, she would not want to wait to feel the radiance of the stone.

No, she had tasted that hunger before—that pit in her stomach—and she did not want to wrestle with those emotions again. So, although she had won this battle, she had resolved to take the stone with her. Her consciousness and her desires quenched for now; she shoved the stone in her pocket, wrapped it in its cloth, and pushed her way out of the bedroom, through the entry room, and out into the cold dark.

The brisk winter air helped revitalize her, and she welcomed the crisp chill she felt on her exposed cheeks. She wrapped herself in her Keeper's cloak, its red trim and amber hue made dull in the weak moonlight. Heading up Hook Street towards the stables, Sophia could see a sprinkling of firelight, a mixture of torches and cooking fires that had sprung up in spontaneity near the palisade. Most likely in response to Alexa and company's triumphant return.

Surely, what news they had brought sparked those greeters to welcome them with food and warmth. Now as an impromptu party took place, Sophia could see groups of people, in various states of celebration, gathered around fires. Their silhouettes made large against the shadows of night. As the sounds of the celebration grew—even despite the dying light—the villagers of Elgion had come out to see what the commotion was about. Until finally, the whole of the village had gathered around the newly made palisade. Gathered in a muddy space normally reserved for the staging of caravans headed out to the north or east.

Sophia approached the party, making for the largest fire that lay central to the gathering. The cold of the night had forced the groups to make many smaller fires in a ramshackle ring around the muddy staging ground. Yet, in that ring, people moved about freely, sharing the first pickled carrots, stews of venison and cabbage, jars of mead and honey, and—to Sophia's delight—hefty portions of wild huckleberry pie.

Sophia, not wanting to get distracted, searched for her sister in the crowd. The people of Elgion were unconcerned with her arrival, either from ignorance or from apathy, and though they were loud in and of themselves it did not take long before she heard the location of her sister. After all, the sergeant that had been sent with her was in the midst of a raucous retelling of the day's events.

"Then she says to me," the sergeant said boisterously. He repeated himself, flagon in hand, whilst slapping the nearest guardsman on the shoulder, "then she says to me, cool as you like—" The man had paused, his face reddened with drink, and his eyes bulged in an exaggerated expression. "Yes, but so are we." The group around him, all in various states of drunkenness, burst into laughter.

To Sophia, the portion she had heard did not warrant such a response, but neither was she present for the whole tale and neither had she indulged as these soldiers had. Then, appearing from the shadows, Sophia saw her sister step into the light.

"Sergeant Prinius, you give me too much credit," the Rangemaster said with respect. Alexa stood tall and proud, and her demeanor was calm, collected, and plainly free of inebriation. Sophia was slightly shocked at her sister's appearance, shocked and proud of the commanding figure that stood in front of her.

"Nah … Mum, you stood there stern-eyed, facing down those *beasts*," Sergeant Prinius replied.

Alexa smiled at the crowd. For a brief second, the onlookers held onto her smile, basking in its warmth.

"Well—" Alexa said as she approached the sergeant, "It's rather easy to stare down orcs when I've been staring at your ugly mug all day."

Sergeant Prinius recoiled from the mockery, the drink slowing his thoughts. Sophia worried that the man might lash out in anger, but to her relief, he instead burst into raucous laughter. The guardsmen and villagers all around joined the big man in his revelry. *That's a relief.*

Sophia managed to catch Alexa's eye whilst this camaraderie played out, and—as cool as you like—Alexa winked at her. Sophia giggled slightly, unprepared for such charisma from the big sister who normally was so callous; so unsure of herself. They didn't approach each other yet, because Sophia sensed that her sister had more to say.

The laughter died to a sensible level and Alexa spoke again, her tone grim, "In all seriousness though, Sergeant Prinius, you and your men made this victory possible. You have given us all hope." The crowd around the central fire, which had pulled the attention of some onlookers, stayed silent in reverence of the words. Alexa raised a clay mug—its lip indented—in salute towards the sergeant.

The sergeant suddenly stern and serious stood straight-backed; slowly, he raised the cup to Alexa in return.

"To the Warriors of August!" Alexa yelled.

"To the Warriors of August!" A chorus of shouts echoed back, and the crowd erupted once more into a cacophony of celebratory noise.

With her cup still raised and surrounded by cheering men and women Alexa looked over to Sophia and jerked her head off to the side, indicating that they should talk somewhere more private. Sophia could not tell the demeanor in which the gesture was delivered for Alexa's face was half shadowed; one side of her round-cheeked face lit by orange firelight and the other obscured in darkness. Nevertheless, the pair meandered out of the crowd, finding a smaller firepit that had two women and one man arguing over how best to cook a huckleberry pie that rested on a cooking stone.

"You got to turn it 'round," one of the women, a heavier-set lady, said.

"No, no, no. It's much too early for that," the other woman, the wife of the man replied in earnest.

The man looked disturbed, and from Sophia's outside perspective it was plain that he agreed with the heavier-set woman, but loyal to his wife he painfully stayed silent. Regardless of the method, Sophia savored the rich aroma of the pie, its tart flavors tantalizing her taste buds.

Alexa must have concluded that they would not bother them and turned towards her. The sisters simply shared a moment in which they looked warmly at one another.

"Seems a little early for celebration," Sophia started.

"Yea, maybe so," Alexa replied. She took another drink from the mug she had used to salute with. "You look well," almost embarrassed by the compliment she gave.

"Thank you … I-I have you to thank for that," Sophia replied earnestly. "However, while I like a cup of ale as much as the next person, don't we have a horde of angry orcs barreling down on us?"

Alexa chuckled, "Yes, maybe it is a little early for celebration." She turned fully towards Sophia now, leaning a little closer, not to whisper, but from excitement. "The way I see it. Is that our people tasted victory today and maybe when we face them tomorrow … or the next day, those big green bastards might not be so scary looking."

"You mean to give them hope?" Sophia asked.

"Yes," Alexa said her voice rising in enthusiasm, "you should have seen it today. We killed at least fifty of their number!"

That was indeed surprising news, for Sophia had thought the ambush would succeed in only killing a few. Apparently, Alexa's plan was way more successful than any could have hoped. "Fifty!?"

"Fifty," Alexa confirmed with a cocky smile. Another roar of cheers sounded behind them. Alexa looked over her shoulder at the commotion and turned back to Sophia. "Look I know that the fight isn't over yet. Maiden's blessings, we all know that, but … look, jus-just blame the fletcher," Alexa exclaimed.

"Blame the fletcher?"

"Yeah, we came riding back in through the palisade to be greeted by the Guard-Captain, and, of course, our report drew the attention of the nervous townsfolk, and well the fletcher must have heard all the ruckus and rolled out two massive kegs of ale out to the street. At first, we all were in shock, but when he finally rolled up to us, he simply tipped one keg up, tapped it, poured a fresh mug of the stuff, took a hefty swig, and handed it to me."

"That man had two kegs of ale? He always seemed so—" Sophia trailed off.

"Grumpy? I know, but, sure as rain, he provided us with refreshment and well you can see how it turned out," Alexa said as she waved her arm around to show the outcome of the kegs.

Sophia pointed her thumb back toward the larger central fire, "Well, it looks like you have been minding yourself ... unlike the sergeant there."

Alexa laughed in response, "Yeah, Sergeant Prinius was all iron and grim duty until he drained the first cup. Now the man would make you think that me and him are old friends." Alexa chuckled, "He's good people though."

"Yea, yea I think he is," Sophia agreed.

Alexa seemed to shake her head slightly as if to refocus herself. "I wondered where you were," she said, some hurt in her voice. "I was going to come look for you, but there you appeared."

Sophia knew why she was delayed, but to not upset her sister, lied, "I am sorry. I got stuck in a particularly engrossing read."

Alexa blew her lips, a mocking expression showing that she knew it had to have been something like that. "That tracks." To her surprise Alexa wrapped her arm around her shoulder and said, "The vest looks *way* better."

She laughed and embraced her sister in kind. "So, what's the next step, *Rangemaster.*"

"Welp, I figure we got one … maybe two days left before those beasts are going to be hitting the palisade. We hurt them pretty bad at the ford so they will be more cautious," Alexa said in an almost practiced tone, like she had been repeating these thoughts over and over in her mind. She continued, "I doubt they will attack the palisade, especially since they can just go around it, but we all expected that. So, that means probably two attacks. One on either side of the palisade ending. I figure that me and the Guard-Captain will split the guard and militia into two groups to defend either point. We will leave a small group of militia to reinforce right here," Alexa said as she pointed to the ground. "And if it all goes belly up, we fall back to the barricades."

"And if the barricades fall?" Sophia prompted.

Alexa launched her response, "Then we pray we can make it to the port. We have already been sending carts of our vulnerable people and critical supplies there for the last couple of days. Of course, that has been somewhat difficult, seeing as how most of the dockworkers have been here with the militia," Alexa said and pointed to a crowd of people, who gathered around a fire, and bore the look of those born to the sea. She finished, "Nevertheless, the port master should be ready to take as many as we can if we evacuate."

Sophia nodded at her sister, proud of the obvious preparation that had gone into the defense and the part Alexa had played in it. Of course, even after the incident with Dunkeath, she had been a part of the planning. The evacuation preparations, the fallback barricades, and the palisade had all been plans Sophia contributed to as well, but it was evident that Alexa had taken this defense as her own. What Sophia had not been a part of was the strategies for the final defense. Her own part to play in the upcoming battle was unknown to her.

"And what about me?" she asked timidly.

Alexa replied nonchalantly, "Well, that's simple. We need someone else to tell the reserves when to charge and when to hold. Both I and the Guard-Captain agreed that you would be the best choice for that."

A chord of fear struck Sophia's heart. She knew that she would have to fight, but, unlike Bella or Alexa, she wasn't as skilled in martial arms. True, a Keeper could use their Embershard amulet to hurl fire, but even the best Keepers could only pull that trick off once every few minutes. And even then the rapid use of any stone tended to either break the object or render its normal products weak and insufficient. Sophia still remembered the unfortunate demise of a novice Keeper while she was training at Augustia's Bastion.

Alexa must have seen the worry on Sophia's face for she placed a hand on her shoulder. "It will be alright sister. We will be with you, and those that will stand next to you are a good lot … as brave as they come," Alexa said in a soothing voice. Sophia closed her eyes trying to find the comfort her sister offered, and in that darkness, she heard a new voice.

"Keeper?" a man's voice asked. Sophia opened her eyes, and there in front of her was the husband of one of the pie cooks. He held in front of him a piece of huckleberry pie on a small clay plate. It's filling steaming and dripping from the center like a delectable morsel. The crust was golden brown and fluffy.

*A perfect piece of pie.*

"This is—this is for you," the man said as he handed the plate of pie to her. "Sorry, we don't have any utensils," he said shrugging in apology.

Sophia was shocked by the gesture, and not entirely sure why he simply offered the pie to her. She figured she would have to bargain with the group, and due to recent events, she figured the price would be high. Yet, here it was, just being offered to her.

The man must have seen her confusion and called out, "For what you did with 'dem gnomes. We have twice as many huckleberries in our larder. Almost like they been picking them themselves!"

"Go on," Alexa encouraged.

Sophia grabbed the plate, holding the slice of pie just beneath her face. The smell wafted up and the aroma of the pie was delightful. She grabbed a small portion, and although it was burning her fingers, she managed to wolf it down. The heat was intense at first but as it cooled in her mouth, the flavor burst into life and a sweet, savory, taste caressed her palate. She closed her eyes once again but this time in contentment.

"Oooh by the look on her face, I will take a piece of that," Alexa said excitedly.

"Certainly, mum," the man replied happily. He clapped his hands and hurried off to grab Alexa a slice.

Sophia ate another bite before she opened her eyes, and, enjoying the flavor, she looked happily at her sister, who had received her own slice. The five people—pie between them all—stood in silence eating in contentment.

A few moments passed in this blissful state, before the heavier-set lady called out, "Well, it must be good because none of you are talking." The group chuckled, nodding in agreement.

"It's delicious," Sophia replied between mouthfuls. "Thank you," she finished earnestly. In that moment, for the briefest of time, she felt an inkling of pure joy.

Yet there hidden in that joy, hidden in the shadows of her mind, was another voice. It called to her, reminding her that she was bound to another joy-bringer. One that would not share.

*Come to me,* it said.

Its voice was a whisper within her mind that only she could hear. There whilst everyone else felt content to simply eat delicious pie, she could only think of the stone in her pocket. The stone that would be able to amplify this moment. An incessant nagging that demanded she just feel its touch one more time.

"Yes, it will be fine," Sophia said suddenly.

Alexa raised her eyebrows in surprise. "The pie was that good?"

Sophia smiled wanly, not wanting to say why she wished to end the conversation. Not daring to tell her sister that she wished to sneak off and take just one more caress of the Magi Stone. She held up an empty plate, speckled with purple remnants of the pie, in response.

Alexa did the same, a shared laugh capping off the gesture.

"Yes … yes the pie was good but knowing you will be there in the vanguard makes me feel a little more at ease," Sophia said with conviction. Which was a lie, but one she told convincingly. She only needed to say one more thing before she could satisfy her addiction. "I wanted to tell you—" She choked on the words. A sudden desire to apologize for everything, to unload her regrets, filled her mind, but she pressed on, "I wanted to tell you, congratulations. I was … worried."

"Thank you," came the reply, and Alexa placed her hand back on Sophia's shoulder. The fires crackled and the sounds of townsfolk conversing surrounded them. Alexa's hand gripped her shoulder, "Look at me."

Sophia looked up into Alexa's eyes, shame trying to pull her gaze away. Her sister's eyes held a small sense of comfort, a refuge from the demands of desire.

"It's gonna be alright … everything will," Alexa said searching Sophia's eyes for recognition.

Sophia blinked away at the emotion of the moment. With tears threatening her face she looked back into Alexa's eyes and nodded in agreement. Not able to hold onto her resolve any longer she broke into a sob.

Alexa embraced her, squeezing her gently; a balm against anguish. The pie makers looked away embarrassed, uncomfortable being a part of something so intimate, especially between two of their leaders.

Sophia—her emotions an unsteady ocean—decided to stay a little while longer with her sister. They returned to the central fire and for an hour or more they listened to stories, shared drinks, and enjoyed delicious food. The town was in a state of happiness before the coming storm. Truly, it was a wonderful celebration, fires against the winter darkness. Slowly, the townsfolk peeled off to go to bed and before long Sophia found herself wishing her sister goodnight.

With a smile on her face, she walked away from the celebration. She found her way to her bed and lay there for a while in silence. The calls of the nighttime creatures were the only sound to break the silence.

"I can make it even better," the sibilant tones of the Magi Stone, of Dolocius, emerged from the darkness. The dead god called out to her, enticing her to the indulgence she had so desperately avoided that night. "Just once more to cap it all off," he promised. Her heart raced as she tried desperately to shut out the demands. The whispers of the stone and her racing mind competed for space, but, in their battle, her mind felt frayed. Anxiety built and she broke into a sweat while she tried desperately to fight off the desire to touch the stone. Yet, every time she squashed them, they would come back; more menacing than before. Slowly, the two competing mindsets built into a crescendo until she thought her head would explode.

"Oh, Ember's breath, who cares!" She surrendered to the demands and placed her hand on the stone. A warmth coursed through her body. A sudden feeling of relief as she resigned herself to the stone's effect. Like quenching a thirst, the drive to fulfill a desire slowly died and, as with all death, her mind drifted into quietude. Her body, now free of the torments of the mind, relaxed. Slowly, her hand upon the stone, she drifted off to sleep.

She awoke to a blaring horn call, a call to arms. Her heart jolted awake as she recognized the lateness of her sleep. Sunlight was breaking through the slats in her windows, and she knew that—in this winter month, she must have slept *far* too long.

She jumped to her feet and raced to the door, but as she reached her hand to the handle a drop of blood splashed on her knuckle. The stark red stopped her in her tracks. She had done it again. She closed her eyes, and a wave of dizziness washed over her. Her heart pounded in her chest as she tried to steady herself. She knew what it was like to face the day after using the stone too heavily, and it was not pretty. Grabbing the sword Alexa had gifted her for the upcoming battle, she went out to find out her fate for the coming day.

As she marched up the muddy street, a pair of militiamen—dockworkers eager to serve—were running towards her. "Mum, mum!" one called to her, his breath short from having to run through the slick mud. "The Rangemaster sent us to find you," he said as they approached. They stopped just short of her, sliding to a stop, and taking a moment to catch their breath.

Sophia, not wanting to show them that she had been late simply from her own folly, lied, "I am sorry I was delayed on Keeper business. Where is the Rangemaster?"

"She's at the eastern defense, or that's what they call the east end of the palisade," the other militiaman replied, his friend who had called out while running was much too winded to speak more.

"Very well, I will meet her there," Sophia replied curtly. The militiamen both stood looking nervously at one another. Their anxious glances betrayed the fact that they had more to say but were too afraid to speak. Sophia who had been walking past them, now stopped, sighed, and asked, "What is it?"

"Um-uh, it's ju-just that—" one spluttered.

"The Rangemaster told us to bring you to the reserve host," the other said, wishing to end the conversation quickly. Both looked to the ground, afraid of reprisal.

Sophia raised her eyebrow at the two, measuring the validity of their words. "Very well. Tell her I am on my way," Sophia replied much to the relief of the militiamen.

"Th-thank you, Keeper," the bolder one said, and they sprinted back off towards the northern end of town, their boots slipping in the frosty mud.

Sophia rushed now, high stepping on the road in an attempt to get to her posting quickly while not slipping in the quagmire of a road. Ahead of her, she saw the central clearing from last night. It now served as a staging ground for the whole of Elgion's forces.

A horn sounded—loud and mournful—across the frosty ground, and Sophia's heart sank at the noise. It sank because it heralded the coming of the enemy, the dreaded foe who she had read about night after night for the last few weeks. For all the accounts she had read, orcs were ruthless in melee combat, and, almost always, straight-up slugging matches with the brutes led to grievous casualties. Now, here on this frontier, they would have to face such a foe with little more than militia and a handful of well-trained troops, and, to top it all off, she was late.

As she approached the reserve host from behind, her steps masked by the horn, she noticed the smoking remnants of the previous night's fires scattered about. The group was about thirty strong, consisting of men and women. They were in between the eastern and western ends of the north-facing palisade. Each end of the unfinished wall was capped off by a group of warriors, who Sophia knew held the strongest of Elgion's fighters. At the western end, she saw the proud standard of Augustia held high, which meant—at least if they stuck to the plan—that Alexa would be to the east.

Each group consisted of approximately sixty soldiers who would use the palisade as protection for their flank. While the group she was to command, the reserve, was there in front of her.

She hoped that her absence would be forgiven, but, just in case, she used the commotion of the horn and moving troops ahead of them to silently make her way roughly into the center of her group. Where she found herself at a comfortable middle ground, standing next to a man on her right and a woman on her left. Both of whom wore makeshift leather armor, carried a spear, and held a simple wooden shield that lacked the proper iron rim needed for long-term use.

*This would have to do.* She glanced around at the group of militiamen and women. They all carried wooden shields, and they all had some form of armor, leather, or for a fortunate few, mail links. She saw that three of them carried swords, their blades well cared for, about ten of them axes, primarily the kind used to split wood, and the rest had spears. This motley crew of warriors was to be Sophia's first command, and quite possibly her last. That grim thought made her realize how hard the town had pushed itself to muster this defense, and, with all the elements of the plan in place, Sophia never felt more unprepared.

Of course, she had been present for one or two of the war councils, she had known of the strategies of defense, and the plan of battle, but now that it was upon her, she felt sick. It was not common for Keepers to command martial elements, but in dire times her order had been called upon when the availability of tested commanders lacked. She shook her head, trying to muster her spirits for the coming fight.

The woman to her left must have seen the head shake for she quite suddenly yelped, "Oh." The surprised expression quickly led into a stuttering speech, "Hello K-K-Keeper. We-uh-we were waiting for you." Her nerves were unsteady, and Sophia thought, *rightly so*. After all, this woman had been given a spear and shield and told to hold the line against one of the most ferocious enemies to grace Telaea.

She looked back at the woman and quite suddenly replied, "You are brave." The words had left her lips before she could process them. It was an involuntary reaction, brought on by the courage of this brave pioneer she looked upon.

Up until now Sophia had felt nothing but fear for the upcoming battle, and yet somehow, looking upon this woman, who was less trained for the upcoming fight than herself but here nonetheless, gave her courage. "What's your name?" she asked quickly to not only cut off the confusion from the bravery comment but also out of genuine curiosity.

"My name is Oliva, mum. I-I-uh-have washed some of your clothes before." The woman shifted her shield-carrying arm.

Sophia felt abashed that she did not recognize her, but she had the faint smell of lavender about her, a hallmark of a launderer. Regardless of her lack of recognition, Sophia could see that the shields were made of thick oak and probably not optimized for long-term use, instead just a tool to fend off a blow or two.

"You can rest that shield for now," Sophia said and now, looking around at her motley crew, she called out, "All of you! Rest your shields on your legs."

Her company looked at her with mild confusion, not sure of her command, but slowly they dropped the heavy round shields. They now looked at her, and recognizing her Keeper's vest, held themselves at a solemn stance. All except for one.

"Hey there, Keeper," A slightly sarcastic voice called out.

Sophia looked at the voice, noting the lack of deference within it. Her heart sank, for there stood Dunkeath, the man she had slammed with a ball of fire not days before.

Her face must have betrayed that surprise for Dunkeath chuckled. "Hey, mum, I don't want no trouble. I think I learned my lesson from the last time," he said holding his hands up in a joking manner. Sophia began to stutter an apology, but he cut her off, "Keeper, look; we all have regrets, right?"

Sophia stared, digesting his meaning, and quizzically she replied, "Yes?"

"Well, I regret being a royal arsehole, and I bet you regret burning my not-so-royal arse with a bit of the 'ol Ember … right?" he asked with shocking familiarity.

There was scattered laughter at his light tone and Sophia, sensing that this was an apology, replied, "Yes. Yes, I do." She smiled, and although she wasn't very used to humor tried anyways, "There wasn't much arse to burn."

Dunkeath let out a bark of laughter and many more of the militia echoed him, especially because it was so uncommon to hear jokes from Sophia, let alone a Keeper. "Quite right," he replied.

Then, although Sophia could see a cloth bandage peeking out from his shirt sleeve, he held up that bandaged arm, spear in hand, and pointed towards the western group of warriors. Just over their heads, Sophia could see the first sight of the enemy. Orcs always varied in size, and now the bigger amongst them were becoming visible, even over the shield wall of their forces.

In the middle, Sophia could make out a monstrous orc. His prodigious size made the features of his face somewhat discernible, making the oddity of a shorn-in-half tusk stand out. The beast held a massive war ax in both hands and like an executioner to the block, he marched stolidly on towards Elgion's vanguard. Sophia wondered how the vanguard, let alone her rag-tag militia, could stand against that.

Dunkeath echoed her thoughts, "Quite right, but what are we going to do about that."

Sophia, not sure of what to say, stayed silent for a while. The enemy getting closer with each breath. She glanced to the eastern end of the palisade and saw some orcs gathering to attack. Sophia remembered the Guard-Captain's warnings against splitting their forces. Alexa however had pointed out that if they didn't defend both sides they would be flanked and overwhelmed. Both, in the end, had agreed that it would have been better to have completed the palisade and thus have only to defend the gate. Yet, needing a plan that didn't just recognize their fallacies, they both settled for an equal force defending a ditch, which would be buffeted by the palisade. If one force were to be free from assault, they would come to the aid of the other. No such aid would come, because on that snowy northern plain two forces of orcs gathered to attack the west and east in equal numbers.

Sophia, to her guilty relief, reckoned that the stronger attack would hit the west, but only because of the massive square-headed orc that headed for that side.

"Well?" Dunkeath prodded her again, not afraid of reprisal.

"Well, I guess we will have to help our friends in the west. But let's not be hasty. We will make sure the east isn't hit by some trickery and then deploy ourselves appropriately," Sophia finished, firming her vest as she did so. She felt threatened in her authority, and the act of straightening her garments gave her a sense of comfort.

"Heck of a plan boss," Dunkeath mocked. Yet his mockery didn't feel as aggressive as before, almost like he admitted that it was really the only plan.

"Thank you, Dunkeath," Sophia said, not wanting to give the young firebrand a chance to speak further. "If it comes to it, I still do have some tricks of my own," she said to the visibly nervous company, but more for her own sake than for theirs.

"What sort of tricks?" Olivia asked with apprehension.

"Ask our friend Dunkeath over there," Sophia said quick-wittedly.

"Oi, that's right," and playing his part perfectly, Dunkeath pulled up his sleeve to expose a bandage with edges of charred skin bordering it. A pang of guilt at his wound wracked Sophia, but the young man must have noticed for he quickly dropped the sleeve.

"Oh-o-ok," the woman stuttered, "is it true you Keepers can bring back the dead?"

Sophia chuckled and was about to reply when an earth-shattering roar bellowed forth from the massive orc. The charge; the battle; their doom had begun. She gripped the hilt of her sword, which until this moment had been nearly forgotten.

It was a comfort, especially since Alexa had given the weapon to her just a few days prior. "It's not the best blade but set it to task and it won't steer you wrong," Alexa had told her.

Now Sophia wondered if that would be one of her last moments with her sister, knowing that one of them may fall that day. As the orcish host, now only meters away from the ditch, roared in an echo of their war boss, a familiar insidious voice called to her.

"You need me," no longer hiding in a whisper but a full proud voice within her mind. Sophia knew that this stone, this fragment of Dolocius, had taken residence within her brain. She felt warmth drip down her face and knew she was bleeding from her nose. A wave of dizziness washed over her, and she fought to steady herself. The urge to touch the stone was overwhelming, and her hand plunged into one of her many pockets. The other stones of the gods clinked in reprisal at their disturbance until she found purchase on the cursed stone and a wave of relief washed over her.

For a moment, time flowed slowly, and she basked in the calming warmth she felt against her palm. Yet a spark within her soul, a piece of her untainted mind had the courage to send out a small prayer to the other gods. She prayed to Hyclepius, the Maiden and healer of all, to Mosyneta, the god of memory, to Hercurius, the god of speed and messengers, and to Ember, the lord of all gods, to save her—to save them all—for she saw the orcish horde charging home.

She was looking east at first, and she watched as the orcs disappeared into the ditch. She watched as the shield wall of Alexa's command shuddered in response to the enemy charge. Soldiers in the second rank jabbed spears forward, in between the gaps in the wall, and ax blows slammed down into the enemy line. From her vantage, the eastern bastion held strong, and their line did not waver. She thanked Ember, who amongst all the gods honored courage the most, for preserving that bastion through the first charge.

Satisfied with the progress of that front, she focused on the western end. "Ember preserve us."

The western orcish force slammed into Captain Vitrusian's vanguard. Their line shuddered at the impact and the soldiers—their heels dug in— were pushed back. A small space must have been cleared at the ditch's edge, because Sophia could see the heads of orcs poking above the shield wall.

"Hold!" she heard the captain bellow, and in reply the massive orc leader roared in challenge. She could only see the above the shoulders that massive beast, but she watched as it launched itself across the ditch. Unlike his comrades he never disappeared below her sight, suggesting that he cleared the ditch entirely with his leap, and, as he did so, he came down with brutal ferocity. His axe shattered a guardsman's shield cleaving into the unfortunate soul's arm. A scream of pain echoed forth as the soldier fell back, cradling his mangled limb. The impact of the chieftain's leap formed a bubble within the shield wall and orc warriors were streaming into the gap.

*They were running out of time.* She released her hold on the Magi Stone, wiped the blood from her face, and girded herself against what she feared for days. She pointed at a group of teenage boys, who were part of her company, "You four, stay here and watch the eastern end. If they break through, sound the retreat."

They nodded with wide-eyed terror.

"The rest of you," Sophia said holding her sword towards the western end. "With me!" There was no delay, the courage of the frontier life was instilled in them, and, although they had just watched that brutish charge, they pushed towards that dire fate. Sophia's heart hammered within, her adrenaline pushing her past the urge to flee, and she roared as they charged forward. Olivia, running alongside her, echoed her leader's cry.

Olivia's spear was the first to reach the enemy, and to the surprise of an orcish warrior, it impaled itself into the soft flesh of its torso. The blade buried itself deep, and Olivia screamed into the orc's face as the force of her charge brought her to within centimeters of its maw.

Sophia, in mid-stride, slashed her blade at an unaware orc's neck. She felt the blade shudder as it bit deep into their spine. Her arm stung from the shock of the blow, and, as the beast fell to its knees, she nearly lost the blade. The bubble that had formed was now being pushed back, and the shield wall was reforming.

"Reform the line!" Captain Vitrusian shouted.

Sophia pulled her blade free, the force needed to loosen the iron was immense.

"Reform the line!" he shouted again as he checked an axe blow of an orc by bodying him with his shield. The orc was pushed back, and the Warriors of August came to the flanks of their leader. The reserve militia's charge, giving them the time needed to reform.

The orc chieftain, who towered above Sophia, was unfortunately not checked. She watched as he swung his massive axe in an arc, taking the head of a guardsmen clean off. A militia man, emboldened by their successful charge, tried to spear the orc chieftain, and the war boss with surprising speed dodged the blade by leaping backward. Its face turned into a malicious grin, and he pulled the militia man towards himself by grabbing the spear. Once his victim was in range he. Sophia heard the crunching sound of a skull between his profaned maw.

"Get back, Keeper!" a guardsman shouted at her. Guardsmen and women pushed what militia had survived back as they locked their shields, ready to push the orcs back down the ditch.

Yet, Sophia figured that would not happen while the massive orc leader survived. *Ember, give me strength,* she prayed internally. She grabbed her Shard and felt its warmth course through her. In response to the comfort, she swore she felt the needling touch of Dolocius, jealous of her wanderings, sending out a corrupting tendril to wrap onto her mind.

Regardless of that jealous god's plans, her militia was holding the second rank and jabbed blade and spear forward through the gaps in the shields.

Olivia's spear was wrenched away, buried in the flesh of yet another orc. A massive cudgel slammed the helmet of the guardsman in front of Olivia, and he collapsed. Now, with the soldier facing him toppled, the once-impaled orc was able to pull the spear that skewered him free. He directed the blade at Olivia and thrust. The fletcher, who unknown to Sophia had been fighting at this deadly western end, slammed his shield into the spear, pushing it just off to the side. His face a defiant roar as his one good eye winced at the shock of the deflecting stroke.

Sophia roared as she jabbed her own sword forward, feeling it deflect off metal. The near death of Olivia giving her the strength to push the deceiver, Dolocius, aside. As she brought her blade back, she gripped the Shard of Ember tight, refocusing on its warmth.

The orcish warchief bellowed and his blade slammed against another shield; a splintering sound of wood as shards of timber flecked her face.

*Time is short.* "Ember, we need you now. We need your strength, aid us in this fight and we will honor you," Sophia beseeched the dead god. She felt the heat pulse through her body, the familiar taste of charcoal on her tongue. Her eyes went alight with the flame, and she looked right at the orcish warchief.

The massive orc, noticing her magical aura, stared back at her. The beast flung a guardswoman that was in front of Sophia aside and raised his axe to strike the Keeper down.

"Protect the Keeper!" she heard Captain Vitrusian shout, but it was unnecessary. For as the orc raised his blade to strike her, she flung her hand forward. The power of Ember coiled around her outstretched arm, and she felt a wave of fire unleash itself from her fingertips. The ball of flame slammed into the orc leader. She only saw smoke at first; the aftermath of her magic obscuring her vision. Blades stopped and the battle lulled as orc and man alike stood in anticipation of the outcome of such strong magic. A breeze blew the smoke away and Sophia no longer saw the chieftain in front of her. The massive orc had been flung clear across the ditch, and although alive, she could see he was grievously wounded.

"Now, kill them!" Captain Vitrusian shouted.

The defenders of Elgion roared in triumph, and they pushed the few remaining orcs from the ditch's top, slaughtering many who did not retreat fast enough. One of the guards, overzealous in their victory, fell into the ditch, and at the bottom was skewered in the back by an orc spear. "Damnit … hold!" the captain bellowed. The rout of the orcs was checked by the death of the lone guardswoman, and now the two forces stared at one another across a muddy ditch. Neither side wished to cross the treacherous chasm to bring their blades to the foe.

Sophia heard a laugh within her mind, a malign chuckle that grew in intensity. "He's coming," Dolocius said to her. Her mind now weakened by the effort to use so much magical force. The Sorrowstone now flashed images of blood and death in her mind, playing havoc on her psyche. The small sanctuary of her consciousness that remained bemoaned what devilry that had made this cursed stone.

Her complaint made the laughter strengthen, "You are all mine now, Keeper. You think I give my power freely? You used my gifts with abandon and now you shall pay them back!"

Her heart sank as the omniscient presence wrestled with what vestiges of control she had.

"When this is done, we will have a reckoning," the Magi Stone said, its voice—only heard by her—grew into a malevolent growl that inspired dread in her heart.

Yet, a flicker of warmth pulsed through her, and like a candle warding off the dark, she managed to hold onto a small piece of her mind.

Dolocius responded with laughter, a booming throaty echo that filled the cavern of her mind. "Oh, you aren't done yet? Well, my friend, Magdris, will break the rest of you," the stone promised ominously.

A whip of frosty wind coursed between the lines, and flurries of snow carried a whisper of something dreadful with them. Sophia's heart quickened as she felt the aura of magic strengthen, an aura not caused by her.

"What in the gods is that!" one of the guards cried. A whisper written in blood now drifting in the air. A sudden wailing scream began, its source the recently skewered guardswoman. Sophia watched in horror as a rivulet of blood ripped itself upwards from the impaled spear in the woman's back.

The blood coursed upwards followed by a choir of screams. The lull in the battle now ended by the macabre, and all around her wounds of the living and dead were wrenched upon as blood drained from them. Streams of red now looking like crimson lightning coursed across the air.

"Keeper!" Sophia heard the captain scream in fear.

She did not answer at first, because this was not a sight she was prepared for. She had expected the defeat of the war chief to herald victory, but now all she saw was defeat. Defeat by the enemy and defeat by the corrupting influence of the Magi Stone.

"Keeper!" he bellowed again.

She watched as a guardsman—his head bloody from some blow—opened his mouth in a silent scream. The helmet on his head lifted off, propelled by the contents of his skull. A fracture there opening up to the tug of the blood that now coalesced in a sphere above him. The man dropped without a word, dead instantly from the magic. And in horror she glanced around, not knowing what to do, until she saw the source of this evil.

An orc more elaborately dressed than the rest, held his arms towards the sky, mouthing some sinister prayer to the god who delivered such foul spells.

"Damnit! Keeper what the hell do we do!?" the captain roared in question.

"Mag-Magdris," Sophia finally managed to say. "This is blood magic. Everyone, fall back, we must get away from the epicenter. Drag any wounded away and they may still live," she ordered quickly, an ignition in her soul allowing her to regain control for a crucial second.

*You are all dead*, Dolocius taunted her.

"You heard her. Get back, drag what wounded we can!" the captain ordered. They fell back to the central ground, carrying the few wounded that had not perished from the pull of Magdris. The four boys Sophia had

left behind must have overheard her commands, because they were helping the survivors of the eastern defense drag their injured away. They had
done their duty well she thought and as she and the survivors of the western defense rallied, she looked for her sister.

Almost in response, she heard Alexa cry out, "Come on, let's get these
wounded looked after!"

Sophia breathed a sigh of relief seeing her sister, who was matted in
blood. The hair on the left side of her head was glued to her scalp, looking
as if it were painted on in a crimson red.

Alexa must have felt her gaze because she looked back, and her appearance coupled with the dread in her eyes made for a gruesome sight.
Without a word, they expressed to one another that they must push on,
but her will drained as she felt another icy pull come from the Sorrowstone.

Sergeant Prinius, still in decent shape—relatively speaking—held the
hand of one of his guards whose stomach lay open. "Hush now, it's gonna
be alright," the sergeant said as the embers from last night's soiree swirled
around him. Once sparks that lit a celebration now a fitting backdrop for
these sullen survivors. All around, screams of agony echoed out, as those
who had only small wounds before felt the anguish of Magdris's pull.

The orcs, who were not immune to the blood magic, had pulled back
as well, and Sophia could not see them in the ditch anymore. She only saw
twin spheres of blood coagulating in the air, which suddenly vanished before her eyes, disappearing into some other realm to feed the desires of a
bloodthirsty tyrant. She knew that the orc shaman's trick had been played.
Now they would have time, albeit fractionally short, before they would be
pushed into the fray again.

She pulled the Maidenstone out of her vest pocket, its marble sheen
stark against the blood and mud that surrounded them. "Maiden, hear me
now! Heal these tortured bodies!" she called, almost begging the god of
mercy to assuage the pain her comrades surely felt. The stone—held

aloft—seemed to shine a little more brightly, and a surprisingly warm gust of wind blew through the scattered forces. The wind caressed her cheek and, for a second, she swore she felt a hand brush across her chin. Almost like a mother comforting an injured child. The screams of the tormented dwindled, and those who were near death fell into sleep, whether to wake or to find mercy was yet to be decided. Sophia felt Alexa's hand drop on her shoulder.

"Good work," Alexa said gently. "Now, all of you! Fall back to the first barricade."

The survivors dragged themselves about thirty paces away from the staging ground, where a rough barricade of crates and furniture were strung along the beginning of Main Street. Those fit to fight dragged the wounded behind that barricade and then formed a thin shield wall a couple of paces behind, hoping that the orcs would be fouled on the loose assortment of obstacles. Ro and Tilde, a guardian and a ranger respectively, climbed up into makeshift platforms that flanked the rear of the barricade. One such platform had been bolted onto the Ranger's Hall that now flanked their left edge, and the other a standalone contraption that stood in front of the blacksmith's forge. Platforms that would give them the ability to rain arrows on the enemy. Although there were still two more such barricades behind them, Sophia felt that they had come to the final stages of their defense.

A sudden sound of timbers straining boomed across the battlefield, and, almost as one, the survivors looked towards the palisade gate. The door was bending in a near rhythmic tone as it was slammed by the enemy.

"That won't hold long," Captain Vitrusian said grimly.

Sophia, knowing the fight was not over, looked around at what remained of her force. Dunkeath and Olivia were behind her, staring wide-eyed towards the palisade. Another fifteen of her troop, still fit to fight, were rallied around her.

"I count … twenty-three guardsmen left captain, not including our-selves," Sergeant Prinius said.

Elira, who must have been with Alexa at the eastern end continued the count, "Matthias and I are safe, and a rough count puts us at about thirty of the militia who served in the vanguard fit to fight."

The leaders of this battle now stood together, centered around Sophia. Seemingly pulled towards the still gleaming Maidenstone which she had held in her hand as she clambered over the barricade. Its marble glow now served as a beacon, rallying them for what likely would be their final de-fense. The gate bowed once more as it received a big blow.

"You got the big bastard good Keeper," Captain Vitrusian said as he rolled his sword arm, relieving some of the strain on his muscles.

"I prayed to the gods when I saw that brute come for you captain," Sergeant Prinius said, his voice hoarse.

"I did too," the captain replied, which warranted a grim laugh from the two veterans.

Alexa, who had been ensuring her rangers were deployed properly, moved to stand next to Sophia. The gate splintered, but still held, as an-other blow landed on its timbers.

"Shield wall," the captain ordered, wiping blood and sweat from his forehead as he did so.

Alexa rolled her shoulders, preparing for another bout with death, and put another arrow to her war bow. "Whatever it is that has you sister, just know that I am here for you," Alexa said, but quietly so that the sergeant and captain could not hear.

Sophia felt her heart skip a beat and felt the pull of the Magi Stone yank at her soul, trying to cling to control. Sophia looked over at her sister who stood ready to face the coming horde. She could see her eyes dart towards her, and although she did not face her, she knew that she looked upon her from her peripherals. The door groaned and, although the locking bar was just slivers of wood, it held. It held but it did not return to a fully closed position. Instead, a gap now showed behind the splintered bar, and, over the waist-high barricade and through the splintered door, Sophia could see the grimacing faces of orc warriors.

Some combination of emotion and an aura of comfort drove her to a resolution she did not know she had in her. Dolocius tugged at her very soul, wrenching her to the limits of tolerance, yet those few words from Alexa sparked a resistance within her, an ember growing into a fire that strove to banish the darkness. "We will get through this, and we will find Bella, and we *will* be whole again," Sophia said with conviction.

Alexa looked at her—surprise on her face, but a surprise that quickly turned into a mirror of the same conviction Sophia felt. "You damn right."

The orcs, seemingly in response to their defiance, burst the door open. A cacophony of roars echoed from the gap, and screaming warriors poured through. Sophia's heart, although determined to fight, sank at how many enemies she still saw.

Roughly eighty orcs, mostly of the larger variety, charged at their shields. Shields that made a single line, fortified by what few militia remained. Those militia held the second rank, brandishing spears and axes to carve into the foe. Alexa, who was to Sophia's right stood behind Sergeant Prinius. Elira and Matthias stood to Alexa's right and Sophia took some comfort from the obvious discipline of the Ranger corps. Matthias's guardian spear held poised for death and Elira—like Alexa—had an arrow knocked. poised to fire with lethal precision.

She glanced to her left, as the enemy reached the barricade, and saw the grim determined face of Olivia nod back at her, a new spear within her grip. In front of Sophia stood the bulky Captain Vitrusian his war helm glinting in the faint sunlight, his shield braced in front of him, and his short sword held like a snake ready to strike.

The force that mustered against the foe, gave Sophia pride, but she knew that it was a pointless defiance. They would all be crushed, and most likely Augustia would not even be warned. They would come in the spring to a village of ashes and bones.

A fragment of thought, brought forth from the chasms of nightmare, flashed within her mind. Her own corpse, mangled and torn, lay in an empty void. The faint laughter of Dolocius mocked her. The damned stone sapped her will, wishing to crush her spirit. "You think you can hide behind those golden gods, Keeper? You think I won't find you hiding in her skirts? You are mine now, and whether you live or die does not matter. I will crush your faith, and with my rage-filled brother's help I will rule this space," The insidious voice of the trickster god promised.

Sophia heard the twang of Elira and Alexa's bows as they fired their shots at the first orcs to crest the barricade top. The beasts fell onto the furniture, *mortar for the crude wall*. The defenders of Elgion braced for the charge and with what little time remained to her she fell into a reverie of revelation.

*This god was using her as a tool for his battle against the Maiden ... against Ember?* It was clear now, the Magi Stone, the Sorrowstone, the stone of Dolocius, or whatever name it so chose, wished to rule; wished to claim victory over its kin, and she was a puppet in this game. With a clarity she had not felt in months she saw with radiant truth, the sparks she felt in her soul; the caress on the wind are his rivals inspiring her to fight back. It was obvious, as it always had been, that she had been manipulated by this 'Magi Stone', that the addictive need was a manifestation of the deceiver. It was obvious now that the warnings against this azure curse were true. Just as true as the necessity of the Keeper's order to try and understand the nature of the gods who gave the stones power.

Shards of those gods were rare, and shards such as the Magi Stone even more so. Their rarity mirrored the Keeper's lack of understanding.

Those who had pondered the depths of Dolocius's deceptions seemed cryptic or unconcerned about the allure of the azure stone. Beyond vague warnings, there was little discussion on the true depth of Dolocius's manipulations. Until last night, as she had battled with her desires, she had not known what bargain she had made when she had begun to use the Sorrowstone. What devil lay in wait for her as she embraced the perception-enhancing powers of the Magi Stone. Yet, there in her addict's refuge, she had, to her horror, read from a book titled *The Shattering* that, and, although briefly, it described Dolocius.

She couldn't be sure at the time of that reading, but somewhere in her soul, she felt sure that that god, that deceiver of all, was the one that poured its power into the azure and purple stone of the magi. Now she was sure of who fought for her mind; who fought to rule this battlefield. Unfortunately, she had run out of time to reflect longer on the nature of that conflict, because although the barricade had given them precious time to fling arrows and spears into the unbalanced enemy, the orcish horde charged home.

An orc warrior slammed against Captain Vitrusian's shield, pushing him back into Sophia. She nearly fell, save for a discarded timber anchoring her against the fall. The beast roared in defiance as it held a double-bladed axe against the captain's shield, sandwiching him between Sophia and the wooden boards. The captain stabbed forward with his short sword, slicing into the beast's flesh.

A roar of anguish and hatred responded to the blows. The beast tried to step back, tried to raise his ax for a blow, but another orc pushed him forward.

Sophia knew that the pressure from the two large warriors could topple the captain completely, and she already felt the once-anchoring log that held her foot slipping in the mud. She stabbed blindly forward hoping to kill one of the beasts before it overwhelmed them. Blood splattered back in her face, the warm liquid stinging her eyes and souring her taste. A scream of desperation was pulled from her lips. She felt her muscles tear in her leg as the weight pushed her back. She stabbed frantically as the blood kept her blind, the specter of death close at hand, mocking laughter in the back of her mind.

She stabbed forward again, and quite suddenly the pressure eased. The captain pushed forward and Sophia, her leg unpinned, was able to stand again. She managed to wipe the blood from her eyes as the captain took a massive blow to his shield. A death scream pierced the air to her right and the guard in front of Elira crumpled. The line bowed inwards; they would only hold for a few more moments.

Yet, the defenders of Elgion kept fighting, stabbing, and slashing at the dreaded orcs with what strength remained. She tried to find another opening at which she could stab at the foe, when an orcish spear lanced through the line, piercing Olivia in the gut. The brave pioneer woman fell back, holding the wound, her once defiant face now a mask of pain and astonishment. Another militia man toppled backward; their numbers were dwindling.

"No," Sophia said to herself, and she stabbed over the captain's shoulder slamming her blade into the open mouth of an orc. She felt the iron cut through flesh and sinew, and she felt the resistance disappear as it pushed clean through the back of the orc's neck. Unfortunately, the hardy nature of the orcish physique did not fall to such a blow and the beast simply chomped down on her sword, nearly severing her hand in the process.

The orc wrenched his head from side to side forcing her to let go. An axe from Sophia's right slammed into the orc's skull, finally ending the beast's resistance. The orc fell back with the sword still in his mouth, wrenched from her grasp.

A scream from Tilde's platform, and that veteran ranger fell into the gathering enemy horde. As the screams of Tilde faltered Sergeant Prinius who had been in front of Alexa was flung back by a massive blow, and, unable to keep his balance, fell back into Sophia, bowling her over.

She fell to the ground, the sergeant's weight pinning her to there. From his loosely hanging limbs, Sophia feared he had been knocked unconscious or, at worst, been pummeled to death. The laughter of Dolocius rang loudly in her mind as she tried to regain focus. "You will not take me," she growled, and with gritted teeth, she pushed the sergeant off her. She stood heavily and her breath was full of exhaustion, but … she … stood.

The final defenders of Elgion were now in a semi-circle with the corpses of the fallen all around them, Ro had managed to flee from his platform and was firing arrows into what gaps he could find. Alexa swung an axe in a desperate arc to fend off an approaching orc, her shield-wielding guard now a discarded lump on the ground.

Amidst the carnage, the wind caressed her cheek and her heart slowed; time ebbing in its flow.

She knew they had only seconds of defiance left, and then they would be overwhelmed and crushed. She closed her eyes and offered a prayer to the gods. She beseeched them for one more chance; one more hope. When she reopened them— as if her focus was forced upon it—the orc shaman who had cast the foul magic of Magdris was there standing tall on the barricade. To her anguish, she saw that his eye sockets were now hollow with only bloody ruin left behind. Blood magic *always* needs a primer. Apparently, to cast such a powerful spell, Magdris had demanded this shaman's eyes as recompense. Now, the beast looked back at her as if he could still see, and Sophia felt a shiver crawl down her spine.

The laughter of Dolocius boomed louder than ever in her mind. "Now is the hour of your doom!"

Yet, she did not feel doomed, for although she stared at such evil, she only felt the warm embrace of the Maiden's touch. In her mind's eye, she saw that glowing goddess smiling down on her. She felt warmth radiate through her body, and suddenly her neck felt hot as the Embershard amulet she wore radiated with renewed energy.

"Today is not your day, Dolocius," Sophia said in defiance, and there in her mind a god recoiled in fear at what he saw.

With grim determination, she grabbed the Magi Stone and held it aloft. The purple glow of the stone, its power waxing at full, bounced off the armor of Elgion's defenders, their blades still slashing forward in defiance. Another soldier fell; their head spinning wickedly to the side as a cudgel slammed into them. Time was dwindling, and so she focused on the orc shaman, who, sensing the changing fates, stumbled backwards. She felt energy surge through her; surge through the amulet, and as an instrument of the gods themselves felt herself become their weapon; their tool in the endless war amongst themselves.

"Ember! Take you!" She roared as she grabbed her amulet and directed the shard's energy at the Magi Stone. Her hand burned as the heat from the shard started to sear her flesh. She felt the primal rage of Ember course through her, the desire to revenge itself on this azure stone becoming plain. Knowing that she would incinerate all in front of her, she pushed Captain Vitrusian—the stalwart defender—to the side and unleashed the torrent of flame.

An inferno belched forth engulfing everything in a fan of death in front of her. The shaman, along with every orc who stood at the cusp of victory, now disappeared into a mist of blackened char. She heard the screams of Dolocius, as one of its vessels on the realm of Telaea was devoured by the dragon god and used as fuel for Sophia's revenge. The once insidious laughter now turned into tormented screams as the trickster god felt the searing flames as if he were there in the flesh. The enemy had been so close to victory; instead, at the edge of defeat—at the edge of despair—Sophia sacrificed the cursed stone—the instrument of her demise—to its deserved fate.

As the inferno died away, Sophia could see plainly down the street, her view unobstructed by barriers; natural or otherwise. A clearing made from cleansing flame that had pushed all filth from sight, and for the briefest of moments had even pushed back the chill air of winter. Now a tunnel of pure air, scorched clean by purifying fire, lay suspended in time, its path showing a clear view of the broken palisade.

This clairvoyant view was only amplified by the sudden clarity of her mind. One moment it had been a raging battleground between malevolent gods, benevolent spirits, and beleaguered consciences. Now it felt free, clear *pure*. She tasted the acrid taste of char on her lips, and although it was bitter and unpleasant it was the purest sensation she had felt in several months. She closed her eyes as the ashes filled in the vacuum of once purified air and breathed a sigh of relief, a sigh of blessed contentment. She was free again.

"Thank the gods," a rather strained-sounding Alexa said.

The ragged voice prompted Sophia to open her eyes. The few orcs who had survived the inferno were fleeing, their courage gone after watching their kin incinerated. They fled with no order towards both the eastern and western ends of the palisade. Mangled lumps were sprawled about those escape routes, casualties of the battle. Sophia could see many of Elgion's bravest and brightest there, once so full of life—so full of spirit—now discarded wrecks of torn flesh. She also saw the unmistakable tint of green flesh within some of the mangled mounds, signs of an enemy slaughtered. Yet the casualties of their own were immense, and as she watched the first of the fleeing orcs disappear down into the ditch, she looked around at what remained.

What pitiful few remained. Backlit by the burning thatch of the black-smith, Alexa, Elira, Matthias, and a paltry smattering of militia and guards stood battered and bruised, their skin, glistening with sweat and slick with blood. A canvas upon which the black soot, swirling in the air, settled eagerly upon.

To her left, where the Ranger's Hall tower platform still stood, she saw Ro, Captain Vitrusian, Sergeant Prinius, who had recovered from his disabling blow, and another small batch of battered defenders.

All told, they numbered around thirty, with around two score either injured or crying out in agony as some wound—fatal or otherwise—besieged them. Those citizens who had not been a part of the martial defense now rushed to them, carrying buckets of water for the flames or bandages and poultices to soothe the wounded or dying. It was not a pretty sight, but war never was.

"Thank the gods indeed," Sophia finally replied, knowing that two battles had been fought that day. One against mortal races and one against bitter rivals of supernatural prowess. She was about to ask what they should do next, when the palisade burst into flame. The sudden flash dazzled her vision, and, when she regained her focus, she saw the worst possible sight she could imagine.

There pushing through the now burning wreckage was the massive orc war leader. His left side appeared charred and battered, the arm hanging loosely on his side—broken. Yet, he still held the massive war ax in his right hand and as he stopped to stare at what remained of his enemies, a score of orcs came to stand at his side, appearing through the rapidly expanding haze of smoke. They stood like a nightmare come to life, the orange glow of the recent inferno reflecting from the backdrop of smoke, giving them a shadowed—malevolent—appearance.

Hefting his shield once again, the Guard-Captain spoke, "Here we go again."

Sergeant Prinius walked to his captain's side knocking his shield into place. "To the very end, captain," the sergeant said with reverential calm. The remaining rangers picked up their weapons, no words spoken, but faces drawn in grim tenacity for the job ahead. Alexa came to stand next to Sophia again.

"It's been a fun journey, sister," Alexa said cheerily.

Sophia, having been recently freed from her torment at the hands of Dolocius, now felt a wave of raw emotion wash over her. Looking out at the grim visage of their doom she could only feel a swell of love and contentment. She was ready for whatever may come, free to march into the future unhindered by the shackles of desire. "To whatever may come," Sophia said as she put a hand on her sister's shoulder.

The orc leader dropped his axe to point toward the stubborn defenders, and what few of his soldiers remained to him started forward. Sophia gritted her teeth knowing that they did not have enough warriors left to survive, knowing that they would die here.

She looked around again; Olivia, her wound being bandaged by a young girl, looked at her in desperate appeal. She saw the remaining people of Elgion, and for a moment wondered if she should yell for their retreat. She didn't think they could make it to the docks in time. So, she decided that they would instead go into that darkness together. Together they would rage against that gruesome foe; that final fate; that mortal coil. "We will prevail," she said to Alexa, and the two nodded at one another, going together into the unknown.

"I only wish Bella were here," another voice said. The surprising tones of the always loyal Blythe, almost comical in their timing, broke the funerary thoughts. But there he was, spear in hand, next to the two sisters.

Alexa must have sensed Sophia's confusion, for she answered her thoughts, "Blythe here is a menace with that spear! He saved me at least once on the eastern end."

Blythe, humble as ever, only nodded to her in recognition.

"I wish she was here too, Blythe," Sophia replied with a warm smile, and then, as if answering them both, a horn sounded in the air. A foreign horn, not of Elgion or orcish make, but a horn all the same. The enemy, once marching to slaughter them all, now stopped in their tracks. Sophia looked at Blythe and Alexa, and they shook their heads to indicate that neither of them knew what blew the horn. All three then looked out towards the source, trying to peer past the smoke that screened the ditch and palisade, wondering what fate lay in store for them.

# Chapter Fourteen

## Bella

Steam rose off the back of her mount, its scaly skin losing its protective layer of moisture to evaporation. A layer of moisture that was being cooked by the raptor's internal heat. A steadily rising temperature throughout the day that came to a point in which Bella could feel the raptors' warmth on her legs.

They had ridden hard the last few days, chasing the trail of their enemy. It had started back in the orc encampment where she had been a prisoner not so long ago. That camp was now nothing but ash and ruin, for she and the saurian riders had laid waste to the few paltry defenders they had found there.

Their force was twenty strong, including Bella, and they enacted a terrible vengeance on the orcish base. Repayment for the murder of their kin. For Bella, repayment for the torment she had endured. They had encountered only a handful of orcs at the camp that were equipped with any discernible weapons, whilst the remaining foes they faced fought more like rabid dogs. At first, they tried to flee, but one by one they had been cut down, turning to animalistic resistance in the end. Bella did not pity them. She had seen too much of what they were, and she knew that there was no good within them. *At least not in this clan, maybe in others, but not this one.*

With the enemy camp laid to ruin, they had ridden in pursuit of the main horde, which had headed south towards Elgion. A hard ride pushed them through the carnage the orcs had made. A path of death and ruin. Every lumber camp had been sacked and burned, whole carcasses of deer and boar lay mangled, half-eaten, and wasted. Signs of filth and excrement were simply strewn about carelessly. She despised them for their ... excess.

Hislock and her had only grown in friendship, using the hunt to further their admiration for one another. They slept little and ate less, seeking to catch up to the horde so that they could plan their next move. Yet, the orcs moved with uncanny haste, and as they woke for the third day, Hislock had shown their worry for her. They had to—just like she did—that the horde was massive, and that it was headed straight for Elgion.

By the second day, Hislock had already sent a pair of riders back to their village for reinforcements, but the main body of the group pressed on, hoping against hope that they could stop the destruction of Elgion. That they could stop this horde from its bloodthirsty rampage.

Now, on a winter's day, the sun glinting off the thin layer of newly fallen snow, Bella and the saurian riders crossed the Farney River Ford at the grain mill. It had been ransacked for any food or valuables.

The horde seemed to want to steal the stockpiled food from Elgion's stores, which had been painstakingly grown, preserved, and stocked for the winter and the early spring. Now, as it always is, some other more violent group wished to take it. She noted that there was little to no trace of the stolen grain or flour, indicating that the mill had been emptied of its contents before the orcs could get to it. This gave her hope, but the sight of smoke thickening on the horizon made that hope flicker and wane. She looked over to Hislock, who like her had seen the smoke, and without a word spoken understood that she wished to go faster.

Hislock raised its spear and called out, "Tok Tok." Words that, although Bella could not replicate due to their excessively throaty nature, she had heard enough now to know they meant something akin to 'speed up' or 'hurry'.

The group—eighteen strong—put their heels to their mounts and surged forward. Bella had gotten used to her mount now and couldn't help but compare them to her own charges. For example, horses were not only faster but had greater endurance, which had been a cause of frustration these last few days. The cold blood of these lizard folk, although charged, unlike their more bestial kin, required more frequent breaks and more time preparing the mounts to ride. The blood, as Hislock had demonstrated, needed to be looked after.

She still remembered the gecko cutting a small slice on its own forearm and had motioned for her to hold out her hand. Hislock had allowed a few drops of their blood to drip on her skin. It was cool to the touch, and as the realization dawned on her, Hislock made a motion showing that they needed to heat up. Now, in the middle of the day they had reached their mounts peak performance. The raptors, who although not as fast as horses were exceptionally lethal and were in that perfect middle ground of warmed blood that gave them their most powerful performance. They raced towards the smoke, and she hoped that it would be enough to save her people … her sisters.

Signs that the orcish host had been here were plain to the eye; snow and mud scuffed in the dragging pattern of their unique—hoof-like—feet. She could see now the cause of the smoke, and she could just discern a wooden palisade through the billowing clouds. They were only a kilometer or so from that wall, and, on the ground, there were signs that the orcish host had arrayed itself for battle.

She clicked her tongue in a mimicry of how Hislock had called to his own mounts. At either end of the palisade, she could see corpses strewn about, some appropriately sized for orcs and some … for humans. They pushed forward seeing an opening in the palisade where a gate once stood; now a broken bunch of timbers that were slowly succumbing to flames. *Curious that they broke the gate and burned it.* She heard a horn blow from one of the saurian riders, a call to inspire fear or courage. They were coming, reinforcements were coming, and she hoped that they were not too late.

She pushed her raptor mount past the palisade gate, and to the beast's credit, it did not hesitate to charge through the thick smoke that enveloped the opposite side of that wall. She held her breath as they pierced the cloud, and when they had breached her breath was checked.

She did not stop moving forward, but, in front of her, she could see a valley of charred ground fanned out in a pattern that originated from a bastion of defense. There she could see defenders, who looked ragged and torn, but were still standing. Yet, even closer, standing amidst piles of ash and soot, she saw the last enemy she wished to face. The massive orcish leader, with his shorn tusk, who had frightened her so in that ramshackle cage.

Her heart skipped as her mount brought her closer and closer to the beast. She saw his massive head turn, exposing a charred and battered torso. She saw the look of surprise on his face as she leveled her spear at his chest. She had been so terrified of this monster, dreading the possibility of seeing him again; *until now*. The fear she saw in his widened eyes gave her the courage to press her charge home.

A jolt ran up her arm and through her shoulder as the spear plunged deep into the orc's chest. A bellow of pain pierced through the sounds of flame and war. The other raptor riders were now amongst the surviving orcs, slaughtering an enemy who had appeared to be on the edge of victory. Now, they cried out in fear, trying to flee the jaws of the raptors and the spears of Hislock's riders.

She had to let go of the spear as her charge brought her past the war chief. Seeing no enemies in front of her, she stopped her mount and turned. The beautifully executed maneuver brought a smile to her face. The orc leader simply fell to his knees, overcome with wounds. He roared in defiance once more as she clicked her tongue to urge her mount forward. The raptor squealed in the high-pitched tones of its kin and leapt—claws outstretched—at the orc. As the raptor bent the chieftain backward with its weight, it bit down with its massive jaws on the orc's head. The chieftain's final cry was cut off by the sound of his skull crunching under the weight of the raptor's jaw.

Bella roared in triumph and felt a surge of emotion wash over her. The terror of her captivity flashed in her mind, and the death of the primary purveyor of that terror overwhelmed her senses. She let the raptor feed on the orcish chieftain.

Hislock approached—their spear reddened—and looked at her. They could see her anguish and her triumph and in sympathy and celebration of their new friend, they raised their spear high and roared in reply to her own. The battle was won before it had begun, thanks in large part to the defenders of Elgion, who had exacted a terrible cost on the enemy force.

She could see now that the chieftain was about to lead the final charge of his remaining forces. A charge that would have been the final blow to a beleaguered defense. All around her, flames licked the buildings and barricades; smoke forming rapidly in the chilly winter air. Then she heard voices; voices that she had clung to in her darkest moments.

"Bella?" Sophia asked in amazement.

"I can't believe it!" Alexa echoed her sister.

She turned on her mount and saw—backlit by the flames of the barricade—her sisters battered and bruised but standing tall. She barked out an impulsive laugh, her emotions overwhelming, and as she opened her mouth to speak, she could only fall into a sob. She leapt out of the saddle, still crying tears of joy, and ran to her sisters. The three embraced in a hug; locked tight by their love, and in that press, the three sisters cried together. They cried at the horrors they had seen, they wept at the pain they had endured, and they sobbed at the survival of their loved ones even when hope had begun to fail. The defenders of Elgion did not interrupt the sisters from their long-awaited reunion. Instead, they looked upon the saurian riders who finished off the remaining orcs, salvation found in what they had thought to be an enemy before.

*

It was warm inside the town hall, lit by roaring fires that raged against the flurry of snow outside. Laughter and boisterous conversation drowned out the crackling logs within the fires. All around there were friends and smiles. Bella looked out at the tables around her and saw, to her delight, the gecko-like saurians sitting at the table of honor to her right. They looked puzzled and confused at their surroundings, but they dove heartily into their food. The remains of mutton and carrot pies strewn about them. Their scaly skin sticky by the honeyed bread so lovingly made by the baker's wife. Strips of dried venison and morsels of fish were dotted about the table. Truly, they ate their fill, delighted by the new flavors they experienced.

Bella laughed aloud as she looked upon Hislock, their snout buried into the bowl of a pie. Hislock looked up at her, a smile plain on their face, and when they saw her laughing, they croaked in response. Of course, the humans and the saurians could not understand one another, but with Bella's fledgling translations and Sophia's intellectual curiosity, they were able to convey enough to show that they were friends.

Friends like Blythe, who now sat to her left, ecstatic at having been reunited with Bella. The stable hand had ridden hard to Elgion after her capture and had served a critical role in warning the village of the orcish threat. Without his steadfast loyalty, Bella doubted that they would be able to sit here enjoying this feast. She still remembered the bear hug he had given her after she had reunited with her sisters, his huge embrace reflective of his simple love—pure and unconditional. A warm memory that only showed Blythe's love and loyalty to those he cared for. The huge man crouched over a delectable-looking roast chicken. She managed to catch his eye and smiled at him as he wrenched massive bites from the bird. Yes, Blythe represented the love that was shared all around them and in equal measure, triumph.

Love that was spread throughout the hall. Sophia, who was just past Blythe, sat next to a pioneer woman named Olivia. A woman who still recovered from a spear wound to her abdomen; the power of the Maiden and some luck saving her life. Bella could plainly see that Sophia and Olivia had become fast friends; their bond forged in the dreadful fires of battle. Sophia also sat next to the miller's boy, who Bella remembered had been scornful of the Keeper. An anger that had started when Sophia had discovered the missing grain they had stolen before all of this had begun. Now, the three sat together as fast friends, and as they drank and ate, merriment obvious in their gestures, Bella smiled at the bond that had been forged.

The smile deepened as she saw Sophia take yet another bite of her favorite, huckleberry pie, pleasure plain on her face. *She must have eaten a whole pie to herself by now,* Bella mused. *Well earned,* she finished that thought as the reports of how Sophia had saved them at the last moment by igniting the Magi Stone bounced around in her mind.

She recalled how Sophia had explained her battle with Dolocius and the events that led to its destruction, "A fight amongst the gods themselves! One a deceiver and one a stalwart warrior." Sophia had said with a touch of enthusiasm only expressed when she was enthralled in some ponderous tome.

When the telling was done, Bella simply hugged her sister and said, "You have us now and always." Pride swelled in her chest as she had embraced her sister, any shadow that had fallen over their relationship was all but a memory now.

The memory made her look to her right where she saw Alexa sitting next to a broken armed Guard-Captain. The two engaged in deep conversation and were rapidly on their way to drunkenness. Bella chuckled as she noted the many drained clay cups around the two.

She saw a sergeant, named Prinius, stumble into Alexa's back. By Alexa's pause and sudden stare at the transgressor, Bella worried that Alexa would hit the man. Instead, Bella found herself laughing aloud as she saw Alexa trick him into looking down only to flick his nose. The captain bellowed in laughter at the trick and the sergeant—looking rather embarrassed—sat heavily next to the two. *They celebrate their victory over death.* Those three had been on the front lines of the battle, risking it all to keep Elgion alive.

Bella caught Alexa's attention and raised her cup to her warrior sister. Alexa, a smile broad on her face, saluted back with her own mug.

The sweet mead swirled pleasantly in her mouth as she heard the governor try desperately to compliment their saurian guests. "What lovely-uh-um-appetites you have," he said with consternation. The governor, flustered at his inability to speak and be understood, simply kept having food brought to the saurian's table, helping them eat the best foods Elgion had to offer. As the governor of the city toiled on, she heard a lute twang discordantly as its string broke. The blacksmith, who was always so cheerful, was now a steadily building bucket of rage as he tried desperately to play the cursed instrument.

That rage was not unwarranted, because to her amusement and to the amusement of many others, the blacksmith was the victim of some gnomish prank. For once he had reset the strings, a little colored hat would bob up and down and, without his knowledge, loosen the newly set string.

The little people had taken a liking to the blacksmith after he had placed a hunk of goat cheese in front of the group. *Gods knew how old that stuff was because they didn't make it here.* Nonetheless, such a great gift brought on high praise from the gnomes who had bobbed frantically up and down at the prize. Now they played pranks on the poor man in a demonstration of their appreciation. A strange folk, but ones that helped make this feast possible. After all, sh had seen the reports from Alexa on the increase in food stores after Sophia's negotiations with them.

Amongst the merriment, there was also loss and sadness. Dillon, an old veteran ranger, sat broodingly next to Ro, Elira, and Matthias. Dillon raised a cup, "She goes now to that Far Range."

Alexa, upon hearing those words, stopped in mid-sentence and stood raising her cup as she did so. Any sign of her drunkenness was gone in a flash, and silence fell across the room at the sudden movement.

She finished the funerary hymn after a solemn nod to Dillon, "Where we all must go. Tilde, our sister … our companion. She was a Warden of the Wilds. A guardian against the unknown. A watcher in the woods, and here we remember her, but here is not where she stays. We will see you again on that Far Range … goodbye." A respectful silence fell across the hall. A log cracked in a fire, and the attendants of the celebration bowed their heads in memory of those they lost.

So *many* had fallen to save Elgion. Bella had been there to clean up the battlefield, and of those who fought—militia or guard—nearly half were now dead. Helped along by the foul blood magic that Sophia had described so vividly. Another half again suffered wounds, ranging from dismember-ment to simple cuts, that would scar with time. Only a few had come away with no major injuries, like Alexa and Ro, but even then, those survivors had looked like death when Bella and the saurians finally came. Regardless of the toll, they sacrificed to save what they held dear. Those survivors now honored the dead, celebrating that precious gift. After a minute of silence, Guard-Captain Vitrusian raised his cup again and yelled, "To the Warriors of August, one and all!"

The hall echoed their captain, "To the Warriors of August!"

All stood in honor of the dead, even Hislock and the saurian riders understood the ritual. Bella saw the gecko-like leader raise its cup to her, showing respect in honoring their customs. Bella smiled at Hislock and raised her cup in kind, thinking that this was a victory for their people as well. People who had lost much to the violent orcs, for the hatred the lizard people showed towards the foul porcine fiends could have only stemmed from grievous insult. Maybe one day she could gather a tally of what they had sacrificed. After all, she had to go back and get Godfrey. She wished the old man was there with her, and, as she drank from her goblet, she said a silent thanks to that sarcastic companion who had so bravely followed her to the edge of death and back. While she said her own thanks, the hall erupted back into conversation, a wave of noise washing away the revered silence.

Yes, so many had fallen—revered in their sacrifice—yet many still lived. Yes, they could have fled to the harbor and taken the ship back to Augustia, but instead, they stood, defying the darkness that surely would have spread across this new land. It was a victory that would mark the foundations of this new world, and show to all those of Telaea, gods and mortals alike, that Elgion would stand against the darkness.

That Elgion would march bravely forward with the guidance of the three sisters. Three sisters who now stood stronger than ever in their bond. One ranger, one Keeper, and—Bella thought with bemusement—*one lucky ruffian*. She looked around the room again and as if her sisters read her mind Alexa and Sophia had both chosen that moment to look at each other. No words were spoken, only that silent love which is held by those that are true to one another.

In that moment, she knew that for whatever may come she would be alright. Whatever fate lay ahead of them, with her sisters by her side, they would prevail.

# About the Author

If you have made it this far, I can only assume you have completed your reading of Shards of Ember. By simply reading this novel you have already shown me support, but if you could leave a review on Amazon, goodreads, or any other book review sites that would help me immensely. If you want to follow my writing career and would like to be involved in my future projects, please subscribe to my mailing list by visiting: mitchelllecoultre.com. or following me on Amazon, Instagram (Mitchell Lecoultre), or Facebook (Mitchell Lecoultre Weaver of Stories) Thank you!

Hello there! My name is Mitchell Lecoultre, but you can call me Mitch. I am, most proudly, a dad to three wonderful daughters, aged nine, six, and six. Yes, that means I have twins! My daughters, my wife, and I reside in Oklahoma where I work as a clinical laboratory scientist, helping physicians treat those who are burdened with diseases such as leukemia. I was born and raised in a small town in northern Idaho where I was raised by a loving family. I learned to love nature and respect the simpler joys of life and thus am more at home with campfire wisdom than cocktail etiquette. When I turned eighteen, I was unsure of what to do in my life and although I was enrolled in college, I joined the US Army instead. I served with honor as a cannon crewmember from 2006-2010. I will however admit that my time deployed overseas, in support of Operation Iraqi Freedom (2007-2008), transformed me, vanquishing the older simpler me. After I finished my term of service, I got married to my beautiful wife, Vanessa, and we went to college at the University of Idaho, where I received a B.S. in Molecular Biology/Biotechnology. I have employed that degree to moderate financial success and am using it now for my current job. I enjoy hiking, walks with my loved ones, miniature painting, video games, reading, well-made television and YouTube content, and audiobooks.

# Sneak Peak for the next book in *Gods Adrift*, "The Godstone Decree"

Navin nearly wept. His little baby looked like no more than a ghost, pale and fragile. His wife looked at him, her eyes pleading. "Save their boy" was the unspoken cry. Tears begging for him, for anyone, to do something; anything. But what *could* he do? He wasn't a doctor, and he surely wasn't a Keeper. So, Navin only looked back at her. The same helpless gaze returned as he stood in the stuffy overly hot room. The same impotency as he listened to the sounds of his six-week-old babe, Demetrius, wheeze as they fought for every breath.

"I have given him some ginger and goblin's finger to ease his cough and fight any fever. Which will help him rest, but unless he gets intervention from the Maiden I don't…I don't think your son will make it," the apothecarian said. Navin hated the hunch-backed diminutive man. There was no cause for this hatred, just sullen anger with nowhere to go. He held his tongue as he looked down at the cowed wrinkled face, eyes downcast so that all Navin saw was a crop of gray hair covering folds of wrinkled skin. Still, Navin knew that this elder spoke the truth, and the sound of his life savings—224 coppers—clinking as they fell into the outstretched hand did little to assuage his quickly building rage. The frail bone-thin hand dropped noticeably under the weight of the bag.

"Thank you," The older man said as he made the satchel disappear into his cloak with a practiced grace. Navin bit the inside of his gum, and before his anger could swell to a crescendo the apothecarian interrupted, "You must bring him to the clinic day. It's…" The elder's mouth moved as he counted silently. "Eight days. Yes, eight days from now. The Keeper's offer their services then, and if we can keep the boy's fever and cough down, he has a chance."

Navin studied the grooved face, its crinkled features staring back at him, the head craned like that of a turtle looking out from its shell. Although the face was impassive, Navin knew, as he knew himself, that Demetrius wouldn't make it that far. This swindler was trying to get him to pay for another treatment on another day, he was trying to capitalize on Navin's hope that his son would survive. No, he needed a solution now, and although this healer had helped, he was only trying to enrich himself at this point.

With tempered grace, that surprised himself, Navin spoke, "Thank you, sir, we will surely bring Demetrius to the clinic day. Now, have a good night." Navin gestured behind him, through the small living room, to the exit door. The healer, obviously seeing that he had not duped the desperate father, sighed and shuffled through the quaint space, making his way past a bench and low table. The wooden home seemed so *insignificant*, even with such a small man as a sense of scale.

"Ember's breath," Navin cursed. At this late hour, this far from the clinic day, he would have to pay for the blessings of the Maiden himself, an expense only the wealthy could afford.

"What…what did he say? What can we do?" Naomi, Navin's wife asked, in an anxious plea.

It was all he could do to not burst into tears as he looked back at her, her countenance of anxiety and grief. "I…he said that we must make it to clinic day." Navin held up a hand as his wife went to protest. "I know, I know that's too far away." He felt helpless, he knew that his boy would most likely die, but he wanted to give Naomi hope. He wanted her to feel like there was a chance. "The healer says that if we keep his fever and cough down that there is a chance Demetrius will make it. He, um, he will be back in a couple of days to administer treatment."

A look of relief fell over his wife's face, her spirit latching on to the morsel that he had given. "Oh, thank the gods." She reached down and kissed their baby boy on the forehead. "You hear that? You are going to get all better, and when you do…we will laugh and play in the sunshine."

Navin looked away, a tear coursing down his cheek. Choosing not to risk his wife seeing the lie, he resolved to go out into the night. His wife had hope—an escape—he needed to find his own. "The healer will need to be paid though," Navin said as he swung his wool coat over his shoulders. His wife looked up from her matronly pose by the bedside, and with a graven expression she nodded. He adjusted the coat on his shoulders, "I am going to see if I can rustle up some coins. I will be back." At this late hour it could only be from a money lender, but Navin saw his wife's desperation, and her solemn nod was all the approval he needed.

With nowhere to go, he gravitated towards the only place that still had lights, still had life, Minollo's Flagon. Like a small candle, the tavern lay near the bottom middle of The Bowl, that natural ridge of hills that ringed Augustia's harbor in a semi-circle. It was what made Augustia such a prime location for a seaport, and, as humans tend to do, a diorama of stratification. Its modest nature and location at the start of the bowl's rise gave it the unique capacity to anonymously serve the rich or the poor. At this late hour, it tended to outlast those taverns which relied on a more regular customer base, and, as such, Navin had no trouble securing a flagon of mead. The earthy tones of the honey infused drink were unique to Minollo's Flagon, and some wondered at the owner's process, for he made it taste like a summer's day.

Navin allowed the rich taste to swirl over his tongue and drown his sorrow. He drank quickly, allowing the alcohol to take him. He knew it was a stupid decision, but he did not care. He took another swig; three heavy gulps sloshed down his throat, the warmth already forming in his belly. As he placed the flagon down, he saw over the spine of the vessel a rather tall—elegant—woman approach. "Ember's breath," he muttered internally, before a wash of guilt flooded over him.

Her slender frame was covered in spotless well-made cloth, and her steps seemed to flutter as they danced towards him. She wore a dark green cloak, its hood shadowing her face, and with a bowed head it was obvious she was trying to be discreet. Even then, Navin couldn't help but notice the radiant beauty, masked in shadow. Her manner screamed of the excesses of the upper class, of one from the upper regions of The Bowl.

"Excuse me sir, may I sit here?" the lady asked pleasantly, like a soft crooning whisper.

Navin, so dumbstruck that she had stopped to talk to him, only sat with the flagon still held in front of his face.

She giggled at his expression. "I heard the mead is quite good here. Apparently, *so* good it robs one of speech."

Navin flushed with another pulse of guilty desire. He tried to wrangle his thoughts back to his family, to Demetrius, but even this lady's laugh was elegant; desirous. A sudden crash from a table of sailor's far into their night's drink, forced him to action. He made to stand, stuttering, "U-u-uh, I'm sorry where muh manners?"

The lady held up a hand, a silver bangle flashing as the cloak's camouflage fell away, "Oh, please don't stand up!" She glanced around nervously recognizing how loudly she had just spoken and then satisfied that no one was the wiser, continued, "I simply wished to have a word with you sir. So, do you mind?" Her hand drifted down to point at the chair opposite him.

Navin, halfway between standing and sitting, made an awkward gesture towards the aforementioned chair, "Not at all." He cleared his throat. "Lady."

With deft grace she seemed to float down into her seat. As she arranged herself, she pulled the hood of the cloak away. A golden ponytail, held with silver bands, fell across her shoulder, and the whites of her teeth flashed at Navin in a broad welcoming smile. Navin, his breath nearly robbed, felt that the small corner of the tavern he had chosen to drink his sorrows away had become a beacon of light. Before he could gather himself, she spoke.

"So, you may be wondering what a woman like me is doing here, yes?" She raised her brows in question, but not with enough of a gap between speech to respond. "Well, you see I don't normally partake in places like this, but I work for someone rather…desperate. Yes, my employer wishes for a simple task. A simple job to be done."

Navin's heart sank slightly, coming to grips with what he already knew. She wasn't there to find love. She was there on business. Of course, a lady like this wouldn't be here for anything else. His guilt surged as he thought of Naomi. He had not even said it aloud in his mind, but his desire had been overwhelming. Somewhere in the secret recesses of his consciousness a thought had taken root, a fantasy of her approaching him for a night's comfort. "Oh yeah? What's that then?" he asked rather gruffly.

She smiled and then produced a small wooden box from beneath the table. She looked around and placed the box gently on the table. Save for a simple depiction of an oak tree in the center it was unremarkable. With her delicate hands still placed on the sides of the box she said, "You look like a *capable* man. So, let me be plain." She glanced around again and leaned in closer.

Navin leaned in as well, his heart thumping, the smell of lavender wafted towards him.

"I need this box delivered somewhere out of town. Could you do this?" She placed a hand on Navin's own and the delicate touch made a shiver run up his arm. "For me?" A blossoming smile flushed across her face; the blush of her cheeks intense.

Navin's heart raced and his thoughts swirled between the despair of his child's illness, his wife's grief, and this new fantasy, this new temptation.

"Of course, you would be compensated for your trouble." The lady produced a small bag, and the clink of coins could be heard as she placed it on the table next to the box. She gently untied the string holding the satchel and exposed its contents to him, inside he could see gleaming Augustian gold marks. His jaw hung slackly.

A small laugh, like the elegant giggle of before, escaped her lips, "There's ten marks in there for you. So, what do ya say?"

Navin was utterly dumbfounded, and he felt like he sat there in silence, his mouth agape, for an eternity. "What…uh…what do…um…you need me to do?" he spluttered.

"That's quite simple. Just take this box here out of town."

"Out of town…where?" he queried. He thought he saw a flash of irritation in the lady's brow at this question, a small tremor on the otherwise pleasant face.

"That information is only for those who wish to be paid."

"Ah, I see." He said, leaning back. He felt like he had been ensnared, but he also knew that ten gold marks would more than pay for the treatment he needed for his son. Ember's breath, it might be enough to get him a better place in the city, somewhere Naomi would be proud of. He felt a pang of grief at the thought of his wife, knowing that she suffered while he flirted with desire. Anger curdled in him, at his own weakness, and looking down at the satchel of coins he resolved to do better for Naomi, for Demetrius. "Fine, I will take yer bargain. Now where to?"

The lady beamed another smile. "Excellent!" Once more she scanned around the room and, satisfied that no one was listening, leaned in. The smell of lavender kissed his senses again and she whispered to him, "I need you to take this to the Broken Stallion Inn. You know the place?"

He nodded.

"Good, take this box there and hand it to the innkeeper. Say it's for someone called," Her voice dropped even further, and Navin strained to hear. "Bloodeye. You must be on your guard, it is in Argolonian territory. You will also *have* to go tonight. Haste is important, understand?" she asked as she pushed the box towards him.

He nodded once again, grabbing the proffered container. It felt rather weightless, he thought, and as he went to pull it into his own pockets, she grabbed his hand again. Her own eyes were a mockery of Naomi's earlier pleading.

The simulacra only served to remind him of his oath to his wife and he knew what he must ask. "I can do this for you, but I need you to take these coins to my wife. I need you to tell her that I will be gone for a bit. Ya see, my son he…he is sick, and I don't think they can wait for me to return. 'Sides what man would I be if I just left 'em, with no explanation, in the middle of the night?"

She nodded in understanding, a glint of sadness gracing her eyes. "Aye, we can do that. Where is your home?"

As he told her his address, he calculated how long it would take to get to the Broken Stallion Inn. Hopefully his son would recover in that time, at least a week and a half of travel on foot. He also wondered what his wife would think when this lady showed up to their door in the middle of the night. Oh, the scolding he would get. Yet, she was not unwarranted, for in the recesses of his mind he asked himself if he would see this elegant beauty again.

If you would like to read more, stay informed on any of my social media platforms and be sure to subscribe to my newsletter for chances to be an Advanced Reader! If that doesn't suit your fancy, then feel free to shoot me an email!

**Website**: mitchelllecoultre.com

**Amazon**: Mitchell Lecoultre – follow the author

**Instagram**: Mitchell Lecoultre

**Facebook**: Mitchell Lecoultre Weaver of Stories

**Email**: mitchleco@hotmail.com

# Thank you!!!

www.ingramcontent.com/pod-product-compliance
Lightning Source LLC
Chambersburg PA
CBHW061917130726

47908CB00017B/1660